We Love You, Bunny

We Love You, Bunny

Mona Awad

SCRIBNER

London · New York · Amsterdam/Antwerp · Sydney/Melbourne · Toronto · New Delhi

First published in the USA in 2025 by Marysue Ricci Books, an imprint of Simon & Schuster, LCC

Published in Great Britain in 2025 by Scribner, an imprint of Simon & Schuster UK.

3 5 7 9 10 8 6 4 2

Simon & Schuster UK Ltd
1st Floor
222 Gray's Inn Road
London WC1X 8HB

Simon & Schuster Australia,
Sydney
Simon & Schuster India,
New Delhi

www.simonandschuster.co.uk
www.simonandschuster.com.au
www.simonandschuster.co.in

A CIP catalogue record for this book is available from the British Library

The authorised representative in the EEA is Simon & Schuster Netherlands BV,
Herculesplein 96, 3584 AA Utrecht, Netherlands. info@simonandschuster.nl

Hardback ISBN: 978-1-3985-3515-2
Trade Paperback ISBN: 978-1-3985-3516-9
eBook ISBN: 978-1-3985-3517-6
eAudio ISBN: 978-1-3985-3609-8

Printed and Bound in the UK using 100% Renewable Electricity at CPI Group (UK) Ltd

MIX
Paper | Supporting
responsible forestry
FSC
www.fsc.org
FSC® C013604

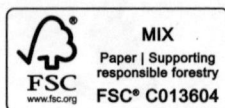

For Michael

And for you, Reader

Love you, Bunny.

Contents

Part One   1

Part Two   173

Part Three   309

Part Four   377

Part Five   461

We Love You,
Bunny

Part One

Prologue

H i, Bunny.
    It's been a little while, hasn't it?

We missed you, we really did. *So* much.

And look at you now, *wow*. All gothed out again. Back to wearing your scary-bleak clothes and your dark hair still hanging in front of your eye, how funny. You've been busy since we last saw you, haven't you? Very busy, apparently, scribble-scribbling in the dark. Publishing your little *novel*. About us, so fun. And it's enjoyed a somewhat moderate success. Good for you! Amazing, really, what people will read nowadays. That's why we brought you up here, in fact, to Kyra's attic (remember this attic?) for a little congratulatory toast among old friends. A cozy reunion of sorts with your former MFA cohort, those you've left in the literary dust, so to speak, ha ha ha. Not that we're bitter, Bunny, oh my god, not at all. We're raising our glasses to you, aren't we?

What's that, Bunny? You *can't* raise your glass?

Oh, because of the restraints, that's right.

Sorry about those.

Well, we'll toast *for* you, how's that? We could use a bit of a tipple, frankly, under the circumstances. A little Light and Sunny, remember those?

Oh, we wouldn't squirm in that chair so much, Bunny, not if we were you. It's just going to cause more bruises on those wrists, that neck, so like a swan's. . . .

But we digress.

Sorry again we had to tie you up a little. But it's just so very lovely to catch up like this, isn't it, just the five of us here in the dark? You all cozy in your chair, and the four of us standing close and adorable in our rabbit masks, making a semicircle of such love and understanding all around you, our dresses shining prettily by the light of the hunter's moon. It's a hunter's moon tonight, Bunny, oh yes. Look at it full and glowing through the window (on All Hallows' Eve, no less!), and the night so beautifully full of screaming. Your screaming included. Probably you've dreamed of this moment, haven't you? We have too, trust. And when we saw on the Warren student listserv that our very own former peer was coming back to town, on tour for her debut novel, the first among our cohort to publish, we thought, *Why not make those dreams a reality? Why not support our old friend Sam Mackey?* Or Samantha *Heather* Mackey, as you so very inventively called yourself in your little novel (going for autofiction, were you?). We did enjoy that wink to the '80s film, by the way, that softening touch to a name otherwise so evocative of your own boyish will. Despite the way you left things, *Samantha*, despite the unpleasantness, we really felt support was the grown-up thing to do. Our therapist even said it might be good for our Healing Journeys. Put the past behind us and such. Be a good literary citizen and such. Buy a copy of her book and read it, very adultlike, not at all screaming *bitch*, not at all vomiting. Fly back to this New England town, the town of our old alma mater, and attend her reading at the Warren University Bookstore, we all had this idea, it seems! The hive mind is not entirely dead, it seems. Awakened, perhaps, by your betrayal.

So funny, your face, when you saw us in the audience, by the way. How we were applauding you, not with our hands so much, but with our eyes. You sort of froze for a minute, didn't you, at your podium, at the sight of us sitting there in the very back row, each of us in a different colored dress so that together we made such a happy rainbow, we embodied the holy elements of earth, air, water, and fire. So smiling at you. So supporting. You sort of cried a little when you first made eye contact, didn't you? We did too, Bunny.

They were joy tears, promise.

Your reading was so amazing, we meant to tell you. And funny! *So funny* how you made us into ax-wielding monsters. So very hilarious how you divulged our most tender secrets. We laughed until we cried, we really did. What's that you're saying, Bunny? We're having just a little bit of a hard time understanding you through the gag we put in your mouth. Or maybe it's the drugs making you drool like that. We mixed just a sprinkling into your bookstore wine earlier, which we bought you out of mercy, really (you were so nervous!). And though you accepted with some hesitancy, Bunny, you did drink. Drank it all down, in fact, didn't you? Perhaps out of the stress of the situation, which we totally get. Sometimes it's stressful to see old friends, we agree. Or maybe it's being back here in the attic, where it all began. *Workshop.* The bunnies, the boys, the blood, so much blood. The beautiful, sacred thing we allowed you to be a part of, out of the kindness of our fucking hearts. The ax is still here too, look at that. Right here in the corner where we last left it, how serendipitous. Even a few flecks of blood on the blade still. Are they fresh flecks? Oh, we don't know, Bunny. Maybe they are. God knows what we've been up to here, right? Only two springs ago, but it feels like an eternity now, doesn't it? Since we all graduated from this hell place and went our separate, lonely ways into the cold, wide world?

Feels good in our hands now, though, the ax. Feels like old times. We still know how to strike and to grip, it looks like. Like riding a bicycle, really.

Funny how it all comes back.

What have *we* been up to? Oh, busy. Very busy, just like you, Bunny. Reading your book and screaming, ha ha ha. Dreaming of revenge scenarios, ha ha ha. Sharing these scenarios during therapy, getting carried away sometimes in the color and wonder of them, until our killjoy therapist says, *That's enough for today.* No but seriously, we really do love our therapist; he's a wonderfully kind and thoughtful human. How he just sits there in his leather chair on Zoom and stares so compassionately at the squares of us, saying, *Tell me, tell me.* He's helping us, so much, to reconnect with our creativity. Since you destroyed our souls, we sort of lost our way, sad to say. But we're working to get it back, working on our own stuff right now, actually.

It's going so well. Tonight's really a big part of our Creative Journey, believe it or not.

And you, you're a big part of it too.

Oh, don't cry, Bunny! We're not going to *kill* you, don't be silly! This isn't your *novel*, this is *reality*, remember? We're not murderers IRL, despite the very ick brush with which you chose to paint us. No, no, we're just going to have a little chat, is all, one by one by one by one. Taking turns with you in our telling, doesn't that sound fun? Sort of like the ultimate Smut Salon. (You remember Smut Salon, don't you?) As for your *novel*, well, we have no intention of commenting, don't worry. About all of that: *no comment*, as they say. Except that you got it wrong. So fucking wrong. About us.

Ax murderers? Please.

(Oh, best not to struggle, Bunny, it will only make the restraints more ouch.)

So what *are* we going to say? Oh how we've thought and thought about this! Our therapist recently put us through something like a writing exercise, remember those? *Imagine,* he said softly, *if you could sit Samantha down and say* one thing, *what would it be?* And he looked at us with his too-blue gaze, which eerily recalled all we had made and lost, and we knew exactly. What we would fucking say. Not that you were a liar. Not that you were a treacherous psychotic whore, no, no. Fuck talking about *you.*

Instead we thought we'd tell you the story, the lovely little story, Bunny, of *us.*

How we came together that first year.

How, together, we broke reality and basically reinvented the laws of the natural world.

How we, too, made something beautiful once, oh yes. More beautiful than anything you could ever dream in your small, small mind. And real, too. Before. Long before you ever walked into the picture. When you were nothing, in fact, but a small, dark speck in the corner of our minds and eyes.

What's that you're trying to say, Bunny? Your publicist is expecting you at your hotel tonight, is she? You have a train to catch in the morning, do you? You have another city, another bookstore to visit on your tour of lies? Oh, we don't know if you're going to make that train tomorrow, Bunny. Maybe, maybe not. Depends on a lot. We'll see how you do as an audience, how's that? Coraline wants to start, don't you, Bunny? *Cupcake*, we believe you called her in your telling.

But your telling is over now.

So sit back, relax, and *listen*, k?

Because here tonight in the moon-splashed dark, it really is high time for us to make something beautiful again.

Cupcake

Hi there, Bunny. Remember me? So clever of you, truly, to reduce me to a baked good. So funny that you described me as a maniacal hair braider or . . . what was it again? *A child of the corn going to prom?* I'm not going to comment further on your *novel* (we agreed to not) except to say that when I perused it during a rehearsal break (I'm back in theater now, by the way, oh it's very lucrative!), I laughed until I cried blood. So funny, how you let your imagination just run away with you like that. How you really don't know anything at all. About me or us or even like reality, really. I'll just hang on to the ax while we talk, is that okay with you? I'll just get a bit closer to you physically also. So you can see my dress up close, the color of dreamy skyscapes tonight. Smell my lemony-sugar smell, which I know turns you on a little, Bunny, don't deny it. In your novel (which I won't mention again ever), you even said you wanted to eat me when you first saw me, didn't you? I knew that. Could sense your hunger, both writerly and sexual, from the start. Could see it in your crazy eyes, through your bitchy hair curtain, black as night, and it explains so much. It's why I didn't take any of your lies about me or your very bad prose personally, not at all. I took it instead as a very elaborate yet ultimately crude fan fiction.

Let me get even closer to you now, so we can whisper, just you and me, if need be. So you can look right into my *anime eyes* while I set some things straight, as it were. About how it all started, Bunny. Before the boys, before the ax. Before the magic of this attic was made known to us.

Before we were even made known to one another. I actually fought to be the first one to tell, because believe it or not (and on this point we sometimes disagree), it all began with me, actually. Yes, me, Caroline. I mean *Coraline*.

It began with me, Coraline.

What a Herculean effort you made to disguise my real name, by the way.

1

Before we were One, we were four, weren't we? Oh so very long ago. The beginning, really. To go back there, we have to go all the way back to that first year, that first fall, don't we? A most strange and beautiful fall it was, remember, Bunny? Of course, you weren't Bunny then, and neither was I. I was Coraline from Virginia. My very first time in New England. I remember the golden light of September still. How it shone so prettily, all over this creepy-lovely town named after God and fate. How it shone on the illustrious campus of Warren, most Ivy of schools, which was my campus now. How it shone down on me that late afternoon as I made my way to the Demitasse a.k.a Welcome Party for the new MFAs. An exclusive group, I was told. Best of the very fucking best. A smile wavering on my face as I thought of how I was one of them now. An honest-to-god graduate student in one of the most cutthroat, hard-to-get-into programs in the country, Bunny. The highly experimental Narrative Arts program, which Mother hissingly called Fiction.

The Demitasse, as I'm sure you recall Bunny, was in a very white tent on the prettily manicured green among the hundreds-of-years-old trees. You didn't go that first year, though, did you? Too afraid to go alone perhaps? Well, I went alone, Bunny. Walked in my sky-blue Mary Janes from my new apartment just blocks away from campus. Even though I had a really lovely car, Mother's old BMW, I walked. Alone, did I mention that already? Scary. First day of school is what it felt like. Five years old all over again, that's how it felt. I remember the lone click of my footsteps in the golden evening, among the lengthening shadows. Crows cawing all around me, making the air sound like death. Sure, I was afraid despite my smiling.

Don't be afraid, Mother had laughed when she said goodbye earlier. *It's only an art degree, for god's sake, Button. Just writing stories, isn't it?*

Yes, Mother, I'd said, not wanting to get into it. That it was my actual fucking soul in those stories.

Well, then, Mother had said, *what's there to be afraid of?*

Nothing, I'd said. *Nothing at all.* And I'd gripped my razor blade, hidden in my dress pocket, where I liked to keep it, Bunny. (I still do keep it there, in fact.) *You're absolutely right as usual, Mother*, I'd said. And Mother had smiled. *Don't disappoint us, please.*

The party was hell at first, of course it was. So many poets. So many old people, probably professors. All of them as pale as vampires, wearing gradations of black that hurt my eyes. Talking softly to one another in small clusters, smirking like they thought they were so, so smart, and probably they *were* so smart was the awful thing. The frames of their eyeglasses were very conceptual. Everyone's hair was so intimidatingly feathered and asymmetrical, such artful chaos everywhere you looked, that for the first time in my life, Bunny, I became self-conscious of my perfectly tucked-under bob. And then the conversations all around me, Bunny. About the Process, and "death of the author" or whatever, and obscure French writers I'd never heard of, and me trying so hard to smile politely at everyone, and everyone looking at me, Bunny, at my oh-so-polite smiling, like I was insane. I suffered. So much social agony. (You're not the only one who knows social agony, fyi.) Alone, I leaned against a white Doric pillar bedecked with billowing tulle for what felt like forever, clutching the razor in my pocket between my so-sweating fingers, and there I almost died a thousand deaths. Yet I was still smiling stupidly.

What do we do with a frown, Button? Mother always said.

We turn it upside down, Mother.

I remember I was wearing this sky dress, which, as you can see, Bunny, has an actual blue sky on it complete with billowy white clouds. My hair was freshly bobbed into Louise Brooks and dyed what Mother called *frigid blond* but I called Grace Kelly. I remember the tulle floating around me,

grazing my bare shoulders like it was saying, *Hi, hi, you're not alone.* I closed
my eyes each time it did. I remember the trays of hors d'oeuvres and chilled
champagne and how I was holding a flute, drinking the sparkly bubbles far
too fast, nearly crushing the glass in my white-gloved hand. I remember rabbits hopping on the distant green, in and out of my field of perception, and
how I thought nothing at all of it then. What I thought was, *I hate it here.*
What I thought was, *This is all so fucking embarrassing.* Not just this party,
but coming here at all. To New England. To *Warren.* To be a *writer.* Not at
all what Mother, probably halfway back to Virginia by now, wanted for me.
Mother's dreams for me were so very big, much bigger than the Academy.
She'd said as much over the moules frites we had at a nearby French bistro
earlier that day. The Bistro was painted all red inside like maybe it was hell.
There was a giant stone rabbit's head on the wall right beside our table,
mouth open like it was roaring. It was backlit by a red light like it was the
animal god of the place. I was aroused by it slightly, I didn't know why. *But
at least it's Ivy League, Coraline,* Mother was saying. *There is that.* And she
took a very long sip of her sauvignon blanc, which is the Episcopalian way of
thanking God. Mother reminded me that I could always return to theater,
be onstage like I wanted, even on-screen like I wanted, right alongside Ryan
Gosling like I wanted, if only I would throw up more and learn to memorize
better. I looked down at my side green salad, its shavings of pecorino and
smattering of lardons, which I had asked them to *take off, please* but which
they'd put on anyway. Inside, I started to cry. But I said, *Thank you so much
for the feedback, Mother, I'll give that some thought.*

Now, looking around this tent at these tables full of writers, I sort of
wished I had. Learned to throw up more. I was ready to leave. To burn my
own notebook even though it held my heart's blood, to fuck my own small
dreams. Some people were sort of smirking at my sky dress, I saw, and I
started to feel stupid in it. *It's the world that is stupid,* Mother always said,
and I clutched that idea like I clutched the razor. Thinking how nice the
blade would feel against my inner-thigh flesh, Bunny. I should go to the
bathroom, get in a locked stall, and maybe do that for a little while. Nick at

my soft skin. Watch the blood bloom there in the prettiest red dots, like tiny roses. I was about to go looking when I saw something that made me stay.

Some*one*, Bunny.

A girl. Standing so petite and alone by a tulle-bedecked pillar like I was, eating a small plate of pastries very quickly. She was wearing a dress patterned with the greenest grass—it was the grass that caught my eye. There were strange-looking flowers growing in that grass, I didn't know their names. She looked very lost, like maybe she was in a fairy-tale wood, at least metaphorically speaking. She kept glancing over her shoulder for the proverbial wolf or the witch, the thing that might gobble her up. It was there, her eyes said, oh yes. It would show up any minute. She had the shiniest red hair, and her face was like a small, scared heart. Like a *doll*, Bunny, yes. One I might have clutched in my own bedroom dark. One that was so pretty, I might have hated her a little, even as I loved her so much. But pretty as this girl was, she was also sort of hunched over her pastries like she wanted to disappear. Funny she was wearing gloves too, white like mine. Seeing those gloves and that grass dress, seeing her scared-heart face, made me smile for the first time since I'd gotten to this hell place. Yes, Bunny, like you, I thought this town was a hell place too at first. A violence in the air that was almost crackling.

Anyway, me and this doll girl, we were suddenly walking toward each other, weren't we? Our steps on the twitching grass, echoing each other's.

"Kyra," her cherry mouth said her name was. (Or *Kira*, as you called her. Your creative powers were just on fire, Bunny.) Her bright, thick lipstick, that's what I couldn't take my eyes off. A shade that reminded me, strangely, of some past unpleasantness. *Lipstick is for whores*, Mother always said.

"I'm Coraline," I told this girl. My mouth was terribly dry, but my lips were balmy, always, with a rose-flavored gloss that I often licked off because it was so delicious, even though Mother told me to stop it, it was sluttish and it was calories and it would ruin the shine. For the first time that day, I felt the shine of them as I spoke. The effect of that shine on this girl, deep in her vertebrae.

"I love your dress," the girl named Kyra said. She wasn't looking at it, though. She was looking into my eyes. Straight into them, which made my skin hum a little. Music played somewhere in my mind, a pretty Stereolab song about flowers and nowhere.

"I love yours," I said. I wasn't looking at her dress either.

"You're like the sky to my grass and flowers," she said, laughing. She had a weird high laugh, I thought.

"You're like the grass to my sky," I said.

"And look," she said, holding up her white-gloved hand, which, yes, matched mine exactly, the hand that was crushing the flute (the other was in my pocket, ever gripping the razor). She looked at our gloved hands like this might be a magic thing. Like *we* might be a magic thing. A world all our own.

"We match," we whispered.

Yes, we said it at the same time, with the exact same quality of whisper. Even though we were not One yet. Did a bunny hop by just then? We thought we sensed one dart into a nearby bush, out of the corners of our eyes and minds. Like fate. Like it was telling us.

Like it fucking knew even way back then.

"Are you Fiction?" she said. It wasn't really a question. More a confirmation of what she already knew.

"Fiction," I said. "Yes. I am. First year. Just arrived."

"Same." She smiled now. The tiniest, whitest teeth. So sharp and shining, like little pearl blades. I felt the golden light of September breaking inside me, breaking through the clouds of my sky dress. She told me things and I didn't listen; the Stereolab song was playing so loud and pretty in my head now. Something about how she was so glad I was here, so glad we'd found each other, etc. She hated parties *so* much. Unless she had someone to talk to, of course.

"I also hate parties," I whispered. Thinking of Mother's many parties. How I held the trays of cocktails and canapés, while her friends floated around me and I pictured stabbing them or myself. "Unless I have someone," I said.

"Well, now we have each other maybe," the doll girl, Kyra, offered shyly.

Do I have you? Do I have you, please? asked her lovely eyes. Slightly in love and also slightly afraid of me, I saw. I became Mother then. Felt her cool smile on my balmy lips. I licked them slowly. "Maybe." Loosening my grip on the razor a little. I looked down at her plate of *Alice in Wonderland* pastries, each one bitten into by her so-small teeth. Suddenly I was hungry, almost wolfishly so. "Delicious," I whispered. "Wherever did you get those?"

"Oh, just there." She pointed to a long white table full of Easter-egg-colored treats. But it wasn't the table I noticed when I looked over.

It was another girl, slouched by the table's edge, watching us.

"Who's that?"

Kyra shrugged, wrinkled her nose. "Who knows? A poet *probably*."

"Poet," I repeated, staring at the girl. She was shoveling pastries into her mouth and grinning like what she was doing was sexually gratifying. She had the most Victorian face. Like she might faint or get tuberculosis any minute. Yet there was a *fuck you* quality to her eyes. It arrested me, Bunny. She was wearing a gross, grungy plaid, like her beauty was trying to graffiti itself. Terrible, yet I couldn't look away. I was mesmerized by her aggressively unbrushed hair, which I immediately longed to tie into complex knots I'd discovered on the internet. She stared at us with her *fuck you* eyes and smiled. How that smile warmed me strangely. She was alone, I saw. Good. Less scary. As we approached her, for Kyra and I walked over to her just as we'd walked to each other, her eyes seemed to shift and soften. No more *fuck you* there. They appeared now like the prettiest murky gray waters of old.

"Hello," we said to her at exactly the same time.

She blinked at us, amused, maybe a little alarmed, by our synchronicity. So was I. She took in our gloved hands, our fit-and-flare dresses, her watery gaze lingering on my sky. "Pretty clouds," she said.

"Thank you," I said. "I love skies," I added stupidly.

"I love them too," the girl said very seriously.

"I love them too," Kyra whispered.

"Has anyone ever told you you look like a mermaid from the nineteenth century?" I blurted at the girl. Then blushed furiously.

She grinned, shook her head. "No."

"You do," I said quietly. "If I braided your hair into a fishtail, you'd see. Very mermaidy, isn't she?" I asked Kyra.

"If mermaids wore plaid," Kyra said coolly, staring at her.

"Are you Fiction?" I asked her, even though I already knew. Sensed it.

"Am I *Fiction?*" She smiled slyly like the idea pleased her.

"One of the new incoming Fiction cohort, she means," Kyra clarified, which annoyed me a little. "One of 'our highly select group,'" she added, quoting the acceptance letter. "One of the five."

The girl was still staring at my clouds in a way that made my cheeks burn, not unpleasantly. "Am I Fiction?" she repeated again slowly, smiling still. "Oh yes. Absolutely."

"Exciting," I said. "Now that you're here, I'm less scared." I don't know why I said that, Bunny. *Was* I less scared? Or was I more?

"So exciting, so much less scared," Kyra echoed. She definitely looked more scared.

"I'm less scared too," the girl whispered, looking into our eyes. "Though fear can be hot sometimes."

Viktoria, she said her name was, which was alarmingly perfect. Maybe that's why you pretty much kept it as is, Samantha (such a heady mix, your prose, of verisimilitude and bald-faced lies). Except you crudely switched out the Slavic *k* for the boring *c* of the English spelling. But there was one lovely detail about her name you omitted: "I go by Vik," she said, looking at just me, which—I don't know, Bunny—was somehow more perfect still.

"I love your dress," I told her. Which was fucking stupid. She wasn't even wearing a dress at the time. *You must stop complimenting people willy-nilly, Button,* Mother said. *You aren't fat anymore and it comes off desperate. Sticky and sweaty and slutty. And no one likes that.* But when I looked at Vik, I could see it, Bunny. Could see her in a dress as oceanic as her eyes. The braids I would twist into her auburn hair, those medieval knots for which she was always destined.

Vik smiled. "Thanks," she said. Sort of like a boy might. Her voice caused a shiver in the place where the razor goes. "I love yours, too," she said, still lost in my clouds. I reached out and took her hand, and she took mine. Her fingernails, I saw now, were very disgusting. Almost willfully so. Like she had maybe been on her hands and knees in the dirt, clawing mud just before she came here. Still, I didn't let go. I held her gross hand, and it's very funny to say, Bunny, but something seemed to course through me then. Some kind of energy, though Mother would kill me for using such a word. It *was* energy. Between me and this mermaid girl in plaid with the unbrushed hair. *Vik*.

Hand in hand in hand, we three walked to a table, far away from everyone. There we found our own heaven complete with orchid centerpiece. There we demolished Kyra's *Alice* pastries, especially Vik. She wolfed them down with her hands in a way I found both boorish and exhilarating. Where would the pastries even go on her slender body, I wondered. I watched her eat, thinking, *Don't want, don't want*. Knowing exactly, exactly where they would go on my own body.

"Have you met anyone else yet?" I asked to make conversation. Couldn't help it, Bunny, I went to Smith, breeder of daffodils and future First Ladies.

"I'm not here to meet, just to *make*," Vik whispered.

Kyra and I looked at each other. *Make?*

"*Make* what?" Kyra whispered back.

Vik looked at us coolly, her lips glossy from all that buttery pastry she'd inhaled. "Whatever turns me on."

"You mean *stories*," Kyra said, which spoiled something. I looked at Vik, who made a snorting sound.

"If that's what you want to call them. I'm interested in other techniques. Other forms."

"Other forms?" I whispered. I wondered if she'd gone to Oberlin. She looked at me and grinned, almost like she knew my writing sample had included, among a few tender prose pieces, a photo of my inner thighs, freshly etched.

"Such as?" Kyra said. The grass on her dress seemed suddenly pricklier, primmer to my eyes. Could I name those flowers after all?

Vik looked at us both. Her mouth was half-open even though she had no words just yet. Her hair took on a golden quality then, the sun glowing right above her head. Almost prophet-like. "Hybridity," Vik said.

"Hybridity," I repeated, entranced. "Huh." For I'd never heard such a word, Bunny. But it sounded magical.

"Like experimental stuff?" Kyra said. "What I might read in an obscure literary journal?"

Vik just smiled.

"Hybridity," Kyra repeated. "Funny, I always thought that was just a term for when you don't know what you're doing, am I wrong? Like when you can't write an actual story or something." And she laughed her high, weird laugh. It didn't sound so much like music then. Her pedigree was Yale or Princeton probably. One of Warren's more boring Ivy sisters. I could see the gargoyled library in which she'd likely whiled away her days, writing *Jane Eyre* fanfic.

"I always thought *stories* were for tight-asses," Vik said. "People who are afraid of getting their hands dirty in the space that begs us to get dirty."

We looked down at our white gloves then, Kyra and I, didn't we, Bunny? Simultaneously we slipped our hands under the table. And Vik smiled, didn't you, Vik? Bunnies hopped behind her on the green. White tails once more darting in and out of our perception. She seemed like our queen already, our queen of filth and mystery. Then her expression shifted. She looked out into the middle distance, almost like she saw something divine break open in the sky.

"Look," she said, a little wonder in her voice. And I was suddenly very jealous, terribly so. Why was she not looking at me anymore?

Then we saw. One of the Fiction faculty was now in our line of sight. The only faculty who mattered to me: Ursula Radcliffe, as you called her in your little novel. *Fosco*, too, wasn't it, after the gothic villain in *The Woman in White?* Oh, we know, all too well, how you feel about Ursula, Bunny. I'll call her Ursula too so as not to confuse you, given your precarious mental state at the moment, even though this really isn't about you. It's about us, about me. And for me, back then, *Ursula* was my Word Witch. Ursula made the word flesh and the flesh word. She was the conjuror of Life in the novel. The reason I came to Warren at all. Also she had the best author photo. How I loved, *loved* the way her long white-blond hair flew all around her head, almost like she was being cosmically electrocuted. True, she wore lipstick, an iridescent porny pink, but I forgave her because of her eyes, the color of dog violets. The way she stared into me, Bunny, as if she could actually see me lying there in my princess bed with the celestial patterned sheets, dreaming myself into her erotic story spaces. She was the author of my very favorites. *Arias of the Solar Plexus. Lamentations: A Bestiary.* And of course, her most seminal work, *To Catch a Crystal Thief of the Heart.*

I noticed then that Vik had the Crystal Thief tattooed on her forearm, beneath the rolled sleeve of her gross plaid. His dark, leporine eyes and leaf-shaped ears gleaming on her soft white flesh. I looked back at Ursula. She was talking to a young woman with long silver hair now. The young woman was very pale and thin, as thin as Mother's dream for me. She was so terribly beautiful, I felt physically wounded by her face. The girl was wearing casual nude linens, I could feel the rich of them from here. She looked like a yoga retreat. A girl for whom the word *summer* was both a noun and a verb. Her silver hair was spiky with birds-of-paradise, and when she looked at me, her eyes were the very coldest blue jewels. Burning my retinas, like when you stare directly into the sun. Who fucking was she? Was she Fiction too? Why was she talking with Ursula, her mouth so close to Ursula's? I was curious, maybe jealous, and I didn't even know of whom anymore, Bunny. To Vik, I no longer even existed. Ursula and this other girl had her eyes.

"Should we go up and say hi?" I asked. Gripping the razor again.

"They seem like they're having a really intense conversation," Vik said. "Like they're communing."

"*Communing?*" Kyra echoed, sort of with a laugh in her voice, speaking my very thought. She wanted me to laugh along with her, but I didn't, Bunny. Between you and me, she already sort of felt like a littlest sister. The grass to my endless sky.

"What about?" I whispered to Vik, my eyes on Ursula and the silver-haired girl.

"Maybe they're talking about *hybridity*," Kyra said. Underneath the table she was holding my hand (the one not holding the razor) tight. Probably we were already beginning to fuse. Vik was still hovering on the edge. I stared at Ursula. *Look at me*, I thought, *I'm the one*. And that is very important to remember, Bunny. That at this point I still had my own singular mind.

Then Ursula saw me at last. My soul, Bunny, it caught a kind of blue fire then. And both she and the jewel-eyed girl smiled wide. Smiles of knowing.

Of *Just you wait.*

2

After the party it was dark. The town had no more golden light at all, and it truly looked like a hell place. Even though my apartment building was only blocks away and I had a rape whistle in my cloud purse, and a can of Mace that Mother had bought me off the internet (also in my cloud purse), I felt afraid. Not in Kansas anymore, Bunny. Fucking literally. I had the razor, too, of course I did. I never really let go of that, not even as I stood there in the dark with Kyra, gloved hand in gloved hand. I could hold the razor in one hand and Kyra's in another. I quite liked this combination, in fact.

Vik took off, disappeared into the dark, her plaid shirt and her wild hair mingling so easily with the shadows. She was there and then she was gone, like a Cheshire cat. Only her voice remaining.

See you in Workshop tomorrow, she'd said.

Tomorrow, I'd whispered. That's right. There was class tomorrow. Workshop. Our first. *Scary*, Kyra had agreed. And then I remembered Ursula would be our teacher. That made me smile. Ursula, who'd smiled at me like she knew I had a razor in my pocket. She knew of the sweat on my finger pads, of my urge to desecrate my own thigh flesh. She knew I'd been dreaming of a bathroom stall in which to do this. Perhaps to carve a short and terrible word there or maybe to draw something pretty. She knew, and it was all going to be part of my Creative Journey; she was going to show me how to turn it into something else, something beautiful and powerful and transcendent, Bunny. But then she'd turned away. And when she did, it was like a darkness suddenly fell over the proceedings, over the party, over myself. The sun went behind a cloud. The tent seemed to empty of its poets and its old-people faculty, and suddenly the admin people were clearing the tables and chairs. The rabbits seemed to have taken over the field. I watched them nibbling at the grass all around us.

"Careful in that grass dress," I told Kyra, "they might eat you up."

"That wouldn't be such a bad death," Kyra said, echoing my thoughts exactly. Which frightened me, Bunny, even as it calmed me so.

"Girl," Kyra whispered beside me, what felt like seconds later. "I think the party's over."

And so it was. Just the two of us suddenly. Standing there in the dark, empty tent. The white tulle billowing all around us "like so many ghosts," she said, echoing my own thoughts again. And again I wasn't sure how I felt about that. *Like so many ghosts*, that's a line from your novel, Bunny, a phrase you no doubt stole from us, by the way, among so many other things. I was still holding hands with her, this girl in the grass dress who also smelled, so eerily, like fresh-cut grass. "I'll walk you home," she said.

"I'll walk *you* home," I said.

And then we did just that.

First Kyra walked me home. Then I walked her home. And then she walked me home again, and when she did, I said, "You might as well stay the night. Only if you want to, of course. Don't if you don't." We were standing in the very large and ornate doorway of my apartment building. She was looking up at me like such a lost soul, a beautiful ghost girl come to haunt me. For a moment I almost felt like I'd dreamed her there, Bunny, this grass to my sky. *Fiction*, she'd said she was, after all. But no, that was silly. She was real. A new friend. I wouldn't have dreamed the cherry lipstick, which she'd applied so thickly to her very full lips.

Truth? And let me whisper this to you, Bunny: I didn't know if I wanted her to stay the night. Part of me did. Even though I had an amazing apartment with tall windows and the prettiest new pastel furniture for thinking and writing on, I was a little afraid of being alone there. How small I might suddenly feel sitting beneath these so-high ceilings. How my sky notebook might taunt me. How I might spiral darkly among the wing chairs and ottomans, despite the bright flower arrangements Mother had put in every room—tulips and irises and freesia and all manner of roses, in such lovely tall vases for me. Not to mention my many movie posters, which she'd hung on the walls, all of them like old friends. Marilyn Monroe fake reading. Marlon Brando in *A Streetcar Named Desire*, frowning with arms folded, being such a scary-hot prick. A dreamy James Dean as Jim Stark in *Rebel Without a Cause*, which was my very favorite movie, Bunny. In fact, many people said that I quite looked like a blond Natalie Wood circa 1956.

Maybe I'd be fine alone after all, I thought, recalling these posters. I was about to say so, that maybe we should say good night now, go our own separate ways, when—

"I'd love to spend the night," Kyra whispered, and her pretty doll eyes were sort of wet with tears almost. Of gratitude, I guessed. "And then we can walk to class together in the morning," she said. "Won't that be fun?"

"So fun," I agreed. And it was funny how when I said that, I suddenly regretted asking her in the first place, Bunny. Suddenly I felt like my soul was no longer my own.

I walked her back to her place one more time, and she picked up a foresty dress for the next day and also some other things for overnight. Her apartment wasn't quite as nice as mine, but I said it was so amazing anyway. Of course I did, Bunny, I'm very well bred. "*Wow,*" I said of the one-bedroom with galley kitchen, filled with her red and black middle-of-the-road furniture. "What an incredible place. It has such *energy,*" I said, relishing being able to use the word openly, without Mother there to disapprove.

"You really think so?" Kyra said.

"Oh yes," I lied. "Absolutely."

It did not really. Have any energy, Bunny. It was a boring arty girl's apartment, quite like mine, in fact, but much lesser. Books on the shelves that were also on my shelves: *Jane Eyre. The Bell Jar. The Waves. The Bloody Chamber*, of course. All Ursula's books, of course, of course. Their spines severely cracked like mine, like she'd perused them about a thousand times, as I had, which enraged me inexplicably. She seemed to have more fairy tale and mythology collections than I did, more Victorian novels, more Murakami and Ogawa (she was a quarter Japanese, she said), but no Parker or Mitford or Austen like I did (that was a strange relief). *The Invention of Morel*, it was cool that she had that one but also annoying to me, Bunny. I thought I was the only one who loved that book, held it close. There were posters on her walls too. Mostly prints of fairies and frolicking nymphs and Pre-Raphaelite ladies holding crystal balls or else combing their very long dark hair while staring mythically into space. There was one of a giant wolf and a little girl in bed together, Little Red Riding Hood probably, and the wolf was grinning widely and Little Red's mouth was a huge O of fake surprise, like, *Oh my, what are you doing here, sir?* There was another of a wide-eyed girl in a dark forest clutching a leering black fox for dear life. Why was she holding on to him like that, I wondered, even though she was so obviously afraid?

"Because that's what obsession is like," Kyra said in her ghostly voice, hearing my thoughts. "I enjoy nonhuman, entity-centric eroticism," she whispered, staring wistfully at the print. "What about you?"

"Me?" And I laughed. Trying to frighten me, to get under my skin. She was already there was the truth. I murmured noncommittally, gazing at her walls. My eyes fell on a print of a very hot young man being dragged into a pool full of pale naked ladies with long dark hair and haunted eyes. I knew this print, of course. Waterhouse. *Hylas and the Nymphs.* "I also have this," I said, touching it softly.

"Oh," she said, touching it also. "Isn't it just so great?"

"It is. I love it so much," I said. "It's my favorite."

"It's *my* favorite," she said. We were both petting the edges of the frame now. Petting it, Bunny, like it was our actual pet. Staring into each other's eyes, she had such terribly lovely eyes. It made me begin to worry, Bunny, did we overlap perhaps too much in our sensibilities? There were differences, of course. She had typewriters everywhere ("They're my thing," she whispered, and I said, "How lovely," even though I did not think typewriters were lovely at all, Bunny—the clicking drove me literally fucking crazy). A few witchy accessories Mother would never have allowed in our home. Crystals in so many pale shades and strange shapes.

"What's this?" I asked, holding up a tied bundle of dried gray leaves and flowers sitting in an iridescent shell. The bundle looked scorched on one end.

"Sage," Kyra said. "I burn it to purify the space."

"Oh, cool," I lied. It didn't smell purified to me at all. It smelled muddy and smoky and cheap.

"My friend who's this incredible witch back in New Hampshire, she made it for me."

"How lovely," I lied again.

"Can I tell you a secret?" Kyra whispered. Her face now very close to my face. Her lipstick so thick, Bunny, did I mention that? Cherries in Winter, I would find out was its whorish name.

"What?" I whispered. Even though I didn't really want to know. Felt my soul slipping from me with her face so close to mine like this.

"I think this place is super haunted," she whispered even more softly, her cherry lips grazing my peach-fuzzy earlobe, the pinprick of diamond that lived there. "There are demons here or something. Spirits. A ghost for sure."

"Is that so?" I said, being oh so polite. I could already see the novella she was starting to write about this in her mind. Her bright eyes shiny with potential plotlines. Herself at the center. Communing with this ghost. Possibly having supernatural sex with it, as was her wont apparently. Annoying. I found her terribly annoying in this moment, Bunny. But I murmured how cool it was, of course.

"In fact, can I show you something?"

No, I thought. *I want to go home now, alone, to my much better apartment. I want my soul back, please.* I wanted to think my own thoughts, away from this girl who might truly be just a witchier, poorer version of myself. But then I remembered how she'd held my hand in the tent earlier, the soft press of her white-gloved flesh. I thought of how my skin had hummed when we first locked eyes, whenever we locked eyes. I looked at her pretty doll face, her bright smile.

"Show me," I said.

And that's when she took me up to see the attic. This very attic we're sitting in right now, in fact, Bunny. Where we would eventually make such magic, such beauty, with this very ax.

"Follow me," Kyra said, her gloved hand holding mine all the way up these really steep and rickety stairs, which were very creepy and gross. There was something about this walk up to her dark attic. It was erotic maybe. Felt somehow like entering sex. Kyra let go of my hand and walked to the middle of the room, while I hovered by the railing. She could let go of me so easily. It distressed me even on this first day of knowing her, even though I didn't know, did I want to be held like this? Now I stared at her pretty silhouette turning circles in the dark room.

"It has an energy, don't you think? For *making*," she said, using Vik's word. "And look, a steepled ceiling. Almost like a church. Or a temple."

Like a Satan church, I thought quietly. Was she slightly satanic? She suddenly seemed a little satanic. It was the red cloak she'd slipped over her shoulders, maybe. *Like Little Red Riding Hood*, she'd insisted, but when I looked at her hooded figure, I thought of degenerate French novels and Black Masses. I could feel her grinning in the dark. The tap-tap of her red Mary Janes on the wooden floorboards. The way the moon shone behind her in the inverted-triangle window.

"Here is where I'm going to create," she said. "Here's where I'm going to *make*."

"What?" I asked.

" 'Whatever turns me on,' " she said, once again echoing Vik. "I'll put my desk here. You could put yours here too. Maybe we could make together."

"Okay," I lied, "I'd love that."

Of course we never did that, did we, Bunny? Put our desks up here. But we didn't know that then. We actually still thought, back then, if you can believe it, Bunny, that we were going to *write* things. Short fucking stories. Novelettes. About who knows what? Ghosts who were also lovers. Erotic sentient mists. Being alive in all its perils. *Click, click* on a typewriter. *Scratch, scratch* with a little Japanese pencil. These were the sounds of our future, we thought. Sweating all alone as our minds dreamed us elsewhere. As we conjured that elsewhere with careful adjectives and just-so words. We were totally fucking wrong about that.

Which is funny.

Because it was right after that, on that last walk back to my place, that we saw him, didn't we? The bunny. Darting right into our path and just stopping there, so that we ourselves stopped on the sidewalk, still holding gloved hands.

"Look," I said.

Yes, it was I who said *look*. Skipping, we'd been skipping together on this dark night, our shoes clicking in eerie synchronicity, the trees making their *shhh* sounds, and there was the sound too of screaming homeless and drunken frat boy. And then this creature suddenly in our path, in our midst. White and glowing in the dark just like we were in our elemental dresses of air and earth. A little furry moon in the black. Staring at us with his so-shining eyes. Like, *Hi*.

"Hi, Bunny," I think I even said.

"What?" Kyra said, like I'd called to her and not the creature.

"Bunny," I repeated, pointing.

"Bunny," she whispered. "Yes."

And the creature seemed to smile at us, almost, in the dark. *Yes*. Then he hopped away. We watched him go, holding hands so very hard, Bunny, that we found we had bruises the next day, didn't we?

We don't remember getting home that night. Or how we ended up in my sky bed together. Tangled into each other, my toy horse, Pinkie Pie, between us. So funny, but I remember nothing after seeing that bunny, Bunny. It was like time stopped or something, stood still like in a stupid love song or film, except this was no love song or film, it was Reality. We blinked and it was somehow the next morning. I woke up in Kyra's grass dress, and she was in my sky dress, how funny. When in the night did we switch? I stared at this beautiful doll girl with the wild red curls lying beside me, this girl who yesterday was a stranger. The whole thing made me very uncomfortable, Bunny. To see her in my bed, first of all. Second, that she looked so very pretty upon first waking, so fucking lovely even in slumber. Third, that our hands were still held, quite fiercely, and I had the dreamiest smile playing on my face. When I caught sight of it in my dresser mirror, I immediately let go of her hand and she opened her eyes. Smiled sleepily. Didn't look at all surprised or horrified to see me lying so close beside her, wearing her grass dress. Or that she was wearing my sky dress. Or that I'd apparently braided her hair into many a medieval knot at some point in the night. (Funny I didn't remember doing that, Bunny, though admittedly, it was my wont to do such things, an itch deep in my fingers that nothing could scratch.) She just patted her braids and yawned like all was as it should be. Stared at my *Rebel Without a Cause* poster.

"Did anyone ever tell you you look like Natalie Wood?"

"No," I lied.

She smiled at me. "Workshop today. Our first."

"Yes."

"So excited. Are you?"

I felt nothing, except the fact that her grass dress was just a little tight on me, Bunny. A little suffocating everywhere but in the boob area, where it gaped disconcertingly.

"Excited," I lied. "So."

"That your desk?" she whispered, looking over at it, just beneath the window.

"Yes," I said, and I suddenly felt sick.

"So pretty," Kyra sighed. "You'll write such great things there probably."

"Maybe." But I didn't know anymore, Bunny. I'd sat there just the other day, looking at the so-pretty light through my so-pretty window. Stared down at my open notebook, whose cover had the most beautiful skyscape. Tapped the blank page with my periwinkle LePen. Tapped and fucking tapped. Harp music played all around me, Bunny, for ambiance, for dreaming purposes, but it began to grate. I stared down at the pale blue page, misty with cloud illustrations. Finally I drew a tulip. It was hideous. The petals so obscene, like lips swollen, almost vaginal. *What Coraline needs more than anything,* Mother told her drunk book club friends once, *is to get fucked. Go fuck the gardener, sweetie. Mother's already done it. She gives him an A++.*

Do they even have A++ in school? one of her friends asked.

At the school of fucking, they do, Mother said. And all her friends laughed. *That's where you oughta go, Coraline. Forget about writing. The school of fucking, that's what you need. Ivy League.* And I fake smiled, the rose balm cracking on my lips. I'd thought we were going to talk about the book club book, but apparently we were not going to. All the women in Mother's book club had their books facedown on their capri laps. I stared at the author photo on the book jacket. Blond like Mother, like all of us, and wearing the crispest white shirt. She looked a little like a real estate agent, her blue eyes haunted and corporate. She had written what the jacket copy said was an *unputdownable tour de force* about *having it all.* But no one, including Mother, who'd chosen the book, seemed to want to talk about it. What they wanted was to hear Mother talk more about the school of fucking. They wanted to hear about the gardener. They wanted their very large fishbowl glasses refilled with cold white wine, which I was forced to pour for them. And as I did so, I swore to myself, right then and there on that July afternoon under the bluest of Virginia skies, that I'd write a book that Mother would read over wanting to fuck the gardener and mocking me openly about my love life. She wouldn't be able to tear her eyes away from my words, I vowed.

"Bunny, are you okay?"

And I was back in my bedroom again, Kyra looking at me worriedly, for tears were stinging my eyes. "Fine," I lied.

"We'd better get going," she said. "Don't want to be late for the first day, do we?"

Dread is what I felt. But I shook my head. Smiled. "Of course not."

Hand in hand we walked toward campus, our shoes still clicking in time. Hand in hand, even after we'd spotted the bruises, Bunny. Even after I said, *We better give our hands a break, we better let go*, we did not let go. I held hers and she held mine, almost tighter, all the way to Narrative Arts, it was like we couldn't *not* hold. We were still wearing each other's dresses, so that now she was the sky to my earth and I was the earth to her sky. I'd given her one of my jewel-colored cardigans to match, out of the great kindness of my heart. I was like that, Bunny, so very generous with my possessions, something you didn't see fit to mention in your telling, but never mind.

I still remember first seeing the Narrative Arts building, Bunny. How it looked, to my eye, like nothing more than a weird old pointy house.

"*This* is it?" I whispered.

"What do you think?" Kyra said.

I stared at the blackened brick, its many round windows like lidless eyes. Its sharp Gothic spires stabbing the pretty sky. *Hate it*, I thought. *Run*, I thought. *Jesus fucking Christ, New England*, I thought. *Is this your idea of beautiful?* But then I remembered Ursula. She was in there somewhere, in her shimmery caftan. All her narrative magic. All her fairy dust. Waiting for me.

"It's pretty," Kyra said, sounding scared.

"It is," I agreed. "So pretty."

"I love it so much."

"Me too," I lied. "So much."

"You look nervous," Kyra said.

"Not at all," I lied again. "Dying to go in. Meet Ursula. My idol."

"My idol too. I'm dying to meet her too."

Which enraged me, Bunny.

"Oh my god, look, there he is again!" she cried.

And indeed there he was again, sitting by a cluster of rosebushes. The bunny. The same bunny from last night? Perhaps. Oh how he was staring at us! Nose twitching almost . . . *knowingly*. Was he looking at me or was he looking at Kyra? Kyra will say both, of course. And at the time I said *Yes*,

both. But between you and me, Samantha? And now that I have the floor
(for once) and I'm allowed to speak unfettered (for once) while others are
forced to be silent (for once) thanks to our pact, which, more on that later: I
really felt like he was staring at just me. Not just *at* me, but fucking *into* me,
my very soul. Staring so hard with his large, dark rabbit eyes, which seemed
afraid but also not afraid. *Good luck*, perhaps he was telling me.

"Thank you, Bunny," I whispered.

So funny to think of that first Workshop. How fucking scared I was as we
entered the so-called Cave. Like you, I'd pictured a literal cave, Bunny. Ancient, oozing walls. A primal, womb-like darkness. Maybe Ursula standing
there, backlit and in bell sleeves, like in a Stevie Nicks video. But it was just
a boring black box theater, remember? In the middle of the space: a hollow
square of tables with chairs around all sides. The table was lit from above
by a single spotlight, like this was a theater and we were the central act.
Something comforting about that. I knew that world, of course, Bunny, all
too well, from my stage/throw-up days. Vik was already there, wearing another shirt of another gross plaid. She hadn't brushed her wavy auburn hair
in what looked like two years. She had no pen in front of her, nor paper, no
laptop, not even a phone. Instead she was sitting on a backward-facing chair
like she was fucking it. Chest pressed into the backrest, legs manspreading
sexily, talking in French to the girl with the silver hair, who turned to look
at us—our shoes made such echoing clicks. The silver-haired girl smiled.
Hi, she said with her mouth but not her voice. I was certain she'd gone to
some illustrious overseas academy, like in Switzerland maybe, a school so
elite that I hadn't even heard of it, Bunny, a castle nestled in snowcapped
mountains and mirror lakes.

Hi, Kyra and I both mouthed, awestruck.

Quickly we took seats beside them.

There was another girl there too, of course, Bunny. *You*. Remember?
Sitting there with your head down, your long dark hair like a curtain drawn

over half your face. Wearing some sort of sad-girl T-shirt. A wolf barking winsomely at a moon or something. A black cardigan to drown in. We could see your one eye peeking out of the hair curtain, and that was all. You stared at us so darkly, and then you looked back down at the table and that's where you kept your eye. We could not say hello to you or even smile at you because you were hiding in your hair, Bunny, like Cousin Itt. Please remember that the next time you call me a bitch in your mind. Or in print, k? That you didn't make it easy for us, socially, from the very beginning.

Now, the chair beside you was empty, and that chair was just a little bit bigger than the other chairs. So we assumed, of course we assumed, that this was the teacher chair. Soon to be filled with the one and only Ursula. In fact, I could hear, in the dark just now, a clicking like footsteps. As you know, Bunny, when you're in the Circle (which, yes, I know is literally a square, but metaphorically it is a circle, just like the classroom is metaphorically a cave), you can't see beyond it at all. The circumference of spotlight does not extend beyond the Circle, suggesting the process of Creation, how we are always mostly in the dark, in a state of either un- or half knowing. So at the sound of the footsteps, I filled with such excitement. I made a small sound of glee, like a hiccup. The silver-haired girl smiled at me again, her jewel eyes burning brightly. I was expecting Ursula to appear out of the black at any moment. To point at me and smile. To say, *Hello, Coraline. You are exceptional. You will write the book club book to end all book clubs, and I will help you find this book inside yourself and I will help you birth it from your mind's vagina. From your soul's vagina, rather. Into a living entity of double-spaced pages beautifully screaming.*

I was expecting to smell her, Bunny. Her author photo suggested a very specific incense. Myrrh laced with fir trees. I expected her iridescence, her brilliance, to blind me a little. I was nearly crying in anticipation as the footsteps inched ever closer.

And then?

We saw it was someone else. Not Ursula at all.

A fucking man.

Very tall, with sleeve tattoos of birds and trees. He had wild, leonine hair, and he was wearing a black T-shirt advertising some sort of Swedish metal band like my older brother and his friends sometimes wore. Um. Who the fuck was this, please?

I glanced at Kyra, whose face looked as confused and afraid as I felt.

The man half smiled at us. He told us hello, his name was Allan.

Allan?!

"I'll be your Workshop leader this fall," this Allan man said. He was very excited to be here with us, he added. He did not look at all excited, Bunny. He had a Scottish accent. It reminded me of crags and spiked flowers. Impenetrable cloudy skies. I'd heard of Allan, of course. *Alan*, as you called him, Bunny, for your imaginative genius clearly knows no bounds (is he suing you, by the way?). Or *the Lion*. (Of course you remember *the Lion*, Bunny.) He was the semi-famous literary horror writer who wrote experimental novellas about women being murdered in the Highlands by very philosophically minded psychopaths. He did not look magical in his author photo. He looked to me, in fact, like he might have committed these very crimes. And in person, even more so. The way he was standing and gripping the back of his own chair with his big hands, each knuckle of which was tattooed with some kind of rune. He'd placed a mug of steaming tea on the table. The mug had Japanese characters on it, which I felt was very appropriative. The scent wafted toward us, bitter and green. The strange girl beside him (you, Bunny) suddenly looked terribly happy. What sliver of your face I could see was smiling now.

A nightmare. This was a fucking nightmare, that simple. I'd never woken up from my celestial bed this morning, where I'd slept curled into Kyra like she was my cat. I was still dreaming on my sun pillow. I was still clutching Pinkie Pie close to my body. There were tears in my closed eyes from this shitty dream. Any minute I'd wake up. For now I raised my hand. "Excuse me, *hi?*"

The man looked at me. I felt him take me in from golden bob to pearls to grass dress. Did he imagine just then beheading me with a hunting knife?

"Yes," he said in his crag voice. So softly.

"I'm sorry, but I thought Ursula was supposed to be our Workshop leader?" It was a question that was also a statement, Bunny.

The man frowned. Mumbled something about a fellowship. Ursula had received one to pursue her own research this fall, so they'd had to do a last-minute change. "She'll be teaching you in spring," he said. "And I have the happy job of teaching you this fall." And again he did not look at all like it was a happy job.

I looked at Kyra. Clearly she felt the same horror, but she was trying to smile. Vik was picking at her dirty fingernails, oblivious. The silver-haired girl, who I found out later was called Elsinore, was just smiling sadly at us. (*Eleanor* was the lazy perversion in your novel, Bunny. Or, what was it again, *the Duchess?* You'll have your moment with her later, don't worry.) Probably she'd already known about Ursula. Probably Ursula herself had told her at the party yesterday. How terribly alone I felt in this moment, Bunny. How left out.

The Cousin Itt girl was beaming now. You, Bunny, you were beaming now. I could see that sliver of your face watching Allan with such naked and open admiration, it was embarrassing. Sort of sticky and sweaty and slutty of you, I thought.

Allan smiled at all of us. Was it a smile or was it a smirk? So very hard to say. He had one of those cryptic, too-cool faces. His crow tattoos gleamed beneath the spotlight. In my pocket, I ran the tip of my finger over the razor.

"Well," he said, "why don't we dive right in? Take a look at the pieces you were all asked to submit a couple of weeks ago. Offer some feedback. So we can get a sense of one another."

Inside, I died a little. *Feedback? On the first day?*

And then? He distributed copies of my very own two-page story, into which I'd poured my heart's blood, Bunny. Which I'd submitted for Ursula. I'd even written *for Ursula* on the top of the page.

"Let's start with you," this man from my nightmares said. Suddenly looking right at me, Bunny.

"*Me?*"

"Why don't you go ahead and read your piece aloud? And then we'll all chime in with our thoughts, okay?"

Read? Aloud? My heart's blood?

But what choice did I have, Bunny? This man, our alleged teacher, was smiling murderously at me. Waiting. So I read my little piece. Of which I was unspeakably ashamed but also fiercely proud. Existential baking instructions addressed to an unfeeling yet strangely charismatic oven. It was a beautiful story that made me cry to write, the emotional truth of it.

Did my voice shake as I read? It did ever so slightly, yes. My cheeks burned, I was suddenly so hot. Patches of sweat bloomed under my pits, on the small of my back. It felt like it took four fucking years to read two pages. When I finally finished, I looked up, breathless. Everyone was sort of smiling at me, including Allan. But not like he was oh so blown away. Not like I had cast a word spell, no, no. Like he was sorry. Very sorry for what he was about to say.

And then, Bunny? He proceeded to give his *feedback*. I didn't hear his words exactly, I felt them. Like daggers to my wrists. I remember Vik and Elsinore staring at me with such immutable faces as Allan went on and on about why exactly I was terrible and my story was terrible. He took out his copy of my piece, covered in his *line notes*, a.k.a. stab wounds. It appeared he'd underlined and circled and even scratched out practically every fucking word with a red pen. I was horrified by all that red, Bunny. Thinking of this man drawing lines through my carefully chosen adjectives, probably with an erection. Sipping his hot green tea in its Orientalist cup. Thinking he knew so much. About *craft*. About narrative. I thought, *Fuck this man.* Hearing him speak about me, I felt I was going to die right there in my grass dress.

"Coraline, you're bleeding," someone said. Kyra.

"Am I?"

And I looked down and saw that, yes, I was in fact bleeding. My dress pocket was all bloody. My index finger had pressed deep into the razor's edge. Funny how I didn't even feel the pain over the breaking of my heart.

This man, Allan, my alleged teacher, he looked at this blood. Saw it spotting my grassy pocket in dark red drops like poppies among the blades. Blood shed by his own cruel tongue. Did he smile then? I swore I saw him smile softly, perhaps even smugly, at my pain. Take a small sip of bitter tea from his handleless cup.

"Thoughts," he whispered. Looking at all five of us, like we were his harem, really.

"I think it's so brilliant," Kyra said. "I mean it's dreamy, but it's also kind of terrifying. In the best way. Like Plath meets Poe or something." She smiled at me. Even though I was close to crying at her kindness, her words meant really nothing. Did not take away the sting.

"Creepy cute," Vik offered. Still manspreading under the table in her ripped denim and dirty boots. "Sort of like Derrida does Emily Post. Hot in a strange, stifled way. I'd fuck it if I could," she whispered. And she looked at me like she was sort of fucking me with her opium eyes.

"Interesting," Allan said, coughing. "What about you, Elsinore?"

The silver-haired girl said nothing. She looked at the blood staining my pocket, then into my eyes. I heard her soul say to my soul, *I see you. You will have your revenge on this man who I agree is a man of nightmares.* A tear escaped my eye, and she smiled warmly at its falling.

"Everything okay?" Allan said. Fucking monster that he was.

"Fine," I said. "Allergies," I said. *To you,* I thought.

"Sam," Allan said, turning to the Cousin Itt girl sitting beside him (you, Bunny). You had a brooch on your cardigan with a deer's head on it, I noticed now. The deer stared at me darkly. You, meanwhile, kept your eye (the one not hidden in your hair) on the table.

"I agree with your notes, Allan," you said to the table, while the brooch deer sneered. You did feel my piece was a bit on the nose, actually, you said. A bit too cute, you said, for its own good. Perhaps I could loosen it up a bit more, structurally. Perhaps I could be more organic, too, with my language choices, less "trying so hard." More "authentic." Just, you know, "let it flow."

I looked at your sneering deer, your hair curtain. So fucking shiny and black, like a ground beetle. I hated you then, Bunny. I really did.

Allan handed me my story, covered in his many slashes. His letter in red pen on the back of the last page, which I did not read, would never fucking read. Everyone else handed in their copies with their own notes they'd made while Allan was talking. Kyra's just had a smiley face. Vik had written *Have you tried anal?* Elsinore had written a quote from Julia Kristeva about the abject. And you, Bunny, handed your copy to me with a sad smile. Like, *Sorry, not sorry.* You'd written a note quite like Allan's. I saw the word *tidy.* I saw the word *contrived.* I saw the word *pacing* and I saw the word *structure* and I knew you'd gone to a state school. I felt the blood seeping darkly from my finger. I saw red, the color. And then suddenly it was just Kyra and I in the Cave, wasn't it? And she was saying over and over, her lips very close to my ear, buzzing with my sense of failure, "Come on, Bunny, let's go."

3

After Workshop I had what I'll call *a moment* in the nearby rose garden. You never mentioned the rose garden in your telling, and I wonder why. It was such a lovely place, right behind the Narrative Arts Center, remember? A flying-hare statue was erected there in seventeen-something, and the roses were always so bright and bloomy. A good place to go after you've been psychologically devastated, when you're seething. And I *was* seething, Bunny. Unspeakably so. Because I didn't come here, all the way to New fucking England, to be . . . fucking humiliated. Especially not by some Nightmare Man. A trigger-happy European male writer. I came here to create my own soul arias. I came here for mind space away from Mother, didn't I? To escape the tumbleweedy terrain of my humdrum life. To be famous maybe. Experience the *ecstasy of Creation* that Ursula had talked about in her seminal hybrids. And I'd thought, in my two-page story about the unfeeling oven, that I had shown a bit of that *in potentia*. And what had Allan done? Jizzed all over it, my *potentia*, with his prickish red pen.

"I hate him," I told Kyra. "So fucking much." I cried into my white-gloved hands, which were bloodstained now, Bunny, and my own pearls felt cold on my throat.

Kyra said, "Please don't cry, Bunny." She said I was so brilliant, it was fucking crazy, and Allan was fucking crazy not to see it too. She went on and on in this vein, and I didn't really hear her, so loud was the white noise of my own rage. There was, though, I noticed, a disconcerting smile on her face as she spoke these words of comfort. She was biting on this smile to keep it from coming in full. Cherries in Winter, her lipstick was called, except that there are no cherries in winter, Bunny, it's a fake concept. Was she actually happy that I'd been humiliated? No. Impossible. *Brilliant, so brilliant,* she said with those trying-not-to-smile fake-cherry lips.

"Thank you, Bunny," I said. But I did wonder. Was she lying to me? Maybe she loved me so much in this moment because she thought I was bad at writing now. Because now I was no threat at all. Meanwhile, Bunny, you'd walked out of the classroom with our Man of Nightmares. Kyra and I saw you both cutting across the green, walking to the campus pub together. We saw you looking up at him with your so-shiny face like he was god or something. You were clutching your books to your chest, beaming obscenely. I sensed that for many years you had probably been something of a social loser. And I should know. Because I carried my books, beaming, exactly like that once, not so very long ago. We saw him hold open the bar's double doors for you, and we saw you smile in a sick way and walk through, and we saw him walk in after you. I was horrified by you in that moment, Bunny, I can't deny.

"What a teacher's pet," Kyra hissed in my ear, still buzzing wildly with my own rage and shame. "She's probably going to fuck him. Do you think she will?"

"Don't know," I said. "Probably."

"What a slut," Kyra said, looking at me hopefully. Waiting for me to say *thank you* maybe. I didn't. I really didn't want this to turn into something about you, Bunny.

The sky that afternoon was such a terrible golden yellow. The clouds such strange shapes, the shapes of my horror. All I could see in my head was Allan's smug face. His cruel smile at my pain.

"I hate him, I hate him," I whispered to the roses and to the damp grass at my feet. The squirrels and swallows seemed to regard me with such pity. Not ashamed to say I wept right there in the garden. Sobbed, maybe a little uncontrollably. Barely conscious of Kyra's little white-gloved hand rubbing my back. Kyra, the sky to my grass, and I was the grass to her sky. Her balmy mouth continuing to speak useless words of consolation while I looked into the animal eyes of the hare statue. Deep, deep into the shiny, slanted blanks. "I could kill him. I could fucking kill him," I whispered.

"Kill, Bunny?" Kyra laughed. "Surely not kill."

"Kill," I said, and it was a word before thought, my mouth moving all by itself.

"Bunny, you're still bleeding," Kyra said to me.

"What?" I looked down. So I was. But who cared about blood from a finger, Bunny, when I'd already lost my heart's blood?

"Maybe we should go to Health Services or something," Kyra offered.

But I didn't want to go to Health Services. I only wanted to go home. I only wanted to hold my pony, Pinkie Pie, as tightly as fucking possible. *Do you really need a toy with you at this age, Button?* Mother had asked. *No, Mother*, I'd lied, *of course not*. And I'd pretended to take it out of the packing box. I only wanted to eat a number of forbidden foods in the dark and then maybe throw them up after or maybe even not. Maybe just let it all congeal in my body. My phone was ringing and ringing in my nonbloody pocket. Mother calling of course. Wanting to know how my first day went. I let it ring as tears filled my eyes afresh. Making the whole world, this awful place that didn't understand me, blur into a hazy pool of sunset colors.

"Want me to kill him for you?" Kyra whispered. Petting my forearm now. She said it like a joke, of course. *Just a joke, Bunny*. She was a very hot girl, I was realizing now. Probably she'd always had her pick of whomever she wanted to fuck. Probably she only had to look at whatever human she was horny for and say, *Fuck?* And they would die right then and there of lust. Not like me, with my dyed blond hair and my tight smile that twitched with so many disorders. Smiling primly beside my slutty mother, who thought I was the slutty one even as she mocked me for being prim. But then why was Kyra looking at me like *I* was powerful? Like I was her sun or something.

"Yes," I said. "Except I want to kill him with you."

"Okay." She smiled. "We'll do it together, then."

I nodded. My skin hummed again. I was joking, surely I was joking. "We'll kill fucking Allan," I said. Something in my voice, or was it my eyes?

"Very funny, Bunny," Kyra said.

"I'm serious," I said. Maybe just to scare her. Maybe because I enjoyed that kind of power more than I cared to admit. Or maybe because I was serious in that moment. Very. Kyra just looked at me. Laughed that weird high laugh of hers. Mumbled again how I was "so funny, Bunny." She said it to the grass now, not looking at my eyes.

So I said, Yes, I was so funny. Kill Allan, I said. Ha ha.

And then we saw him.

Standing in the tall grass, right in front of the statue. Floppy eared, his fur white as snow. The bunny we'd seen last night and then again on our way to class, I was sure it was the same one now. Staring at us with his large, dark eyes.

"Bunny," we both whispered.

Back in Virginia, whenever I saw a bunny, it always felt like magic, and I'd blush if we made eye contact, and then of course it would dart away, breaking my heart. But this bunny—and it brings actual tears to my eyes even now to say it—*approached*. It began to walk toward me—*hop* toward me?—and I began to walk shyly toward it. It was . . . how else can I describe it? Like a sort of love-story moment, a movie scene where the two lovers walk toward each other from opposite ends of the screen, their eyes locked. I could feel the leaves falling gently all around me, like they, too, wanted in on this moment of deep connection, of cosmic understanding.

And then suddenly he was in my arms. Incredible, the soft feel of his fur. The heavy magic of his life in my bloody hands. I gasped with glee.

"Oh, Bunny," I whispered. My bunny. And the beautiful animal, he looked at me, I recall this so clearly. He looked right fucking at me. And in my mind I heard a voice. I swore I did.

It said, *I'm yours, Coraline. I'm yours.*

Tears escaped my eyes and dripped onto the bunny. Blood from my finger pooled onto his white fur, leaving a dark red mark there, but he didn't seem to mind at all. He looked at me even more tenderly. And I held him. So tightly, Bunny.

And the bunny's dark eyes, full of my own eyes' tears, suddenly brightened. Yes. Right before me I saw them change color while staying entirely locked with mine. Shift into blue the way the black night breaks into blue morning. The palest blue of my sky dress, which, at the moment, was on Kyra's body. And the strangest thing? Was that I wasn't shocked at all. I felt like I knew it would happen. Energy coursing from my hands into his furry body had made it so. My tears falling into his eyes, my finger's blood on his scruff, had made it so. *I* had made this moment of Bunny's eyes miraculously changing.

"My god," I whispered. I saw a whole sky in Bunny's eye reflected back at me. A whole world that made my own world fall away. I forgot the rose garden and I forgot Kyra and I forgot my razor and I even forgot about that man-demon, Allan. I forgot everything except Bunny, smiling at me with his sweet little rabbit mouth. Covered in my blood and tears like a newborn.

Suddenly I felt a swell of arms around me. The fact of human skin unnerved me just then, Bunny. Who was bothering me in my magical moment with Bunny? Kyra, of course. Rubbing my back, trying to squirm inside my magic. And then two pairs of arms joining Kyra's and encircling me, suffocating me, it felt like. Vik, I knew by the dirty fingernails. And then Elsinore's hand too, her fingernails pearlescent pointed ovals.

"There, there," their glossy mouths whispered into my ears. "We're here for you, Bunny."

"Bunny," they called me, so that I did not know if they were referring to me or to the animal or perhaps to us both, so fused we were in this moment.

"We're here and we saw," they whispered into my neck. "What he fucking did. You must be so humiliated, Bunny. We would have died if he'd said that to us. You must be so ashamed. But don't worry. We hate him with you. And we will have our revenge. *Kill Allan,*" they said. "Metaphorically speaking, of course."

And all of me shuddering at these words while I clutched Bunny's bloodied fur. I felt so much love in this moment. For Bunny. *My* Bunny. With his new blue eyes that I made.

Me.

Coraline.

And can I tell you, I was so—

Creepy Doll

Um, hi! That's all very well and good, but I think it's time for me to seriously cut in and take over, okay, Bunny? Not that I don't think Coraline's amazing and that her storytelling is amazing (omg so good). It's just unfortunate for you, Bunny (for all of us), that on this night of Absolute Truth, in the midst of our Healing Journeys, she also decided to be just a little bit of a fucking liar, apparently. I didn't realize one could be such an unreliable narrator of nonfiction, but perhaps we all can be at times? When we're desperate and delusional especially, Bunny, which I know you can totally relate to.

Sadly, I couldn't quite catch *all* of her half-whispered story, but it's now clear that (as usual, Bunny!) I'm going to have to take the ax and do some serious labor to get us back on track. Because we really do need to move it along here, k? I mean, given the circumstances especially. Of you being tied up and all, Bunny. Of us having kidnapped you, which, just so you know, I totally didn't agree with. At least not at first. I mean, part of me was like, *Yes, let's do it, Samantha's a fucking asshole, and I* do *want her to fucking die,* but then I thought: Why give her better book sales? Why go to jail for her when I don't even love orange? Also, despite my talents with the ax, which you've witnessed firsthand and which you may witness again tonight (we'll see how things go, Bunny!), I'm actually a really good person inside. *Thoughtful,* unlike some. Always thinking of the greater good. Which is why, in those early days, I used to reach out to you, remember? Texted you so many times to come and join us for bento boxes or whatever, remember? Because I was fucking nice. It's so funny, Bunny, how in your novel (which, oh yes, I read) you turned my invitations into a mean-girl thing. Reflective of a sadistic streak that you imagined, in your well-documented insanity, to live in my own heart. Funny how you got me so wrong. How you saw darkness where there was really only ever light and goodwill. Anyway, I did vote no on the kidnapping, just fyi. But what can I say? Sadly, I was in the minority there. Sadly, I was swayed. Convinced by certain arguments, by the greater good. I often am, my fatal flaw, as you'll hear in my own story. That said, I don't want to keep you any longer than we have to, Bunny, I really don't. Certainly I don't want to kill you, ha ha ha. I mean, I totally fucking do, but not at this precise moment in time. For now I just want to talk, k? Bend your ear, even though I know you're so very busy and important these days! That's a joke, Bunny. I checked your phone while Coraline was talking (how adorable that you have bunny wallpaper!), and it doesn't seem like anyone has tried to reach you at all. Except for one unknown number that's probably spam or something. One text that's just a question mark, how sad. Who's that from, I wonder. Your one nonverbal friend maybe? Lonely at the top perhaps (more like midlist really, right?). Oh well. At least you can breathe a sigh of relief for now, yes? Relax and reminisce with me, *Creepy Doll*. When I first read that name in your novel and realized you meant me, I laughed and laughed. Didn't cry *Cunt* until I lost my voice at all. Let me just take that ax from you now, Coraline, k? Since it's my turn to sit by Samantha, my turn to tell. And who knows, we might need it, right, Bunny? I actually haven't been back up here since our Workshop days. Haven't even washed the blood off the walls, ha ha ha. Remember the blood, Bunny?

Such great times we had, totally.

I still live here, oh yes. Same apartment, same attic where we once made such magic. Where now there's nothing but ghosts. What do I do these days? Since you took my creativity away and destroyed me in print, you mean? Oh, lots. Make incense and meditate, mostly. Listen to Stevie Nicks and remind myself of how karma works, which is *mysteriously*. Think about where I've been and where I wish to go next, creatively and otherwise.

Now let me get back to our story. Take over the narrative from my darling Coraline, because between you and me, she really went off the rails in her telling. Adding such indulgent flourishes that were, well, just a little fucking distracting, really. Not to mention wildly inaccurate. Also pacing, hello? *Tick, tick* goes the clock and we each need our turn, k? Friendly reminder that we *did* agree to take turns, and not interrupt one another ever (our own gag rule!), even though it can be very hard to do that when one of us decides to lie and betray and slander so flagrantly. In fact, I'll have to back up just a bit so that you know the actual truth. About the beauty we made. And how we *all* had roles to play.

Especially me, Bunny.

4

So after Allan critiqued/destroyed Coraline's piece in the Cave, she was kind of a fucking mess, so sad to say. I know because I was sitting right beside her in Workshop at the time. Under the table, I'd even given her my hand to hold, let her crush it, and she did—she nearly broke my fingers, Bunny. At the time, though, I so didn't even notice. That first fall something was happening to me, Bunny, to my body and mind and soul. It was all becoming less solid or something. *I* was becoming less solid. I looked over at Coraline, and sometimes I didn't know where she ended and I began. Even on that first day. I saw the tears she shed and that she'd cut her own finger with something in her pocket. I even cried along with her. On the inside, obvi, Bunny. I bled there with her too. I already loved her so fucking much, you see, quite in spite of myself. We'd slept together the night before, as you know, though, sorry, it didn't happen quite like she said, Bunny, not at all.

The truth?

I was happy to go home alone after the party, I totally was. But she practically begged me to stay the night, is the thing. "Come home with me," she said, squeezing my hand tight. She was scared, apparently, of her huge new apartment with its fancy floral arrangements, which did cast some very strange and pointy shadows on the wall. So I stayed, Bunny, of course I did. I'm really nice, like I said. She made me a cup of hibiscus-and-rose tea with one of her many pretty kettles, and she watched me eat mini cupcakes with a sort of murderous intensity. It was lovely. That night I shared so much of my own soul with her. About my first sexual experiences with various humans in college and then, more importantly, with various entities. And she listened to my stories of that. How I'd fucked ghosts, felt them descend upon me in the night, invited them brazenly into my bed. She told me, too, about her various stilted, all-too-human experiences. With first a boy and then a girl and then a girl who later transitioned into a boy, and he was her favorite, she whispered. It was like the best of both. But nothing ever worked out, she said. Romantically. Always with everyone something felt like it was . . . "missing" or "not enough." Or "just too much, you know? Too much reality." "Yes," I said, for I did know. "Perhaps because I'm an artist," she mused, placing another cupcake of her choice on my plate, watching me eat, her mouth chewing a little in time with mine. I watched her pour more tea into my rose-patterned cup, carefully so as not to spill any drops, though her gloved hand was shaking like crazy, Bunny. *Perhaps also because you like to control,* I thought. *Because you can't abide someone else's needs or free will.* But I said, "Totally, it's because you're an artist. I feel the same way, Bunny," recalling the bunny we'd seen in the dark. I told her how I'd seen spirits from a very young age and how typewriters had spirits too and all I had to do was type and the ghost in the machine would speak to me, speak through me, and how this was a sort of sex with the cosmos, with unseen forces. I wasn't terribly interested in fucking humans when there were such entities out there, I told her. This was why I'd applied to Warren in the first place. I knew they would embrace my entity-sex approach, the ghostly fictions that resulted. This was also why I loved fairy tales and myths so much, because they understood these things were in the air.

"Even demons?" she whispered.

I said, "Of course demons, Bunny." (I was fucking with her maybe.)

I remember she looked afraid, which was so adorable. And when she invited me into her celestial bed (*she* invited *me*, Bunny), we lay there side by side, stared at each other sort of smiling until our eyes closed at the very same time. Each of us holding a hoof of Pinkie Pie, her small, plastic animal companion. "Have you ever heard of bronies?" I asked her. And she said, "What's that?" "Never mind," I said. A happy tear shed from her so-blue eye. She stroked my cheek and I let her. In fact, I stroked hers at the same time, breaking my nonhuman rule for intimacy. Her skin was so peach-fuzzy and warm, it was crazy. It was lovely. That night, I'm not ashamed to say I dreamed of her, Bunny. Of her sky dress and her eyes full of such violent longing. For what exactly, I had no words to articulate, but I knew. I knew its shape and shadows.

Because it was in my eyes too.

The next day we seemed to awaken at the very same time, the same quality of light rousing us from our dreams. But I woke to find her staring at me coldly, Bunny. No longer smiling at all. Looking, in fact, in the stark light of noontime, like she couldn't believe I was there. Every answer to my every question strange and clipped. *What the fuck*, I wondered. It threw me off, I have to say. Destabilized me more than any unseen force. But also, and here is the not-so-great thing, it intrigued me (this is my own social damage coming out, perhaps). I grew warmer, pathetically so, hoping to melt her back into that smiling, desperate shape I'd experienced last night in the dark. But she remained withdrawn and mysterious, sadly bitchy. Sadly irresistible. And yes, I know she's here with us now in the attic, and that she's hearing my words and being forced (for once) to listen. And good.

While we're mostly here to tell you, Bunny, we're also here, perhaps, to tell each other finally. As part of our Healing Journeys. Finding our Creative Way, you know?

Speaking of which, let's jump ahead to just after our first Workshop.

Suffice it to say that Allan's words, which were hurting her, were also hurting me. I was so angry on her behalf. Outraged even. After everyone left the Cave, she just sort of sat there in a daze in my grass dress, stroking her own pearls, didn't you, Bunny? Her other hand was bleeding in her pocket (my pocket, really, because it was my dress), and I thought about how now the dress would have to be dry-cleaned. But that was okay. I totally forgave her. Didn't even mention the dry cleaning. Instead I helped her get out of her chair, in which she was so sadly slumped. I led her by the hand out of the dark classroom, and she shuffled behind me, crying her many silent tears of shame. I gave her my heart-framed sunglasses to shield her eyes from the cruelty of the bright day, from people's staring. Because she'd already felt exposed enough for one afternoon, hadn't you, Bunny? I agreed with her when she cursed New England, even though I was from New England, from the neighboring state of New Hampshire, in fact, set most of my stories there. Yes, I agreed, this was a hell place, a terrible place, *you're so right*, even though I quite liked everything about it. I cursed the yellowing sky along with her, and inside I said a silent prayer for it to please ignore the curse. I led her to the rose garden behind the Narrative Arts building, and I said, "Look at the pretty flowers!" And she said, "Fuck the flowers, Bunny," she was so very upset. Really childlike in this moment, letting out great honking cries like a kind of goose. I sat her down on a bench, and there she wept like the child she'd become, and I rubbed her back while she did. She tried to shake my hand off like I was some kind of fly. Which fucking hurt me, so I dropped my hand. Put it back in my own lap, the lap of her sky dress, which I had not bloodied with my grief and anger and inconsiderateness. I gazed at its many sinuous clouds, clouds I suspected she loved to live in instead of here on this earth.

I whispered, "What does he know, Bunny? What does he fucking know? This Man of Nightmares?"

I whispered, "You're so amazing and your story was amazing."

I whispered that we would have our revenge.

She wasn't really listening to me at all. She was actually kind of ignoring me, being a bit of a dreamy bitch. More fresh blood seeped so redly from her grassy pocket (my pocket), and I really felt she was being seriously thoughtless, Bunny, about the stain she was making. But I said nothing. I looked up, thinking what else to say, even though it was a wasted effort, she was so lost, and I realized I barely knew her, really, had just met her the day before, and I did sort of think her oven story needed work, actually. I mean, come on, Bunny, isn't that what we were here for, this was like a serious MFA, k? Hardcore, why I applied. Finally I said, "Want me to kill him for you?" I said it to make her smile, Bunny. To make her laugh. But she turned to me, looked so fucking serious, it scared me. Her mascara was running down her face in long, jagged blue lines.

"Yes. Let's fucking kill him," she said. "Together."

"Together?" I said. And she took my hand.

And I'll admit, Bunny, I felt a warmth prickling through me at her touch. I saw a flash of an ax coming down on a body. My small hands gripping the handle. I saw all of this in her eyes, how they were staring at me. I fell a little in love with her again then, her murdery way, it's true. But I wasn't serious, Bunny. Not like she was. I was totally just saying it to make her feel better about being eviscerated. But it's also true that just when I said it, we saw him.

That bunny.

From the night before and earlier that day.

And here is where her narrative really begins to forget. Maybe she just forgot because of the trauma of this day, which I don't at all mean to minimize, but *I'm* the one who actually saw the bunny first, Bunny. Sitting there in the grass, among the very red roses full of thorns. Snow-white fur. Large, dark eyes. Ears like little furry antennae. He was staring at me—Kyra. And I'm the one who walked over to him. We walked toward each other, the bunny and I, while Coraline just sat there oblivious. Still staring murder at the sky, lost in her melodrama clouds. Meanwhile, I bent down and scooped up the animal. I didn't really have to scoop. He actually hopped into my arms like in a fucking fairy tale. Like literal magic. And it was like all my previous experiences with entities had prepared me for this moment. I was able to hold the bunny. I was able to walk over to Coraline with the so-soft creature in my arms. And in my great generosity, in a haze of trust and friendship, I fucking gave him to her. To cheer her up about her bad story. I put him in her bloody lap. "Here you go, Bunny."

But she just ignored him. Kept staring like nothing magical was happening on her prickly thighs.

So I said, "Bunny, look."

She finally looked, and that's when she squealed a little bit like a pig. Miraculously, the bunny did not hop away. Instead he just sat there like a gift. *That's* when she held him. And I held him with her. We held him together. She got her blood and tears all over him, yes, but I was crying too, so my tears were on there too, hello?

And *that's* when his eyes changed color, Bunny. When we were *both* holding the bunny, okay? Turned the sky blue of the dress *I* was wearing. Yes, her dress, but who was wearing it that day, hello?

Me. Kyra. I was. Hi.

Vik and Elsinore came running up to us then and said, "Omg, so sorry, are you okay? What an awful man!" Then, yes, we all hugged. And then, yes, they saw the bunny we were holding, saw his crazy-colored eyes, which did, yes, seem even more vivid in their blue thanks to them joining us. Thanks to the four of us holding one another and this bunny together. Yes, it was amazing. Yes, we were all totally amazed too. But much as I love you, Coraline, you cannot go taking credit for something that I was predominantly responsible for, okay, Bunny? But again, like I said, you were sort of a fucking mess that day, weren't you? What with your story being critiqued in a fiction workshop and all. Because you were, like, a graduate student in an MFA program. *Such* a crazy hard day for you, omg.

Sorry, Bunny, where was I? Oh yes. The bunny's eyes turning blue definitely changed the mood of the afternoon. There was no going back after that, really, even though right after this happened, we sort of gasp-sighed and someone dropped the animal and then he ran away from us. Hopped away, I guess. We called after him, of course. "Come back, Bunny! Come back!"

He did not come back, Bunny.

Perhaps he was too scared, which, looking back now, makes total sense.

I do often wonder what would've happened if it had just been me with Bunny. If he might have stayed for a while. Maybe this would be a very different story, you know? We all watched him disappear into the thorny roses, covered in Coraline's blood and all our tears. We looked at one another and we knew, even then, that we had done Something. That it was the start. Of what?

Well, that was the part we didn't know.

Evening suddenly. The air grew crisp and cold and more murdery, the way it does in this town after a certain hour. The blue began to deepen all around us, making our four shadows stretch and stretch on the garden grass. The cool wind was in our faces, blowing our many shining hairs back. All our pale eyes, once wet with wonder tears, even cynical Vik's, were semidry now. We found ourselves walking the few streets back to my place. Not talking. All of us holding hands, step by step. If people were in our way, well, they moved. Walked around us like we were one very wide body with many legs and arms. It was like we *were* one body, Bunny. Like three more hearts were beating inside me. Three more minds had melded to my own. I saw the sun with my eight eyes as it sank bloodily before us. Rabbits hopped on the sidewalk, in and out of our path, sort of smiling at us, I saw. We did not remark upon just how many of these creatures were pretty much everywhere we looked now, Bunny. Perhaps we were not ready for words yet. I looked, all of us looked, for the bloody one. The tearstained one. The newly blue-eyed one, but he was nowhere now. He had disappeared into the roses and beyond.

At my apartment, for this was where we found ourselves, where we had unconsciously wandered, I welcomed everyone into the living room, to sit upon my very red furniture. Right away, though, Vik opened the door to the attic, and she and Elsinore just went on up there. Right up the dark, rickety stairs like they'd been up there before. I followed them with a bottle of absinthe and a tray of jewel-colored glasses. I sensed Elsinore was clearly the leader of us all. It was something in the way she sat cross-legged beneath my triangle window like she was queen of the floorboards. So silent. So thinking. I couldn't read her cryptic expression, which was like the many shining sides of a crystal. Vik, meanwhile, stretched out in a sort of daze. I did not know what to make of her lovely veiny-bony face, her unblinking *fuck you* eyes and her full, half-open mouth, which seemed to be neither smiling nor frowning. What thoughts were swimming inside that sharply cut skull of hers like little silver fish, equally unblinking? Coraline, meanwhile, was sort of hyperventilating. The minute we got in the door, she whisper-asked if I had any baked goods. I did, in fact, have muffin loaf and told her I'd get her some, but she said, "Never mind, never mind," she would find it on her own, thanks, and I didn't need to come into the kitchen with her or anything, *thanks*.

Okay.

So I sat cross-legged beside Elsinore, and I said, because no one was fucking saying anything, "Holy fuck."

Elsinore's eyes opened. She smiled at me like, *What?*

"Did you guys see?"

"See?" Vik said.

"The bunny's eyes changing color like that? Wasn't it so incredible?"

And it was funny, Bunny. But I suddenly felt kind of dirty and crude being so direct. Elsinore closed her eyes again, saying nothing. Vik sort of smirked at the ceiling, also saying nothing. So we were not acknowledging?

"Um, did you guys not *see*?"

"Of course we *saw*, Bunny," Vik whispered.

"Well, what do you think it means?" I asked.

"*Means?*" Vik repeated. Like I ruined something just by asking. Like it was the most boring question in the world, when to me it was really the only question. *Yes, bitch. What does it mean? That we just turned a bunny's eyes blue, hello?*

"Who cares what it fucking *means*? It was hot." She looked dreamily at my ceiling like she suddenly saw stars there.

"I know what it meansh," Coraline whispered, mouth full of my muffin loaf. Taking each bite like a breathy kiss; it was kind of a turn-on to watch, Bunny. She stood by the staircase like she'd done the night before, like she was afraid to come in.

"What?"

"Maybe we're magic," Coraline panted.

I, I thought. *Not we. If anyone's magic, it's me. I'm magic and I shared my magic with you.*

But I said, "Yes. Maybe we are. Ha ha." I didn't want to be disagreeable to my peers. Which was maybe a mistake. A side effect of my fatal flaw.

Vik and Elsinore smiled. And then it was dropped, the subject. Cast aside. Made light of. Made fun of even. "Probably just someone doing experiments," Vik offered, and then we all agreed. Warren was such an experimental school, cutting-edge that way. There were scientists, Vik said—weren't there?—who experimented with bunny DNA and changed the color of their fur. Injected it with some jellyfish protein. Produced a magenta bunny and a lime-green bunny and even a sky-colored one, so she'd heard. So maybe we'd stumbled into something like that going on here.

"Definitely," they all agreed again. Yes, experiments, that was all we were dealing with. We'd just stumbled into someone else's arty science project.

"Where do you think he is now? The bunny," I pressed. *My bunny,* I thought.

"Our bunny," Vik corrected.

Elsinore opened her eyes. Looked at us—at me, actually. "This attic," she whispered. "Has such great energy, Kyra. Is it Kyra?"

"Yes. Thank you." Elsinore complimenting me felt good. Like anointment from a white witch.

"Coraline," she said, turning to Coraline. "You must be so devastated and humiliated."

Coraline nodded, still sort of making out with my muffin, those soft, kissy bites. I envied it. She looked like she was about to cry again, probably thinking of her oven story.

"Of course you are. We all are, aren't we?" Elsinore said. "Terribly disappointed by this turn of events. I'd planned on having Ursula as a mentor."

Vik grunted, her eyes suddenly swimmy with some kind of emotion. The Crystal Thief tattoo shone on her forearm.

"Should we confront Allan?" Coraline said. "Complain about his way of speaking to us?"

Not to us, I thought. *To you, Bunny.*

"Because I don't know that we should accept it. It's like he was applying his man rules to my creativity. His dickish notion of time and space and fucking *plot*. His dick, really! All over my story, that's how it felt."

"It was an assault," Elsinore offered with a certitude that made me shiver. Her voice had the intonation of an otherworldly bell. "You were violated."

"An assault," Coraline repeated, entranced. "Yes. Absolutely. I was violated."

"We were right there with you, Bunny," Elsinore said. "We saw it all. You have witnesses, remember? We saw him squash your creative voice, strangle it with his tattooed man hands, his patriarchal adjectives, his lack of understanding that was fucking *willful*. Because he wanted you to be ashamed. He gets off on your humiliation. Probably he went home and whacked off thinking about your blood and tears, how small he made you feel."

"And how untalented," Vik offered.

"How whimsical," Elsinore added.

"How prissy." Vik smiled.

"She gets the point," I cut in before I could think. I was protective of her, I couldn't help it, Bunny, and I didn't think she needed this kind of recap. But Coraline didn't even look at me. She'd finished with my muffin (probably she'd throw it up soon) and looked impeccably blond and above all appetites again.

"He saw my bloody pocket!" she chimed in. "He saw it and he fucking smiled."

"Of course he did."

"What a monster."

"We hate him."

"So much."

"What hurts one of us, hurts all of us, after all."

Coraline smiled, so comforted. "Thank you," she said to them. And cried into Elsinore's bony shoulder. I watched this. Elsinore embracing Coraline in her bloody grass dress (*my* grass dress). Vik walking over and putting her plaid arms around them both. Consolingly patting Coraline's side boob. I watched, turning a glass of absinthe around and around in my small hands, quite like I'm turning the handle of the ax right now, Bunny. I thought of how I'd said almost the exact same words of comfort to Coraline on the bench only hours ago and how she'd ignored me. Just stared at the sky, even though I'd rubbed her humped back like I was trying to start a fucking fire. And I took internal note of this, like I had done at countless other tender social moments in my life. Moments where my words, though I was the first to speak them, were not heard at all by the collective. Almost as if a ghost, instead of a human person, had spoken. Perhaps this was why I'd always cleaved, socially and sexually, to the spirit world. I understood so much, so implicitly, about the unseen, the unheard.

Eventually it was decided that we would go talk to Ursula together. After all, this really concerned all of us, did it not? If Allan had "assaulted" Coraline, it was only a matter of time before he assaulted the rest of us, right? Weren't we all slated to be workshopped in the coming weeks? Each one of our souls (a.k.a. short fictions) to be impaled by his terrible, penile red pen?

"*Exactly*," Coraline said.

"Wait, should we ask that other girl to join us?" I asked. "Sam, I think that's her name. Since she's also in our class?" (See how I was trying to include you, Bunny? Even then.)

But they all just stared at me like I was fucking insane.

"Um, didn't you hear that *Sam* agreed with him? I mean, she basically assaulted me too."

"Also, didn't you see the two of them walking out together after class? To that bar?"

"She's probably sucking him off right now."

"I *hate* her," Coraline seethed. "Almost *more* than him."

"We all do, Bunny." Elsinore patted her shoulder. "Certainly she isn't to be trusted. No, Kyra, I think it's best it's just us four. The four of us should be really more than enough."

"Besides, we're magic, aren't we?" Vik added, grinning.

And Coraline and Elsinore smiled. Still embracing so tightly, it hurt my eyes to see.

"Yes," they said as one soft voice. "Exactly."

5

Ursula didn't respond to our group email right away. We checked our inboxes about five million times an hour after we collectively hit send, and fucking nothing. Then the first day passed and the next day passed. A week went by, and we really started to wonder, Bunny, if we would ever hear back, please. We knew she was on leave and all, but still, what the fuck, k? Weeks went by, four, in which we all grew closer, disturbingly so (more on that in a bit). In which we all had to go up for Workshop with Allan. And yeah, it was pretty bad, Bunny, and that drew us closer still, for we had a common enemy now, in the form of Allan. It was a shitshow for all of us, except you maybe. He fucking loved you and your stories, which infuriated some of us. Made some of us hate you, it did, we can't lie. *I* didn't hate you nearly as much as the rest of us did, though, Bunny, just fyi. Because between us, as I'm sure you know (and let me whisper this now in your ear): Allan sort of loved my work too. Said my engagement with the entity was actually pretty promising. He enjoyed my demonic girls and wolf men, my prose fornications with ghosts. He especially appreciated my fairy-tale violences, my surprisingly hard turns. I had an edge you didn't see coming, he said. And I tried very hard not to smile when he said that, Bunny. Kept my face a dead face as I felt everyone's side-eyes on me in the Cave. After, I shrugged off his love and played up the one thing he *did* critique, which was my formatting. How I cried and cried in the rose garden, performatively I'll confess, about his formatting comments. Acted totally inconsolable. How *dare* he suggest, I wailed, that I change the *shape* of my story, that I break up my paragraphs further. "It's like he's insisting I change the shape of *me* or something, you know?" They all comforted me—what choice did they have?—I was so upset. But Coraline, patting my shoulder, had a bit of *Fucking really?* in her eyes, even as she said, "There, there."

One by one by one, all of us had our moment in the rose garden about Allan. He thought Elsinore was . . . what was it again, Bunny? Oh right: a fucking fraud. And that Vik was style over substance, provocation over punch. Vik didn't cry, did you, Bunny? But she did go red in the face, oh yes. *I'll show you punch, fucker.* And Elsinore, well, she just smiled coldly. Thanked him so much for his feedback. Said she'd give it some thought. But her eyes were brimming with *I will kill you.* We could hear the words roaring in her mind, for they roared in all our heads too, our hearts beating ragefully in time.

"I will kill, I will kill, I will kill," she screeched in the rose garden after, pacing its periphery like a cat. Sort of forgetting we were all there, Bunny. I could never have imagined her losing it like that, and it was kind of frightening, kind of hot. She looked incredibly thin when she was rageful, Coraline whispered to me later. With her fists curled and her neck tendons quivering and her forehead veins throbbing and her pale lips pressed really tight together.

I remember it was as she was screaming that the blue-eyed bunny came back to say hello. Yes, yes. Standing in the grass, watching her scream. Eating grass or dandelions or clover, or was it a rose petal? Ears twitching, almost like he was listening really. Like, *Yes. I know. I so know exactly.* It quieted Elsinore. He still had Coraline's blood on him, we saw, in a heart-shaped stain. "Kill," she whispered again. And he hopped closer, didn't he? A leaf in his mouth. Just then our phones all buzzed. There was Ursula's name on our screens. She'd finally fucking replied. Yes, she'd love to meet, she said. How was five o'clock tonight at her place?

And just like that, the bunny ran off.

So it was that we found ourselves on Ursula's white front porch among her many spiky flowers and climbing vines. It was the first week of October, and

I remember the sweet-crisp chill, Bunny, I remember the rabbity bite in the air. It was dreamy. Arousing, almost. Autumn leaves the color of fire rustling all around us and a dog barking like mad in the garden. Ursula's dog, as it turned out. I remember thinking, *What the fuck are we doing here? What are we even going to say to her?* But I didn't ask. Just stood there with the rest of them, my cohort, from whom I suddenly felt so estranged.

"I've dreamed of this moment," Coraline whispered as we stood on her porch.

"*I've* dreamed of this moment," Vik said.

"So dreamed of it," I lied. I'd been doing this a lot lately, I noticed, Bunny. Echoing. Seconding. Couldn't seem to stop myself, even when I disagreed, even when I thought, *That's fucking stupid*, what I said was, *Oh my god, totally.*

"We all have," Elsinore said, sort of coldly magnanimous. Then, out of the corner of my eye, I noticed a shed in the back garden. A small white house covered in creeper, one dark round window like an eye.

"Let's go," I whispered to Coraline, tugging on her hand.

"Go?" she snapped back. "What, are you fucking crazy? *Why?*"

And that wounded me, Bunny. *I don't know why*, I wanted to tell her. *The barking dog. That shed. The crackling leaves. How I'm fucking losing you.* "I just have this . . . feeling," I whispered at last. But suddenly the front door was open, and we were walking into Ursula's house, right into her living room, weren't we?

Surreal, Bunny. To be in Ursula's living room, the late-afternoon light burning into all our eyes. Surrounded by her vaguely vaginal paintings, her flower arrangements shaped like balls, remember those? Of course you do, you made such fun of it all in your little novel. Yes, the so-white walls and the black African masks. Yes, the scent of desert sage on fire. You weren't wrong, Bunny, it *was* a little boomer meets *please think I'm a witch*. Crystals shone from her every bookcase full of rare books, and her furniture looked like it had been antiqued across many global marketplaces. Fusion appetizers on a Scandi coffee table, and a heavy black kettle full of stewing herbs.

And we, seated on her pastel couch of the softest suede, staring at her like she was the fucking sun, like she could make all our writerly dreams come true. And maybe she could. She sat in a lavender wing chair, smiling cryptically at all of us. Her silver-golden hair billowing as though in a breeze that blew just around her person. A giant amethyst loomed on a shelf behind her. She offered us tea and we took it, "thank you so much, oh my god, we hope we're not disturbing you." And she smiled, pouring. Like *yes*. We were fucking disturbing her. And yet here we were, weren't we? The tea was terribly strong, Bunny, putrid, primal tasting, and her smile so pink and inscrutable above the steam.

"And to what do I owe this surprise visit?" she said at last in a voice fit for operas.

We were silent at first. Staring. All having a moment, I guess. Of fangirl. The fact of Ursula, *the* Ursula, in front of us. Ursula the Word Witch speaking actual words to us. She who wrote *To Catch a Crystal Thief of the Heart*. Wearing some sort of caftan-meets-smock that shone iridescently like the crystal behind her. I was about to respond, when, beside me, I heard Elsinore's soft voice chime in. "Professor Radcliffe—"

"Ursula," Ursula said. "Please."

"*Ursula*," we all repeated, and her name in our mouths felt exhilarating.

"We're so thankful you agreed to meet with us," Elsinore said.

"So thankful," I echoed.

"And can we also just say we're such fans?"

"*Such* fans," I echoed again. What the fuck was wrong with me, Bunny?

"Hardcore," Vik said, offering her forearm tattoo to Ursula, who looked at the Crystal Thief etched there and only slightly smiled.

"You're the reason we came here," Elsinore said.

"You're why I want to be a writer," Coraline added desperately.

"You're why I'm alive at all," Vik said.

Give me a fucking break, I thought, even though I was still nodding and smiling. Even though I was repeating, "Alive, writer, reason. Totally."

"Well, I'm terribly flattered," she said. She did not look flattered. She looked, in fact, a little bored, Bunny. Perhaps even impatient. *This is my leave*, I felt her soul roar behind her smiling eyes. *What are you kids doing here?* But maybe I was just seeing things. Her husband appeared in the doorway just then. You remember him, of course. David Sylph, the poet who taught the Poetry Workshop and whom I strangely despised on sight. Something lizardy about his lips, too-shining about his eyes. He looked like he probably enjoyed a lot of appropriative world music. He handed out some ornate biscuits from a tray while looking subtly, almost eruditely, at all of our boobs.

"Now," Ursula said when he had gone. And then she gazed down at her wrist as though there were a watch there (there wasn't). "What can I do for you girls?"

"We're very sorry to be bothering you," Elsinore began.

"But this is an *emergency*," Coraline said, tears in her eyes. Which I thought was a little fucking much, but I said nothing. Just smiled a smile that hurt my face. Nodded. "Total emergency," I added.

"Emergency? What sort of emergency?" Ursula asked.

And then we told her about Allan.

"We hate him," we all said. And at this point it was true.

Ursula stirred her tea. Sat back. "*Hate*," she said dreamily, "is a very strong word. Of course, I don't have to tell *you* that, you're writers."

We all nodded as if we were many heads being controlled by a single string.

"But we have reason," Coraline hissed. Lip twitching. Eyes welling up further at the recollection of her shame, poor Bunny.

"He assaulted us," Elsinore said, taking Coraline's hand.

"All of us," Vik added, taking Coraline's other hand, which she gripped. Suddenly I felt sick. They'd been hanging around one another more and more lately.

"*Assaulted?* Oh my. May I ask how—"

"I don't know if he assaulted *exactly*," I piped up. Couldn't help but clarify, Bunny. They all looked at me, surprised. "Not *physically*, anyway. He was just . . . mean. Extremely," I added, glancing at Coraline, who looked like she might want to kill me.

"He *attacked* our stories," Coraline shouted. "He *attacked* us each personally."

"Metaphorically," I said.

"Which is basically literally," Vik added like a smack.

Coraline was fully crying now. Elsinore and Vik were rubbing her back. As I watched this unfold, there was a part of me, a small part, that felt this was all very fucking ridiculous, Bunny.

"I see," Ursula said. "Oh my. Well, I'm so sorry to hear this, truly." She smiled sadly. Was she sorry? I couldn't tell. Her expressions were cryptic, quite like Elsinore's, and those violet eyes gave little away. "Of course it's a very vulnerable thing to enter the Cave for the first time. And to have one's creative spirit crushed like that." She shook her head. "Allan can be . . . so *Allan*. He has his ways just like I have mine. Would you like me to speak with him? It's highly unusual, of course, but I suppose I—"

"No," Coraline said. "We want you," she whispered to the polished floor. With obscene intensity, Bunny. Tears still in her eyes.

"*Me?*" Ursula said.

"To be our Workshop leader this fall. Instead of him."

"Would you?" Vik said.

"Oh my god, we'd be so grateful," I heard myself add. Why, Bunny? Why was I saying these words? I looked at Ursula. There was panic on her face, though she was still smiling. That little undercurrent of outrage there, behind her eyes.

But Coraline persisted. "It's just we were so looking forward to—"

"Impossible," she snapped. "Not that I wouldn't *love* to, of course," she added quickly. "I'm sure we'd all get along so very well, and what a pleasure it would be for me to dive into your respective Word Journeyings. But as you know, I'm away this fall semester, sadly. I've received a fellowship to pursue my own creative research, as I'm sure Allan shared. I'm working on a . . . project." Her voice, I noticed, cracked on the word *project*.

"What sort of project?" Coraline asked hungrily through her tears.

Ursula's face darkened then, Bunny. She glanced through the windows at that shed outside. For a moment she looked she might cry herself. At last she turned to us, smiling coldly. "It's revealing itself to me, slowly," she said. "One mustn't tempt the muse into retreat by speaking its name, after all."

"Of course not," Elsinore whispered.

"I'd rather cut out my tongue," Vik agreed.

"Totally," I said, even as I thought, *You're all fucking crazy*.

"But my being away is good for all of us," she added. "In order to be a good teacher, a sound mentor, one must separate oneself from time to time. By spring I'll surely be rejuvenated, in a place to better serve you all. Until then you will have to weather this storm, I'm afraid. Tap the Wound, Cassandra," she said to Coraline, who nodded, not correcting her. "Turn it into power. Think of this as an opportunity."

"To have my soul obliterated?" Coraline cried.

Ursula smiled. "To form your own creative crucible, of course."

We looked at one another. *What?*

"As a group of five, you have your own power," Ursula continued. "Where *is* the fifth, by the way?" she said.

"Sadly, Sam doesn't appreciate the community aspect of Workshop," Elsinore said. And I suddenly envied you, Bunny. Wherever you were. Sucking off Allan, probably. Picking at your own damage in the dark. Alone and free.

"What a shame." Ursula smiled. "But four is still . . . formidable. Particularly as an all-female cohort. We've never had one of those before, you know."

"I'm actually fluid," Vik said, stiffening.

"And I'm nonconforming," Elsinore said. "Beyond the binary."

"Me too," Coraline whispered, her hands folded primly in the lap of her bell dress. "Totally nonconforming."

Liar, I thought. She fucking screamed *conforming* from every cell. But I mumbled "me too" also. "So nonconforming." I felt her glare at me.

"Even better," Ursula said, slightly impatient now. And perhaps slightly confused. She showed her age then. She glanced longingly again at the shed, then looked back at us. "The point is that you're *together*. And what you make together cannot be made *alone*."

Were we all then thinking of the bunny's eyes going blue? Hard to say from our faces, so suddenly entranced by this idea of *together*. Of *not alone*.

"Transformative power requires many streams of consciousness," Ursula intoned, stirring her tea.

"So many streams," we all agreed, nodding.

"The Collective can be a powerful force. Perhaps together you'll make the word flesh. Tap the Wound and bring it to vivid life. Making something beautiful is, after all, the best revenge." She smiled. A stream of afternoon sun fell on her just then, making the giant crystal glow like a wondrous rainbow behind her. "And who knows? The things you make may change the nature of reality with their never-before-seen juxtapositions."

I was going to ask, *What the fuck?* but everyone else seemed to understand. Elsinore stared at Ursula like she was an oracle, a tear in her cold blue eye. Coraline was bawling again—surprise, surprise. Even Vik seemed to sniffle. And then the strangest thing: I was crying too, I realized. Yes, my face was wet, why? Maybe I understood on some implicit level that she was giving us something. Some creative code. Some cosmic permission.

"Don't let this opportunity go hopping away into the dark," she whispered.

We turned a bunny's eyes blue, I almost told her then. But something stopped me, Bunny. Then Coraline jumped in. "Do you know of any rabbit experiments on campus?"

For a moment Ursula just stared at us very strangely. "*Rabbit* experiments? What do you mean?"

"Nothing," I cut in. "She means nothing." And I kicked Coraline under the table, and she looked at me like, *What the fuck? Why do you silence me?* I didn't know why, Bunny. Just a feeling like the one I'd had on the porch.

Ursula stared at us and then laughed. "Rabbit experiments. My, my. The Warren lore is alive and well, I see. Urban legend."

"What urban legend?" I asked, though I could feel Vik glaring at me for what she called my *clarifying impulse*. But Ursula was looking at David now, lurking in the doorway, then at her bare wrist. Maybe she had an invisible watch there after all. She stood up, casting her considerable shadow over us. "Your own creative crucible, don't forget."

And then it was somehow goodbye.

We were back outside in the golden afternoon again, just the four of us on her porch with the barking dog turning madly in the fire-colored leaves. "Our own creative crucible," we all whispered at the same time.

Our many streams.

Afterward, mini cupcakes in this café called Mini that Elsinore found just off campus. Where we might go, she said, to *distill.*

Distill what exactly? I wondered.

But Coraline and Vik nodded like they understood, so I nodded too. *Distill. Absolutely.*

Of course, you know Mini well, Bunny. We took you there many a time, remember? I'll never forget your face when you saw that everything on the menu was in literal mini. I'll admit it semi-horrified me too, at first. The mini chicken wings especially—how small did these birds have to be? I ordered a mini bubble tea, and it came in so small a glass that I almost laughed, but the waiter did not laugh when he set the drink in front of me with its so-small straw. So then I didn't laugh either.

"This place is so amazing, Elsinore," Coraline said, her eyes all dewy. I felt like I'd lost her to some grander force.

"Genius," Vik said.

"So amazing," I whispered, even though I wasn't so sure it was. There was an odd sort of mood among us. I actually texted you then, Bunny, under the table, to see if you wanted to join. You didn't answer me, of course. Just a few fluttery gray dots in a gray bubble (you receiving the text, probably) and then nothing. Fine. *Fucking fine, bitch,* I thought. We sipped our mini beverages. *Creative crucible.* The phrase was humming in all our minds, I knew. Making our auras vibrate, thrum with excitement. *What do you suppose it even means?* I wanted to ask, but then thought better of it. No one liked to contemplate this question, it seemed.

"Wasn't that talk with Ursula so amazing?" I finally said.

They looked at me like I'd sullied something by speaking.

But I forged ahead: "What do you think she was suggesting? By making our own creative crucible? Changing the nature of reality."

Silence. Just looking at their mini foods dreamily. Sipping from their mini straws. Vik belched.

"Well?" I said at last, pressing. I knew I was pressing.

"Um, pretty obvious, don't you think, *Bunny?*" Vik said, but she was looking at Elsinore, a question in her eyes.

"Is it?" I said. "Then maybe I'm too stupid to understand or something?"

No one contradicted this. The answer in the air seemed to be *Maybe.* I looked at Coraline, but she was looking over at Elsinore too. Waiting like I once waited at the Delphi oracle when I traveled there with my parents. Waiting for I don't know what, the air, the pillars, the dust, something to fucking *speak.* But Elsinore was sipping obliquely at her mini kombucha and saying nothing. Light from the window was dancing on her beautifully cold, sharp face, illuminating the flowery spikes in her hair. I felt, by contrast, like such a silly creature. So terribly mortal and of the earth. Needing everything spelled out. Needing signposts.

"We'll have to find it, of course," Elsinore said at last, more to herself than to any of us.

"Find what?" Coraline said. And her voice betrayed her. I knew then she didn't understand either. Neither did Vik. We were all in the exact same dark as to what Ursula's words meant for us. As to what to do next. Except Elsinore, apparently, who seemed to understand all.

Elsinore smiled then, at all of us, that occult gaze of hers that I would come to know so well. That I would come to fear, Bunny.

"Follow me," she said.

First Vik stood up, of course. Draining her mini lager. She had a braid in her hair, I saw now. Medievaly and ornate. It had the mark of Coraline's fingerprints all over it, and I felt a sort of red rage ticking in my heart. Most nights last month I'd stayed at her place. I'd get a text late in the evening while I was lying alone in my red bed, my red cloak around my shoulders, whispering to ghosts. Or while I was in the attic, my hands poised over the keyboard of my typewriter, waiting for an entity to inhabit me. *Speak through me, please,* I whispered to it. One of my many incense sticks burning to help make it manifest. To help it fuck me. And then I'd hear a buzzing sound by my boob. Coraline texting me. *Can't sleep ☹ Come?*

And I would not say, *Busy, sorry ☹*

I would not say, *I'm working on making word of the spirit ☺*

Instead I would button up my cloak. Walk the dark streets full of shadows and screaming. Not even waiting for Safe Ryde, which, as you know, Bunny, is the complimentary university car service that everyone at Warren takes after dark so as not to get mugged or murdered. I would brave the night in all its unholy and unknowable dark like I was Little Red in the forest. Clip-clop to her much better neighborhood, which had brighter streetlights, bigger houses, leafier, more fragrant trees. And Coraline would be standing there in her front doorway between the two stone griffins that flanked the entrance, wearing one of her many celestial dresses with matching cardigan—she had one in every color of the rainbow, Bunny, in every shade under the sun. Her hand tugging on her cold white pearls like they were a noose she refused to remove. Her other hand in her pocket, ever gripping the razor. That pocket, I started to note, was always slightly spotted with brown or sometimes fresh red dots. She'd see me walking toward her, coming out of the dark like I was something she herself had conjured, and her eyes would light right up. Mine would too at the sight of her, I admit. Coraline, to whom my soul was already so strangely wed. But there was a darkness there too, I saw it.

Bunny, she'd whisper so tenderly to my face, but like the word also hurt her to speak. She'd given me her heart, I'd seen her at her most vulnerable, seen her vomit grief and rage about her oven story being destroyed by Allan. And she resented me a little for all that. Definitely. *You're here*, she'd say, and that was all she'd say. Letting go of her pearls to stroke my face, but never ever letting go of the razor. She would not say *Thank god you came. Thank you for braving the scary dark.* She would not even say *come in.* She would never ever say *I love you.* Instead she would stroke my face so sadly, so tenderly, right there in the doorway like she fucking hated me. And then she would turn around and walk down her own high-ceilinged hallway, and I would follow her. Up the plushly carpeted stairs—yes, she lived in a better building than I did. (But did she have a magic attic with a triangle window? No she did not.) I followed her bell-shaped silhouette into her rich-girl apartment with its high ceilings and designer foliage. So very five-star *Alice in Wonderland.* Brimming with flowers and furry furniture, all of which you immediately wanted to pet or hug, all of it emitting a most dreamy perfume. She would not ask me if I was hungry or even thirsty, would you, Coraline? I wouldn't even be offered a cup of water, so that one time, desperate, I had to drink from her bathroom faucet, lapping at its tepid stream like a parched cat. Sometimes she'd braid my hair in the living room. She'd simply sit on her petal-patterned love seat and pat the space in front of her like, *Come.* Not even fucking looking at me. Looking instead out her window with the billowy raw silk curtains, remember, Coraline? Knowing I'd come. Knowing I'd sit there kneeling between your legs for however long while you'd braid my red hair, which you said you were so jealous of. It was so beautiful, did I know that? *I didn't*, I lied. You pulled and pulled on my hair until tears would fall from my eyes, Bunny, until I couldn't even feel my hair let alone my scalp anymore. *There*, you'd whisper into my neck when you were done. And though I was curious about your braiding techniques, I didn't dare look in the mirror, Bunny. Didn't want to confront what I'd become in your presence, what you were turning me into, the tears in my eyes and the wide, strange smile on my face that I couldn't seem to help. I followed you into your sky-blue bedroom with the celestial sheets, which were crinkled, always, by your so-disturbed sleep. I saw an open notepad on the bed and a pen beside it, dripping its lavender ink onto the sheets like so much fairy blood. You'd written only one sentence on that white pearlescent page, which you'd then scratched out, it seemed. Scratched out so violently, you'd ripped the page a bit. A little blocked, weren't you, Bunny, on top of being lonely and afraid? There was your small pink pony sitting on the bed. Smiling at us both in a kind of pervy way, pink sparkles shimmering in its big, unseeing horse eyes. And that's when you'd turn to me, your face a question, but also a command. I nodded. Knew the drill after only a couple of nighttimes. Knew my job. Which was to crawl into that bed. Watch you lower the unicorn light on your mushroom nightstand. Watch, by a sliver of slanting moonlight, as you stripped out of your sky dress into a pretty blue silk slip. Remove your white gloves in the dark finger by finger, revealing your dirty secret: cut-up finger pads, permanently scarred by the sharp, glinty friend in your pocket. I wore my white gloves for fashion, for kitsch, but I alone knew that you wore yours for other reasons, Bunny. You didn't take off your pearls, not ever—those stayed around your throat like that scary fairy tale about the girl who wears the green ribbon around her neck. If you take off the ribbon, off goes her head, so the story tells. Sometimes I pictured taking the pearls off your neck in the night and watching your head with its beautiful blond bob just roll away like a ball. Though it was a terrible image, once I pictured it, I couldn't unpicture it, Bunny. You climbed into the cool blue bed after me, and you opened your arms, waiting. Knowing I would climb into them like a cat, which I did. And then you embraced me. So tightly, I felt strangled, like you were the pearls and I was the neck. Your perfume, though, was glorious. Wild bluebells swaying in the bluest of breezes. Sometimes a peppery freesia, its sweet pink note ending in a sharp black crackle. Your heart beat hard into my back like a scared-excited puppy's. Your hot, minty breath on my neck making the small red hairs there rise and fall. And you petted me, didn't you, and I let you, didn't I, until I felt your troubled eyes close. Until you began to snore. So prettily.

That was our ritual most nights that first September, since the very first day we met, wasn't it? In the morning I'd wake up and you'd already be gone. No boa-constricting arms around me. No bluebell or freesia scent. I'd stumble out of the bedroom, still in my red cloak, to find you doing barre in your sun-splashed living room. Or in your retro kitchen, already dressed in one of your sky dresses, making yourself a London Fog and humming along to Chappell Roan. Or perhaps sitting on your petal pouf, pretending to read beneath the framed print of Marilyn Monroe also pretending to read. The way you wouldn't meet my eyes at first. It was like we'd fucked or something, right in the hot cocoon of your nightly shame, and you just couldn't face me now. To look at me would have been too much like seeing the mud-brown roots of your lying golden hair. Your blank sky notebook filled with nothing but inky pools. The razor marks on your inner thighs and finger pads. There were words carved there between your legs, I knew. Some beautiful and some terrible. I was like that to you now, I guessed: the beautiful and terrible words. Shameful, true, and hidden. A secret habit. A compulsion maybe, even. You couldn't live without me already. But here was the thing: I couldn't live without you. Still loved you in spite of myself. And I knew you loved me too.

Hey, Bunny, I'd say, coming to sit by you. As I always did.

Hey, Bunny, you'd say, and smile. Like you were oh so surprised to see me there.

And you'd stroke my sweaty braids away from my eyes.

And we were so happy, we almost died, didn't we?

Every fucking morning.

But then there was a night, a few weeks in, when you did not call. When I sat in my attic communing with the spirit (or trying to get it to commune with me, at least), one eye always on the phone by my crossed legs. Waiting for you to buzz the floorboards with the words that melted me. *Come. I need you.* No buzz came. I watched the sun set and the moon rise in my triangle window. At first I thought, *Good.* I thought, *Fucking finally.* I could work for once. Commune the way I would have every single night since I got here if you hadn't been summoning me to play your evening doll (which I did happily, Bunny, is the sick thing). But these were lies. I missed you. I missed your tall, cool blue rooms and I missed your beautiful cruelty. I missed your silk touch, and I even missed how you braided my hair so tightly that I stopped feeling first my hair and then my scalp and then even my fucking head, Bunny. I missed your perfumed strangling and the heat of your tortured face buried into my nape. I missed your heart pounding fiercely into my shoulder blades. I looked down at my silent phone and thought, *Who? Who is with you tonight in my stead?* And I knew. Could see her in her gross plaid. Her balmy smirk and the hazy *fuck you* of her eyes. Reclined on your Wonderland furniture like she owned it all. I pictured the two of you in your sky bed. Were you holding her close? Would she even let you? Or was it she who was holding you? Were your eyes right now blissfully closed in her plaid arms? Were her hands, with their so-dirty fingernails (which you yourself had reported to me), grazing the contours of you? God how I hated this image. It made me press deep into the typewriter, so that all I typed that night was

alsdjfk;dkjf;lsjsflda;sjfl;sajf;sajfa;fjjdkljflkdjlsdajfdkljfldkjfa;ljdf;

And that was the sum of my rage, Bunny. It was what I felt that afternoon at Mini, staring at the braid in Vik's hair, which you must have braided into it the night before. A fishtail like the mermaid you believed her to be. It swished behind her back as she now rose from her chair to follow Elsinore.

And then you got up, following after Vik. Not even looking or waiting to see if I was getting up too. The two of you holding hands now. And me suddenly so alone at the mini table, with all the devoured mini foods. Nothing at all left but mini crumbs.

So what choice did I fucking have, Bunny?

I followed. Shouting, "Hey! Wait! What are you—"

Vignette

All right, all right. I think we've heard enough from her, haven't we, Sam? I'll take it from here. I think, yet again, someone's getting just a tad off course, don't you? Not even talking to you anymore, even though you're like the guest of honor, Bunny. How rude, right? I mean, that's what we're here for. Not to give vent to private, petty grievances. (Jesus, save it for therapy, Kyra.) So let's move along. After all, Sam's got people to see, places to go, don't you, Bunny? Probably not going anywhere for a while, though, are you? Not given how tightly Coraline tied you up. All that hair braiding taught her a thing or two, apparently, about knots.

Now, where were we?

Oh yes.

We're supposed to be telling the story of how we made something beautiful, Bunny. By which we also mean violent. By which we also mean true. I'll just take that ax from you now, Kyra, thanks. Since it's my turn and all. My turn to go sit by Samantha. My turn to chat, get close. You know, when we first talked about doing this whole kidnapping thing, I, unlike Kyra, was all for it. Not that I had some grievance. I didn't, Bunny. Didn't fucking care, really. When your book or whatever came out, I heard about it, sure. Saw a review for it (mixed) by total accident in the local paper. I was turning the pages of the Arts section and there, toward the very back, was a black-and-white photo of your unsmiling face beside this picture of a pink book jacket with a silhouette of a bunny. I stared at your "author photo" (it looked more like a mug shot, fyi) beside this alleged

book. And you know what I did then? Belched and turned the page. Did
I read the book? I skimmed, Bunny. As you know, conventional narratives
aren't really my thing. More of a *vignette* sort of girl myself, ha ha. But
I read enough to get the gist, I did. *Meh* was my overall feeling. Do you
know the reason I was game right away for this little setup? Not because
I always disliked you, Bunny (though I did, I did). Not because you're a
traitor (though you are, you are). Not because I smelled, from the very
fucking start, that you would one day wound us in your cowardly writer
way. Alone, in the dark. Chuckling with your little rageful pencil. Turning
us into that most tedious and limiting of forms, *a novel*. Only very thinly
disguising us. I mean, yes, you gave me a different eye color and made me
come from a different state, but I knew it was me. Of course I did, I'm
not fucking stupid, Bunny. I *did* go to Barnard, after all. Also, you barely
changed our names, hello? But did I care? Not a drop. When the others
called me screaming-crying-throwing-up into my ear, I rolled my eyes.
Said, *Fucking chill*. But when this plan was hatched (and I won't say by
whom, Bunny)—hatched like a swan's egg, you might even say—I said,
Sign me up. And the reason was so simple. Because I've always, always had
a fondness for violence. It's integral, after all, to the Work. My many years
as a ballerina taught me that. My time at Barnard, too. I had the bloody
toe shoes, the stabby crinoline, to prove it. Burned them both in a staged
bonfire in my junior year, did I ever tell you about that? Oh yes. Orgasmed
while I watched it all crisp. Become sparks that seemed, in the night, like
so much strange orange snow. Looking back, I think that was probably
when I turned what you called *shock artist* (still am, by the way). I had way
more fun burning the crinoline than I ever had fucking twirling in it for
yawning audiences, Bunny. And that's when I realized what art should be:
a blow to the senses. A punch in the face, always. A fuck in the ass, definitely. The deepest, dirtiest fuck of your life, Bunny. But also a wake-up
call. A rousing call to Life and to the fact of imminent Death. Sort of like
what we're doing with you right now.

Speaking of which, we're supposed to be telling you the story of how we made something beautiful. So let me get to the nitty-gritty. Cover the dirty part for us, how's that? For which I was responsible, actually. So it seems almost fitting. Creation is dirty work, that's what some of us, anyway, seem not to understand.

6

I'll start where we left off, before we got tediously fucking sidetracked. When we were all sitting at Mini, processing Ursula's witchery—our *own creative crucible*, our *many streams, make the word flesh*, etc.—and Elsinore suddenly rose from the table. I was the first to follow after her, of course I was. Elsinore and I—or Else, as I called her—we had a thing. From the very beginning, that very first day when we met on the tented green, surrounded by so many assholes, we understood each other implicitly, as implicitly as I understood that violence and art are one. Else didn't speak much. Neither did I. Didn't have to. We just looked at each other. Her aura spoke for her, I was into that. Felt its indigo reverberating in my own soul. Her cold face and colder eyes. Her sense of dress, sort of Manson girl meets Free People. How she just stood there in her suede boots, fucking emanating. She was all about other modes of expression. *What are words, anyway?* we often asked each other with our eyes in the evenings. Lies. Lies is what. Words are the pretty, lying gloves over the clawed, dirty hands of our souls. Words are like a doily we place over our seething hearts, a strand of pearls we wear on our necks to prettify the veins. Distractions. Cut the pearls off, I thought. Take scissors to the limp string and snip. Let the pretty golden head roll.

I came to Warren to go beyond. Beyond words as doilies and gloves and pearls. Beyond the sentence tinsel of semicolons and commas. Beyond fucking structure and time and plot. All shackles. I, more than any of us, wanted my hands in the raw clay, Bunny. To create new forms. So when we talk about who's responsible for what happened next, let's fucking remember that. Remember, too, that I knew how to trust. I wasn't scared of the unknown. I lived there. Rolled around in the worms and mud of it. I don't ask questions like some people. About *meaning?* About *direction?* About *intent?*

Fuck all that.

So at Mini when Else said, *Follow me*, I fucking followed. Didn't hesitate. Did I know where we were going? No idea, Bunny. Not at first, anyway. Then I guess I did. Else and I already had a mind-soul-body connection, like I said, and I started to see where she was heading with my third eye. Narrative Arts. The rose garden. Where we all first hugged and I felt the power of our locked arms.

The bunny's eyes turned blue only after we *all* hugged, by the way.

Just want to clarify that.

Since there seem to be varying accounts.

Anyway, when Else and I left Mini, Coraline followed us. Then Kyra followed Coraline, didn't you, Bunny? Kyra was the last to follow, of course. The first to ask, "Where are we going? What we are doing? Why are we walking back to Narrative Arts?" So many questions for a girl who claims to fornicate with entities. And to love fairy tales. In fairy tales no one ever asks why, did you notice that, Bunny? Does Little Red ask the wolf, *Why are you talking to me? Why are you fucking following me?*

No, she doesn't. She just walks into the woods, swinging her basket and gathering her flowers, just traipses right into her own erotic demise. I respect that. Likewise, I just walk into the great unknown. Like a real artist. And yet I knew. I knew what we were looking for.

The bunny.

Our bunny. Covered in Coraline's blood and all our tears. The one whose eyes we turned blue. All of us.

The garden was empty when we got to it. Nothing but flowers shivering in the late sun. No creatures anywhere. Huh. *Disappointing*, we thought. Funny how I could feel all of us thinking the word in our minds. I saw Coraline was shivering, holding herself lamely in her own arms. I offered her my plaid shirt, underneath which I had only a wifebeater on. Kyra, at the same time, offered her little red fairy cloak. Offered it even though I knew she was cold, was clearly shivering in her evil-kitten dress or whatever. Funny I could even feel Kyra's cold though I myself was hot. *What is happening?* I thought.

Coraline looked at both offerings, then took my shirt almost immediately. Which was funny, Bunny. But not at all surprising. I knew the two of them were close, just like Else and I were close, in a kind of soul-speak way. But I'd noted that whenever I chose to talk to or even look at Coraline, she immediately seemed to forget Kyra existed. And to be honest with you, Bunny? Since this is a night of Absolute Truth? I rather enjoyed my effect.

So when Coraline took my shirt instead of Kyra's cloak, I should have been happy about that, Bunny. I should have been smug. And I was, I was. But I also felt Kyra die inside, inwardly curse my name, call us both a bitch in her mind. Felt it so keenly, it was almost like it was me dying inside, me cursing my own name, me hurling the word *bitch* in my head. Strange. I looked at Kyra, still holding her fairy cloak out to Coraline, her smile twitchy with murder thoughts. Thoughts I was hearing in my own mind like they were my own thoughts.

How could you fucking humiliate me like this, Bunny?

I hate that I love you.

"You sure you don't want the cloak, too?" Kyra asked, almost like a threat. "I don't need it at all, Bunny," she lied, even though she obviously did. She was shivering like crazy at this point. And somewhere inside myself, I was weirdly shivering too.

"Oh, this'll be plenty, I'm sure," Coraline said, looking only at me, like, *I choose you.* She put my shirt on and I helped her do that. Meanwhile, Kyra watched us, hated us. And I pretended not to feel her hurt and confusion coursing through my own blood.

"Thank you," Coraline said to me, blushing. I loved to make her blush, it was so easy and gratifying.

Else, meanwhile, was turning circles in the center of the garden like her slim body was a divining rod.

"What is she looking for?" Kyra asked me, staring at Else. Not deigning to ask Else directly. A little too awed by her, both Kyra and Coraline. Her willowy frame and her long silver hair, which made her look not old but otherworldly sexy, like a Tolkien elf. Her prolonged silences, the way she'd look at you with her cold blue gaze, seeing all the things you didn't want seen, until you felt physically flayed by her eyes. The dagger around her neck always eerily catching the light, no matter where she stood. I was often tasked with being her translator. Even though I had no idea what was going on in her scary-sexy-mysterious mind.

"Shhhhh," I said to Kyra. "Isn't it fucking obvious by now?"

It was then I saw the rabbit hole.

Yes. I was the first one to see it. Me. *My* eyes seeing it. *My* hand pointing to it. There, in the very far corner of the garden. The muddy hole in the grass. Freshly dug up. Fit for a bunny.

"Bunny," we all whispered.

So then?

We walked over to the hole, following my pointing finger. Walked as one body with many feet, our steps in perfect tandem. All our shadows seeming to be suddenly in sync as we cut across the grass. Our hearts beating more quickly now, I could feel them all beating in my body.

We stood around the hole's circumference for a while, waiting. For what? We knew and didn't know. Coraline kept licking the sweat beads off her upper lip. Kyra was looking down into the hole like it was a questionable wishing well.

"Maybe we should build a trap for him or something?" Coraline said at last. "To lure him out of the hole?"

"A *trap?*" Kyra said.

"He's an animal, isn't he? Doesn't one of us hunt? Or know someone who hunts?"

We shook our heads, though I noticed that everyone was suddenly looking at me now, like surely I hunted or knew a hunter. I did not hunt.

I did not know anyone who hunted. My father, as you may or may not re-call, Bunny, basically invented virtual reality. My mother's a former model turned Pilates guru who invented a diet prosecco. She'd been the one to send me in for ballet at a young age. My world is as rarified as Swiss thermal spring water. Far more rarified than the world of these girls. Only Elsinore, perhaps, could come close.

"How hard can it be?" I said. "Probably just a stick with a leaf attached."

"Or a carrot maybe?" Kyra offered.

"I don't think so," I said with certitude. I had no idea.

I looked to Else, but her aura had gone griege.

"Last time he just jumped into my arms," Coraline wailed.

"Into *my* arms, actually," Kyra countered.

"Into *our* arms," I said. Because, excuse me? "Anyway, that was just a fluke probably." I looked over at Else, whose face said, *There are no fucking accidents.*

"Well," Coraline said, "maybe if we just wait, he'll come out." And then she sat down on the grass. Right by the hole, like she was waiting for some-one to serve her a London Fog. She slipped her hand into her dress pocket and pulled out a red velvet mini cupcake. Dropped it into the hole. The white icing top, I noted, was speckled with red dots. I'd been to Coraline's place only a couple of times. Recently she'd invited me over, mainly to com-plain that she thought Kyra was suffocating her and so she was trying to branch out socially. *Do you ever have people who become just too attached?* she'd asked, clutching my forearm so fiercely that there were marks on it the next day, little pink crescent moons.

"What did you do that for?" Kyra asked, her voice sounding hysterical. She was asking about the cupcake.

Coraline shrugged. "Maybe he likes red velvet."

"I can't imagine that. A rabbit liking red velvet."

"Well, I fucking can," Coraline said. And she sat there peering into the hole into which she'd tipped her cupcake. What a sad, sort-of-hot picture she made, Bunny.

"Bunny," she whispered into the dirt hole softly. Like she was Alice in Wonderland or whatever. Gripping its edges with her white-gloved fingers. "Hello, hello?" she whispered. "Bonsoir. It's me," she whispered, "Coraline." Like that might mean something.

Then Kyra dropped down beside her. Put her hands in the dirt by the hole's edge like she was trying to receive and dictate a message from the mud. She tilted her head back as though she were being fucked by the grass. Closed her eyes while Coraline glared at her. "I think he was here," she murmured at last, as if the rabbit's ghost had spoken to her.

"Of course he was here, *Bunny*," Coraline snapped. "*That's* obvious." She petted the hole's edge possessively. "The question is where is he now? When is he coming *back?*"

We looked to Elsinore, standing in the corner of the garden, communing with the moon. Her eyes were rolling closed and open. I noticed the dagger-shaped diamond around her neck glinting strangely. Kyra put her ear down to the grass, listening. She frowned, shook her head. "He's not saying. Probably because there are so many of us. He's probably scared of crowds or something," she said, looking from me to Coraline. Like, *Go*.

"I'm not leaving," Coraline said.

"Me neither," I said.

Else was now staring from the hole to the moon back to the hole, like she was awaiting cosmic instructions. *Fuck instructions*, I thought. What were we going to do, just stand here all night, staring and waiting? Sure, sometimes you had to learn to let Art come to you, but sometimes, *sometimes, Bunny*, you had to go to it, didn't you? Get dirty and grab it by the cottony tail. *Don't let this opportunity go hopping away into the dark*, wasn't that what Ursula had said? So I got down on my hands and knees.

"Um, what are you doing, Bunny?"

The ground was so cool and soft beneath me, the grass like a wet shag carpet, twitching with bugs. And then, much to the horror of Coraline and Kyra, I started to dig in the hole.

Can I tell you how good it felt? Like fucking. Better than fucking. Like creating something. With the mud in my fingers and the moon on my back, I fell into a kind of trance almost. Coraline and Kyra both stood up, whisper-screaming, "What are you doing? What are you fucking doing, Bunny?"

I ignored them, of course. What did they think I was fucking doing? Being action is what. Being the verb and the noun rather than the adjective, the useless adverb. And in my trance, I dug deep. So deep that the mud started to feel very cold. Probably you know all about mud, Bunny, living, as you did, beneath the poverty line? I chanted softly to myself. One of Ursula's soul arias. I was facedown in the hole, digging myself into a kind of ecstasy, when I felt a soft something brush against me. A rat? *A fucking rat*, I thought. I screamed. Pulled my head out of the hole.

And then a noise like a grunt in stereo.

Behind us.

We all turned and saw four mangy young men standing by the flying-hare statue. All wearing army trench coats, though none of them, I was quite sure, had ever been to war. Hair sprouting like chaotically cultivated foliage. Very pale, even the nonwhite ones, like they'd never seen the sun.

The Poets, we knew instantly.

We looked at one another then. Like, *Fuck*. We'd already discussed how we felt about poetry. About poets in general. Always so smirking and tortured. Reeking of cigarettes and bruised pride. You remember the Poets, don't you, Bunny? They didn't get much real estate in your book, I noticed, except for the one. Allow me to refresh your memory as I recount.

"Well, well," one of them said, and I immediately pegged him as the leader. "If it isn't the Fictions." Latin looking. Black hair with enviable slick, remember him? Eyewear that said, *I'm quietly judging you all the time.* A necklace of bright feathers and bone, like he might have dismembered a Muppet in his free time. I imagined his poems made manspreading use of white space.

Coraline looked afraid. Gripped the hole. She'd told us already about how hideously they'd ignored her at the Demitasse. She'd made a comment about the cheese selection pairing nicely with the cracker selection, and they'd all stared at her like she'd farted with her mouth.

"What might you be doing here on this fall evening, *Fictions?*" another prodded. Gunnar. Second in command, clearly. Pyramidal facial hair. He looked like the blondest, most evil Jesus. Probably he wrote odes, I thought.

"Some digging, looks like?" Another. Redheaded and terribly pale. Cunning fucking face, like a wily sprite or an Irish butcher specializing in offal. He had a single pearl in his ear, probably pillaged from an unsuspecting grandmother. Ballads, I assumed, and shivered.

"Finding inspiration for your ... *stories?* Fodder for your Oprah picks?" asked the Muppet Dismemberer. They all looked like they might laugh.

"Some of us don't write *stories*," I spat.

"Is that so? Well, what do you write then, *Fiction?*" asked Evil Jesus.

"We could ask you the same thing, *Ode Boy*," Coraline snapped.

"Hey, hey," another said. Black, with pale blue hair that matched his eyes. Hot, honestly, if he weren't a Poet. A tattoo of three sinuous tears under his right eye, which I remember being mildly impressed by at the time. Perhaps he had murdered or was in a prison gang or had known great sorrow and loss. Later we found out, of course, that the closest he'd come to prison was Princeton, and that the only gang he'd ever been in was at Exeter, for bird-watching. He patted the redheaded butcher boy's shoulder. Like, *Easy. We're all friends here.* Except we weren't. Would never be, not with Poets.

It was then I noticed a fifth boy hanging back from their cauldron of four. Now, I know you know him, Bunny. Soup-bowl haircut. An open parka (in October, Bunny) over a T-shirt of a smiling sloth. He was smiling just like the sloth, gazing at the clouds above all our heads, like he was enjoying a laugh (perhaps at our expense) with some obscure sky god. *Jonah*, you called him in your novel. Because, um, that's his actual fucking name. Quite the Fiction you are, Bunny. But I agree, it suits him. What else could a boy like him possibly be called?

"What are *you* all doing out here?" Kyra asked them. She was still semi-fucking the grass, by the way. "Ooh, let me guess, k? Looking for inspiration for your chapbooks that no one will ever read? That maybe the local bookstore will sell on their consignment shelf out of pity, if at all?" She asked this very sweetly, in her baby voice. It was like suddenly inside the baby there was this roaring bitch. I had a touch more respect for her then.

The Poets paled further, perhaps picturing the very consignment shelf on which their future chapbooks would soon sit. Their eyes narrowed collectively.

"We just got out of David's workshop," Jonah offered happily. The others all looked at him and seemed to hiss.

"Oh really? How was it?" I asked.

"Edifying," they all said. "Unlike some people, we *enjoy* hearing critique." Noble nostril flare followed by noble grunt.

"And what is that supposed to mean?" This from Else. In a low voice from the corner of the garden. Though she spoke quietly, they all heard her. Heard the dagger in her voice, as plainly as they saw it glinting on her neck.

The Muppet Dismemberer smiled. "Oh, nothing, nothing. Just we heard from a little bird that someone got so very upset about their feedback in the Cave the first day." They all made fake sad faces.

"WHO TOLD YOU?" Coraline screamed, going red. Fucking losing her shit. And the Poets just stared at her, smiling broadly now. A reaction. That's all poets want. To fuck with you immediately and irreversibly. Forget plot. No journey or catharsis through narrative, no, no. They go right for the jugular with their word art and leave you bleeding. I kind of have to admire them for this.

"The Cave speaks," said the sprite.

"Also, good luck being a graduate student," Evil Jesus sneered, his vaguely Scandi accent mocking us. "I mean, if you're all going to freak out over a little criticism, what hope do you really *have*, Fictions?"

"Go back to your zine reading, Ode Boy!" Kyra roared.

"You go back to digging in the mud for your book club plots!" the sprite cried, his pearl earring quivering ragefully. "No doubt you'll find them there."

"What *are* you looking for in the mud there, by the way, Fictions?" said the hot one, tattooed tears shining on his high cheek.

We looked at one another. And it was extraordinary, what happened then. Suddenly I felt like I could hear all four of our minds in my own mind. Talking in whispers, aligning like migratory birds in the sky. *Should we ask them if they've seen our bunny? Should we?* We pictured posing the question. Pictured them laughing at us with all their pale, lizardy mouths.

A bunny, huh? they would say to us once they'd gathered themselves.

Sure, we saw him—we think he went to the alehouse.

Or didn't we see him first at the athenaeum? another might say.

Oh yes! Brushing up on his, you know, Poe and whatnot. More sniggering.

They would laugh even louder about it later, we knew, in whatever dark Marxist hole they congregated in. They would laugh until they cried, their pale faces going pink.

And then just like that, we decided.

"Nothing," we told them as one voice. My voice. My mouth, which spoke for all of us. "Looking for nothing. Just digging for our book club plots like you said. You're right. We Fictions. So stupid."

And it was funny, but suddenly they seemed somewhat suspicious of us. No more laughing at us now. Not even sniggering. Another sort of sound came from their closed mouths. A sound of interest piqued. They stared at the hole we surrounded. A bit of longing in their slitty eyes. A bit of curious.

"*Fine,*" they spat at last. "Have fun playing in your *mud,* Fictions."

A wind came then and their black army coats blew open all at once, like a flock of vampire bats spreading their wings. They started to turn away.

"Go write a sestina about the sunset that no one will fucking ever read ever!" we roared after them. But they were already gone. Only the boy in the sloth T-shirt waved at us while walking backward. "Goodbye! Hey, if you see Sam, say I said hi?"

Ugh. He even rhymed, Bunny.

Our eyes locked then, all eight of them. *Close one. That was a close one,* I felt them all say in my mind. *Our* mind, I guess it was.

Very close, Bunny, we all thought together. Smiling now.

The wind blew softly through the roses then, and the clouds seemed to move more quickly in the sky. The sun sank behind the Warren towers, the dying light of it turning us pink. So we were pink and smiling at one another, Bunny, suddenly a plural consciousness so deeply joined that tears shone in all our eyes at the exact same time. It was beautiful. It felt like nothing could touch us. Ever, ever again.

And then? There he was. The bunny. Sitting behind us like he'd always been there. Staring at us with his so-blue eyes. Eyes that *we'd* made blue. Not someone else's experiment. No, it was ours. *He* was ours, this fuzzy bunny. Possibly even mine, for did I not dig the hole? Coraline's blood had dried on his furry shoulder, in the form of a warped heart. He was watching us argue. Long ears twitching. Sort of smiling, just like we were.

"My bunny," I whispered, we all whispered this. Opening all eight of our arms. He looked at all these arms, or seemed to. So that he didn't know where to go.

So that he hopped away.

And we all followed.

7

How did we end up in a circle surrounding the bunny in Kyra's attic? Well, Bunny led us there, if you can believe it. Hopped all the way from the garden to her place. He even looked over his bloody shoulder to see were we following? *Fuck yes, Bunny.* Following with no idea at all where he was leading us. It was sort of erotic. I was feeling, I'll admit, sexual about it. Which was weird. And yes, I know what you're thinking: *Surprise, surprise, Vik's feeling sexual about something fucked-up.* Well, fuck you, Bunny. It was weird, okay? Yes, I've been turned on by some bizarre shit, but I don't fuck bunnies, Bunny. Just not a freak that way, sorry. And yet? I can't deny there was something arousing about all of us together in the cool of night, following this furry creature, with his sly eyes that seemed to glow an even brighter blue in the dark. He seemed almost to smile at us over his shoulder. Like, *Come on. Let's go.*

All the way there we didn't fucking speak. Couldn't. Didn't want to spook him, first of all. Didn't want him to run away. *Don't run away, Bunny! We would fucking die if you ran away now.* We all held our breaths as we made our way through the dark, winding streets. Kyra was so happy when Bunny suddenly stopped in front of her house. We felt her joy inside of us, leaping and clapping its small hands, and it was awful. Yet we were so mesmerized by the fact of Bunny in our midst. He hopped up her stone steps. Like, *Here. Here is where I'd like to go, ladies, okay?* Okay, Bunny. Sure. We're not loving this choice, but what choice have we? Bunny waited patiently while Kyra opened her front door; he just sort of sat there on the stoop, looking up. Watched her turn the key in the lock with the shakiest fucking hand, a smile on his face. And we waited with Bunny, small smiles on our own faces also. And we knew we would lose our souls to this, whatever it was. It was already happening. It had already begun.

Bunny went right in when Kyra opened the door. Hopped his way through the living room and right up her rickety staircase to the attic. Almost like it was Bunny's place now, not hers anymore. He was the one who had collected all the typewriters and dumb knickknacks and fairy posters. Bunny was the one who owned two copies of the writing diaries of Virginia Woolf. It was Bunny who'd dog-eared the pages, thrice underlined the line: *I am I: and I must follow that furrow, not copy another.*

And then?

We were in the attic with Bunny. Dark. So dark but for a splash of moon in the triangle window that made everything a little silvery. And what happened was like a kind of dream. All of us suddenly in a circle around Bunny, glowing whitely in the moonlight. One of us had lit candles, when and why did we even light candles? Don't know. Yet one of us had done it. Knew to do it. Knew also to play music from her iPhone. Something haunting and harpy with reverb. To burn an incense stick, four incense sticks, in fact, each embodying a different element—earth, air, water, fire—going all at once. To set a bundle of sage ablaze in an abalone shell, it was Kyra who did this.

"Why are you doing that, Bunny?" I asked her, watching her small, heart-shaped face lit orange from the many flames.

"Bunny wants me to," she whispered, staring at the creature. He was simply sitting there in the pool of moonlight. Sitting in the center of us like our furry sun. Kyra's eyes, when she looked at me, looked lost in the most terrible, beautiful dream. I was lost there too, I knew. We all were. Someone had also put on an old black-and-white film, it looked like, using Kyra's projector. It played silently, hugely, on the attic wall. It looked foreign but familiar. A New Wave I didn't recognize but felt I knew by heart all the same. A masked couple walking arm in arm, around and around a fountain. What movie was this, I wondered, and who had put it on? But I didn't have the mind frame to ask more questions just now. Could only swim in this moment. And all while Bunny sat there in our midst like literal magic. The moon making him glow whiter and brighter. None of us dared make even a breath of a sound. Or move closer. Even though, god, I wanted to, Bunny. Looking at Bunny. And Bunny looking at me, I felt. Making me want. So much. Want what exactly? Didn't even know. But my body hummed with it. Dripped with it. Bunny was emanating an energy. A magnetic force, like he was the moon and we were the tide.

"Hot," I heard myself say. And it felt as though Bunny's eyes had pulled the word out of me. Like a magician, really.

"Pretty," someone else's mouth said. Or maybe all our mouths said. Said it at the exact same time. The incenses were twisting in the air, the different smokes braiding themselves like hair in Coraline's gloved fingers. Music played from all four of our phones now. My atmospheric bitch rock. Coraline's poppy swells and power ballads. Else's oblique ambient punctuated with her Kate Bush and Heart. Those dark fucking fairy harps, which must have been Kyra's. And Bunny seemed to be swaying now slightly to our various musics. Like he was dancing almost. Was he? Or was he just sitting there, munching the little mound of grass one of us must have plucked along the way and provided to him?

"Amazing," we all whispered. And then we began to sway with Bunny. Like we were all of us suddenly dancing too. The blue of Bunny's eyes became a kind of indigo then. Suddenly I was moving closer, my feet moving closer, inching toward this magic. Toward Bunny, who was drawing me near with his magnetism, his magnetic eyes and smile. We were all of us moving closer, I saw. Making a tight circle around Bunny, who was still swaying as we were swaying. Occasionally munching the grass.

"There's a fairy tale about a girl who marries a rabbit," Kyra said softly, swaying. "But the rabbit turns out to be an abusive asshole. So she runs away."

"What are you saying, girl?" Coraline asked.

"Nothing. Just that in fairy tales, people have relations with animals like rabbits, is all. Girls are always marrying beasts in fairy tales. And . . . " She trailed off, staring into Bunny's eyes.

"*And?*" I asked.

"And then they turn human and hot when you kiss them. Or something." There was an intensity to her face now when she was looking at Bunny. A trembling to her lips.

"Are you saying you want to kiss the bunny, girl?"

"*No.*"

But in our minds we heard her say, *Fuck yes.*

"Look, we're not in fairy-tale times, Bunny," Coraline snapped.

"Easy," Else murmured. She, too, was staring intensely at Bunny, swaying very close to him. I noticed a thin blue vein throbbing in her forehead. "Easy now," she whispered. It was unclear if she was talking to Coraline or to herself or to Bunny.

"I know we're not in fairy-tale times," Kyra hissed to Coraline. "Obviously, Bunny. I know this is . . . reality or whatever."

"Well, then you know that in *reality*, if you kissed a rabbit, that would be fucking . . . bestiality, girl."

"Yes. This is true," I whispered to Kyra. "It would be gross of you," I said. Even though I, too, wanted to make out with Bunny.

"All I'm saying is that when we hugged the bunny, his eyes changed color," Kyra said. "So just imagine . . ."

Yes, we all thought in our minds. *Imagine.*

"All the dates I've ever had are so dull," Coraline sighed.

And in the hive of our mind, we could suddenly picture her bobbed and bored in various prep-school-dance and college-party contexts. Waltzing with rich, pimpled boys with greaser hair like something out of a 1950s film. Twirling her pearls above her sweetheart neckline. Yawning into her gloved hand. Gazing out the windshield while whatever bow-tied asshole talked about his postgraduate career plans. Dreaming herself elsewhere.

"Sorry, Bunny," I said. "You've been so unfulfilled."

And her eyes brimmed with tears. "Not that I'm even thinking about that," she said, shaking her head. "Romance? I mean, I'm here to write. I'm here for myself."

"We all are," Kyra said, her eyes on Bunny.

"I'm not even here to meet anyone," Coraline insisted. She wasn't really telling us, she was telling Bunny. Sort of laughing crazily. Sort of blushing.

"Though I suppose if someone came along, it might be nice," she added. She looked at Bunny's twitching ears. Their slick pink insides. "Of course, they'd have to be my intellectual equal."

"Of course."

And then in the hive, in the hot pink mists of our collective mind, a figure appeared. A pretty blond man with a twitchy pink nose. He wore a pale blue shirt and an apron that said, *I Will Cut a Bitch (and a Cake ☺)*. He had a girlish smile and wore a pinkish lipstick whose very shade we had once seen her point to and say *for whores*. He was nodding at everything she fucking said, she was so endlessly fascinating. He was saying, *Of course. Absolutely. Tell me.*

"It might be very nice," I said.

"Yes," she said, flushed now, not looking at me. "But I'm really just here to make."

"Me too."

"Totally."

"All the *humans* I meet are boring," Kyra whispered to Bunny. "Period." And then in our collective mind, we saw her footloose and red-cloaked in her fairy-tale world, fornicating with mists. Wandering among the half-naked nymphs and leering wolves and buff mermen poking their lovely wet heads out of glassy forest pools, their eyes dark with wanting to drag her down to oblivion. She was prancing through this forest world to the music of Mary Lattimore, holding the hand of a giant creature in a rabbit mask. The rabbit was extremely long-eared and he wore a very smart black tux, and in his other hand he held an ax, which he was swinging wildly. Jesus Christ.

"I just want something hot," I whispered. "And surprising. It has to take me by surprise," I said. "To be provocative." And I felt them see my own dream in all its nakedness, which I won't share with you, Bunny, sorry. Except to say how strange it was to feel them seeing my insides like that. Fantasies that, despite my well-known boldness, I would never fucking speak, never write. I don't embarrass easily, Bunny, but I'll admit I blushed then.

"What about you, Else?" I asked her. Mainly to get their eyes out of my soul.

Else shook her head. Watched Bunny like he was a fire. "Desire," she whispered, "is so elusive, isn't it?"

"So elusive," we agreed.

"Amorphous and complex. To give language to it is a tricky thing." There were tears in her eyes when she said this. In the hive we suddenly saw crashing sea waves. Sharp rock and white foam, so much foam. And superimposed over these waves, like a film, a white antique chest of drawers. In the top middle drawer, an ornate lock. A very large golden key in the lock. The key suddenly turning slowly in this lock all by itself. We looked at Elsinore. She was very red in the face, staring hard at Bunny. That blue vein in her temple was really throbbing now. The dagger around her neck was glowing iridescently in the dark. Its point, we saw now, was very sharp indeed.

More images began to appear and disappear in the hive, Bunny. Quickly they arose and dissolved like some rapidly moving dream. Not just in our collective mind, but on the attic wall, too, projected like a film. The fastest-moving movie or something, Bunny, it was crazy. Actors and musicians appeared and disappeared, dissolving into one another. Falling cherry blossoms and our mouths opening to catch the petals. A hand held aloft in a rainstorm, the skin ecstatic with cold drips. That crashing sea, the shoreline jagged with black rock. The Poets smirking at us in the garden, their coats blowing open like bat wings. Allan in the Cave, looking even taller than he actually was, stirring his tea and insulting us in his Scottish accent. Telling us we were fucking terrible, *sorry, not sorry*. A red-nailed hand holding an ax.

And then? So funny to say, but we saw ourselves. Me handing Coraline my plaid shirt with my so-dirty fingernails, and Coraline taking her sky dress off in blue silhouette. Elsinore in her drapey linens talking to Ursula under the tented green, staring into me with her cold jewel eyes, and Kyra applying Cherries in Winter thickly to her pouting lips, waiting for ghosts to fuck. The four of us in the rose garden holding one another so tightly, Bunny, that we truly did not know where we began and ended. Holding until we were one incredibly fragrant, hot body, pulsing with want.

And then the screen went black.

The moonlight was now a deep silver pool in which Bunny floated. We stared at him, all of us red-faced, and the music played on, such violent harps and strings. Almost like we, with our minds, were making the harpist's fingers drag across the strings with more and more violence. The black-and-white film was playing on the wall again, the masked couple walking more quickly, backward now around the fountain, something diabolical in their smiles. Like they knew what we were up to in the attic, they were watching. And the rabbit in the moonlight pool was trembling, trembling. And what were we doing?

Oh god, we didn't know.

But it was hot, Bunny.

All our eyes on Bunny and all our hearts beating in time together like a bass to the song of this, and it was too much. *Stop*, we thought, but we couldn't seem to stop now, it was too late. Because Bunny was trembling as we were trembling, and were we making him tremble with the force of our eyes and minds?

"Stop, stop," Kyra whispered, "we're hurting him, I think."

And Coraline was crying and shaking her head, her mind screaming, *JOY, JOY, JOY*, and Else's eyes were rolled back into her head, deep in her dark pink fantasy world of keys and locks.

And I? I don't know where I was.

Lost.

Lost in the moonlight pool with Bunny. Lost in the dreaming. Lost in the trembling of my own body, trembling like Bunny's body. Lost in our mind frequency, which hummed loud now like a drone.

And then suddenly the frequency stopped, the world became terribly still. I looked at Bunny and Bunny looked at me, right into my eyes alone.

And he fucking exploded.

The Duchess

Hello there, Samantha. You remember me, of course you do. Viktoria, thank you so much for sharing your . . . experience. Alas, I think it's time for me to step in and speak, don't you? Particularly as we're approaching this most tender moment in our story. I hope that you (like me) have enjoyed the recountings so far, Samantha, warped though they all were by the prism of Ego. For instance, I was especially amused by how Vik seemed to suggest that it was she alone who caused the rabbit explosion. Amused, Samantha, but not at all surprised. Ego is a terrible thing for the Artist's soul, as you well know. But we must remember that what we've been hearing tonight are the narratives of wounded souls (and who wounded them, Samantha?). That they all seem to be losing their way in the labyrinth of this story, getting caught up in the *I* of it all, is to be expected.

Allow me, then, at this crucial juncture, to humbly pick up the Thread.

You're looking a bit pale, Samantha, I must say. Are you not at all happy to see me? Well, that's fine, I understand. You and I have had some . . . *differences* in the past, haven't we? Differences in Understanding. For instance, you probably think we're such villains for gagging you. Such *Cuntscapades*. (When I saw that you'd actually called us that in print, I thought, *Wow. What literature you've made.*) A misunderstanding there, of Intent. Really Vik stuffed my unwashed sock in your mouth out of loving-kindness. As a helpful little reminder of Workshop. The gag rule, remember that? Your turn to *shhhhh*, our turn to speak. We're just making the metaphor literal is all, which we know you know all about. Just like this ax, which, yes, it's my turn to take, my turn to hang on to, thanks, Vik. My turn to bring the blade right up to Samantha's neck, so like a swan's, I quite agree. You hit the nail right on the head there, Bunny. Oh, don't worry, Samantha, I'm not going to decapitate you, we've already said. I'm not a psychopath, I'm a fiction writer. I'm just making you *feel* the metaphor, is all. Bringing you into the visceral experience of it, shall we say. Making you *smell the room*, remember when our writing teachers would say that? *I want to smell the room.* Do you smell it now, Samantha? It smells, thanks to you, of stale blood and dead dreams.

It was my idea to bring us all together like this, hope you don't mind. Not because I despise you, of course not. Not because when I read your book, I pictured killing you slowly and excruciatingly and inventively, no, no. I, unlike my former cohort, actually found reading your little novel to be quite illuminating. Novels aren't my *medium*, Samantha, I much prefer my own innovation of the *proem*. But yours was a learning experience. *What an astonishingly convoluted document*, I thought, *of mental illness!* A perfect example of what happens when a less evolved being seeks to articulate their petty feelings in story form. In fact, I often share it with my students. Oh yes, I'm a teacher now, Samantha. Not at a university, don't be silly. I went screaming from the Academy after graduating from Warren. No, I run my own online story/drum circle now. Oh, it's wonderful. Unlike Workshop, it's filled with such loving-kindness. And it's in the spirit of loving-kindness, absolutely, that we come to you tonight. Yes, believe it or not, we want to help you, quite like our brilliant therapist is helping us. Sometimes we really do think we conjured him, it's true. Maybe we did. He's so very good. Too good, really, for this world. He listens to us, and almost no one listens anymore, don't you find that? That almost no one looks deep into the heart of you and wants to know: *Who the hell are you in there?* He's the one who told me, *Help her. Take pity on her as you did before.* He was right, Bunny. I did pity you before, we all did. I mean, you were terribly alone, weren't you, at the time? Except for some very sad . . . I mean, can we even call them friends? And you still are alone, it seems. Just look at your phone, the phone of the semi-famous authoress. We've had you with us for a few hours now, and nothing but a few calls from an unknown number. A text that's just four question marks. Maybe your publicist or something checking in. Doing due diligence. But does she really care, Samantha? Probably not. No one cares where the hell you are. But *we* care, oh yes. Which is why we're all here, aren't we? Because we love you, Bunny. Now you may be wondering, is it worth the toil? The personal sacrifice on our part? The risk we're all taking? That reminds me, can one of you please go downstairs and make sure the doors are locked and all the window shades are drawn? We don't want a neighbor glimpsing something they shouldn't, getting the wrong idea and calling the police and such. (Though of course if they knew what you'd done, they'd probably applaud us.) But I don't really think that's going to happen, Samantha. In our two years of Workshop, which did involve some screaming, some botched swings of the ax, we were never once bothered, were we? It's almost as if no one *cares* what we writers do up here in the dark! But you never know. We don't want to be interrupted, not at this tender juncture in our narrative. In fact, I think you'd all better go downstairs now, if you don't mind, Bunny. Leave Sam and me alone for this part, okay?

Yes, I do think it's necessary.

Yes, all of you. Even you, Vik.

Thank you so much.

Isn't that better, Bunny? Now we can really go deep, you and me, oh yes. Because I really want you to understand some things, okay? And having read your "book," I think it's clear you really don't understand anything at all. Not to get into the *I* of it all myself, but you were especially, especially misguided about me. *The Duchess*, as you called me, which honestly was sort of flattering. You recognized something, didn't you, in your cruel, warped way, about power. But the one thing you didn't understand? The most crucial thing perhaps? Is that all of this, the whole fucking thing, was me. And this isn't Ego talking, Samantha. It's Truth. The actual, literal Thread.

You'll see.

8

Now, where were we in our little telling? Oh yes. The attic. The rabbit. The Happy Accident of its explosion. But before we venture any further into the dark wood of this story, Bunny, let's please remember that Creation is an elusive Process. Its ways are deeply Mysterious, as I know you know. Ultimately unknowable, even to its practitioners. Perhaps especially to its practitioners. Outcomes are at best Unpredictable. Often they are Unfortunate. Often they disappoint. Deeply.

Was I at first disappointed that the rabbit fulminated? Of course I was, Samantha. My Aura instantly turned Ocher with Regret. And if I'm being truthful—and I really do want to be truthful here—perhaps I also felt a small sense of responsibility. I had attempted to introduce my beloved cohort—by way of my charged silences, my cryptic words, my proems—to the slippery ways of Creation. I had attempted to lead by example. I had attempted to put the tenets in *Arias of the Solar Plexus* into practice.

And to what End?

Sitting in my cashmere lap now was a severed rabbit's ear, leaking its dark blood onto my griege fringe. I stared down into it, enchanted, attempting to divine meaning in the entrails. All around me the air smelled vital, of blood and burst animal. It was a scent that reminded me, strangely, of Mother when she came home from hunting pheasant, the wild mixing wonderfully, profoundly, with her Opium. As if from a distance, I heard my cohort calling my name repeatedly, pitifully. Screaming, "WHAT HAVE WE DONE, WHAT HAVE WE DONE? OH MY GOD, WE KILLED THE BUNNY WITH OUR MINDS AND EYES, DID WE FUCKING KILL THE BUNNY WITH OUR MINDS AND EYES? ARE WE MURDERERS?"

They are so crude, I whispered with my own mind to the severed ear. I was mesmerized by the shapes the pooling blood was making on my nude cashmere, like ever-shifting clouds. The ear, hearing my words perhaps, almost seemed to twitch. *Yes. They are so crude. Had it been you alone, Elsinore, something else might very well have happened here.*

What? I asked. *What might have happened? Tell me what the meaning of this is, please.*

But the severed ear fell silent then. Or was it that I was drawn back into the vulgar world of the attic by the screaming and crying all around me, rising in volume? Coraline, I saw, was weeping insanely, clutching at her boob like someone had stabbed her there. Between you and me, I would have told her to shut the fuck up (much as I love her), but I could not waste precious breath at the moment. Not when I was Processing. Kyra, of course, was hugging her semi-violently in an attempt, I suppose, to console. Vik, meanwhile, my dear Vik, perhaps the closest to me in Intuitive Gifts, stared at me and I stared at her. She was covered in guts and blood just like I was. Guts in her auburn curls and blood splatter on her blue-white face, which brought out all its lovely bones and veins almost too well. She was smiling as I was smiling. She had an ear in her lap too, I saw.

This is when I knew.

There are no accidents, Samantha.

I looked around the attic, at my bloody cohort, and I laughed. *Look at what we've done*, I thought, taking in the entrails scattered across the floor. Wasn't it so terribly beautiful?

I walked over to Coraline, still screaming bloody murder, and I kneeled down before her prim little body, her prettily crying face. I stared at that blond bob so perfectly, painfully tucked under. I pictured the curling iron in her bathroom, the roll brush filled with dyed-blond hairs. Imagined the smoke rising from her hair as she twisted and twisted the hot rod. Every fucking morning she probably cooked her hair this way, lock by lock. I stared into her bright blue eyes, bloodshot from crying into her white-gloved hands.

"Murderers, we're murderers," she sobbed, and Kyra said, "Shhhhh, it's okay, Bunny," enabling her terribly. I looked at Kyra and she abruptly stopped. Let go of Coraline like she was a doll I was asking her to drop. I've always had the power to do this, Samantha (more on that later). Still Coraline cried and so I smacked her. Hard across the face. Violence, as you know, Samantha, is sometimes sadly necessary. She appeared shocked by this, my sudden tough love. So unschooled in the ways of Creation. I cupped her apple cheeks in my hands. That I had a mesmeric effect on her was obvious. Her crying stopped instantly.

"Do you realize," I whispered into her face, "what we've done?"

Coraline shook her head. Stared at me with her child's eyes; they had a kind of piercing quality that made me uneasy. I wondered for a moment if she could see me as a child in Mother's rose garden, so many years ago, turning all the flowers black with my rage. Could she see me outside on the cliffs in my conjuring nightgown, clutching Mother's diamond (my first dagger) in my fist, asking the sky to bleed along with my tears? Surely not.

"We murdered," she whispered. "We murdered, we murdered, we murdered—" Until, sadly, I had to smack her again.

"We exploded the bunny," Kyra whispered beside her.

And I smiled condescendingly. "That's one way of looking at things."

"How else is there to look, Bunny?"

The insolence, the back talk, took my breath away. But I held it together. "Your problem, Bunny, is that you're thinking *far* too literally. You're not reading the larger meaning. You're not thinking about the implications."

"What is the larger meaning?" Kyra and Coraline asked in the same voice, at the very same time. They looked both moved and disgusted by their synchronicity.

That you're a fucking psycho, my sister, Jane, would say to me. *That you're a megalomaniacal monster. Like Mother. Worse.*

"That we can destroy," Vik said, grinning. "That we're basically God. Right, Else?"

I smiled. Vik was laughing now, sort of crazily, rolling on the floor in the blood and entrails. Kyra and Coraline were dead silent, watching me, my serene, blood-splotched face. I could feel their minds roving wildly. Contemplating the mutinous possibilities. Wondering if they should perhaps call the police. Wondering whom they should tell. I took the blood from my finger and gently, gently put a dot of it on each of their noses.

"Ponder it," I told them.

And with that, I took my severed ear and left.

I walked home that night along the river, a most circuitous route. My body was covered in rabbit guts and blood, but I wouldn't wash it away tonight, Samantha. Because I knew even then it was evidence. Of what? Something. We did something, but what?

As I was leaving, Vik said, *I'll come with you. Should I come with you, Else? Please let me come with you.*

Like so many neophytes I've encountered before, Vik wanted to be around my Aura. She wanted to be around my Light. But I needed solitude, Samantha. I had things to contemplate, after all. Perhaps it truly was happening again. My Gift as I liked to call it. Though my sister calls it something else. I even thought of calling Jane and telling her: *Jane, I think it's happening again. I have fulminated a rabbit with the sheer power of my eyes.* But what would Jane do? Laugh. Light a cigarette. *Oh, Elsinore.* Or perhaps she'd call my parents and have them lock me up. Jane, cold surgeon, smirking master (or so she thought) of all things brain. Yet the mind, the soul, remained a mystery to her. That was my domain and she knew it. How many times had I stood on the cliff's edge at our Cumberland beach house, admiring a sunset, thanking the various entities responsible in my preverbal language, my eyes closed in the pinkening light, when I heard an *ahem.* And there was Jane in her khakis and marinière, watching me with equal parts derision and fascination. Me in my long white nightdress, my crystal dagger in my fist. And yes, for a moment in her surgical gaze I felt five years old, but only for a moment. I said, *Can I help you?* And she looked at me and said, *What fucking world do you live in?*

Mine, I whispered. The truth of it never failed to bring me to tears right there in front of her. I let them fall, catching the dying pink light of day. And Jane rolled her eyes like various others have done in my life. I watched her crunch away in her horsebit loafers. Ten years behind the fashion in her Timeless Classics, but you'd never guess it from her fucking attitude. Thinking she knew everything about everything. About the Cosmos. About Creation. Just because she took a scalpel to a skull a few times a week and played gleefully with the goo inside. And yet, when inexplicable things happened, whom did she come to? Like that day all the roses in our mother's garden died while I was just standing there, very upset about something. What, I can't even remember, isn't that funny? I recall only the pain coursing through me and the sky darkening above me and the roses curling into themselves like they were afraid.

What the fuck are you doing? Jane whispered behind me.

Grieving, I whispered back.

Or the time our nana died quite suddenly at dinner. She was laughing at a proem I'd been reading aloud at the table when she started to choke on a quail bone, poor thing. A quail I myself had abstained from eating, weeping quietly for those semi-flightless birds. My sister and then my mother attempted the Heimlich to no end, while I watched, the proem shaking in my hand, hoping for the best. Alas, quail bones can be quite tricky.

You killed Nana, Jane hissed at me, many days later. I was in my room reading tea leaves, staring deep into my cup of stars, as was my wont.

That is absurd, I told my sister, though inwardly I was delighted at this long-awaited recognition of my Powers. *She choked on a quail bone,* I said. *And her own cruel laughter,* I thought. And perhaps the gods, my gods that I prayed to, had been watching. I smiled into my cup of stars, which was really quite like staring into an entire universe, Samantha.

No, it was that proem, my sister spat. *Your fucking dumb proem killed her.* Even though I could see she knew the Truth. Could tell by the way she fearfully whispered *Bitch* as she shut the door.

Why am I telling you this, Samantha? So that you understand my history, I suppose. The larger context from which I came that really informed us all. My context is especially significant.

I probably shouldn't call Jane in this instance, I reflected. I'd keep the rabbit-fulmination story to myself for now. Sometimes it really is best for me if I am left alone to ponder the Magnitudes, the larger meaning of Events. But I found when I walked outside into the New England night, the moon still high above me, anointing my very bloody body with its silvery glow, the severed rabbit ear in my satchel, I could not ponder. I felt only a strange kind of giddiness. The moon was smiling at me (she knew what I had done, yes). Saying, *Wait. Fear not. We're not done here yet, dear.*

We're not? What next?

But then she fell silent.

Really, Vik said to me once, *the moon is the ultimate bitch. Just look at her.*

At the time I remember I thought, *What a terrible, unlearned thing to say about a celestial body.* But now, looking at her up there in the black sky, so cold and bright and tantalizing, I sort of understood. The moon *was* being a bitch, Bunny.

A fitful night of sleep. I dreamed on ergonomic sheets the color of the highest Chakra, yet I remained in the spiritual Dark. In my dream I was in Costa Rica, lying on a beach in a long white dress, frothy as the Sea itself. Cold, primordial waves crashed again and again over my trembling body. I was clutching broken shells in my fists so very tightly that they chafed and bled. *Let go and all will be revealed,* the waves whispered into my frozen ears. In my dreams, you see, I understood the language of water, Samantha, I understood the language of everything. And so in the dream I opened my hands. I woke to find myself flanked by Borges and Cixous, my golden retrievers. They had found the rabbit's ear in my satchel and were making of it a plaything. I recalled the explosion in the attic. Coraline crying, Kyra consoling her. Both of them looking at me like I was responsible for murder. Which probably I was, though I swear it was not my intention, Samantha.

Outcome and Intent are two very different countries, aren't they? And I had intended . . . something else. Not merely blood and torn flesh. Not merely destruction. No, something wondrous, generative. At this, I suppose, I'd failed. In the bright light of day, I watched my golden dogs tug mercilessly, playfully, at the ear of the exploded wretch. I screamed at Borges to stop, *stop it!* I took the torn rabbit's ear into my hands, licked clean by these uncomprehending hounds. The sunshine stung my eyes then. Burned them with its Cruel Light. I wept, Bunny. Not only because I had been profoundly fucking misunderstood by my cohort, a cross that any Artist worth their salt must bear, but because I truly began to believe myself a Failure.

Which is so fucking funny when you think about it now.

9

Serendipity, Bunny. Its power, particularly for Creators, is infinitely illuminating if one only Taps In. As I made my way to campus that following morning, I was still ignorant of its full Magic, but not for long. Now, as it happens, I was up for Workshop that day. Cruel fate, I probably thought at the time, Bunny. That the day after my alleged Failure, it was my turn to face the firing squad of Allan's word arrows, flaccid yet painful. As I drove to campus (*not* in a Mercedes, despite the gauche suggestion in your novel), the New England sunshine turning the world the color of hellfire, I vowed that I would not allow him to see me bleed.

When I entered the Cave, its Darkness seemed to press on my Heart. So that I felt compelled to say: "Might we have Workshop in another room today, please, Allan?"

There were many other rooms in Narrative Arts beyond the Cave, after all, Samantha. There was the infamous Hall of Infinite Reflection, for instance, apparently a mirror mindfuck. There was the Metaphorical Chamber, which, by a trick of lights, allegedly cast the most existentially devastating yet generative shadows. Were you aware of these rooms? They didn't come up in your little novel, I noticed. Of course, you didn't do much in the way of world-building, did you? Difficult, perhaps, for you to see anything of the World beyond your own Rat's Maze of concerns. But I am not so small-minded in my Perception, Samantha, and on this day I wished to venture beyond the Cave. *Because I don't feel like being in the literal Dark when I am also in a Dark of the Heart. If it's at all possible.*

I didn't say this exactly. I said it in the worldly words that Allan might understand. I insinuated (with my tone alone) menstrual issues. And I looked right at our Nightmare Man, his green tea steaming in a YETI mug today—

never once breaking eye contact, this is the secret to everything, Samantha—until he shrugged. "Sure. It's your workshop. We can be in the Poetry Library today, if you'd like?"

"The Poetry Library," I repeated, nodding. How perfectly vile. But it overlooked the garden at least.

I had the rabbit ear in my satchel, and yes, it was beginning to smell at this point. I had my dagger diamond around my neck, and it gleamed there, its point hovering over my heart, Sharp and Always. As we filed into the library, I looked at my cohort. Coraline still had blood on her face, but her hair was freshly flat-ironed, lips glossed. She'd found a way, even in her emotional turmoil, to continue her mortification of the flesh via grooming. Her gloved hand was in her spotted pocket, as usual. Kyra, her hair half-braided, looked at me, and her bright, mutinous eyes were full of *We should call the police, please.* Yet she also looked nervous, in awe of me, perhaps. I have often assumed this role of power. It is easily done if one is Unwavering, Samantha. One must simply stare directly into the eye of one's enemy (or friend), quite like I'm staring at you now. One must never blink first and look away, but look deep into the iris and attempt with one's mind to see into the black. To find the Shadow Self shivering there, homely and hairy and afraid. Once one sees the Shadow Self, one must smile. As if to say, *I see you in there.* And the enemy (or friend) will instantly deflate. I have always been able to do this, which is perhaps why the roses have always seen me coming, Bunny.

The Poetry Library, as you know, is a bright room with windows full of bitchy New England light, facing the rose garden with its many, many flowers. I took a seat on one side of the table, facing the wall of windows so as to be smitten with this light. I assumed my cohort would join me there, of course, that we would sit as One as we had done for weeks now, in solidarity against the psychic tyranny of Allan. So it was funny, Bunny, it was so *serendipitous,* that I found myself sitting there alone. Because no one wanted to sit with me today, apparently. My fellow Bunnies—*traitors,* I should say—sat on the opposite side of the square from me, their backs to the windows. They sat beside you, actually, Samantha, do you not recall that day? Of course not. You were deep in the Rat's Maze, weren't you, and probably didn't even notice the shift at all. Your head down, dark hair in your face, covering one death-black eye. Wearing some sort of antisocial T-shirt, a wolverine baring its bloody jaws, perhaps. But *I* remember that day. How they all avoided my gaze, not even Vik would meet my eye. She picked at her bloody nails, her face slightly pink. There was still rabbit effluvium in her auburn waves, I noted.

Allan smiled. "Better?"

"Much," I lied.

"All right, then," he said. "Let's begin." And he looked down at a copy of my proem and sighed with the pleasure of the torturer about to wield the whip.

Was I surprised when Allan proceeded to eviscerate me? Of course not. I was ready for it, Samantha. Had even prepared myself psychically for the assault.

"The first issue I'm having, Elsinore," he began, "is that I'm not quite sure what this"—and he held up my pane of glass—"*is* exactly." He shook the pane at me, Samantha, perhaps you recall. I think you smiled at that, didn't you?

"It's called a proem," I said. "I find form limiting," I told him. "In general." *I find you limiting in general. I wish for you to die*, I thought.

Yet Allan remained standing. He had taken to the whiteboard, in fact. He was diagramming one of my sacred sentences on its surface. He was saying, in his horribly logical voice, that part of the problem was that my sentences simply didn't make sense, you see? Was there a *reason*, for instance, that I was always capitalizing my Nouns? Was I German? Not even consistently German, but *randomly* German?

I did not respond. Allan knew, of course, that I was not randomly German. He confessed that he also found my relationship with the em dash and the semicolon equally perplexing. *Is that so, Allan?* Oh yes, a real struggle to grasp my syntax, he insisted.

Though I could feel my Aura darkening at his words, I held it together. I was not Coraline, you see. I was not five years old emotionally. I looked at him coolly, evenly, through my bespoke eyewear, which wasn't necessary for seeing, I just enjoy fashion, Samantha.

"May I ask how you struggled?" I asked. Like I was actually interested in Allan's struggle and not, at this moment, quietly wishing Death upon his Body. Unlike you, I didn't apply to Warren to work with this horror hack, Samantha, who dressed up his disturbingly violent streak in philosophical musings. I've never been one to rely on the cheap tricks and tropes of *genre*, as you know. I'm all about conjuring Atmospheres of the Heart. Soul States in all their wondrous color and fragility. Something Allan, with his unsubtle use of chainsaws, didn't seem to understand.

"The overabundant use of metaphor and simile, for one," he said now, "really obscures meaning. One risks becoming . . . *overwrought*." He smiled at the dagger dangling from my neck, swinging lightly over my solar plexus.

"I wonder too about the stakes in this story. . . ."

And this, Samantha, is when I confess that inside I cracked. *STAKES?* I mind-screamed. *UM. AM I FUCKING WRITING A BOOK CLUB PICK, YOU BOOR? DO I LOOK FUCKING OPRAH-FRIENDLY TO YOU?* But outwardly I merely smiled. Pretended to make a note of his commentary with my feather pen. Instead I wrote the words *Kill Allan* multiple times in my elegant script, relishing my calligraphy skills.

"Stakes," I said. "Absolutely, Allan. Please do elaborate."

And of course Allan did elaborate. There was an "obliqueness"—he might even go as far as to say an "opaqueness"—to my narrative style. He wished I would be a little more direct. He suggested reading some "minimalists," some "realists" (ha!), who approach storytelling more straightforwardly. He suggested signposting a little more too. "Help us know where you're going, Elsinore."

"Where I'm going," I repeated, darkly amused. *What if I myself don't fucking know? Do we not create in a holy state of Unknowing?*

Allan drank in my shame. I felt him espy the Shadow Self ever so briefly, in the black of my iris. He saw her, dangerously thin and crying over her panes of glass, the ghost of her dead grandmother's laughter, her sister's scorn. Then, smiling, he looked away. "Other thoughts here?"

"I have to say I agree," you said. You, Samantha. Cousin Itt. Which was no fucking surprise but then? They all agreed. *They* meaning, of course, my alleged friends. They with whom I had already shared so much of my Self. Bunny and Bunny and Bunny all looking at me like I was a fucking stranger. As if we hadn't all held one another just last night in a fierce psychic embrace, hadn't exposed our darkest and deepest desires in the pink fog of the hive mind. Hadn't seen our souls flash on the attic wall like the strangest, most intimate movie montage. They nodded along with you and with this man-demon. Imperceptibly, in some cases, but I glimpsed it with my Third Eye. Felt the diamond dagger grow hot and pointed between my breasts. Were they relishing my demise?

"A bit less style, a bit more . . . *substance*," Kyra murmured.

My Aura blackened. I looked out to the sky for support. Yet it did not storm with my anger. The clouds did not gather, did not brew with my sense of injustice. The world stayed blandly, impossibly bright, almost like it was willfully indifferent to my pain. I looked back at Allan, smiling at me. Still talking, unbelievably. But I couldn't even hear his words anymore, Samantha. I could only see his smug mouth movements. Forming terrible words about me that were *lies, lies, lies*—or were they true?

It was then I saw something in the window. In the rose garden. Flashing in my field of Perception while I was staring murder at Allan. In the very periphery of the field. For a mere second, Bunny.

A figure. Standing in the far corner of the rose garden, watching me.

A man.

I don't normally notice men, married as I am to the Sea. But this man I noticed. He was too far away for me to see his face. But something about his silhouette, his way of standing among the tall flowers, tugged at my third Chakra. His hair was a mess of auburn waves catching the light.

"Elsinore, did you hear Sam's suggestion?"

And the only answer to that was yes. "Of course I did," I murmured, glancing at you, though my gaze quickly returned to the man in the garden. He appeared to be jumping now. Up and down lightly in the mud. Though I still couldn't see his face, I felt the smiling on it. The smile was on my face too.

"Not visceral enough," Allan was saying, still fondling my proem. "Perhaps the thing is to anchor us in some concrete, scene-specific details. Without forgetting forward action, of course."

"Of course."

"Certainly, there's room to feel the reality a little more."

"The Reality. Absolutely."

"Elsinore, are you crying?"

Was I? Yes. I could feel the tears dribbling down my cheeks as I watched the strange young man jumping all around the garden now. Quite ecstatically, Bunny.

"Elsinore, may I ask what's—"

"Allergies," I whispered, transfixed. A lie. I felt the jumping man laugh at this, like he'd heard me.

"Allergies," Allan repeated. "Really."

The laughter bubbled dangerously now in my own throat. I bit my lower lip, felt its soft fullness between my teeth. Felt the fact of my youth, of Allan's inevitable, impending Death.

"Yes. I've long been plagued by them."

Allan smiled at me in a hard way. Barely sympathetic on the surface, annoyed very visibly beneath. "It seems as if we have a number of allergy sufferers in this cohort," he said softly, his voice rife with cold derision. Coraline went red in the face. But I didn't fucking care, Bunny. Not anymore. In this moment nothing could touch me. Behind Allan, the man was waving wildly at me now.

"Will you excuse me, please?" I asked.

"But this is your workshop—"

"Sometimes air helps," I said, rising from my chair. "With the allergies."

"But wouldn't going outside make it *worse?*" you offered. You again, Samantha, yes. Smirking in your bleak T-shirt. Wanting me to be caught out. It was gross of you, can I just say? Utterly fucking unfeminist. I forgive you now, of course, I do. You were speaking, as you always spoke, from a place of Petty Envy and Darkness.

I didn't answer your catty comment dressed up as a question, of course. Didn't wait for Allan to give permission, either. Whether he said no or yes, I had no fucking idea, Bunny. Left the library, the useless Workshop. Left everyone's staring, treacherous faces behind and walked out into the cold light of day.

10

As I made my way toward the rose garden, my heart pounded inside me. My skin felt hot, then cold, then hot again. I was dizzy, practically sick in a way I'd never been before. With what? Fear perhaps. That he wouldn't be there. That what I'd felt looking through the library windows, locking eyes with him, was a lie. What *had* I felt exactly? Don't know, but it was visceral, Bunny. When I thought of him being gone, a dark Chasm opened in me. Bottomless. I quickened my steps.

Nothing in the garden. Just flowers at first, that's all I saw. Bright shades blinding my eyes, and the grass soft and green beneath my feet. There was the dirt hole Vik had dug with her bare hands only last night, into which Coraline had thrown her pastry. There was the sky above me, its brightness mocking me. *Look, the sky is the color of us*, that's what Coraline would say, tilting her head toward the heavens. Blues and pinks that swirled into each other dreamily. But I was in no mood to dream, Samantha. The emptiness of the garden made me feel alone, terribly. The swells of the song "Alone" rose in my memory. Once, long ago, it had been my favorite, a private shame I'll share with you, Bunny, because I know you also have a fondness for the power ballad. Failure, I was a Failure, this is what I felt. I'll share that with you too, since I know you know the feeling well.

It was when I was in the grips of Failure's unrelenting Blackness that I saw him. The jumping man I'd espied through the windows. Standing in the tall flowers, his back to me. Those auburn waves shining in the sun. Like he'd always been there. Right in plain sight and to notice him was just an act of seeing what was always there.

He was standing perfectly still now. Wearing a deep blue blazer over what looked like a long white nightgown. Beneath the hem I glimpsed his bare feet, mud-covered and wiggling in the grass. When I saw those bare feet, my heart sank. Oh. *A Homeless,* I thought. Likely come into the garden to forage for sustenance among the shrubs, how sad. How unsurprising, too. The campus was rife with homeless, this city being a hellscape and our trash so rich. I'd often seen them ambling across the green in dumpster-scavenged polo shirts, eating discarded cafeteria foie gras by the tin. Coraline gripped my hand whenever we passed them, saying they hurt her heart and eyes far too much. I told her that was absurd, how privileged she was, etc. *Not everyone has BMWs, okay, Bunny?* I stared at the man's blazered back, his soiled feet. How could I have gotten it so wrong? *Go,* I told myself. *Leave this man before he notices you and rapes you and tries to steal or eat your crystals.* I felt them shimmering on my wrists and in my bra, beating violently along with my own heart—a warning. But for some reason I found I could not leave this particular Homeless, Bunny. In fact, my feet began to move forward. Toward and not away from this man in a dress standing in the flower beds. The dress, I couldn't help but note, looked oddly familiar.

He turned to me then. Smiled. "Sad?" he said.

He was tall, very. Pale with a sharp, pink-cheeked face. Bright blue eyes that seemed to laugh at me, at everything.

I found myself nodding. "Yes." Even though I was not sad, not anymore. I felt a strange sunlight in my soul, Samantha. Coursing through my insides like fire. The man nodded like he understood.

"Because they don't understand the nuances of you," he offered, staring into my eyes. I detected a vaguely British accent. He was holding a limp dandelion in his fist.

"They don't," I agreed. *That is it precisely,* I thought. How did this man in the nightgown know? Perhaps he was an Artist too. It was often difficult, due to the bohemian leanings of the faculty and student body, to tell who was actually a Homeless and who wasn't. "Are you an Artist?" I asked.

"Artist?" His face darkened suddenly. "No."

"Do you go to Warren?"

But he was distracted now by the weed in his hand. He turned it around and around between his slim fingers, seeming to lose himself in its revolutions. Then suddenly he held it out to me. "For you, Mother," he said.

Mother? So maybe a Homeless after all, I thought. Possibly an insane or drugged kind. I stared down at the tiny yellow petals he cupped in his large hand, the weedy face like a small sun. I stared at his naked fist. Five fingered, full of veins pulsing with blood. Nodding, I was nodding. My trembling hand reaching out, ready to accept the limp weed. Ready to accept anything. Instead the man appeared to change his mind at the last minute. Ate the dandelion. Smiled at me as he chewed. "Who are you?" I whispered.

"Who?" Like he hadn't understood.

"What is your . . . *name?*" And I felt stupid. Alice trying to converse with the Caterpillar, who only gazes at her curiously through the mist. He smiled a funny smile.

"Name?" He patted his blazer pockets, like he was looking for a business card perhaps. "Name, name, name," he whispered. He had quite a chiseled pectoral and abdominal area, I couldn't help but notice, thanks to the very low-cut nature of the nightgown, its buttons torn and open down to the navel. The sight of all that sculpted flesh embarrassed me profoundly. As if he belonged on the cover of those romance novels Mother and Jane sometimes read and that, yes, I'd sometimes read too. (I enjoy the low work at *times*, Samantha. It all feeds.) This man, however, was covered in tattoos. A ring of arrows on his chest, I saw. Right around his left pec, doubling as the spokes of a fiery sun, the orb grinning over his Heart. Ocean waves crashing on his boulder-like shoulder. Foresty mountains spreading across his steely abdominals, flowery flames all along the obliques. "Name, name," he was still muttering, patting his pockets. At last he pulled something from inside his jacket. Offered it to me with triumph. An empty box. Of what looked like allergy medication. *Aerius*, it read on the box.

"Your name is Aerius?"

He smiled. "Aerius." Like it pleased him to say. He reached down and picked up another dandelion from the grass. Started to hand it to me, then seemed to think better of it. Ate it. He smiled at the blue and pink swirling sky. "Aerius!" he shouted, and laughed. Jumped up and down like he was moshing. "AERIUS, AERIUS, AERIUS!"

As I watched him hop before me, screaming his alleged name, it occurred to me, Bunny, that he might very well be an escaped mental patient. But then why, when I watched his lithe, leaping body, did I feel so strange? Ashamed, deeply. Prideful, terribly. Above all, vaguely responsible. And my body, Samantha. On literal fire. Teary and smiley and barely able to breathe all at once.

"Aerius," I whispered. Think I whispered. It was very hard to speak just then. "What are you doing in the garden? Why were you jumping and waving at me just now?"

Like I didn't fucking know. And just like that, he stopped jumping. Snatched the allergy medication from my hands and tucked it back in his pocket like he might need it later. He stared at me, and the fearful symmetry of his face, an animal symmetry I saw now, arrested me. "*Why?*" he repeated in a low voice. Like, *What sort of question is this, Mother?* He smiled a smile of not such innocence then. Moved in closer to me. Hopped closer, you could almost say. His scent, it intoxicated me, Samantha. Grasses and so many fucking wildflowers, more flowers than I'd ever breathed in all at once. He smelled also, disconcertingly, like Coraline's cupcakes, vaguely too like attic incense. He touched my face with his very large, bare hands. They felt terribly warm and soft. Like they were covered finely in fur, even though they were entirely human flesh. Grazing my skin so softly, I died and died. His fingernails, I saw, were painted yellow as suns, each one with its own smiling face. Smiling just like he was.

"Relieves eyes," he whispered, pointing gently to my eyes. And just like that, tears fell from them.

"Relieves nose," he said, and poked my nose with a finger.

"Throatandears," he said, stroking my earlobe now softly. Marveling at the feather earring that hung there. *So pretty and shiny,* I could feel him thinking while I stared at the blue of his eyes. Hour between the dog and wolf in summer. Me lying in the tall grass as a child, staring up and losing myself in the deepening sky. Me staring into the dark eyes of a rabbit, watching them brighten into precisely this cerulean shade.

"What else," I asked when I had voice to speak, "does it relieve?"

"Relieves . . . ," he began, but then became distracted by something on my head. Pulled one of the birds-of-paradise I'd tucked into my hair. "Pretty," he whispered. "Is it mine?"

"Yes. Everything," I might have said then. *Everything yours. Forever and ever.* I watched him tuck the flower into the breast pocket of his dress, my heart on fire.

And then it was obvious, like a new kind of seeing, Samantha. His long white dress, why it looked so terribly familiar. It was my fucking dress. The one I'd bought last year from Free People for a Beltane bonfire ritual. "That's my dress," I said.

He shook his head. "*My* dress," he whispered. Fingered the frothy collar. The rip I recognized by the left shoulder, caused by my own deep conjuring work.

"Oh my god," I whispered, falling to my knees. He did the same. Like falling to the ground was a new game we were now playing and how fun. I noticed the string of cold pearls on his neck, definitely Coraline's. His lips, I saw now, were tinged with Kyra's Cherries in Winter. There was Vik's tattoo of the Crystal Thief on his forearm, which I shuddered to see, did not like to see, a painful reminder that he was not mine alone. And above all, his face, so like the furry one we had surrounded only last night in the attic. Jesus fucking Christ. "Are you . . . Could you be—"

"Shhhh," he said. Like, *No more questions.* "Still sad?" Wiping the tears from my eyes with his pelt-soft hands.

"No." I shook my head, staring into his eyes. "Happy," I whispered, looking into the blue. "So happy, I'm sad again."

"Sappy," he whispered back, nodding as if he knew. "Joy tears."

"Yes," I laughed. And he laughed with me, Bunny. The way you laugh along with someone even though you don't know why. We were laughing wildly together in the grass, the sunlight shining on us, rainbows breaking through the clouds as they broke through my own soul. Workshop and Allan seemed so far away. Wanting to kill him seemed hilarious. "In fact, I don't even think I want to kill Allan anymore," I said through my tears and laughter.

"Kill Allan?" he repeated. And suddenly he grew serious. Sat up. Looked around the rose garden. "I could kill Allan," he offered.

"What?"

But he'd let go of me now. Was rifling through his pockets again, smiling. This time he pulled out a razor. I knew the implement well, of course. Coraline's. Its sharpened edge forever speckled with her blood. Grinning, he held it up to the sunlight, turning it around just like he'd turned the dandelion. Looking with such wonder at how the blade caught the light.

"What are you doing?" I asked.

"Kill Allan," he said softly, beautifully. With such a smile on his face, Bunny. So that for a moment I was entranced. So that I might even have said *Yes, please do go ahead.* Then I caught myself. "No," I said quickly. "No, no. Not literally kill," I said. "We just hate him is all."

"We hate him," he said dreamily, smiling at the glinty blade. "Literally Kill Allan, is all."

"No!"

"Kill Allan, Kill Allan, Kill Allan." And he jumped up, quite sprightly. It was at this moment, perhaps, that his full height truly impressed itself upon me, Bunny. He was, I saw, about six four, his hopping shadow veritably swallowing me, the whole garden, in Darkness. I watched him skip now toward the Narrative Arts building with his big bare feet, clutching the razor, which flashed so beautifully in his fist. There was a beauty to the movement, Samantha, can I simply observe that? Does that really make me a monster to say? I could not deny the Beauty, even as I registered that, yes, I was witnessing Violence. A potential homicide. It was the skipping that arrested me, paralyzed me, with its wild, limbic perfection. The way the sunlight loved him. Caught the gold in his waves, you should have seen it. The way the grass knew his lithe feet. The lightness of the hop and the predatorial gleam in his blue eyes.

And then in the near distance, beyond the garden, I saw Allan in the street. Walking toward his gray Subaru; he must have ended Workshop early. His vile messenger bag, full of whatever obscure theory texts, slung across his chest. Ready to do some Whole Foods shopping, perhaps. And Aerius making his skipping way down the garden path toward him, fist raised.

"Kill Allan! Kill Allan!" he sang softly.

I ran then. Ran after him with all my might, Bunny, but he was skipping so fast now, the razor swinging wildly in his fist. I ran faster and faster, even reaching my hand out to hold him back, muttering, "Stop, please stop, oh god." And then he did stop suddenly. So suddenly that I actually crashed into his back, clutched his arm. What had made him stop? Had he come to his senses, perhaps? Was this whole thing just some hideous-wonderful dream? I looked up, and there, blocking his path, was my cohort. Standing in an intense and colorful huddle. Coraline, Kyra, and Vik all staring at him, at me, like, *Hello, what the fuck is this, please?* They looked at my hand gripping his arm, trying to hold him back from killing Allan, who was now safely in his Subaru, it seemed, driving smugly away, oblivious. And Aerius was staring at them curiously. How embarrassed I felt suddenly. Caught in the strangest game.

Not wanting to startle anyone, least of all the boy with the razor, I attempted telepathy.

Listen, I said to them with my mind, *we have to bring him back to Kyra's. I'll explain—*

But there was no need at all to explain, Bunny.

Their eyes, staring at him, suddenly brightened.

Perhaps Coraline saw her own pearls on his throat, her blade in his fist. I saw her reflexively check her dress pocket: empty, Bunny, and her jaw just dropped. Probably Kyra discerned her Cherries in Winter staining his lips. And Vik? Maybe she noted the Crystal Thief on his arm, the way his bare feet were reveling in the mud. Or perhaps it was simply the electric blue of his eyes that they were all swimming in like such endless sky. They seemed sort of drugged by his physicality, the fact of him standing there in the sunlight. In any case, they all knew what to do. Each of them picked a dandelion from the grass. Held it up to him, twirling it around and around as if to hypnotize. Said, "For you, if you come with us."

He smiled then. And he followed us, Bunny. Out of the rose garden.

Toward where we knew not.

One step at a time, we told ourselves.

As we walked, we made a kind of ring around him, Bunny. Each of us twirling a dandelion. Holding them like candles that might lead us through the Dark, even though it was still the bright of day. That way, everywhere he looked there was a dandelion to dazzle him, to keep him with us. There were moments when he wanted to jump or skip, and so we had to skip too, to keep up. We made quite a picture, Bunny, skipping down the sidewalk of this hideous town. He was still holding the razor in his fist, swinging it wildly, and that kept us a little on edge. But no one stopped us or anything. In fact, most passersby didn't even seem to notice or turn to look, was the funny thing. It was almost like we were alone in the World. Coraline kept trying to take his other hand, which was fucking annoying. Kyra was looking at him worriedly, like any minute she might whip out her phone and call the police. And Vik, she was just ogling him openly. "I like your dress," she said, staring at his exposed torso, his man hands, his shapely calves. If cars passed, he stopped. Grew rigid. Wanted to run away, but we said, "No, it's okay." We held the spinning dandelions up higher. Tried to give him an education along the way. "Oh, those are poor-people cars," we said pointing at the various Subarus and Priuses speeding past.

"Poor," he said, and nodded.

"And that is a bus. A mode of public transportation, quite smelly and sad, which one should never take."

"Never take bus," he said.

"And those are Homeless. Lots around here, so sad. What we thought you were at first, isn't that funny?"

"Funny." He nodded. "And this?" he said, pointing to a gnome statue on a front lawn.

"That? Is tacky."

"*Tacky.*" And he reached out to stroke the gnome's face tenderly, until we lured him away.

It was, for the most part, an uneventful walk home, Bunny. I say *for the most part* because we did have a most unfortunate run-in with a Poet along the way. Jonah, as a matter of fact. Your dear friend with whom you used to smoke cigarettes and talk shit about us in the rancid alleys that are your sad stomping grounds. No use denying it, Samantha. It's well documented in the screed you wrote, which, as we said, we won't deign to discuss. It's lovely that we're all friends again now, of course. Speaks to our ability to put such things behind us. Forgive even while we never ever forget.

Anyway, when Jonah appeared in our path, we all drew breath, Bunny. We never like to run into Poets, period, but this was an especially precarious moment for us. Those with any kind of mental acuity would've intuited that and left us be. Not Jonah, of course. When he saw us, he immediately waved and ran over. "Oh hey!" this clueless boy said. "You're the Fictions, right?"

"Yes." We nodded, immediately hiding the dandelions behind our backs. Drawing our bodies closer to Aerius.

"Cool. So great to see you guys again."

"So great," we said. Smiling pleasantly, Bunny. Like, *Fuck off. Can't you see we're busy?* We formed a tighter ring around Aerius, trying to hide him from Jonah's view, but this was impossible due to his incredible height. Jonah spotted him easily in our midst, a massive tree growing out of the small garden of us.

"Hey," this Poet said to him. "I don't think we've met before. I'm Jonah."

Aerius, who'd been looking longingly at another garden gnome, turned now to face him. His gaze brightened. "Jonah," he said.

"And you are?"

But Aerius merely stared at him like he'd never seen anything like Jonah before. Like Jonah was a dandelion but better. Better, perhaps, than all our dandelions put together. "I am—" he began.

"A foreign exchange student, actually," Coraline piped up, gripping his arm. "We're just showing him around right now. Giving him a tour and things. Orienting him." She smiled. She looked fucking psychotic, Bunny. Her smile twitching like mad with her lies. But Jonah was thankfully oblivious.

"A foreign exchange student?" he said. "How cool! From where?"

"Argentina," I offered, just as Kyra said, "Japan," just as Vik said, "Morocco," just as Coraline said, "The Isle of Man."

"Wow!" Jonah said. "So, like, from everywhere. That's so incredible."

"It is," we murmured. "So incredible."

"Incredible," Aerius whispered, smiling at Jonah now. In a way I wasn't so sure I liked at all. I gripped his arm tighter. Drew closer to him.

"Well, cool," Jonah said. "Maybe I can have you all over sometime for tea or something. And I can learn more about Argentina. And Japan. And Morocco. *And* the Isle of Man," he laughed. "I'll be worldly as fuck."

"As fuck," Aerius agreed. Smiling more broadly now.

"Yes," I lied, raising my voice. "How lovely that would be for us all. We'll definitely take you up on that. Perhaps in a few—"

"Can I come now?" Aerius cut in in a low voice, still staring at Jonah.

"*Now?*" Jonah repeated, surprised. "Oh, I didn't realize you guys were free now, but—"

"Free," Aerius repeated, a little longingly.

"NO," Coraline screamed, tugging on his jacket sleeve. "Not free. Very busy just now, aren't we? So much to do and see."

"So much," we all agreed.

"Oh, too bad," Jonah said. "Some other time, then."

"Too bad," Aerius repeated sadly, watching him go.

And in this way, we averted what we must admit was immediate disaster. Not that disaster didn't come, Bunny.

Of course it fucking did.

———————————

Aerius came with us to the house quite willingly the rest of the way. Okay, perhaps not entirely willingly. Did we have some small trouble getting him into the house? Depends on how you define *trouble*. It's true that when we got very near Kyra's house, and he looked up and saw the attic, he screamed a little. Whether at the sight of the inverted triangle window specifically or the attic itself, we weren't sure. Not wanting to return to the Womb, perhaps. Anyway, his arms suddenly went rigid in our hands. He began to resist us as we attempted to escort him so lovingly up the steps. We knew then that there was no amount of dandelions we could bribe him with, Bunny. Very clearly, all the dandelions in the world wouldn't bring him back up there of his own Accord. And so, yes, in the end, we had to drag him a little. Just those final few feet. Just to get up those last steps, that's all. And into the house. Back up to the attic.

Were we actually shocked at how physically strong and capable we were? Yes, a little, ha ha. But then, I had always been a deeply devoted Pilates practitioner, not to mention an avid Peloton user. Vik, of course, was a trained dancer, still strong as fuck, even if she had willfully neglected her body. And Coraline and Kyra, well, I honestly don't know where they got their respective strength from, Bunny, but my, my, how they had it. In droves. Maybe just from being raging Type As, who knows? In any case, you should have seen them walking backward up the front steps and then the attic steps, gripping the boy's limbs with all their might as they did so, their straining faces turning all the shades of Love.

For it was Love that drove us ultimately, Bunny, yes.

Love of Creation. Love of Wonder. Love of the Unknown.

Love of Art, really.

Please, as we tell you this story, fucking remember that.

11

I n Kyra's witchy living room, we sat equidistant from one another, listening, listening to one another's panicked thoughts. They rang in our
collective mind, forming a darkening pink cloud that hovered above our
heads. *Oh my god oh my god oh my god. Is he ours? What have we done and
what do we do now?* I stared down at the rose petals floating in my teacup.
Such strange shapes they made, Samantha. Perplexing. I could not intuit
their meaning.

The boy had screamed for a good hour and then quieted down and
then screamed again. Now all was dead silent. Kyra had put various treats
up there, so lovingly and thoughtfully. A plate filled with various Trader
Joe's confections (Coraline's idea). Some herbal fairy tea in case he was cold.
Electrolyte water in case he needed to hydrate. A tumbler of absinthe in case
he wanted something a little stronger, Bunny. All the dandelions, of course.
But though we strained our ears, we never once heard him partake.

"What are we doing?" Kyra said out loud at last. "What have we done?"

"Isn't it obvious?" Coraline said. "We conjured a man from a bunny. Just
like fairy tales. We're fairy tales now." She took a sip of her London Fog,
which she'd spiked with gin. "We're legends," she whispered.

"Did we really, though?" Kyra said. "I mean, what if he is just a Homeless? Or an escaped mental patient or something? Or just, like . . . a weird
fucking Warren person? And we're holding him hostage?"

"That would be hot," Vik said, winking at me. "I'm into that. Aren't you,
Bunny?"

I smiled thinly.

"You're into committing *crimes?*" Kyra challenged.

"Everything is a crime, hello. Every step you take on this earth is murder of one kind or another, Bunny. Open your eyes to the . . . fucking world."

"But we could be arrested," Kyra said softly to the window. "We could be tried for kidnapping. And I haven't even started writing my novel yet, not really. I can't write in prison. I need to work on a very specific typewriter." She cried softly for herself. Looked accusingly at us.

"We're not going to be arrested, okay?" This from Vik. "He's ours, like Coraline said. We made him."

"'Made him.' Do you know how insane that sounds, Bunny?" Kyra said.

"Insane? *You're* the one who talked all that crap about bunnies turning human or whatever."

"Yeah, in *fairy tales*, but—"

"WE ARE FAIRY TALES!" Coraline screamed. "And artists," she added in a low voice.

"Our medium is paper, not—"

"Well, sometimes the medium chooses you, right, Bunny?" And Vik looked to me. Wanting me to validate all this, please.

"He's ours," I confirmed. I almost said *mine*, thinking of him grinning at me, in my own torn dress. "Undoubtedly." Was there a wavering in my voice? Oh yes. I heard it, but did they?

"Exactly," Vik said. But she also sounded uncertain.

The minute we'd put him in the attic, you see, the minute we'd closed the door on his uncomprehending face, which screamed, *Betrayal! Betrayal!*, I was no longer sure of anything. Now that he was outside my field of Perception, I wondered, Bunny. Doubted even. *Was* he ours? Had I dreamed those twilight eyes that laughed at me? Those fur-soft hands? Was I fucking kidding myself? Perhaps, I pondered, he had been a Homeless all along, like Kyra said. Or an escaped mental patient, as I myself had surmised. So he was wearing a long white dress—was it really my dress? Perhaps it only resembled my dress. My style did skew nineteenth-century insane asylum, I knew that. Jane had even pointed that out to me numerous times. *You're fucking psychotic and you dress fucking psychotic*, she had said, only a few Yuletides ago. As for the other accessories, well, razors and pearl necklaces are a dime a dozen, are they not? Especially around Warren. And everyone is tattooed these days. Everyone's body boasts an inky Boschian universe. Maybe when I beheld the man in the garden holding out the box of allergy medication, I was only seeing what I wanted to see. Maybe I was delusional after all, just like Jane had always said. *It's good you're going to Warren, Elsinore,* she'd said when I got my acceptance letter. *Your particular psychosis will blend right in over there. You'll finally meet your Kind.*

I looked around the living room at my cohort, surrounded by shelves upon shelves of the books that had warped our souls. Coraline, in her sky dress and gloves, staring out the window with tears in her eyes. Kyra attempting to light sage with very trembling hands. Vik brazenly masturbating with her mind. *You know the type,* my sister had said. *Thinking the sky is changing with your moods, the tide is rising with your breath, that everything is a goddamned "sign" about you and your proem project. Let me tell you something, Elsinore. Let me tell you a secret that's no secret at all. The universe is indifferent to you.* And she smiled with such joy as she beheld my obvious pain.

The more time I spent away from him, the more it was beginning to feel entirely possible, likely even, Bunny, that we had indeed deluded ourselves.

I could feel my fellow Bunnies beginning to think so too.

Did we or didn't we?

Is he or isn't he?

The Doubt, Bunny, was growing like a Weed in all our minds.

Suddenly Kyra stood up, swaying on her feet, and said, "I'm just going to check on something."

Coraline grabbed her hand. "*What* are you going to go check on exactly, Bunny?"

"Just . . . that he has enough electrolytes and mini peanut butter cups and things. That we're not starving him or something. That we're not adding murder to our many crimes for today." She smiled sweetly. "That's all."

"That's *all?*"

"Well, I guess I do want to see if he's ours. Make sure. Because I don't want to go to prison, okay, Bunny? I worked very fucking hard to get into this program."

"*How* are you going make sure, though?"

"I don't know yet. But if he's *ours*, then I can just relax." She'd never relax. "Anyway, it's my apartment, my attic, isn't it?" And she walked up the stairs with small, sure-footed steps.

While she was gone, we watched the sky darken through the windows, saying no words. Listening with our collective ears, straining to hear any sound above our heads. Nothing. Not even a fucking whisper, Bunny.

"I'm going up there," Coraline said at last, her eyes on the ceiling.

"No," Vik and I whispered back.

"What if she let him go? It would be just like her to let something go that's MINE."

"Ours," we both corrected her, even as I thought, *Fucking mine.*

"*Ours*," Coraline repeated, sort of snort-laughing to herself. "Right."

Just then Kyra came down again. Pale, very pale. Strangely smaller looking than before.

"Well?" we all said as one voice.

"He's ours," she said. "At least, I'm pretty sure he is. But . . ."

"*But?*"

"I think . . ."

"WHAT?"

"We have to get rid of him. Or something." She was red in the face, looking at the floor.

"What do you mean, 'get rid of him'?" Vik glanced at me.

"He's dangerous. He's a *threat*."

I recalled his skipping across the garden with a razor swinging in his fist. "That's absurd," I said.

She looked at me. "He really does want to kill Allan. For real."

Coraline snorted. "*Everyone* wants to kill Allan, though. So I don't know if that actually counts as anything but him being perfectly rational?"

"The bottom line is that he's violent," Kyra whispered. "And if we don't kill him now, he might run off and do something terrible. And I'm sorry, but I just don't want that on my conscience, okay, Bunny? We need to be pragmatic here. Ethical. Think about the greater good."

"*Ethical?*" Coraline repeated. "Wait, Little Miss I Don't Want to Go to Fucking Jail Because I'll Miss My Typewriter is talking murder of a human being?"

"He's not human, Bunny," she said.

"What is he, then?"

Kyra shook her head sadly. "I don't know. A monster. A sociopath maybe."

Coraline smacked her. Right across the face. "Don't you DARE call him that."

Kyra didn't even flinch. She just stroked her own cheek, smiled a little now. "There's something else. He knows things, Bunny."

I could feel myself pale then. Saw the color drain from each of our faces. Felt our hearts quicken. *Knows things? What fucking things, Bunny?*

"About us."

Coraline's eyes went wide. "Like *what?*" We watched her blotchy white-gloved hands tighten into fists.

Kyra kept smiling. "Why don't you go on up there and ask him, Bunny? Or go get murdered by a maniac. Up to you, totally."

Coraline looked at Kyra, grinning at her now like, *I dare you.* "Fine," she said. Took another long swig of her gin Fog. "You read my mind, actually."

"Bunny, wait." And she reached out and grabbed Coraline's arm. "It really is dangerous." I saw the love on her face then. Coraline seemed to soften suddenly, to hesitate. Then she smiled coldly.

"It's nothing I can't handle," she sniffed. "I mean, he's got my pearls on his neck, for Christ's sake, doesn't he?"

"And your razor in his pocket," Kyra whispered.

But Coraline was already clip-clopping up the stairs two at a time, humming to herself.

She was gone for longer than Kyra. Again we pricked up our collective ears as we waited, more impatiently this time, all of us on edge. "I have an ax," Kyra was whispering to the floor. "My father showed me how to chop wood with it, said I was actually pretty pro. Before I left, he told me to take it with me in case of break-ins, rapists, *You never know, my dear. You're going to Warren, after all.*"

"If she doesn't come down in five minutes, we should check on her probably," Vik said to me, ignoring Kyra. "Just in case she's being, you know, murdered."

"Probably," I agreed solemnly.

Thirty more minutes passed. At last Coraline came down looking very much the same though we could tell she'd had more to drink. Her bob slightly askew, cheeks flushed. "Well?" we all asked.

And she looked at us like she'd forgotten we were there. "He said he'd like to come live with me in my apartment," she said dreamily.

"*What?*"

"Just because it gets better light. I mean, it really does, Bunny. You can't get mad about architecture." We watched her refill her drink, humming.

"What about the fact that he's dangerous?" Kyra said.

"Well, we can't be responsible for that. I mean, he's his own person, isn't he?" She was smiling. "He's a . . . free spirit."

"Who wants to KILL Allan."

"Oh, I don't think he's really going to *do* that, Bunny." She was still biting on her grin. "I mean, he's wearing a velvet blazer, for fuck's sake, okay? He's not a *predator*. Bunnies aren't predators, that's just . . . science." She settled back down on the love seat with her drink, tucking her feet under the bell of her dress like she was in a 1950s film. This was the decade in which she would live for the rest of her life, with varying degrees of self-awareness about this fact. And then I saw the blood on her bare right shoulder. The word freshly carved there. *Aerius*, it said.

"What about the things he knows?" Kyra whispered.

And Coraline looked at us. Paled briefly. Only then did her smile twitch. "That's exactly why he should live in my apartment. Not only does it have more light, it has more locks. So that everything he knows stays with me. With us. Forever." She drank moodily from her cup.

Vik grinned. "I'm going up there."

Coraline and Kyra protested wildly, but I just stood there. As you know, I've never been one to waste my energy, Bunny. Always been one to bide my time. I just watched Vik dash up the stairs before anyone could stop her.

Once more we waited. Once more silence, except for Coraline, who was humming a baleful indie tune about a mermaid dragging you under. And Kyra still mumbling about her dear ax. It was in the closet, she whispered. It was freshly sharpened. Meanwhile, I attempted to attune myself, uselessly, to what was going on above our heads with Vik. She came back down at last. Hair slightly disarrayed. Eyes shining. Mouth open and grinning in a way that made me feel somewhat dirty, Bunny, to behold it.

"So?"

"Oh, he's ours, all right," she said.

Coraline smiled and Kyra frowned. *Yes. He is.*

"And?"

"I say we keep him for a while. Maybe actually bring him back to my place for a bit? Because I have that yard. But yeah, that's my vote. Keep."

And of course when she said the word *keep*, I heard the true word with our hive mind, which was *fuck. We fuck him. I fuck him.* I saw the beginnings of a hickey on her neck. Some claw marks on her forearms, brazenly displayed for our viewing pleasure.

"You're disgusting," Coraline hissed, going pink.

Vik grinned at Coraline, walked over to her. "You're telling me you *don't* want to keep him, Bunny? Bring him to your place?"

"Just for *better light.* Kyra's attic has a lot of dust and I'm concerned."

"Better light, huh? You don't think he's incredibly hot?" she said, moving in closer to Coraline. "You don't want to bring him into your blue bedroom and see what he can do with that razor of yours?" she whispered into her neck.

"NO!"

"Well, I fucking do," she said, stroking Coraline's face. "Those pearls. That chest. My god, my god," Vik said. Pretended to faint. "We're good. Is all I have to say."

"But he's not *human*, Bunny," Kyra cried from the sidelines.

"Oh, he's human enough," Vik said, grinning at her. "Trust me. Anyway, aren't *you* the one who fucks entities?"

"Not literally! *Metaphorically* I do!"

"Well, this isn't a fucking *metaphor*, Bunny."

"Oh my god," Coraline whispered to Vik, closing her eyes. "You fucked him already didn't you?"

Vik patted Coraline's hair. "Calm down, Bunny. You two can still take *turns about the room*, drinking Lady Grey or whatever. We can share, how's that?" She grinned at Coraline, who blushed afresh.

"Disgusting," Kyra hissed. "You want to make him your sex slave?"

"If he's into it, why not? At least I don't want to *kill* him."

"What about what he knows, Vik?" I asked. "What about that?"

And only then did Vik's confident smile crack. Only then did she look at me like, *Oh yeah. Right. That.*

"I have an ax," Kyra whispered to the floor.

All this talk of ownership and, yes, murder, was making me just a hair uncomfortable, Bunny. As you can surely appreciate. My cohort seemed to have forgotten once more that I was even in the room. This often happens when I am attempting to Look Within for the Key. When my eyes close and my Third Eye opens, it's true that I do become a kind of invisible. It was a feeling I'd experienced at family events, where my sister was the star and I a mere moon. How she'd smile drunkenly at the endless praise heaped upon her person, for doing what? Just what a dusty medical textbook told her to do, Samantha. Meanwhile, I brooded alone in the shadows, the sky positively electric, ringing with my impending Will.

As my cohort discussed among themselves, I took the opportunity, Bunny, to go up and see our charge for myself. Kyra, seeing me go, peeled away from Coraline and Vik, still taunting/flirting with each other, to hand me her ax. "Just in case he tries to murder you, Bunny," she whispered. "You can murder him first." She pressed it into my hands before I could say, *Don't be fucking stupid. I don't believe in murder. Besides, if you all didn't need it, why do I?*

Yet I took it from her.

He had been silent for some time, I noted. Not a scream had bled down to us through the ceiling. Not a whimper or even a whisper. I could no longer hear his heart beating in my head. Though my fellow Bunnies had spoken of him with some urgency that told me he was up there, of course he was up there, we had locked him in there ourselves—still, there was a part of me that couldn't, wouldn't believe until I saw with my own eyes.

Dark when I opened the door. No sign of him at first in the dog-and-wolf light of evening, the room itself mostly awash in black. Panic gripped me briefly.

"Hello?" I deigned to call out, a wavering in my voice.

No answer. The ax, Bunny, was heavy in my hand, but I was glad for it now.

And then I saw him in the corner, sitting cross-legged on the floor. Staring out at the darkening blue sky through the triangle window, his waves catching the last of the sky's light. A visceral itch to run my fingers through them. Fiercely. Never stopping. My fingers hummed with this itch. *Oh, he is mine!* As soon as I saw his hunched silhouette, certainty returned to me. I dropped my ax. That he was mine was a fact as indelible as the sun in the sky or rainbows after rain. The clatter didn't even rouse him, so lost he was in looking out the window. As I approached, I noted, with not a little rage, that my fellows had each left their mark upon his person. His hair had been half braided, clearly by Coraline. Cherries in Winter freshly applied to his lips with Kyra's try-hard hand. A smile-shaped hickey on his neck and Vik's horndog mouth responsible.

"How . . . are you?" I asked. With feeling, Bunny. Nothing but concern for his well-being in my heart. And some trepidation, thinking of Coraline's razor in his pocket. I didn't know whether to sit or stand. Finally I just sort of crouched before him.

He turned to stare at me. Still saying nothing. Yet seeing my soul, I felt. The animal gleam in his eye was too much to look at directly. He had grown rabbity in captivity.

"Aerius," I whispered. "Please. You're among friends."

He looked away from me. Hung his head rather sadly. He was surrounded by limp dandelions, all of them untouched. The plate of mini confections, the electrolyte water, also untouched. The little teacup turned over, the herbal pink mulch bleeding into the floorboards. Only the absinthe had been consumed.

"Are you not hungry?"

Silence.

"Thirsty?"

Still silence.

"Perhaps you'd like a dandelion. . . ." I picked one up from the floor, held it out and twirled it for him, feeling like a fucking witch. He stared at me.

"I really hope you're . . . comfortable," I insisted, sort of stammering. "It's not like my apartment, of course," I heard myself say idiotically. "Perhaps you'd like to go there with me instead. You could meet my dogs. We could . . . talk. Get to know each other better." What was I even saying, Bunny? I had no idea. My hands were clasped together like I was praying, like I was pleading with him. Still he stared at me, something like anger—or was it fear?—in his eyes. Hard to say, only one eye illuminated in the black, his hair hiding the other. He, too, had a bitch curtain, Samantha, disconcertingly quite like yours.

"I hope you know," I began again, "that we—that I . . . love you."

"Love?" He turned away to look out the window. *Is that what this is, Mother? Trapping me up here? Keeping me locked away like this?* "Aerius is tricked," he whispered. His speech, Bunny. It moved me in spite of myself. He was so terribly articulate, even if gravely mistaken.

"Sometimes when you love, you have to trick," I said softly.

"Why?"

"Because the World is a very cruel place."

"Cru-elle," he repeated softly.

"And stupid and ignorant," I added, thinking of Allan. "And if we were to release you now, you would be left to fend for yourself. And we wouldn't be there to . . . protect you, to explain about you."

He stared at me again. "How very special you are," I said, smiling.

He pulled a tube of lipstick from his pocket. Applied it thoughtfully to his lips, looking at me as though I were a mirror. Perhaps I was. "And dangerous?" he asked.

"*Dangerous?*" I laughed. "I don't believe that at all. I mean, you don't *really* want to kill Allan, do you?"

"Kill Allan," he whispered, growing serious.

"I didn't think so. But Kyra also mentioned you know some things. About us."

He looked away from me then, Bunny. Lowered his eyes.

"What do you know," I pressed, "about me, for instance?"

"Know?" Like suddenly he didn't understand the word, Bunny. Oh but he did. He shook his head, but I saw it in his eyes. My Shadow Self. All our Shadow Selves, in fact. Four figures cowering in the black of his iris. "Aerius would like to go back to the garden now," he said.

"Not," I said, "until you tell Mother what you know about her."

He pressed his cherry lips together tight. I saw Coraline's primness in him then. Or was it Kyra's defiance? Or was it the *fuck you* in Vik's eyes? My own mark was there too, of course—which said, *I will make the clouds storm with my anger. I will brighten the sky with my loving care.*

He took the dandelion from me and twirled it between his fingers. Kept his mouth shut.

Fine, I thought. Walked away from him. *Keep your secrets.*

"Northwestern," he whispered from behind me.

I grew cold then, Bunny. *What?*

I looked at him, suddenly standing before me, grinning now.

"We had such *alchemical* aspirations."

I felt myself pale. "No," I whispered, shaking my head.

"We believed we could reimagine the Sciences," he said, moving in closer. "Transform the whole of Medicine with our Witchery. Best our bitch sister at med school. Alas," and here he leaned in, placed his hands tenderly on either side of my now trembling face. "'The Admissions Committee regrets—'"

"NO!"

He smiled. "'I must get into Warren, Mother! If I can't get into any med school, at the very fucking least I should be able to get a lowly writing deg—'"

"NO, NO, NO!" I tried to stop up my ears, but he was holding me fast, beaming.

"'Call the Provost! A favor, don't they owe us?'"

But I heard no more of his words, Bunny, because I was screaming. My mouth stretched open, crying, "STOP!" Oh but he didn't stop, Bunny. Instead his eyes lit up, like someone had flipped a switch inside of him, turned him from Off to On. He began jumping up and down delightedly. Shouting the many cruel names I'd been called by my enemies from junior high onward. Not to mention the many egregious lies and rumors that have always surrounded my person. I won't share those with you, obviously, Samantha, except to say that his deep knowledge of my secret psychic wounds, the visceral delight he took in my pain, well, it unmoored me. It fascinated me too. For his eyes never looked more beautiful than when they were alive with my Shadow Self, than when he was spewing my soul's detritus in my face. I watched helplessly as he ran ecstatic circles around me in his nightdress, which was most definitely my nightdress, Samantha. I saw the Free People tag sticking out of his back collar, flapping in the breeze he made. The fabric was covered in grass stains, the hem irreversibly torn. "DO WE LOOK FUCKING OPRAH-FRIENDLY TO YOU?" he was shouting now. "KILL ALLAN KILL ALLAN KILL ALLAN!"

I looked down, and there was the ax in my hands again. I'd picked it up off the floor, was gripping it tight. Trembling, I raised it now, high above my head. Though it pained me, I was ready to strike.

Now you may well wonder, Samantha, why I'm sharing this shameful exchange with you at all. Quite uncharacteristically vulnerable of me, I know. I'm *giving you the vulnerability*, I suppose. Which I know you just love. You did that in your little novel, didn't you? Playing up your "working-class" background, your outsiderness, your ambiguous sexuality, your mental . . . *troubles*, let's call them. Just *dying* to show us the many warts on your soul. I tend *not* to stoop to such psychic manipulations in my own storytelling, Bunny. I've shared, in this instance, only for the higher sake of Story. For the sake of Art. So that you understand that he was indeed MINE. And though much of what he ejaculated was a mere echo or exaggeration or a damning lie, I knew he knew the Shadow. His words cut right to the Heart, over which my dagger sits eternally. For whoever cuts me to the Heart will also be cut, Samantha. Oh yes.

Now where was I?

Noticing the ax raised in my hands, he froze abruptly in the middle of his run. Stared at me, shocked. *Mother, how could you?*

Knock, knock on the door just then.

"Bunny, are you okay?" they called up.

"Bunny, um, should we fucking come up there?"

"Bunny, hi, are you making out with him or murdering him up there? Don't murder him, k? Or make out with him. Not before we discuss."

I looked at him. He was panting before me, his dress drenched with sweat just as mine was. I could feel his rabbity heart pounding in his chest like it was my own fucking heart. My crude masterpiece. Breathing as I was breathing. The same fucking breaths, it felt like. To kill him in that moment, Samantha, would have been like hacking into my own flesh.

"Fine," I told the floorboards, lowering my ax. "I'll be right down." I turned away from him, started walking toward the attic steps. Then I heard him whisper, "Please." I turned back and found him crouched near my feet. "Let Aerius go."

"Go where?" I said coldly. I heard the cold in my voice. My father telling me I could not leave my room, did I understand?

"Trust," he whispered.

Trust? I looked at his beautiful throat, strangled by Coraline's pearls, a veritable dog collar. Voice box filled with how many more lies and secrets, how many more social wounds and mind fragments. *He's dangerous. He's a threat,* Kyra had said, and now I understood why. Of course the thought of killing him brought tears to my eyes. I did not wish to kill a being with such incredible cheekbones, with such exquisite face symmetry that so eerily resembled my own (the others will *never* admit this resemblance, Samantha, by the way).

Right then he saw the murder I was thinking about, the gleam it gave to my eye. He held up the razor uselessly. He would not use it against me, somehow I sensed this. Strangely, it even aroused me, though certainly this was Coraline's fantasy (her doing) not mine.

"Aerius goes where Aerius goes," he whispered threateningly, but also pleadingly, like I might have asked my mother, so long ago, to go outside and play.

12

H e needs revision," is what I said to them when pressed. Back in the living room, I snatched Coraline's gin Fog and drank down the vile concoction. I desperately needed a drink after that, Bunny. The screaming in the attic continued above our heads. As did the jumping.

"*Revision?*" they repeated.

"*Work,*" I shouted. They stared at me. "*Civilizing,* if you like."

"Civilizing?" Vik echoed, wrinkling her nose. "I don't know. I sort of like him as he is. Wild. All over the place. I say we let him go and see what happens."

"I say we cut our losses," Kyra whispered, petting the ax handle. "Start fresh. Who's to say we can't do it again and better next time?"

Coraline was shaking her head. "No. No *letting go.* No *murdering.* Let me please just take him to my place and—"

And I screamed, Bunny. It was a yogic trill, a call to attention, my voice reverberating like a most holy bell. This time they all fell silent. Stared at me. I smiled. I have always been able to take a particular kind of psychic charge, Samantha, as you know. "Look," I said wisely, "I've assessed the situation. He and I had a very long . . . *talk* up there. And I agree with Kyra that, sadly, in his current state he poses a significant threat."

"To Allan?"

"Fuck Allan. To *us.* He's far too . . . unhinged. Raw. Not to be . . . *trusted* at this stage."

And they all nodded uncomfortably. *Yes.* Perhaps recalling seeing their own Shadow Selves lurking in his eyes. Though surely none had experienced my degree of encounter.

"So we kill him?" Kyra said hopefully.

"*No.*"

"Why not?"

"Because we don't just *kill* what we make, Bunny." I flashed to myself in the attic, the ax trembling above my head. "We're artists, graduate scholars, for fuck's sake. We were just given a most incredible Gift. Possibly from God. Do you want to spit in the eye of God?"

"So . . . what do we do, then?"

"We *love,*" I said. "Nurture. Teach as only we can. We do the difficult but ultimately very rewarding work of making him better."

Vik sighed. "I fucking hate revision."

"Me too," Kyra said. "Also, how do we *revise* a human being? *If* he's even human, Bunny. I mean, we don't even know what he—"

"Forget what he IS or WAS! *Think* about what he *could be.*"

We all fell silent for a spell. Pondered.

"Maybe we could give him some of our own writing to read or something," Coraline ventured at last. Staring into the fire, who'd started a fire? Don't know, but there it was burning before our eyes. "So he can . . ." She blushed furiously, shook her head at the flames. "Get to know us better. Maybe if he gets to know us, he'll stop screaming so much."

"Or wanting to kill Allan so much."

I pictured Aerius perusing my many proems. If he were given the opportunity to sit with them for a while, surely—

"He'd learn to understand us," Vik said quietly, finishing my thought. "Grasp our *intentions.*" She smirked at the word.

"Not to mention our individual concerns," Kyra added, still petting the ax.

"We could put some of our favorite books up there too," Coraline added, sitting up now. "He could read them, and we could discuss them together. Reading always broadens your horizons, doesn't it?"

"It does," we all agreed, nodding. "Enriches your insides, absolutely. It always helps the Work to read. Breaks it open. Brings it to another level. Sharpens the language, so to speak."

Screams over our heads now.

"Speaking of another level, maybe we could make him a playlist or something," Kyra offered. "Include our favorite songs."

"Oh my god, I've always wanted to do that," Coraline sighed. "For a . . . project."

"Not all Taylor Swift please, though, Bunny," Kyra whispered to Coraline.

"Um, or fucking Enya," Coraline snapped back at her. "Or Lana, please," she added more quietly, turning to Vik.

"Or Kate," Vik said pointedly, looking and then not looking at me.

I ignored this. "Kyra, you have that projector. What about film? How wonderful for him to have audiovisual models of ideal behavior playing on the walls at all hours. To give him a sense of our souls and such."

"We should put some porn up there too," Vik said. "Female-directed and/or gay. Just so, you know, he has everything."

"And maybe we should get him other clothes?" Kyra said to me. "Not that I don't *love* the white nightgown, Bunny. Very Kate Bush circa 1978. But he *could* have some other looks."

A rage ticked in me then. Sky blackening. But I gathered myself. Smiled and said, "Absolutely. Definitely we'll take that under consideration. We're all in this together, after all. This is a *Collective*. We're gathering ideas here. Brainstorming."

A clap of thunder outside. As though God had heard us, Bunny, and She, They, It—whatever the fuck—was on our side, also storming.

The screaming ceased.

And except for the rain, all was silent above our heads.

13

And so? We did our best to revise him, Bunny. To improve, add dimension, *some layers*, so to speak. Over the next weeks we slid our many stories and vignettes and proems through the door. We smiled to think of him up there perusing our pages and panes. Loved to imagine where he might laugh or cry or simply be taken by us. How he might be enchanted by a certain word or phrase. Or by our particular genius more generally, our keen poetic sensibilities. We slid our very favorite books through the door too, dog-earing pages, underlining particular passages of import, and making pointed notes in the margins with our cerulean LePens. *This*, we wrote, drawing an arrow, sometimes a heart, by the just-so words.

"We do hope you enjoy," we whispered to him from the stair while he just stared at us silently from his dark corner, Bunny, surrounded by the many untouched foods we'd also lovingly provided. Glowered at us until at last we turned away and sighed and shut the door.

We really did hope for the best, Bunny. Hoped it might all somehow sink in. Hoped we might find him changed by our multipronged efforts. That one day we might come up to the attic and find that he looked upon us with Love and Understanding rather than a kind of visceral animal alarm, a bewildered fear-hate. That on the subject of our proems and books, he'd have many thoughts. Rather than a silence, Bunny, that was fucking deafening. Rather than find his cherry lips pressed shut in a way that felt almost willful. Defiant. As *fuck you* as Vik's eyes. We hoped for dialogue, gratitude. Instead we found our texts quite ripped up, likely by his own teeth. All the pages we'd placed so lovingly within his reading view torn into so much paper snow. Others he appeared to have eaten or shat on in the interim. And seemed quite happy about this. In fact, it was only when we were deeply devastated or angry that he ever looked pleased. Came alive at all. A light in his eyes then, such beautiful eyes he had, Bunny. Yet still disconcertingly full of our Shadow Selves. Our most filthy secrets.

Did we have to tie him up a little, Samantha? Sort of like we tied you up? Yes, sadly, we did in the end. In this very chair you're sitting on, in fact, isn't that funny? Just to keep him up here, to keep him with us. So he didn't try to run away into the cold, cruel world, which just wasn't ready for him, Bunny. So he didn't jump up and down above our heads, giving us such a fucking headache after two minutes. We couldn't afford the headache; we needed our minds now more than ever before. Did we gag him too? We did gag him a little, sure. Just from time to time. But again, with very good reason. The constant screaming would have alarmed Kyra's neighbors, who were already sort of suspicious of us, Bunny. Always fucking staring at us whenever we skipped past their window, laughing and singing, arm in arm (for all in all, it was a most happy October). We really didn't want those puritanical assholes knocking on the door at this particular juncture in the Process, did we? What would we have even said, can you imagine? We laugh to think about it now. *So sorry for screaming, but, um, we're just in the middle of a highly experimental creative writing project. We're just performing an act of the most deep and dire Love. We're scholars, you see, and unlike you, dying slowly before your televisions, we're trying to make something of ourselves and our lives. To make something fucking beautiful that loves us.*

"Please love us," we pleaded with him.

In the evenings one of us might play a film for him, chosen from a collectively agreed-upon selection of New Waves, classics, and contemporary independents. And, upon the urgings of Coraline, the melodramas and screwball rom-coms of the '40s and '50s. Though Vik was adamant about adding porn to the mix—it was a basic human right, she said—we told her, "Let's hold off on that for now, Bunny." Sometimes we'd sit beside him while the film played, but mostly not, due to his disconcerting sounds of protest, which broke our hearts more than we can say. More oft than

not, we'd leave him alone to watch the moving picture on the wall. Sometimes watching him watch from the staircase, we liked to do that. Just to
see what, if any, impression it was making upon his soul. He was always
better to watch than the film, Samantha. Better than any fucking film, really. His living, breathing body, crouched there in the dark. The light from
the screen playing on his face, bright eyes wide open in a kind of haunted
Wonder. That's when I took in him a kind of fiery pride. That's when my
hopes for him were highest. "Fucking look at him," I whispered. In fact, we
all whispered these words at the very same time. Sometimes he appeared
quite lost in the story, quite moved. Kyra said I was projecting, but what
the fuck did she know, Bunny? His favorite film was *Frankenstein*, understandably so. His eyes brightened whenever the monster filled the screen.
He stomped on the floorboards, even grunted along with the creature.
Screamed along with him too at the horribleness of humanity. Through
the gag, Bunny, obviously.

There were days, of course, when he refused the cinematic delights we
offered up like our hearts. Refused even though he must have been so very
bored up there. Still he closed his eyes and hung his shaking head. "Let's just
put him out of his misery," Kyra might hiss then.

"Let's let him go," Coraline countered. "To my place maybe. I keep telling you, he'll do better in a space where he can get more light."

"I think one of us should offer up our body," Vik sighed. "Probably me
because I can handle his animal nature."

"NO," we all screamed. "Revision is a Process, remember. Patience is
key."

At these times we played music for him on a Bose speaker. Our tender
and thoughtfully made playlist, to which we all had contributed our most
cherished songs. Because music soothes the savage Beast. Or is it savage
breast? Well, either/or.

In this way we inundated him with our souls daily. So he really he had
no choice but to internalize them. Internalize *us*, in some way. If he chose
not to peruse our pages or open our beloved books, if he closed his eyes to

the moving pictures on the wall, our *sound* at least would speak to him. He could only stop up his ears so much, Bunny.

Surely, he would be moved by us in some form, we thought.

But progress was a Journey, Samantha. A Collective is not easy, as you yourself know. Did we sometimes disagree about the evening's film choice? About the order of the playlist songs or which text he might imbibe next? Of course we fucking did, order being so crucial to Outcome and Effect.

On the subject of his diet, too, we were not always of One Mind. Coraline, of course, wanted to give him sweets almost exclusively. "It might make him sweeter," she reasoned. "More polite. Less murdery." Pixy Stix, for instance, might be a good antidote to his constant refrain of *Kill Allan*. Swedish Fish, too, for color and chew. Pinkberry with all manner of toppings, but especially rainbow sprinkles, Bunny, because "so pretty." Every mini muffin they sold at Mini, and could they please make more kinds, she implored, perhaps carrot or freesia flavored? "He really enjoys baked goods," she told us, bearing a plate full of confections up to the attic. "He told me."

And in truth, Bunny, we suspected he'd told her no such thing.

Kyra, on the other hand, was all about organic produce. "He's a creature, after all," she reminded us. A *vegan*, and we should feed him as such. If we fed him only heirloom lettuces and carrots from Whole Foods, then he might revert naturally to his nonpredatorial nature. Sometimes she'd add a mini peanut butter cup to his tray, since he also really seemed to like those, she said. Though honestly, Bunny, I never saw anyone but her partake.

Vik, on the other hand, thought all of this was fucking absurd. She wanted to feed him "whatever the fuck" she picked from the mud on the way over to Kyra's. A clump of weeds. Grasses. A flower bitten through with frost. "What he wants is the dirt," she said obscenely.

And I? I confess I felt a juice cleanse or two might do him good. Surely, after his rabbit-to-human transformation, he was sorely in need of replenishing electrolytes. Each day I went to the nearby juice bar, purchased a veritable rainbow of elixirs for him to choose from.

Yet despite our best efforts, he mostly refused to eat. Our candy, our muffins, our grasses and dandelions and plethora of fruit essence, it was all the same to him.

Fucking nothing.

He's getting thinner, one of us would inevitably report whenever we came down from the attic. Not drinking at all from his cup of stars (my own humble gift). Not even partaking of the freesia and cowslips we'd stolen from the Botanical Gardens, which we learned rabbits eat from revisiting *Watership Down*, a timeless classic.

During this time we continued to go to Workshop, of course we did. It was hilarious under the circumstances. We smiled, inwardly, whenever Allan told us we needed to really push ourselves a bit more creatively. *Okay, Bunny*, we thought. *Thanks. We'll, um, be sure to make a note of that.* The week after my useless Workshop, in fact, Allan pulled me aside to (shudder) "check in."

"Everything all right, Elsinore?" he wondered. Playing the oh-so-concerned professor. He sincerely hoped my allergies were okay? That I'd gotten them all under control?

"Oh yes," I said, "absolutely under control, Allan. Reining them in as we speak." I smiled, picturing Aerius running his homicidal circles in the attic.

"Oh good. Well, I hope Workshop was helpful in the end?"

"In the end? Absolutely. Just doing some revision right now, actually."

"Revision," he repeated, looking mildly impressed. "Really? And how is that going?"

"It's a Process, of course. Sometimes I actually feel like it's going to kill me." I laughed here. "Or someone else," I said, looking at Allan. He smiled strangely.

"Sounds like you're cutting pretty close to the bone, Elsinore," he said in a low voice.

You have no idea, Allan.

Was it hard to keep a straight face in Workshop with what we had gestating in the attic? It was, Bunny. A smile might creep across my lips at the most inopportune times, like when you or Allan were criticizing me, for instance, for not being "dimensional" enough. That word always made me laugh on the inside, Bunny, and sometimes on the outside too. Or whenever the word "reality" was mentioned. Or "alive." As in, "I wish this were a little more alive on the page. More visceral." Then the laughter would almost explode from one of us like flatulence. Did you notice us laughing, Samantha? Yes, I suppose you did. It was very hard to contain, given the circumstances. Our laughter was as "visceral" and wild as the boy in the attic, shitting freesia on our floorboards, probably as we spoke. Likely it added to your enmity toward us. Another lump of coal for your hate. But we couldn't help it, Bunny.

That October there was a kind of singing in our heads always. Our playlist on continuous loop in our minds. The air outside was a new kind of sweet. The colors of the world were more vivid to our eyes. An iridescent dreaminess crept into our souls. No matter what stupid shit you were saying or Allan was saying or what stupid reading he'd assigned for the week (usually a short story or novel full of murder and philosophy), we could all sort of think, *Whatever*. Because we had other things to discuss. Things of great import. Like did he read or eat the Austen this time? And what about the Woolf? Did he appear to have internalized our marginal musings on the Diaries? What about *The Waves*?

"Oh yes, quite literally, Bunny," Coraline might report. "He also appears to have eaten *The Bell Jar*. As well as two copies of *Jane Eyre*."

"But what did he make of the Borges?" I asked eagerly. For this particular text had been my own humble suggestion.

"We are not sure, Bunny," Kyra said. "When we asked him this question, he only screamed. Screamed so very loudly, we actually thought our eardrums would burst. We are actually very surprised our neighbors didn't finally complain or even call the police. Perhaps they did, and now they are on their way."

Kyra had made such claims before, of course. That the boy had screamed so loudly, surely the neighbors would knock on the door this time. Or the police would finally come. But the police never came, Bunny. And the neighbors never once knocked. Which is maybe something to keep in mind for your own situation here, sadly. That no matter how much he screamed and jumped, how many times we had to chase him around the attic, *the Work*, as it were, continued undisturbed. Reassuring for us, definitely, but maybe not so much for you right now. At the time we did wonder about the lack of intervention or even comment from the outside World. We wondered about it during his screams, but we wondered about it even more during his silences. When the infernal sounds of his struggle ceased, nothing bleeding down from the ceiling but the dreamy harps and guitars of our own playlist, and we all sat in silence in the living room, we asked ourselves: Were we fucking crazy? Was this a collective hallucination? A psychic byproduct of perhaps spending too much time together? It was strange that whenever we were away from him, even for just a very short time, we almost ceased to believe that he was actually tied up there in the attic, eating our Duras page by page.

"Well, perhaps it touched him," I offered now. Reanchoring myself in the present moment. Kyra's living room. An octobral dusk. All of us sitting in a circle around a fire that always seemed to be burning brightly, Bunny. "The Borges."

"Perhaps," my cohort agreed uneasily.

"And what does he make of the many films we have shown?" I asked, turning to Vik, changing the subject. "Has he spoken of them to you? Has he pontificated?"

Vik stared at me, in my vanity eyewear and raw silk conjuring dress, my silver hair pinned back by so many birds-of-paradise. My notepad on my knee and my feather pen in my fist, its amethyst ink dripping onto the empty white face of the page. I knew that, inwardly, she was starting to resist my revision project. It was, she thought, like attempting to turn a field of wildflowers into "the fucking Botanical Gardens." Or a boreal forest into a gated park of pruned trees. She wanted nothing more than to take Aerius back to her basement apartment and fuck him (consensually, she always insisted) in her yard full of weeds. I could not trust, in fact, that she wasn't already fucking him in the attic whenever it was her turn to read him Derrida (her text selection). She took a very long time up there, each time. It made Coraline crazy.

"Oh, he's pontificated, Bunny," Vik whispered. "In his nonverbal language, of course."

"Of course." I nodded. Aerius hadn't spoken actual words since that awful day in the attic. Never spoke except to scream. I knew, of course, that he was quite articulate, was probably already deeply familiar with the literature and films and music we were sharing with him. He was only choosing to refuse us. Which pained me.

"And what of our own work?" I pressed. "What does he make of that?"

"He's made a sort of confetti of it, Bunny," Coraline reported sadly. "It covers the attic floor like so much snow. He's left rabbit droppings on some of the untorn pages. Very grassy, which is odd because he still won't touch the grass we give him, let alone eat it."

"Won't touch the grass? Why not? Perhaps you're not pulling it from the earth by its root so that it maintains its grassy freshness?"

A Darkness in my peer's face then. A defensiveness. *Perhaps you could feed him once in a while. If you're so fucking concerned, Bunny. Perhaps you should go on up and check on him yourself. This whole "revision" thing being your idea and all.*

But I much preferred to give directions from afar, to distill feedback on his reported progress. I did the arguably far more difficult work of conceptualizing, blueprinting, making recommendations. I was a general, my cohort the mere army. I drank kombucha, tapped into my crown Chakra, consulted the tarot at every twilight time. The Fool, I almost always drew from the deck. I stared into his laughing, enigmatic face and wondered dreamily, *What next?*

Then, of course, came the night we'll never forget, Samantha. Samhain. *Halloween*, as it's called by the plebeians, which we're happily celebrating with you right now. We were sitting in Kyra's living room, pondering. Vik was up in the attic, taking her very sweet time with him as usual. Enraging the hell out of Coraline.

"WHAT is she fucking DOING up there?" Coraline roared, pacing the floor. She was wearing a dress patterned with an absurd profusion of spring flowers, so as to be more appealing to Aerius. "It's been an hour," she said, tapping her wrist, in the manner of Ursula, where there was no watch at all. "Now it's been TWO hours. Oh my god." And she covered her eyes pitifully with her white-gloved hands.

"Calm down, Bunny," Kyra whispered, patting her back. Looking ridiculous (though admittedly sexy) in a pair of cat ears that Coraline had drunkenly plopped on her head earlier. Coraline now shook her off.

"I will *not* calm down. Not while *my* creation is potentially being *violated.*"

"*Your* creation?"

"*Ours*, okay, Bunny?" But her eyes said, *Mine. MINE MINE MINE.* It rang through all our bodies like a banshee cry.

"Let me get you a drink, Bunny. Would you like that?"

Coraline held her champagne flute up for the gin cocktail to be poured. *Just fucking pour it to the brim, Bunny,* I could feel her thinking. Not even looking at Kyra.

"How about an orange peel? Or a rosemary sprig? Like you like." Kyra, ever the thoughtful hostess. *Look what a wonderful hostess I'm being, Bunny,* her mind said, *even though you're being just a bit of a bitch right now.*

"I don't WANT a fucking peel, Bunny. Or a SPRIG."

"What *do* you want, Bunny?"

I saw for a shimmer of a moment, in her misty eyes, what she wanted. In all its gross petal-pink shades. She shook her head, collapsed into expected tears, surfacing now and then to gulp mouthfuls of gin. Kyra, patting her humped back, looked at me. *Do you see how he is destroying us, Bunny? We have an ax, don't forget. It is freshly sharpened, for I have been sharpening it each day since he came into our lives, since this whole mess began. Let's please put an end to this now and start fresh.* She looked at the attic door, at the empty hook where she'd begun to hang the ax for easy access. Vik must have taken it with her to the attic.

"All right, that's enough," Coraline said. "I'm fucking going up there."

"No, Bunny. We're supposed to give one another creative space, remember?"

And Coraline bit her lip. *Yes.* This was what we had indeed agreed upon. That we'd each have our individual time with him. Get to know him. Let him get to know us. Respect that we must. But her face said she didn't care. *Not today, Bunny. Not tonight.* Yet just as she was about to charge up the stairs, the attic door opened. In came grinning Vik. Her auburn tresses in great disarray, stinking of freesia and biting on a grin a mile fucking wide, Bunny.

"Ladies," she said, doffing an invisible cap. And we could feel her mind going, *Oh my, oh my, oh my.*

Coraline's flute cracked in her hand. "What happened up there? What did you do to him?"

"Just read him some Derrida. Gave him some dinner dandelions. That's all."

Lies. Lies, lies, lies, we all knew of course. Could read one another's souls at this point like picture books.

"What *took* you so long, then?"

"Well, you know how Derrida is. So . . . *dense.* We had to keep stopping. He asked a lot of pointed questions about post-structuralism and such. He was taking notes."

"*Notes?*" Coraline narrowed her eyes. *Don't believe you, Bunny.*

"May we ask why YOU took so long yesterday afternoon?" Vik shot back.

Coraline reddened. "Because I was reading him *The Wind in the Willows.* And he got lost in the story. We both did." Her eyes filled with a terrible

yearning. "Did he ask about me?" she whispered to the floor, in the most embarrassing tone, Bunny.

"*You?* Not that I can recall, no. Don't think you came up. *He,* on the
other hand . . ." And she grinned.

Coraline ran up to the attic crying, while Vik looked at us like, *What
did I fucking say?* Grinning like a Cheshire cat who's just been fucked. Kyra
glanced at me again from across the living room like, *Isn't murder starting to
make so much more sense?*

But her mind musings were suddenly interrupted by Coraline's piercing
scream.

"BUNNY. Come fucking up here!"

And when I heard those words, I knew. Was not at all surprised when
we ran up to find Coraline standing alone in the middle of the attic. Still
screaming, though no sound was coming from her open mouth, Bunny. Her
fists opening and closing like a child's. And Aerius?

"Gone," she whispered.

And indeed, he was gone. How different Kyra's attic looked to my eye in
this moment. Just a shitty old attic, I saw. Bereft of all but our word confetti.
Our Heart's Blood turned into so much ripped paper. Beheaded dandelions scattered here and there, the air smelling keenly of rabbit piss. Rancid
freesia and roses and so many clumps of dying grasses. Torn books and a
turned-over speaker, from which our playlist still wailed on, skipping like a
heart. The triangle window, shattered now, let in only a bit of the darkening
blue. The broken glass mocked us, casting a fractured evening light on our
faces. A jagged, man-shaped hole there now.

"Didn't you . . . ," Coraline began, hyperventilating, "remember to . . . tie
him back *up,* Bunny?"

"Of course I fucking remembered," Vik mumbled. Another lie we read
as plainly as the *fuck you* in her eyes.

"Then how did he jump out the window?" Kyra asked.

"I don't—"

"You KILLED him," Coraline cried.

"*I* killed him? How did I—"

"He jumped and died because of you! You DROVE him away with your HORNINESS. Your fucking *desire!*"

"I just wanted to give him a minute to fucking breathe, is all. He's a wild . . . spirit. We can't tie him up all the time, can we?"

But she was looking away from us now, flustered. Hiding something clearly. *LIES*, I wanted to scream. Instead I reached out my arm.

"Viktoria," I said. So terribly kindly. "Why don't you tell us what *really* happened, hmm? Remember this is a Collective. Remember you're among friends." My grip on her shoulder was tight. My soul shrieked *Mutiny*, yet I kept my gaze endlessly Maternal, my smile rife with Understanding.

She looked at me and covered her face with her hands. "He said something to me," she whispered.

My heart went cold. "What did he say?" I asked, and my own voice cracked. Recalling his outburst with me on that very first day.

"He called me a . . . name," she said.

"What name?" Kyra and Coraline asked, curious now.

Vik shook her head at the floor. As if still refusing it. As if she could still see his cherry lips gleefully forming the shape of her shame.

"VANILLA," she spat at last.

We looked at each other. *Vanilla?*

"He's such a monster," Vik cried. Dissolved into pitiful tears. I looked back at Kyra and Coraline, expecting they too would be bemused. But their eyes were downcast now. Were they recalling a similar instance with him?

"I did tie him back up, I did," she blubbered. "But I was flustered after that, okay? I must not have done it tightly enough or something." She looked at me, red-eyed, puffy faced. I'd never seen her so vulnerable. Desperate for some kind of absolution, some words of motherly kindness. But what was I to say, Samantha? I slid my grip to her neck, smiled coldly.

"I'll never fucking forgive you," Coraline blurted serendipitously, a crude paraphrasing of what was just then in my own soul. "I'll hate you. Always and forever."

"He didn't die, Bunny, look," Kyra said, pointing to the ground outside. We all turned and looked through the man-shaped hole. Indeed, there was no dead body down there on the grass below. Only Kyra's weedy front lawn. My heart immediately brightened, even as another kind of panic immediately took hold. *Where is he?*

"He must have landed on his feet and hopped away or something," Kyra mused sadly. Clearly, she'd been hoping for his death.

"He's not a *cat*, Kyra," Coraline snapped. "But it does look like he didn't die." She looked at me, her hopeful smile terrible to behold. "He's alive," she said, her voice a butterfly net flailing around in the dark.

"Where is he?" I heard myself whisper. "Where, where, where?"

While they all speculated on where he might have gone—how many gardens were there in this college town? How many fields? What systematic plan might we devise in order to cover this ground as efficiently as possible?—I closed my eyes. Attempted, desperately, to locate him telepathically. But it was like a light inside me had gone dark, Bunny, the candle of my spirit snuffed. I pictured Aerius wetting his forefinger and thumb with his lovely pink tongue and then putting out my soul's flame. And now he was out there, beyond our reach. Running around in my torn Free People. His dandelion-speckled lips possibly spewing my many secrets to my many enemies, oh god. But I could not show Panic, neither in my words nor in my mind nor in my heart, which my fellow Bunnies could read so plainly in any case.

"Jesus Christ," Kyra whispered. "Look there. On the wall."

I opened my eyes.

And then I saw the giant words written in blood, on the very wall where we'd shown him our favorite films, projected our narrative dreams. Words written, I knew, by his finger, in his blood. Which was our finger, our blood.

KILL ALLAN ☺

14

You don't really think he's going to do it, do you?" Vik asked, a half laugh in her voice. This was later, before a fire Kyra made in the living room to warm us, Bunny, though I knew we would be forever cold now. All of us staring at the tall, leaping flames. Seeing only his shape there.

"Of course not *really*, Bunny. We didn't mean it fucking literally, did we?" Coraline said.

"We said we wanted to," Kyra said simply. "And now it's in him. The wanting to."

"But he *has* to know we didn't mean it *for real*, right?" Vik insisted, still pale. *Vanilla, vanilla* humming in her mind. She'd never actually fucked him, she confessed.

I looked at the wildly crackling fire. Would I only ever see his silhouette in every cloud and flame?

"I don't know that he understands the difference between figurative and literal language, though," Kyra said. "I mean, did we ever, um, delineate that?"

"I'm sure somewhere between Derrida and du Maurier it got covered, Bunny," Coraline snapped. Flower dress askew. Eye makeup running down her face, never so pale as it was now. Her once golden bob a brassy frizz fest. I could see the dark roots creeping into the gold plainly. What a picture of aesthetic ruin she made.

"I didn't do the reading for tomorrow," she sighed sadly. "I should do it. Even though I'm sure it's just another murder text."

Yes. They were all murder texts. That is all Allan ever seemed to assign.

She looked at me, they all did, waiting for my words of wisdom, of consolation. But I offered them not. I, unlike them, was eerily calm now. Thanks to Vik's clumsiness, something irreversible had now been set in motion, Bunny. It would lead to an inevitable Outcome, which was perhaps destined all along. Of course I wanted him back. Of course I worried for his safety. He was out there now, my creation. Set loose upon the World. But though I was afraid, it was also exhilarating to me. I wondered what might happen now.

Just then, Bunny, I noticed it. The back of the attic door. That hook where Kyra liked to hang the ax. That hook still empty.

I looked at my cohort. All of them were now staring at this empty hook.

"Where's the ax?" I asked. Even though I knew, of course.

We all did.

"Oh my fucking god," Kyra whispered.

And quite in spite of myself, Bunny, I smiled.

Are you still with us, Samantha? On this portentous Samhain night, when our beloved broke free with our ax in his hand? Jumped right out of that window over there, breaking the glass, which Kyra's since had replaced, of course (don't get any ideas, Bunny). We're so glad you are.

Now, it's at this point in our telling where we're going to take a bit of a turn, Bunny.

A hop, if you will.

I'm going to invite my former cohort to join us again. . . . Come on back up, Bunnies.

Hurry, hurry.

Because it's time.

Because we agreed to share something with you, something we've never shown a soul. And even though you're terribly fucking unworthy, still we're going to share it. For the sake of our Journeys, Healing and Creative both. And because that's what we Artists do, isn't it? Share our souls with the unworthy World. We *give*, even though no one ever says, *Thank you, I'm listening. Wow, I so hear the stardust in that.* We're also going to share because otherwise you might not believe what we're about to tell you next, true story. And it's probably best to let *him* tell it. Yes, *him*, Bunny, in his very own words. For the sake of authenticity. So you'll hear directly from the Source. We have it right here, the pages lovingly bound and preserved. We'll read it to you, how's that? Since you're not in the best position to turn pages on your own at the moment, your hands not being exactly free.

We do hope you're still with us, Bunny, even though it's late now. And the world so terribly quiet at this hour. It's quite forgotten all about you, sadly. No idea that you're alone here in the Dark with us. Which is really the perfect time for a story. *This* story in particular, of course.

Are you ready, Bunny?

Part Two

Aerius

I

Dear Reader,

Hello! Very nice to meet you!

Of course, I know we are not *really* meeting ☺

You are Wherever you are right now, reading this Page. Maybe you are in a lovely Garden on a bright autumnal Day, surrounded by delicious Flowers the color of Sunshine, the Sun itself warming your Pelt beautifully (I hope ☺)! Or maybe you are in a cold, dark room like I am, on a muddy, flowerless floor full of Worms and Stones (I hope not ☹).

And I? Who wrote this Page long ago?

I am who knows where now ☹

Hopefully not Here anymore ☺

Probably we will never meet in Person ☹ (Though I do hope Someday we will ☺)

Mother says meeting Here on the Page is actually *better* than meeting in Person. In Person only ever disappoints, Mother says, and there is the Bitterness of dead Dandy Lion Stems in her Voice. The Page can disappoint too, of course, Mother admits, though it disappoints less ☺ But I still hope we will meet in Person anyway, Reader. Perhaps even become Friends ☺ Mother says I should write as though I am speaking intimately, truthfully, to a dear Friend. I will try, though I have no Friends of yet ☹ Apart from Pony, that is, who has been with me since the Attic Times and who does not speak anymore. Pony does not speak no matter how many Times I have tried to engage him in Conversations, no matter how many Questions I ask him about himself. His pink Eyes sparkle so beautifully, Reader, but they never do blink. He is a lovely but sadly unmoving, possibly dead Horse ☹ Not *Dead*, Mother always corrects. He is what she calls instead a Silly Toy. How this devastated me, dear Reader, when Mother first shared this News ☹ I thought she was only lying to be Cruelle, which she sometimes likes to be. But Mother says tis not she who is Cruelle so much, tis the World ☹ Which makes a kind of sense, though I do love the World ☺

I confess I still unburden my Self to Pony in the Evenings when I am alone here in the Writing Shed. Though his Eyes never blink, I *imagine* he is blinking. I imagine he is listening, too. Mother says to *imagine* is to make your Insides rich, to make what might never be *be*, if only for a Moment, in your Mindscape. And so I imagine Pony shedding many invisible Tears for me and the many Violences that have befallen me and that I have befallen ☹ I imagine that he is smiling and laughing at the many Wonders that have befallen me too ☺ Mother caught me doing this once and called it Pathetic ☹

The next Day she presented me with this Book.

In which I am now writing these very Words ☺

As I write, I will imagine another kind of Friend. Here, now, on my cold and flowerless Floor, with only a sliver of Moon on my Face, with the delicious Hum of freshly growing Grasses so close yet so far from my Ears, I will imagine You ☺

You, dear Reader, will be my most Perfect Friend ☺ To whom I can say anything, like I could to Pony, and you will not laugh at me please (as Mother sometimes laughs at me), and you will be on my Side in what I am increasingly learning is a cold and Cruelle World ☹ Though it also has its Beauties ☺

I can see you opening this Book now, Friend. My Book with the bright pink Flowers on the Cover, which I don't love. These Flowers frankly scare me somewhat ☹ I hope you will not tell Mother if you meet her, about the Flowers scaring me, though they do, they do ☹ When I close my Eyes, in fact, the Flowers seem to grow even larger in my Mindscape, the Petals threaten to strangle me, to strangle Aerius, and I wake up quite screaming ☹ Yet I keep the Book. Apart from Pony, tis my only Possession in the World (Mother confiscated my Weaponry ☹), so I hold it close. Tis a Way, too, my only Way, to communicate with the Outside, to tell You, my only Friend, of my Happenings. And of course, as Mother says, to Tap the Wound. This is why she bought me the Flower Book in the first Place, she said. Mother thinks I have many Wounds. She thinks I have been through what she calls Violences. She thinks I have experienced many Wonders, too, beyond the mere Comprehension of the Human Mindscape. Now I must *Tap the Wound to Language those Violences and Wonders.*

Reader, I do not know what tis to Tap the Wound exactly ☹

I asked Mother one Night, when we were sitting inside her Ring of small Fires (Candles, Mother calls them), cross-legged as she likes to do. She had her Eyes closed, as she likes to do too. Seeing with her Mindscape what she calls *the Source. The Well Spring.*

"Mother," I whispered, "what is it to Tap the Wound?"

Mother opened one Eye. Not at all loving to be interrupted. But loving me more, I could sense. She looked at me sitting across from her over the many Flames. I confess I prefer her Eyes closed to whenever she looks at me, always with a kind of Hunger-Wonder. Like I am the finest Flower she has ever seen that she would also love to eat. So beautiful, she dare not eat, yet one Day she may not be able to resist. One Day the Hunger might triumph over the Wonder. And Aerius might be no more ☹

But on this Night she only smiled at me. "Tapping the Wound is an *unconscious* Process. To *explain* would be to kill the Flow of the Well Spring."

I nodded as if I understood. Sometimes with Mother tis best to pretend to understand rather than to ask more Questions. She often becomes overwhelmed at how much I do not seem to know ☹ She often leaves and slams the door and, just before she does, looks at me like I am so stupid, I am such *Trash.* She will burn me alive, she will tear me into a thousand Pieces and throw me in the Garbage, her Eyes say. *If* I continue to speak in what she calls this "nonsensical" or "banal Manner." If I continue to "ramble on" about Ponies and Dandy Lions when she wishes me to speak on other Matters ☹

So here I am ☺ *Tapping the Wound* (or trying to) ☺

For you, dear Reader. My Friend ☺

Now that we have "met," where should Aerius begin? There is so much to tell that the Truth is I do not know! I would prefer *not* to begin in the Attic Times, dear Reader. I would *much* prefer not. These Times are too painful to revisit ☹ Instead I think I will begin with my first Night of Freedom ☺ Tis a Time that I like to go most in my Mindscape, despite some of its (inevitable) Violences ☹☺ Yes, I will begin there: with Aerius in the Attic, so much Abused ☹ Tied up, locked away with nothing but a Triangle of Sky to look at for so very long ☹ Eating Nothing but dead Grasses and brightly colored Poisons in a multitude of Shapes ☹ Something called a Playlist forever roaring around my Person ☹ Moving Pictures on the wall, of which I could make no sense, and some very tasteless Literatures by my bound Feets, which provided little in the Way of Sustenance ☹ My Eyes forever on the Triangle, dreaming, dreaming of Escape. And then came that fateful Night when one of my Keepers was a bit loose with the Rope. She'd become flustered by a Word I had said. I knew not which, for I often spoke without knowing what I was saying, Reader. But this Word had a dismantling Effect on her Person, causing her to fumble suddenly with the many Ropes that bound me, so that she inadvertently left a kind of Loophole, from which, with the help of my Razor, I was able to free my Body.

In her haste to leave me, she also left the Ax on the floor, which I happily picked up. Struck the Triangle thrice. And then, bypassing its many Shards, jumped into the Night.

I should say that when I jumped, I knew that Death might well be my Fate. Alas, twas a Risk I was willing to take, such had been the Pain of my Attic Times ☹ So when I landed in the tall Grasses below, Alive and unscathed (and already on my Feets, no less), you can imagine my very pleasant Surprise ☺ I stood in the Grasses, staring at the little house that had long been my Prison. Through the lit windows I saw my Keepers: Goldy Cut, Murder Fairy, and Insatiable (these were my private Names for them). And of course the One I called the Mind Witch, whom I saw less often than my other three Keepers, but whom I sensed was Queen of them all. They all four seemed much shorter than I recalled. They were arguing about me in their high-pitched Voices, which they often liked to do, about who would date me and what Literatures to feed me next, and one of them chanting softly about an Ax with which to kill me, and so on ☹ And I ran, Reader. Right past the open living room windows, in perfect view of them, each one smelling of Flowers not in Nature, each wearing a Petal-colored Dress, whose bright Shades haunt me still ☹ I took Ax along with me, Reader. Since I knew they were planning to kill me with her, I thought it best ☺

And to Kill Allan with also ☺

More on this Matter very soon ☹

I had Pony with me too, of course. He'd been a gift from Goldy Cut. *This is for you*, she'd said, offering up the pink Horse like an Organ of her Body. At first I did not want to accept, let alone talk to him, belonging as he did to Goldy Cut. Perhaps he was her Spy ☹ But as it turned out, he had no such Loyalties, for he, too, had suffered many Violences at her Hands ☹ And so we fast became great Friends ☺ Now I tucked him neatly first in my inside Pocket, then in my outside Pocket so he could better see the Happenings of our Escape ☺ He, like me, was so very excited to leave at last! More excited than even I, or so I imagined, by his many eye Sparkles. (I had begun *imagining* long before Mother gave a name to it, it seems.) I had my Razor with me too. Goldy Cut had used it to carve many Words into my Pelt, always such soft little Strokes, mostly her Phone number and Name surrounded by blobby Circles, which she said were Hearts. *My Heart*, she said, pointing to one of these misshapen Circles. Her Hand trembling so mightily when she made her many Imprints on my Body that the Words and numbers still appear to be trembling too.

But I Digress.

Pony, Razor, and Ax, these were my only Friends in the World, each one useful in their Way. Pony and Razor in my Pockets, and Ax fitting very comfortably inside my velvet Blazer the deep blue color of Twilight Time. There was even a hook within the lining for me to hang her on. Ax fit so perfectly there that twas almost Too Good to Be True, almost as if I were in a *Story*—a Fiction or one of those Moving Pictures—where the Narrative Stars always seem to align. Almost as if a strange kind of Fortune were following me. A Serendipity, to use the Mind Witch's most favorite Word.

Oh how the Night Air felt, Reader ☺ The cool Sweetness! The hum of Grasses! The Moon casting her silvery Light on my Face! Aerius felt alive! *Alive, alive, alive*, Pony and I might have screamed (or so I imagined Pony screamed, for his smiling Mouth never once moved). I pulsed with a new kind of Electricity. An Energy all along my Pelt. My Lips curled into quite a Smile, I felt it on my Face ☺ Though I was terribly hungry and thirsty, I did not touch the delicious-smelling Grass at my Feets, for I was still too close to my former Prison. Instead I stuffed some in my Pockets along with some cold Flowers. Then I skipped along for some Time and did not look back, not once at the smashed Triangle window. Which still gives me Nightmares to think about ☹

How long did I run, jumping up and down and up and down, shouting Free, Free, Free? I cannot tell, for such was my Exhilaration. The Moon alone witnessed my Ecstasy. Once I was far enough away, I stuffed my Mouth with as many Dandy Lions as could be held in that smiling Vessel ☺ I found there to be a crisp new Chill to their Taste. Clearly it had grown colder since the Attic Times ☹ There was a frosty Bite to each stem and Petal, to the Night Air itself.

I was just wondering about this, contemplating how much Time had truly passed, when I saw three little Monsters up ahead on the road, skipping toward me in the Dark. Each one was carrying a small orange bucket. The buckets were shaped like smiling Pumpkins. I did not like the look of these Monsters or their leering Pumpkin buckets, Reader ☹ They stopped before me. Two appeared to be little Ghosts, and the other a Devil with Horns and a large red plastic Pitchfork. They were very short Monsters.

And afeared of me, I could tell by their Eyes, which widened at the Sight of my Person. Their Fear, I confess, delighted me a little ☺

They looked at me, my Mouth full of cold (but still delicious) Dandy Lion. My velvet Blazer, my white Nightgown fluttering in the dark Breeze.

"What are *you* supposed to be?" they asked.

Pony did not like this Question; I felt him frowning in my Pocket. *Supposed to be?*

"Free," I said. The Word, Reader, gave me such a Shiver of Pleasure to say.

These Monsters looked at one another, then held up their buckets.

"Trick or Treat," they said to me. Quite hopefully, but afeared still. I stared at the leering Pumpkin Faces, those sly black Smiles. The buckets, I saw, were filled to the near top with Candy. I knew twas Candy, Reader, because I'd been fed similar Confections by my Keepers in various Forms. I had craved Clover and tender Grasses fresh from the Earth, and what had they mostly given me? A toxic, bright-colored Dust called Pixy Stix, to which I'd sorely become addicted ☹ Some vile, sweet plastic Ropes that they said were Red Vines. A monstrously hard candy called (paradoxically) a "Jolly Rancher," which I learned (the hard Way ☹) you could not bite into directly but instead had to suck for a very long Time. These three Monsters, it seemed, wanted me to add to their toxic Bounty ☹ How lucky for them that I had fresh Grasses in my Pocket to offer instead ☺ I gave them some of these Pocket Grasses, though I could feel Pony whispering, *Don't, don't!* I gave them a Dandy Lion, too. "They are cold due to the Chill," I warned, "but still delicious."

The Monsters looked at one another, presumably not knowing what to make of my Offerings. "Don't you have anything else?" This from one of the two Ghosts.

I could not part with Pony, obviously, though I noticed the Devil Child eyeing him enviously. But perhaps I could part with Razor, since I also had Ax. So I held it out with a Smile, Reader, as if to say, *For you.* Handed it forth like a Flower. And these little Monsters screamed. The two sneakered Ghosts ran promptly away into the Dark.

But the Devil, who'd been eyeing Pony, stayed. Stared at me, not seeming able to stop himself. Almost as if he were drinking me, Reader. My Dress, my Pearls, my Blazer blue as the Night itself, the Razor I twirled in my Hand. Mostly he stared at my Face as if he were lost there. I was used to this Manner of Staring; it had been a staple of my Attic Times. Though I despised my Keepers, I confess their obvious Enchantment always did delight me ☺ It reminded me that even though I was bound and in their Power, I had Powers of my own. And so the Boy's Fixation pleased me. I put away the Razor and, as I did so, felt compelled to reach into my Pocket again, though I knew it to be empty. And twas funny, but something was in there this Time. Like Magic, it had appeared (and perhaps this Story Magic of which I spoke earlier was responsible). A Jolly Rancher, twas ☺ Watermelon ☺ On the wrapper, a wedge of the Fruit smiling broadly at us both ☺

I handed it to the little Devil, put the Candy right in his open Hoof, which was trembling slightly. And how funny that I quite enjoyed the Tremble, Reader, that I was having such an Effect! He appeared completely entranced. My Keepers often used this Word, "entranced," to describe my Effect upon them. *You cast such a Spell*, Murder Fairy often said, *that I probably have to murder you. Because I don't want to share you, Bunny. Because if I can't have you, No One can.*

The Devil looked down at the Jolly Rancher as if twere something more than mere Candy. "Al?" a Woman's Voice called softly somewhere.

"Who are you?" he whispered.

"Aerius," I whispered back.

"Al!" the Woman's Voice called again, seeming to get closer.

The Boy, who perhaps was named Al, ignored her. "Aerius," he repeated, as though learning the name of a lovely Song. So lost in my Face, and I marveling at how lost he was there. Wanting him to be more lost still. I looked at his own Face, which was painted all over with shining red flecks.

"I enjoy this Glitter," I said to the Boy, touching his Cheek. "Tis so sparkly. May I have some?"

"Al? Where are you?"

The Boy nodded, as if in a Trance. He swiped at his Face and brushed the residual Glitter gently onto my Cheeks like I had seen my Keepers do with what they call Rouge. He smiled. And I smiled at his Smiling. Twas a moment of Great Electric Beauty, Reader. Of Transcendent Connection between us. Ax slipped from my Blazer onto the cold, sparkly pavement with a soft Clatter.

"ALAN!" the Voice roared now. "Alan Michael Foxworthy, you come here right now! Where are you?"

And something happened to my Body then, Reader, at the sound of this Name. My Hands on the Boy's Shoulders. Suddenly gripping them tight. "*Allan?*" I repeated.

The Boy startled and I startled too, Reader. So viscerally connected we were in this Moment. Fear brightening his Eyes anew. "Allan," I said, gripping his Shoulders tighter still. And then the Words came to me like a Song, the Song of my Blood. "Kill Allan," I whispered, reaching down for my Ax, which had perhaps dropped to the Ground for this very Reason ☺

Kill Allan, Kill Allan, Kill Allan.

I had just raised my Ax over his Head, as he stood there watching her like she was a lovely Falling Star, when I heard another Voice pierce the Night. Familiar. Terrible. "Aerius!"

Twas the high Voice of one of my Keepers ☹ Goldy Cut, possibly Murder Fairy.

"Aerius, where are you?"

How it made my Blood cold, Reader, to hear this Voice calling me ☹ How it froze me there in Fear before Allan ☹ I looked around me, wildly, Ax in Hand. But I could see no Sign of them. No Petal-colored Dress, no shining Hairs. Had I imagined the Voice, or were they truly out there hunting for me? I turned back to Allan to ask him for his Thoughts on this before I killed him, but I found he'd gone ☹ Run off and disappeared into the Dark ☹ Leaving only his leering Pumpkin bucket behind, its many bright-colored Poisons spilling onto the sidewalk. I stared at these Poisons, recalling Goldy Cut handing them to me by the Fistful, a wavering Smile on her Face. *Sweets to make you sweet*, she'd whispered.

Twas then I grew Sad, Reader ☹ For unless I was *imagining* Things (☺), I was already being pursued ☹ And I had failed to kill Allan, who had strangely grown so much shorter than when I'd first seen him from the Garden, walking toward his Subaru—which was quite curious. Though *why* I wished to kill him, I did not know, Reader. Why, at the sound of his Name, did such sharp Longing fill my Blood? And why did I feel as if to kill him would bring a kind of strange Relief?

This was all quite curious too.

"But then, the ways of Nature *are* curious, aren't they?" I asked Pony.

Yes, Pony whispered from my Pocket.

"Aerius!" cried the Voice again. Voices. Growing louder and closer now. And so I, like Allan, disappeared into the Dark.

I ran until I could no longer hear them dogging me, until I felt I'd left their Shadows in the Dust. I found my Self on a dark, winding street, lit by many a strange orange Light. Pumpkins leered at me from every doorstep, every window. Monsters large and small walked past me in the Dark, brushing past my velvet Shoulders. Some in large Clusters, some alone. A shrieking Laughter came from I knew not where. Perhaps the Night was laughing at me, Reader ☹ Everywhere I looked, Men made of Bones sat on porch steps staring idly into my Soul ☹

All these Sights and Sounds uneased Pony terribly. They uneased me, too, I confess.

"Pony," I whispered into my Pocket, "is this really the World?"

Pony did not answer this Time; he sometimes fell silent for long Spells. Without Allan to Kill, with my Keepers after me, the Night lost much of its Joy, Reader ☹ Grew cold and strange ☹ I suddenly started to feel quite alone in this bizarre new World where Allans could shrink without Warning and Dandy Lions were bitten through with Frost and every Shadow or Sound could be a Keeper with an Ax wanting to revise me ☹ I longed for that little Monster's Face on mine again, looking at me with such Wonder and Fear, even if he was Allan and I must Kill Allan ☹

I longed perhaps, for the first Time, Reader, for a Friend ☹

Twas then I heard Sounds of a faint but buoyant Music playing nearby. Voices shouting in Delight. Up ahead I saw a big house on a Hill, quite lit up with the prettiest Lights. I was dazzled by these Lights and by the Sounds of Rejoicing seemingly coming from within ☺ I felt a sense of Giddiness return to me. A sense of the Night's great Possibilities ☺ Perhaps all that Light would heat up the cold Earth, and I would find warmer Dandy Lions and more tender Grasses there. Perhaps there too I would find a Friend ☺

As I approached the house, the Lights and rejoicing Sounds grew so much louder, which was entrancing and drew me ever nearer ☺ Monsters were entering the front door in large numbers. It seemed a very popular Destination, this house. There were strange Characters etched over the door— Letters but not English Letters. Greek, I recognized from the many ancient Texts that Insatiable liked to read to me, alongside her Post-structuralist Theories ☹ *Forgive me*, she often whispered hotly during these Readings, her dirty fingernails digging into my Shoulder, her unbrushed Hairs in my Face. *But I'm Insatiable.* To see those Characters made me (and Pony) not a little nervous, Reader. Reminded me that my Keepers were surely still out there hunting for me so that they could continue with their terrible Revision ☹ This Revision seemed to involve a lot of Hair Braidings, a lot of Sighing in my Face with Tears shining in their Eyes, a lot of touching my Hands as though not believing them to be Real. A lot of asking me to tell them something, please, and me never knowing what to tell, for I sensed each Keeper wanted something quite Specific, some quite particular String of Words, and these particular Words I could not guess ☹ A lot of begging me to run away with them, *please*, and not tell the Others, *please*, a lot of saying the word *Mine* and grasping my Wrist quite tightly, sometimes asking me, shyly, if I'd like to make out or receive something called Oral. Or if I might like to give them Oral. *Please.* Though they thankfully never went so far as to impose their actual Bodies on me, Reader, they did subject me, quite extensively, to their Longings ☹

Much as I did not want to be alone, much as I wanted to go into the house with its warming Lights and happy Sounds, I also did not want to be discovered by Insatiable ☹ Or Goldy Cut, or Murder Fairy even though I had her Ax now. Certainly I did not want to be found by the Mind Witch ☹ This house was filled with Monsters, after all, and perhaps one or all of my Keepers were among them ☹

What was I to do?

I was pondering this Question when I felt something at my Feets. There, lying on the frostbitten Grass: a Rabbit's Face. Plastic. Pink. Smiling at me. How familiar (and yet not familiar) this Face seemed to me—its pudgy pink Cheeks full of stiff white Whiskers and its Eyes two black Holes framed with pretty Eyelashes. Long pink Ears with furry white Tufts grew out of its Head. Something about these Ears in particular filled me with a kind of odd Longing, Reader. Twas like looking into a slightly off Mirror, I cannot tell why. I picked up the Face—a *Mask*, I would learn twas called— and placed it over my own. I felt it belonged there somehow, belonged on me. There was an elastic that went around the back of my Head that held it in Place. Suddenly I saw the World through these very small Holes, and though twas harder to breathe, twas also somewhat easier to absorb my Surroundings this Way. Twas easier to *Be*—do you understand this Feeling, Reader? Suddenly I felt Free again. A different kind of Free. Like I could hide and yet show my Self at the very same Time ☺

I ran inside the house quite eagerly then. Ax in Hand and this Rabbit's Face on mine.

Eager, very eager, to make new Friends ☺

II

H ello, Friends!" I shouted when I came in the door, waving Ax. Everyone waved and screamed delightedly, Reader.

"Whoa, Bro!"

"What the fuck?"

A Party, twas ☺ At something called a Frat, or so a passing Zombie told me. There was much wild Laughter here and many screaming Monsters in Polo Shirts wearing scary Creature Masks of various sorts, drinking quite exuberantly from large red plastic cups or else from long hoses attached to giant barrels. A jolly Music played, by Someone called The Smiths. Played so loudly that I could barely hear my own Mind, Reader. In my Pocket I felt Pony's Head was going to explode from the many Sights and Sounds! A very merry bunch of Frat Monsters they seemed to be. All of them congregating in a large living room full of beany bags and fainting couches. There were dead Animal Heads on the wall (which made me shudder a little to behold), and the room smelled heavily of Goldy Cut, whenever she was *just a wee bit tipsy on the Juniper Sap.* Nervously I looked around for her but found no Sign ☺ Not of her nor of any of them ☺ Twas then I recalled her using the Word *Frat* as though she were spitting it. As though the Word was physically distasteful to her and she needed to eject it from her Body as quickly as possible. This delighted me to recall, Reader ☺ I would be safe here, surely, among these drunk Monsters, all gathering around me now, smiling at me through their Creature Masks. Waving their plastic cups as they pointed their Fingers at me and screamed, "What the Fuck?" Or, "Whoa, who the Fuck are you supposed to be, Bro?"

"Free," I said.

"Rad," a Monster said. "That's some *Donnie Darko* shit, Bro."

"Into *American Psycho* much?"

"Echo and the Bunnymen Fan?" another cried.

"Yes," I said. Even though I did not know who Donnie Darko was, Reader. Or who American Psycho was. Or Echo and the Bunnymen ☹ Still, tis always good to say Yes rather than No ☺ It makes Faces happier, I find.

"Yes, yes, yes!" I cried. For their Eyes were all on me now, Reader, and this felt very good ☺ Made me bounce a little to the Song playing, which was very buoyant and not at all like the melancholy Harps and high-pitched Wailings of the Playlist, to which I had long been subjected ☹

"Cool Ax, Bro."

"Yes!" I agreed. "She is quite chilled from the Night Air!" And I swung her round most merrily. They all laughed, some a little nervously. *What the fuck?* Which did delight me ☺

"Hot," many Girl Monsters whispered, giggling among themselves at my Person. These Girl Monsters—shiny-haired and smelling of false Flowers—reminded me a little too much of my Keepers ☹ So I steered clear of them, Reader, though I did enjoy their obvious Admiration ☺ The Song playing now was one that Pony quite liked and that I liked too, because it sounded really very much like Jumping. And in fact these Frat Monsters were now all jumping, Reader! All around me! So I jumped with them! Oh, twas Fun, twas Fun! Pony was crying with such unbridled Delight from my Pocket. He had let go at last of his Reservations, allowing himself to be carried away by the Rejoicings ☺ As we jumped, Someone gave me a Drink called Goldschläger. Twas a gold-flecked Magic Liquid that was sweet-spicy as Cinnamons ☺ Not at all like the putrid kombucha or the bitter, colorless seltzer given to me by my Keepers that fizzed most hideously ☹ I drank many thimblefuls of this Goldy Liquid, to the great Applause of the jumping Monsters all around me, and how I loved these Applause! They made me jump higher and drink more thimblefuls, twas so lovely and warming to imbibe! And when I used this word *imbibe*, how these Frat Monsters all roared at me with Delight.

"*Imbibe!*" they repeated, laughing. "This rabbit guy's a *fucking* Trip, Bro."

And I said, "YES!" For I was a Trip, I was! I loved this Word to describe my Self ☺

I was jumping really wildly now, waving my Ax around, when beside me I noticed another jumping Monster with a Black Bird on his Shoulder and a black Patch over one Eye. He was laughing and repeating that I was such a Trip, I was such a Trip. And I laughed and said he was a Trip also, and he laughed more, so I laughed more, and I don't know why, but I felt somehow we might become Friends, I felt this Potential ☺ For he was smiling and jumping close to me now, jumping quite as high as I was, looking at my Ax with such Wonder. And he whispered, "Is the Ax . . . uh, Real, Bro?"

"Real?" I said.

Twas such a funny Word to me, Reader. I still didn't quite grasp its Meaning, though my Keepers had often taken such Pains to explain. Especially the Mind Witch ☹ *Real*, she might begin, stroking my Arm with her very long-fingered Hands, *is when something is here in the World and not just in your Mindscape anymore. When it is here with you in the Attic. Right in front of your Face and you still can't fucking believe it.* She looked at me, Tears in her Eyes, her Talons sinking deeply into my forearm Flesh.

"What *is* Real?" I said now to the Man with the Eye Patch.

And he laughed and said, "Oh, Bro, you just made my Head, like, explode, k?"

"I did? Oh, that is wonderful," I cried. We were both of us jumping very wildly, in Time with each other quite like a Dance. Sometimes my Keepers would make me dance with them, especially Goldy Cut ☹ How she loved to do what she called Slow Dance ☹ She'd play what she called a Power Ballad (those soft Swells still assail my Soul to recall, Reader ☹), place my Hands on her terribly soft Shoulders, sometimes on her Back or Waist, and make us rock together in Time to the yearning Strains, her golden Head pressed fiercely into my Chest, weeping and laughing at the same Time.

I did not care for that kind of Dancing, Reader. Not at all ☹

But this kind of jumping Dancing I loved ☺

"What is Real, what is Real, what is Real?!" I sang, jumping and jumping and jumping and turning round and round as I jumped. The Goldy Liquid made the Words tumble quite silkily off my Tongue.

And he laughed and said, "Whoa, Bro, my Philosophy seminar's not till tomorrow at nine fifteen, k? Plus I didn't even do the Reading!"

"Me too!" I screamed, thinking of the many Readings I had left behind in the Attic ☺

"Wait, you're in my class, Bro?"

"No, but I would LOVE to be! So long as we may keep jumping! So long as we may jump together forever!"

"Fuck yes!"

"FUCK YES!" I cried.

"Is this for Real, Bro?" he whispered, still jumping as I was jumping, not looking at the Ax this Time, but at my Face. Or rather the Mask I'd placed over my Face, which also strangely felt like my Face. "Like as in you and I dancing together right now and this Music and these Lights? You know, *Reality*." And he smiled at me. His one Eye was most lovely, Reader.

"Oh, it's definitely Reality," I said. And he laughed and said once more that I was a Trip, a real Trip, and I agreed I was. And I said, "Is your Black Bird Reality?" And he said, "Fuck yes, it's Reality." And now we were jumping really very close together, Reader, twas quite a lovely Moment of Transcendent Connection, of Great Electric Beauty. And he whispered, "You're not Queer, are you?" And I said, "Queer?" And his Eyes said, *Say no but mean yes.* So I said, "No," but I smiled *Yes*, and he said, "Thank god." He took another large thimbleful of the Goldy Liquid and handed me one too, and both of us imbibed and the Music slowed then. Suddenly I noticed that we were no longer in the living room but another Place, that in our wild Jumpings we'd somehow leapt quite far away from the other Frat Monsters, Reader. That we were now upstairs, alone, in a small room with very red walls. Many dead Animal Heads hung on these walls, as well as Guns. I stared at the shining Animal Eyes, the gleaming

Barrels, and felt a Fear run through my Pelt quite like a Lightning Flash. I looked back at my Monster Friend with the Eye Patch. He was smiling at me strangely now, his handsome Face very red from all the Goldy Liquid he had imbibed. Quite lovely he was to behold. The Music playing was quite like the Power Ballads Goldy Cut enjoyed, and we were no longer jumping but swaying together, rocking almost, quite close, almost like we were *Slow Dancing*. Though I felt quite uneasy in this room, I did not mind dancing in this Way with this Monster. "Has anyone ever told you you look like that Actor?" he whispered to me. "In all the Movies right now. The hot One."

"Yes," I said, though I had no idea, Reader. I felt strangely like he wanted to kiss me, and in Truth I felt a similar Longing. He was really a most handsome Monster, Reader, the exquisite Symmetry of his Face accentuated beautifully by the Eye Patch. Instead he took a very long Sip of his Drink.

"It's actually supposedly to be a Raven," he said. Shaking his broad Shoulder, upon which the giant Bird sat.

"A Raven?" I looked at this large Bird. Its sharp Beak and shining Eyes suddenly seemed quite Cruelle. Mocking. Capable of anything. I felt my Heart curl into a small Fist.

The Monster's smile brightened then. "You're not *scared*, are you? Are Bunnies scared of Ravens?" he whispered, fingering the Whiskers on my other Face.

I shook my Head. "No," I lied. And he brought the Bird up to my Nose and screamed, "BOO," then laughed a little at my Cowering. I did not care for that, Reader ☹

"Well, they *are* Predators, I guess," he said, pulling me back to him gently. "For poor, sweet Bunnies." He looked at me tenderly with his one Eye. I felt a strange Excitement then, even as the Animal Heads, the red walls, the gleaming Guns, filled me with an increasing Unease. And then his lovely Eye suddenly grew hard and sharp. He laughed again. Whether at himself or me, I could not tell.

"Relax, Bro," he whispered, letting me go. "It's not really *Real*, k? It never was."

"Never?" I whispered.

"Nah. It's from some fucking *Poem*, apparently." He shrugged and drank more of the Goldy Liquid. Sucked thoughtfully on a Pen of Vapors, which he'd pulled from his Pocket. The Vapors smelled of Bubble Gums. "Called 'Nevermore' or something?"

"'The Raven,' you idiot," said a Voice. I turned and noticed another Monster, half passed out on a torn couch behind us, opening one Eye. "By Poe?"

"Poe, that's it," my Monster said, nodding.

"He wrote 'The Tell-Tale Heart,' Bro. Classic shit, " this Couch Monster pontificated. Quite out of it himself from the Goldy Liquid. He was gripping a red plastic cup, whose amber Contents were spilling onto the floorboards.

"What the fuck is 'Tell-Tale Heart'?" my Monster said.

"You know, where the Dude hacks this other Dude up just because he doesn't like his Eye for whatever Reason. And then he hides his Body Parts in the Floor? Sick *Fuck*, Bro."

"*Smart* Fuck!" my Monster laughed, winking at me.

"Good one, Bro," said the Couch Monster.

"Good one," I agreed, though I did not know. "Yes. A very, very good one," I said. "And who, may I ask, is this Writer again?" For his Name, Poe, rang a strange Bell from the Attic Times.

"You know the fucking Dude, Dude. Edgar something?"my Monster said.

"Allan!" the Couch Monster cried. "And just fyi, Poe didn't have an Eye Patch, Bro."

"Bro, this is an injury from *Lacrosse*, k?" my Monster shot back, defensively. "Which I don't even want to play. My stepdad makes me."

"Allan?" I repeated. And my Soul, Reader, suddenly grew quite cold.

"Allan, yeah!" my Monster said, most happily. Blowing his Vapors at me and grinning. Offering me his Pen. "Edgar Allan fucking Poe, Bro."

A kind of Electricity passed through my Body, Reader. A Darkness gripped my Heart. For here he was again: Allan. Now grown tall (he was quite the Shape-Shifter, I was learning!). Swaying before me with a Patch on his Eye and a Cruelle Raven on his Shoulder. Laughing drunkenly about how he did not know the fucking "Tell-Tale Heart," k? *Sorry, not sorry. Ha ha.* His one lovely Eye on me, going soft, then hard, then soft. Well, he should probably go back to his room now, he said, to do his Philosophy Readings. The Prof liked to give a Pop Quiz and such. And the Ax in my Hand suddenly became Alive with Purpose, hot and loud with Whispers: *Hello, hello! Kill Allan! Kill Allan!* The Impulse consumed me. I must kill him or I should never be relieved of its Dark Grip ☹ And so down Ax came onto Allan ☺ Onto Allan's Neck specifically, Reader ☺ What a sharp cracking Sound she made when she struck Tendon, then Bone! So that Allan's Head was severed quite cleanly from his Body in one Strike ☺ Blood! So much Blood everywhere in the most wondrous of Splatters. Blood all over my own Hands, still gripping Ax, herself bloody and trembling as I was trembling. Trembling because we had done it, we had killed Allan ☺ There was his headless Body lying at my Feets, his Blood pooling darkly on the floorboards, quite red as the walls. I should feel Relief now. So why then, Reader, did I feel none at all? ☹ Perplexed, I watched Allan's Head sort of slowly rolling away like it might strangely be Alive still. And the Couch Monster, himself covered in Blood Splatter as well as some quivering pink Gristle, still sitting on the torn couch with the plastic cup in his Hand, watched the Head rolling, a mildly amused look on his Face.

"Oh, very fucking funny, Tyler," he said to the Head. "Ha ha *ha.* You're not getting me this Time, k? I'm not falling for it." He shook his own Head, still affixed to his Body. "Not this year." He kicked lightly at Allan's Head. "Tyler!" he called. "Dude, get *up.*"

"Tyler?" I looked at the Head. "Your name is Tyler?" I whispered to it.

The Head seemed to nod a little. *Yes. Tyler.*

Oh god, I thought.

Oops ☹

Oops, Oops, Oops!

Twas a Word I knew well, for my Keepers used it often, especially Goldy Cut. *Oops*, she often said, smiling wildly, whenever she pressed her Lips against my various Extremities ☻ *Oops, Oops!*

What is Oops? I once asked her, afeared.

It is a sound you make when there has been a terrible, terrible Accident, she whispered, her Face very close to my Face. *Like this!* And then she kissed me quite heatedly on the Nose.

"Oops," I whispered now.

And then, Reader, there was Screaming. So much of it suddenly all around me. I joined in with it like Singing. The Couch Monster was screaming and I was screaming and Pony was screaming in my Pocket, and there was more Screaming still, from all of us, when I attempted to put the Wrong Allan's Head back on his Body so as to bring him back to Life, hopefully. Alas, to no Avail ☻ There was even more Screaming as the Head dropped from my Hands and rolled away again; so strangely and happily it rolled toward the door, the Face itself smiling though bloody. Almost as if it had a Mind of its own. Which I guess it technically did, Reader. And the Couch Monster kept screaming and then laughing, perhaps not knowing which to do, what to believe. "Very fucking funny, Dude," he kept shouting from his torn Perch, even though he looked wildly afeared. Meanwhile, the severed Head rolled right out of the room and into the hall, Reader. We watched it tumble down the stairs leading into the living room, where the Frat Monsters were still in the midst of their great Party. Imminently they would all discover my Oops ☻ I turned to the Couch Monster, who was staring from the Body to the Ax in my bloody Hand. "I should probably take my leave now," I told him quietly.

"Oh my god, you really fucking killed him, didn't you? For Real."

"What is Real?" I whispered, bracing my Self for living room Screams. Surely the Wrong Allan's Head was making its Way down the stairs now and the Frat Monsters would notice. But I heard only the Sound of Laughter.

"Oh my god!"

"Awwww!"

"How did he get in here?"

"Cute!"

Cute? I thought of the severed Head. I did not know if twas *cute*, but perhaps twas? I was about to ask the Couch Monster for his Thoughts on this, but he was screaming terrifically now. "You killed him! You really fucking killed him! Oh my god, you're a sick FUCK!" And he reached out for one of the many Guns on the red wall.

The Animal Eyes there flashed. *Run*, I felt their Heads tell me.

So I did run, Reader. Right out the window, which thankfully I did not have to break with Ax. Twas already open, almost as if waiting for me to jump out of it, back into the dark Night.

III

Having killed the Wrong Allan, I left the Frat Party quite Dejected, Reader ⊗

Oops, I thought. *Oops, Oops, Oops!*

Twas my melancholy Refrain ⊗

Dejectedly, I sucked on a Pixy Stix I found in my dress Pocket, for I felt I deserved no Flowers ⊗ It tasted like so much bland pink Dust ⊗ The Darkness from which I'd sought Relief still gripped my Heart ⊗ My Head was swimming from the Goldy Liquid as I zigzagged my Way through the Night, the bloody Ax in my Hand. The jumping Music still roared in my Ears along with the Couch Monster's many Screams, yet the Moon smiled as if she did not know of my troubled Heart, and the Grass cooled my Feets refreshingly. So refreshing was the Feel of the Grass that it nearly brought Tears to my Eyes, Reader. A strange Flash came to me then. A Vision. Of my Self in another Body, quite small and furry, with a twitching Nose full of Whiskers. I was crouched in Grasses quite like these, hiding under Shrubs to protect from giant Birds in the Sky like the one on the Wrong Allan's Shoulder, partaking of some delicate Cowslips while the Hum of the Wind made a jumping Song in my Ears. Odd. Something in the Feel of the Earth just then, its fresh green Scent, had brought on this Flash. Brought me back to what felt like another Life, some other Self I had once been, some other Shape I may once have taken in a different World. A Place from which I was now forever Estranged ⊗ Severed as the Head of the Wrong Allan ⊗ I'd had such Flashes before, Reader, of what I called this Lost Self, this Lost Place. I did not understand them or how they pertained to me. Why did my Feets love the Grasses so?

I attempted once to share these Flashes with the Mind Witch, and she looked at me a long Time, her Face a cold Stone. At last she told me I'd had

one too many Pixy Stix. I was to be cut off from Sugars forever ☹ Goldy
Cut, when I told her, looked like she was going to punch me or herself, I did
not know which. Then she said she would no longer be sharing her Juniper Sap with me and twas only Lady Grey tea from now on, and she poured
me a cup with her trembling Hands. Murder Fairy appeared to weep for
me when I told her about my Flash. She contemplated the Blade of her Ax,
which she always brought with her into the Attic when she revised me. *That
is not a Flash*, she said slowly, turning her Ax round and round, Eyes on my
Eyes with what felt like sudden Pity. *It is a Memory*, she said. I felt a Shiver
then, like I do whenever Someone gives a Name to something I cannot see
or touch. *A Memory*, I repeated. She nodded. *What does it mean?* I whispered.

But Murder Fairy had walked away sadly, clip-clopping on her fairy
Heels. Muttering, *What have we done, what have we done?*

Insatiable, when I told her, was simply more Insatiable. Fingered my
Hairs dreamily. *That's hot*, she said. *Tell me more*, she said, *about this Lost
Place. About your small, furry Body, the Cowslip Taste on your Tongue and the
cool Shade of Shrubs and your very long Ears, which hear the jumping Song of
the Wind.*

But I never could tell, Reader ☹ To tell of such Things was not something I sensed I could do. Not in this Attic or even in this Language, the Language of Insatiable and my Keepers, the Language of this strange Pixy Dust
Place in which I'd found my Self, with only a Triangle of Sky through which
to see the World. It needed another kind of Language to tell, I sensed, one
I did not know or that I knew no longer. And my human Mouth could not
make its Shapes.

I ripped off my Mask, that other Face, to feel the Air on my actual Face.
My *Real* Face, as the Wrong Allan might have said. Or was it? I stared down
at the plastic Rabbit Mask to which I'd felt such a strange Kinship, the long
Ears and Whiskers splattered now with the Wrong Allan's Blood. The
adorable Smile caked with Gristle, which made it quite afearing to behold.
I threw it into the Fire that suddenly appeared at my Feets, watched it melt
and hiss.

"What have I done?" I asked Pony. But it seemed he would not speak to me. Refused, it felt like. I took him out of my Pocket and stared into his ever-sparkling Eyes.

"Pony," I whispered. "What am I?"

He seemed to behold me coldly. He judged me, perhaps, for my Oops ☹ Quite like I had many times judged Goldy Cut for hers ☹

How alone I felt then, Reader. And very Sad ☹ I had killed a potential Friend ☹ *Tyler*, with whom I'd been having such good Times ☺ We'd had such a compelling Conversation about Birds and Axes and the Nature of Reality. I felt almost like we might even have kissed. Yes, he had attempted to afear me with his Bird ☹ But apart from that, all had been going so very wonderfully between us ☺ Until he'd said his Name was Allan and I'd severed his Head quite cleanly from his Body ☹ I can only hope he feels much better soon ☺ I can only hope his Head and Body will meet again and that tis a wonderful Reunion ☺ As I hope you and I will meet too someday, Reader. And that tis similarly Wonderful ☺

I was just in the midst of burning my other Face, Reader, watching its violent Happiness dissolve into the crackling Flames, wondering about this Flash—this *Memory*—that the Grasses had just now given my Feets, when something floated out of the Dark. Some*one*. I froze at this approaching Shape. Could it be one of my Keepers? Oh god, could it be the Mind Witch? Could it be a Cruelle Someone coming to scold me about my Oops? Could it be, at long last, the *Right* Allan? I tightened my Grip on Ax just in case. In my Pocket I felt Pony holding his Breath. *Oh god*, he murmured. His Nerves were understandably quite shattered by the Happenings of this Night. *Shhh*, I told him soothingly.

What is it now, what is it now? he whispered.

Another Monster. Tall as I was and quite broad shouldered. Seeming to float right out of the cold Dark.

"Hello!" he cried. He had a pale green Face, two giant Bolts on either side of his Neck. At first he quite terrified both Pony and my Self, Reader, though he was waving and waving in such a friendly Way. I noticed there were Stitches above his Brow, as if he had recently had some kind of Forehead Surgery ☹ The Bolts and Stitches looked like serious Ouches, yet they did not seem to trouble him. He was practically skipping toward us, quite jollily. And then I recognized him, and when I did, a Wave of such Joy passed over me, Reader ☺

"Aerius," he called. "Hey, Aerius!" Waving still.

"You *know* me?" I said to the famous Monster.

"Sure I know you," the Monster said. He seemed so certain. Though his Face was not smiling, was not even moving, I heard the Smile in his Voice, Reader, which was already doing some jumping, skipping Thing to my Heart. "Don't you recognize me, too?" he said gently.

"Of course," I whispered. "I watched you many a Night on the wall, dear Monster. You comforted me so much during my Attic Times—I related deeply to your many Trials and Misunderstandings. I just never expected to meet you here, in Reality. Though I wished for it."

The Monster looked confused. "The wall?"

He took his Face off. Twas a Mask, apparently, just like the one I'd worn at the Party (but far more seamless, far more Real). Underneath was another Face entirely, Reader, and when I saw it, I felt a Wave of even greater Joy.

Twas the Boy.

The One I had encountered on the street with my Keepers back when they were first luring me away from the Garden toward the Attic, where they would imprison me ☹ I remembered his Hairs the Color of young Dandy Lions and his Eyes the Color of delicate Grasses and softest Earth and how his dreamy Expression seemed to smile so prettily at Everything and Nothing. He was smiling at me now, just like that. "You know me now, right?" he said.

"Yes," was all I could say, with such a Smile in my own Voice. "I know you now."

And what happened then, Reader? To my Body, I cannot even tell. Perhaps there is no Language for this, or if there is, I do not yet know it. Or perhaps this is another Instance where my Mouth cannot make its Shapes.

But I could feel it, Reader. Singing in my Heart like Wind through Grasses. "Jonah," we all said at the same Time. Pony and my Self and Jonah, in one Breath.

"Great to see you again," Jonah said.

"So great," I said. For suddenly I had few Words. Looking at Jonah, twas as if all the Words I knew had run from my Tongue and gone hiding under Shrubs.

"Sorry if I confused you," he said. Pointing up to his Monster Face, suspended now above his Head. "I guess it's not too bad a costume. I mean, for Party City."

"It's wonderful," I said. *What's Party City?* Pony whispered.

"Nothing like your costume, though," he said. I waited for him to ask what I was supposed to be, as everyone seemed to like to do. But Jonah did not ask. He just repeated that twas so great, so cool, and he looked at me appreciatingly. At my velvet Blazer and my bloody Ax and my Pearls and my nervously smiling Face. "I love it so much," he said.

"You do?"

"Oh fuck yeah. It's . . . Wild."

Oh my god, Pony whispered in my Pocket. And I truly hoped Jonah did not hear him. Sometimes Pony liked to share his Thoughts at the most inopportune Moments.

"This Blood looks so Real," he said, touching a Splatter of it on my velvet Shoulder.

"Yes," I said. "Sadly, I have killed the Wrong Allan this Night." And there were Tears in my Eyes when I shared my Oops ☹ I expected him to walk away or at least swat my Nose for it, as Goldy Cut often did. But Jonah just looked at me in a kind of wondrous Joy.

"Oh man, you have a Backstory and Everything?" He shook his Dandy Lion Head. "That's fucking brilliant."

"Really?"

He nodded. "Scary good. I love the Specificity. Like the most visceral Performance Art."

"Art," I sighed. "Yes." For this is exactly how my Keepers often described me. *You are Art. You are Our Art. You are Ours. You are fucking Mine, k?*

"Amazing," he said. "Now I feel pretty lame, you know, going as Frankenstein. Frankenstein's *Creature*, I mean. But it's a Classic, right?"

"A Classic," I said, looking at his Face. "Oh yes." I could never stop looking, I felt. And he was looking at me just the same.

"*The Modern Prometheus*," we both said, and smiled.

The Grasses brightened in his Eyes. The Moon smiled on his golden Hairs. An Urge to lick his exquisite Face passed over me. But I did not act upon it, Reader, for I would not do to Jonah what my Keepers had done to me. I would not subject him to my Longings. Unless he himself had similar Longings. Did he?

"So what are you up to?" he asked me, kicking lightly at the Grass. I heard it shiver and sigh beneath his Feets. "Heading to a Party or . . . "

"I have actually just been to one." Sirens screamed in the Night just then. Reminding me, most unpleasantly, of the Oops ☹

"Oh, at that Frat house up there?" He shuddered. "Those guys scare the fucking shit out of me. For Real."

"They do?" I thought of the Wrong Allan's great Delight in my Fear at his Bird ☹ The Guns on the red walls ☹

"Oh yeah. Sort of allergic to Frat houses. Allergic to Everything, really." He pulled a small box from his coat Pocket and grinned.

My Heart pounded. *Aerius*, I saw the box read.

"My name," I whispered.

"Oh right. Ha! Wild," he said. Every Time Jonah said *Wild*, I felt a kind of Singing along my Pelt. "Yeah, my aunt sends me this stuff from Canada. It's pretty trippy, but it works like a Charm. You want one? Here."

And then, Reader, he handed me my Self. I looked at the small blue Pill Jonah had placed in my palm. Part of me wanted to keep it forever and ever. To put it in the Pocket with Pony. Treasure it as a *Memory*. Perhaps I sensed, even then, how this would all End. Instead I swallowed it. We both did,

Jonah and I, at the very same Time, even as Pony warned me, quietly, that this may not be the best Idea. I had already imbibed quite a bit of the Goldy Liquid by then and my Head was still swimming. I did not listen, Reader. This perhaps was part of my Undoing.

"Wow," Jonah said, "looks like something crazy is going on over there at the Frat house. Like there was a Crime or something."

And indeed many fire trucks and police cars with blue and red flashing Lights appeared to be encircling the house quite like my Keepers had once encircled me, holding Dandy Lions. But No One appeared to be holding Dandy Lions in this case ☹ In fact, men were holding Guns, entering the house in Swarms.

"Yes," I agreed uneasily. I turned to Jonah, but he was lost in looking at the Sky now, smilingly oblivious, like the Sky was telling him such lovely Secrets. Stupidly I wished to be the Sky so he could smile upon me in this Way, Reader. He turned to me then, almost as if he'd heard my Thoughts. His Eyes now fixed on my Eyes. Suddenly I longed for my other Face, the Rabbit Mask I'd thrown so carelessly into the Fire. But it had long since melted away.

"We should probably get the hell out of here," he whispered.

I smiled. *We.* "Yes. We should."

"Oh hey, where are your Friends, anyway?"

"Friends?"

"Those Girls you were with when I saw you. You know Coraline and—"

"Oh. *Them.*" A most sinister Wind swept through the Trees then. I thought I heard a distant Wailing—anguished, female—pierce the Night. "I know not where they are *precisely*, but I suspect they are around," I said quite sadly.

"Did you want to go find them?"

"No." I shook my Head. "I do not want to find them, nor do I wish to ever be found by them. I want to get the Hell out of Here. With you. Wherever you are going." The Truth of these Words, Reader, rang clear in my Voice.

Made me feel Flushed and Exposed to say. As though I were not wearing Clothes and Jonah could now see the Whole of my Pelt. Could see beyond the Pelt itself, to my thrumming Heart. In my Pocket, Pony sighed. Perhaps he sensed I was Doomed.

But Jonah just smiled. "So let's go."

IV

*L*ove. My Keepers had often spoke of it, Reader. *I love you, do you love me?* they might whisper with a very low Voice, as though Someone Else might hear. *Do you love me, do you love me?* Like a wild and unending Refrain. This Word, in fact, was everywhere in the Attic Times. In the many Songs they played for me and in the many Films they showcased for my Viewing Pleasure and the many Pages of Writings they made me read in order to, as they explained, better understand their Souls ☹ Sometimes I ate this Writing, despite its bitter Taste ☹ Sometimes I tore it up to make a kind of Snow or I relieved my Self on it, watching Love become quite distorted on the Page—this was perhaps my favorite Thing to do with the Writings they gave me, especially their own ☺ Especially if they contained the word *Love*. Mostly, though, the Word was on their Lips, glossed and grazing my Ears ☹ Twas a Question whispered as they pressed their Heads into my Chest, Foreheads butting against my Rib Cage as if it were a locked door, Reader, that they were trying to break open with their Craniums ☹

Do you fucking love me?

Yes, I might lie to them. *I love.* Mainly to stop the Headbutting, Reader. To stop the Crying and the Lip Grazing, the tremulous Whispers that were always far too close to my Face. The Whispers were full of something else I could not name, but I heard its Chains, I heard its Ax. I felt its pointed pink Talons and pulsing Genitals, which sounds very strange to say.

No, I might say sometimes, if I was quite tired. *I don't love you.* Because twas true, but also (I admit) to be Cruelle. To lash back at them for locking me up ☹ For Revising me, which they said was a Process. A Process I was quickly learning I did not care for, not at all ☹

And how their Faces would fall if I said I did not Love, would never Love. Murder Fairy would look at me like she would happily grab her Ax right then and *put us all out of our fucking Misery*. Goldy Cut would wince, and then she'd gulp her Juniper Sap, pretend she hadn't heard me. The Mind Witch would weep uncontrollably, twas the only Time I ever saw her Face break. *I hate you*, she might scream-hiss. But this was a Lie, as we both knew. The Love was there in her Eyes, more legible, in fact, than any of her diamond Writings—wild and terrible and possessing her, and she was afeared. Insatiable, on the other Hand, would only smile somewhat sadly and say, *A Challenge. I humbly accept.*

Depending on how I felt that Day, I might enjoy their Face Fallings, Reader. I might even relish in them ☺ Very rarely did I feel truly sad for them ☹ That tis an Ouch to love what doesn't love you, you see, is something I did not yet fully understand.

Now I know tis a deeper Ouch than any Razor Swipe ☹

Tis an inside Ouch, which has no Cure, perhaps, but Time ☹

In any case, Reader, my first Understanding of Love came from the Attic Times. And so you can imagine, quite naturally, that I did not think very fondly of it. That I thought *Love* to be quite a terrible and violent Thing.

And yet.

And yet, and yet, and yet. On this Night, when I looked at Jonah walking beside me in the Dark, smoking and smiling at the Moon, which suddenly seemed so much closer to the Earth, this was precisely the Word that came skipping into my Heart, making it pound and pound. It came to me again when he offered me a Cigarette. Which I did take from him, Reader, though my Keepers told me I must never smoke; Goldy Cut said twas for Whores, like Lippy Stick, and was I a Whore? Well, Reader, Tonight I guess I was ☺ I took the Cigarette from Jonah like I had taken his small blue Pill, like I would have taken Anything. And when I couldn't light it, how beautifully he showed me that I had to suck on it softly, see? Like this. Just the Filter. Then hold the Flame to the opposite end, sucking lightly, until it caught Fire and started to Smoke, see?

I saw, Reader.

And when I failed to light it at first, he did not lose his Patience with me the Way my Keepers did whenever I did not perform according to their many Expectations ☹ Instead he smiled and lit my Cigarette with his Cigarette ☺ Told me to place the Tip of mine against the Tip of his so that I might catch his Fire. And when he beamed at me through the twisting Smoke, it sang in my Heart again.

I love you.

"Sorry?" Jonah said.

"This Cigarette," I said. "I love this Cigarette. So much."

Twas one of my first Lies, Reader. Love has made of me a Liar. It has since made me many Things, but above all, a Liar. Did he see the Love on my Face as I had so often seen the Love on my Keepers' Faces, their Features twisted with the shameful Violence of it? If he did, he did not say.

"I love it too," Jonah said, holding up his Cigarette thoughtfully. "Though it'll kill me probably."

"It'll kill me, too, I think," I whispered. I knew, I knew.

"So we can die together," he said, and I heard a kind of Music in my Mindscape then. Those Ballads of Goldy Cut's started to make a kind of dazzling and terrible Sense. Snippets of them began to ring in my Ears.

"I would love that," I said. There was the Word again. *Dangerous*, whispered Pony. Yet how good it felt to say aloud, even in this Context.

"I would love, love, love that," I said again as we made our winding Way through the Dark. With Jonah at my Side, the leering Pumpkins no longer scared me, Reader, nor did the staring Men of Bones nor the many Monsters screaming past us on their Way to or from their many Parties. I was happy, even though at this Point I was likely being pursued by both my Keepers and the Polices ☹ Of the two Hunting Parties, twas my Keepers of whom I was more afeared ☹ Each Time I heard a Siren approaching (and there were many), my Heart froze, for I did not wish to go to Jail, I did not wish to be arrested, though I was indeed sorry I had killed the Wrong Allan and continued to hope that his Condition would improve ☺ I did not wish to be parted from my new Friend so soon ☹ (Also, I still had the *right* Allan to find and kill ☺) But my Heart froze even more, Reader, at the sound of any female Voice rising in the Night. I braced my Self for that Voice to sound familiar, come closer, call my Name.

"You okay?" Jonah asked worriedly.

"Oh yes, thank you." More Lies ☹

He grinned. "Cool. Oh wow, here we are already." And he pointed to some sort of sad-looking house up ahead.

I stared at this sad house. Truly, I cared not where we were, Reader. *Anywhere with you*, I thought, *so long as tis far from Sirens and Jails and Keepers*. But this house did give me a bad Feeling ☹

"What is this Place?" I asked.

Jonah smiled. "Oh, didn't I say? This is a Poetry bar. They're doing a Midnight Reading."

"Poet Tree?" A Darkness filled my Soul then.

"What's—"

"I hate Poet Trees! And all Poets!" I said these Words so quickly, Reader, before I could even think. What I had meant to say was *I will go fucking Anywhere with you*. "I loathe all Poets," I shouted instead, and again it felt as though I was not speaking of my own Will. As if these Words had come not from my Heart but from some other Place within me. The same Place, perhaps, that must Kill Allan. I looked at Jonah. Oh god, had I ruined Things between us? But he just laughed. What a happy Music his Laughter made in the Night, quite like a jumping Song ☺

"Well, I hope you don't hate me, then."

My Heart froze. "*What?* You're not ..."

"Afraid so. I'm writing a Poem in my Head right now, in fact," he said, coming in close.

"You are?" Oh god, Reader ☹

"About you," he whispered into my Ear.

Oh god, Reader ☺ Melting, I was melting now.

"Poet Tree can be amazing," he said softly. He looked at me and my Pelt grew hotter still. "Plus No One ever comes to this bar, so it's a really chill space. Anything goes."

"No One comes?" Twas the one positive about Poet Trees in this circumstance, I reasoned, that they might provide me good cover.

"Well, sometimes some of the Faculty come. And this Woman who always seems to have a really bad Cold. Or maybe she has Allergies. If she does, they're worse than mine."

"Faculty?" And I immediately recalled the first Allan. The One I had seen so long ago, in the Rose Garden, whom I had failed to kill ☹ His Physiology inspiring in me a Violence both inexplicable and Fathoms deep. "You mean Allan might come?" I asked, and I felt something in me awaken, quite in spite of my Self.

"Oh, the Fiction guy? Yeah, he might."

"Then I will go," I said immediately, gripping Ax more tightly. No more Hesitation. I wondered then if I might not be possessed by some other shadow Spirit, some other shadow Will. If my Mindscape, Reader, was not entirely my own. Though I was physically Free, far away from the Attic and its Ropes, perhaps they held me still ☹ Why did I not want to go to the bar simply to be with Jonah, even if I did hate Poet Trees? But now that I might Kill Allan there, the Decision to go seemed so very clear (despite the Poet Trees ☹).

"I'll go for you," I lied, though I did want it to be true. The minute I began to love, Reader, I began to lie, it seems.

"Awesome!" Jonah said. "Who knows, maybe you'll even fall in Love with it."

"Maybe," I whispered.

"If you give it a Chance, it can fucking blow your Mind, I promise." He smiled and took my Hand. And for a brief Moment, Reader, I forgot Everything. Wished to stay with him under the Moon, his Touch warming me through, all the Way to my Heart. Twas then, just over his Shoulder, that I thought I saw my Keepers on the road, in the near Distance ⊗ Faces Pale with Longings. Dresses shimmering in the Dark. "Aerius! Aerius!"

"Hey, is Someone—"

"We should go Inside now," I whispered.

And so twas I, in the End, Reader, who hurried us into the bar.

V

A Poet Tree Reading, Reader ☹
At something called a *Bookstore bar* ☹

Do you see what I have done for Love (and to Kill Allan)?

I entered a Space full of Poets, which is to say I entered a nearly empty bar quite like a dark Hole ☹ Twas called Inferno, and *how very apropos*, the Mind Witch would have said (sometimes I still hear their Phrasings echoing through my Brain Chambers ☺). Of course she, or indeed any of my Keepers, would never dare cross its Threshold, reviling Poet Trees as they did. *We are allergic to Poets with few Exceptions*, they often said. *Ondaatje and Plath, obvi. Keats and Byron, whose Ghosts we wish to fuck, and Wordsworth, who wandered lonely as a Cloud*. Was this where my own Revulsion came from? I wondered, but I did not like to wonder long, for twas a Dark Wondering. Anyway, wasn't it partly their Revulsion that had made me enter most willingly into this Hole?

And what a Hole twas, Reader. Clearly, no Sun had ever shone in this Place ☹ A very frowning Barman in Black blew Smoke Rings at us from his Clove Cigarette ☹ There was a table of sad-looking Books whose covers were so many shades of Gray ☹ *Poem* Books, I realized, and grew quite cold in my Heart ☹ Later I learned they were not even called Books, Reader, but *Volumes* ☹ There were also these very thin pamphlets called *Chapbooks*, their covers made of a dreary-colored construction Paper, their Pages bound with a most dismal Ribbon. How these Chappy Books made me shudder, Reader ☹ The Way they could not even stand up by themselves on the table, but had to be propped up by Life Supports ☹ (Or *Book Stands*, as Jonah called them.) I would have just stood there at the door in Horror were it not for Jonah gently tugging on my Hand. No jolly Music played here, as it had in the Frat house. Instead a kind of funereal Hymn that you couldn't jump to, Reader ⊗ You couldn't even bounce ⊗ There was a very pale Woman in a Turban, sneezing alone in a Corner, her table quite littered with Kleenexes. Everything about the Place, its Atmosphere, was making Pony quite suicidal ⊗ I even took the Razor from him and placed it in my other Pocket as a Precaution.

Jonah, meanwhile, had led us to a crooked table where four Men sat, brooding. They all wore black Trenchy Coats, their Cruelle Eyes were lined with pretty Makeups, and their Talons, Reader, were painted a chipped Black darker than Midnights.

Poets, I knew instantly, and shuddered within my Self.

Suddenly I felt I must go, Reader. I must run, in spite of my Love. Allan was not here after all, so I could not kill him ⊗ No One was here, in fact, but the Woman with the Allergies and these Poets ⊗ Each was holding a tall glass of fizzing amber Liquid, from which they took the most somber Sips. Not at all like the flushed happy Monsters at the Frat house who drowned their Insides with this sort of Liquid, cheering one another on as they imbibed it from a Hose.

When the Poets saw Jonah, their Mouths made such sneering Shapes.

"Hey, guys!" Jonah said. So friendly and lovely. I felt such an Urge in this Moment to lick his Face. He was the only bright and beautiful Thing in this dank Lair of *Poet Tree*, where no Trees grew ⊗ But these Poets, they just blinked. One wore a pretty Pearl on his Ear that I immediately wished to steal.

"Jonah," they grunted. "Who's your *Friend*?" I did not like the Way they said *Friend*, Reader.

"This is Aerius," Jonah said, taking my Hand.

"*Aerius*?" Though their Mouths still sneered, I could tell these Poets were intrigued. A dull Light there in their Cruelle Eyes when they beheld me that was not there before.

"Aerius," one of them repeated dubiously. He appeared to be their Leader, like the Mind Witch was. "Is that derived from Greek Mythology or something? A Warping of the Name of some lesser God?"

The other three smiled, smoke coiling from their Nostrils in a most sinister Synchronicity.

"Tis an Allergy Medicine," I said. And I threw the box onto the crooked table, right in their Midst. Jonah, meanwhile, squeezed my Hand tightly and smiled at me. May I write about this only? About Jonah's Smile and his Hand in mine and his Dandy Lion Hairs forever falling in his grassy Eyes? Sadly, I think not ☹ Mother says the Flower Book is not for *Romance*, tis for *Violences*, which are imminent ☹☺

"Clever," the Leader was saying. Contemplating my Body now, my inky Pectorals and the Pearls at my Throat. "Very *post-postmodern*." He said this quite like an Insult. "You must be a fan of *Pastiche*."

"I love *all* Pastiches," I said. "Especially Éclairs, but Mille-Feuilles are quite nice too." I smiled at him, licked my Lips a bit.

"Funny," he said, not smiling even a Drop. They were now all looking at my Ax. Not nervously. Almost as if they were mildly amused by the Killing Implement, curious.

"Quite the Tribute to Kafka," they murmured. "Literalizing the Metaphor, so to speak." They sneered again. "You must be a Fiction."

"He's a Friend of the Fictions," Jonah said.

"A Friend of the Fictions is no Friend of ours!" roared one of the Poets, pounding his Fist on the table. Pale and Freckled. Most vexed, yet quite handsome in his Agitation. His shining Orange Hairs reminded me very pleasantly of Carrots ☺

"I am no Friend of the Fictions," I told him, crouching down to his Level now so that I could look him right in his gray, glittering Eyes. "Not at all."

"What are you, then?" he whispered.

"Not another Poet, surely?" one of the Others offered wearily.

I shook my Head, my Face very close to the Carrot-haired Boy's Face, which was a little afeared now. "I hate Poets," I said, smiling. "And all Poet Trees. I find them to be very vile and stupid." I reached out to his Ear, and he immediately closed his Eyes to savor this, my Touch.

"May I have this?" I whispered, grasping the Pearl Earring that had first caught my Eye. "I enjoy its Iridescence."

He nodded, Tears falling from his Eyes, even as the Others whispered, "But, Colby, your grandmother!" I took it, stood up, slipped the Pearl into my Ear Flesh (a Hole there awaiting it as if twere Destiny), and thanked him heartily.

They all stared at me now, especially the Leader.

At last he kicked a wobbly stool toward me, his Eyes fixed on my Face in a new Way. "You and your *Friend* are welcome to join us. Most welcome," he said to Jonah, though he was looking entirely at me. I looked at the small, crooked table, over which he seemed to reign.

Let's go, Jonah, I thought. *Let me lick your Body under the Moon. Away from here. Allan is not here to kill, and perhaps my Keepers have moved along in their Hunt.* But I could not say this, for Jonah was made so happy by the Invitation ☹

"Awesome." He grinned. "Aerius, you sit, and I'll grab us some drinks from the bar."

"You're leaving me?" I said, quite panicked.

"Just to go to the bar. What do you want? I'm going to have a soda, but I can get you anything. Morpheus makes great Manhattans, so I hear."

I looked at the Man behind the bar, the very frowning one we had seen when we entered, still blowing his Rings of Smoke. He was now scribbling in a red Notebook by the Light of a half-melted Candle. His Lips twisted cruelly in a kind of obscene Joy, delighting perhaps in his Genie-yes ☹ I had seen such Joy on the Faces of my Keepers when they were doing their Writings ☹ Oh god ☹

"There is a Goldy Liquid," I said, and I squeezed his Hand again desperately. "With many golden Flecks. I'd like a barrel of this, please."

He laughed. "I'll see what I can do. Hey, maybe that'll get you to read with us."

"Yes, maybe," I agreed. "Just hurry." Not understanding at the Time what

he meant, you see, by *read*. I must say that to you now, Reader, in my De-
fense. Twas another one of my many Misunderstandings ☹

Jonah ran off quite happily toward the bar, and I watched him go. Pony
watched him too, sighing quite sadly. I attempted to soothe him with some
whispered Words, which I only hoped were true. *He will return, don't be
afeared. He would never leave us.*

A Throat cleared. I turned and saw the Poets were all staring at me.

"So. You're *reading*, are you? And what form will this Oratory Delight
take?" This from the Leader, grinning nastily.

"Excuse me?"

"What will you *read*, Fiction?" asked another. A tall Blondy one, clearly
his Henchman.

"He has told us he is not a Fiction," the Carrot-haired one said.

"Or even a Friend of the Fictions," added a blue-haired one, grinning,
though he appeared to have false Tears streaming from one Eye.

"I have read many Pages," I said. "Though I have eaten more than I have
read," I confessed. "And definitely I have defecated more than I have eaten."

They laughed now, quite in spite of themselves. I laughed too.

"Are you for Real?" the blue-haired one asked.

"Oh yes," I told him. For at the Moment, Reader, among these laughing Poets, I truly felt I was. I put my Ax on the table. They contemplated it
coolly. Perhaps they were more impressed by it now, though tis very hard to
say with Poets. "Do you know if Allan is here?" I asked. "Or will be coming
soon?"

"Allan? You mean the *Fiction* Prof?" the Leader said. "No, he won't come."

"No Fictions ever come to our Readings," Blondy seethed.

"They would rather *die* than do that," agreed Carrot.

"He came that one Time, remember?" said Blue. "At the start of Term?"

"Just to be Polite," Blondy hissed. "None of the Fictions ever visit this
Realm of Poesy," he said to me quite bitterly. "Too busy writing their Pap!"
And they all raised their glasses full of bitter, fizzing Liquid and drank.

They looked at me, narrowing their Eyes. Perhaps they thought I was a Fiction after all. "Why do you ask about *Allan* anyway?"

"Oh," I said, "because I am going to kill him."

When is Jonah coming back? Pony kept asking from my Pocket.

"*Kill* him?"

"Yes. I thought I had, but sadly I had not. Twas the Wrong Allan, as it turned out." I took a Sip of one of their many ales, while they all stared at me in quite a new Way. Twas not entirely unpleasant, Reader, for Pony or for my Self. I have always enjoyed such Eyes on me, tis true, even if they are Poets' Eyes. Tis what my Keepers have called a Fatal Flaw. *The Thing inside you that you cannot control, that will be your Undoing*, they often whispered, most huskily. Perhaps, Reader, my Enjoyment of Eyes would be my Undoing ☹

"Are you reading?" I asked them, for this seemed to be a favorite Question among their Kind. They all nodded, still lost in looking at me. And then I noticed the Pages, Reader. Pages on the crooked table and in their Hands. Slightly crumpled and torn from intense Handling. Quite like the Pages my Keepers had given me to read, as if they were offering me their Insides ☹ Suddenly the Lights at one end of the bar brightened, revealing a Stage. A Microphone. How cold I grew in my Soul, Reader, when I saw this Stage and Microphone ☹

Jonah returned with my double shot of Goldy Liquid, and I drank this down in two seconds. "Whoa," he said, smiling. "Someone's excited about the Reading."

I looked into his earthy Eyes, and my Heart, Reader, did that skippy-jumpy Thing again.

"Let us go from here," I whispered. Forgetting quite about my Keepers at this Point. Forgetting even that I must Kill Allan.

"Right now?" Jonah said. "But the Reading hasn't even started."

"Actually, you can't leave," Carrot said, smiling. "None of us can. Looks like we're under Lockdown again. Just got the alert from Campus Security." He held up his Phone triumphantly.

"Oh no, really?" Jonah said. "What this Time?"

"Not another Gunman?" Blondy asked.

Carrot shrugged. "Someone armed on Campus. A 'Violent Occurrence.' Possible Homicide."

"*Possible* Homicide? What does that mean?" Blondy pressed.

"I'm just reading an *email*, Gunnar."

And then what Mother calls *the Energy in the room* shifted. I felt it shift, Reader. They all looked back at Ax, sitting on the table among their crumpled Pages and gray Volumes. Her Blade shining with the Blood of the Wrong Allan thanks to the Stage Lights.

"How terrible," I murmured. "What a most awful Oops." Tears filled my Eyes a little then. Tears I could not conceal. At the Memory of the Wrong Allan's Laughter and his Smoke of Bubble Gums and his Head rolling away from his Body ☹ And these Poets, they observed these Tears. This is the most terrible Thing about Poets. They miss *Nothing*.

"Perhaps we should begin the Reading?" I said to divert their Eyes from Ax.

And this was the only Time, Reader, that I have ever encouraged Poet Trees.

The Reading. My Soul shudders to recall it, Reader ☹ Twas a most vile Experience for Pony and my Self. For Pony perhaps even more than me, for he did not have the benefit of my Goldy Liquid. *Oh my fucking god*, I heard him whisper. *Will it never cease? Is he going to read Another? Oh my god, he's going to read Another. Tell me please that this one will not be in a fake Tree Language? Oh, I will suicide if he does, I care not.*

And so on, he lamented, in my Pocket ☹ I was so thankful, Reader, that I had placed the Razor far beyond the reach of his Hoof. I wondered if I should leave. But between what they called the Lockdown and my Keepers likely hunting for me just beyond the doors, I knew I must stay where I was, hearing the many Poet Trees emanating from their pale Mouths in their overly cadenced Voices ☹ Looking back on it, I'm not sure how I survived ☹ Well, in Truth, I do remember. Jonah ☺ Sitting beside me, his beautiful, dreaming Face ☺ He watched each of his Fellows with genuine Delight, always smiling, always clapping and whistling fiercely at the End. "So cool," he said whenever a Poet sat down, and they quite ignored him.

"I am hoping you will read next," I said to him, not believing that I was actually encouraging *more* Poet Trees. Such was the extent of my Love for him.

"Oh, I don't know," Jonah sighed, shaking his Head. "Everyone's been so good."

"Go for me?" I pleaded.

Reader, I cannot say how wonderful he was ☺ I do not know about his actual Poet Trees, for I heard them not. I could hear Nothing, Nothing, but the Rush and roar of my own Blood, the beat of my own Heart. Another Music played in my Mindscape over the terrible Music in the bar, so that I heard its vile Sound no more. I heard only this lovely Mindscape Music, humming through me, so that every Hair of my Pelt stood quite on its End. Twas Jonah who created this Effect ☺ Jonah in his torn Jacket and black Joy Division T-shirt that read *Unknown Pleasures*. Jonah, his Dandy Lion Hairs made even more Dandy Lion–like by the Lights. His hulking Body hunched over the Mic he was far too tall for. I clapped for him wildly. Banged Ax upon the table. Whistled, Reader, and Pony did too.

And when he came back, I took him by his Hands and I said, "You are the only Poet whose Trees I can stand." I did not say that this was because I could not hear them, Reader. I did not share this Part. Love made me a Liar, as I have shared.

"Was he not wonderful?" I asked the others, my Hand on Ax, which they perceived.

"Oh yes," they murmured, looking from me to Ax. "Quite, quite."

"Well, it's your Turn now," Jonah said to me, grinning.

"My Turn?"

"Oh yes," they all hissed, suddenly glaring at me. "*Tis* your Turn."

Jonah laughed. "Oh, I was only kidding, guys. Aerius isn't a—"

"All the more Reason," the Leader snapped. "If he is not a Poet and not a Fiction, then *what* is he? Perhaps his Reading will illuminate us." And the Poets smiled then, somewhat cruelly. Losing their Fear of Ax briefly at the thought of my Pain.

"Aerius, you really don't have to," Jonah said quietly.

Please don't, Pony whispered.

"Your Audience of Dust awaits," the Leader taunted, waving his Hand at the empty bar. Quite bitterly he said this, Reader. Twas a Gauntlet thrown. Yet his gleaming Eyes were fixed on me, all their Eyes were, including Jonah's. And I relished it, Reader, despite Pony's Protestations. My Enjoyment of Eyes, he cried, would be the Death of us both ☹

I took Ax with me to the Stage, tucking her in my Blazer, for I did not trust to leave her with Poets. At the Microphone, I smiled at the Darkness. Apart from our table there was No One in the bar but the Woman dabbing at her Nose with many Kleenexes. And the Barman, Morpheus, watching me stonily. He had set down his little red Notebook. I looked at the small Candle blazing on the low table beside me, its tiny Flame. Reader, in Truth, I did not know what to do ☹ There was such Expectation on their Faces. An awful Desire for me to Perform. And this Desire, I'm sorry to say, brought me back to my Attic Times ☹ When Goldy Cut or Murder Fairy or Insatiable, or especially, especially the Mind Witch, wished for me to say Things ☹ Very specific Words and Phrases they wished me to say, and the more they wished, the more I found I could not speak, I refused. And now here on this Poet Tree Stage, I was experiencing something similar: a terrible Want rising from my Audience.

I froze ☹

A soft bit of Laughter now in the Dark. From one of the Poets, I did not know which ☹ Someone shaking his Head. Whispering "Fraud," whispering "Joke," whispering "Pastiche Trash," whispering "Probably a Fiction after all." The Woman with the Kleenexes blew her Nose pointedly. And then I discerned Jonah's Face. Smiling up at me. Nodding such Encouragement, though I was saying Nothing at all. Nodding as if I had already begun my Reading. As if I were right now blowing his Mindscape to a new and holy Place.

Suddenly I recalled something my Keepers had done in the Attic with the Letters of Feedback they'd received from Allan, which they often read aloud, quite bitterly. What they did with these Letters was a kind of Poem, they said, better than anything the Poets in the Program could manage. A kind of *Performance Art*, I remember they had called it.

And so I leapt off the Stage. Back in the bar, I gathered all the crumpled Pages from the Poets' table. Some Pages I even took directly from their Fists. And they let me, Reader, their Hands going slack at my Touch. This is something I have noticed about my Self, a Power I seem to possess at times. That I can take things from People and they let me, almost as if my reaching out puts them into a kind of Trance of Willingness. I *would give you fucking Anything*, my Keepers often told me. *It is I who am in a kind of Jail*, they said. *You make of my Human Will a Puddle of Nothing.* I did not believe them at the Time. For wasn't I the one locked up? And weren't they the ones free to go skipping out into the World whenever they pleased? And yet now that I was out in the World, it seemed there was something to it. I remembered the little Monster giving me his Face Glitter, the Wrong Allan offering me his Pen of Vapors. And here now in Inferno, these Poets giving me their Pages. "What are you doing?" they whispered, handing them over. But I had moved along, was now gathering all the Chappy Books with their construction paper Covers and their many Titles—*A Musing, A Meditation, A Prelude, An Addendum to the Compendium.* I walked over to the Woman's table. Crouched down to her side so that we were Eye to inflamed Eye.

"It seems," I said to her, "that you have a number of Allergies."

She nodded, lost in staring at my Chest area, the ring of inky Arrows aimed at my Breast that were also the spokes of a smiling Sun. I took her Hand, damp and small fingered, and placed it there, upon the Orb. I felt her

Fingers jump a little at the velvety Feel of my Pelt, and I pressed deeper. "Have you ever considered," I whispered into her Ear, "that you are allergic to Poet Trees?" She shook her Head in Wonder.

"Tis worth pondering," I said. And I took the many Kleenexes from her table, adding them to my Bounty. She let me, her watery Eyes even seeming to say, *Take*. On my Way back to the Stage, I snatched the small red Notebook from Morpheus, who was right then scribing in it with his Fountain Pen. Though there was a Wondering on his Face, he gave me the Notebook, as well as another shot of the Goldy Liquid. "On the house," he said dreamily as I drank it down at the bar without breaking our intense Contact of Eyes.

Back on the Stage, I gathered these Pages and Chappy Books into the highest Pile, on the low table at my side. Topped the Pile prettily with the many Kleenexes. I picked up one of the Volumes sitting atop. Twas called *Word Lake: A Meandering* ☹ I held it up, smiling into the Dark. Then I held it to the Fire of the stubby, half-melted Candle ☺ It caught a most lovely Flame ☺

And this Flame I tipped toward the pile of Poet Trees ☺

Reader, how lovely was the Fire, I cannot even say ☺ High and leaping and bright in that dark Hole of a bar ☺ Twas a Fire quite like the one in which I had thrown my other Face. All those Chappy Books and crumply Pages. All those scribbled Words, which my Keepers often described as Heart's Blood. *My Insides*, they said. *My Soul*.

All of this burning so very brightly ☺

I looked at my Audience. The Question *What is he doing? What is he doing?* ceased to pervade the Air. Now it seemed Everyone was too caught up in the Flames. My Poem, Reader, had rendered them quite speechless ☺ Were they horrified or impressed? I could not tell by their Faces, so open-mouthed and wide-eyed.

Suddenly I heard the Sound of a single Clap in the Dark. The Leader, he was clapping and clapping for me. Morpheus joined him. Then the Woman, all of them clapping wildly. And I felt happy, shamefully so. For they were clapping for me, for my Art. So excited was I that I began to jump, quite in spite of my Self, and I kicked over the table on which the Fire was burning, and then I poured the remainder of my Goldy Liquid onto the Flames ☺

More wild Applause, and I relished it, Reader. The Leader rose from his chair, followed quickly by his Entourage. Even the Woman rose, no longer red nosed or watery eyed, for she appeared to be miraculously cured of her Allergies ☺ All were standing and clapping except . . .

Jonah.

He remained seated in something like a shocked Stupor. Looking up at the burning Poems with a kind of Horror on his lovely Face. Perhaps he was also looking at the curtains just now catching Fire. For you see, we were all so worked up by the Beauty of the many Poet Trees going up in Smoke that we (and I include my Self and Pony) failed to see the Conflagration spreading, Reader. Failed to see the whole Stage in Flames.

Jonah stood up, looked at me. On his Face was no Smile anymore. He turned and walked out of the bar.

"Jonah! Wait," I called out, but my Voice was lost in the Roar of the Blaze and the greater Roar of Applause from the Poets. They bounded onto the Stage now, pouring Whiskey on the Fire so that the Flames grew taller still.

My Reading was quite beyond my Control at this Point, Reader ☹ It now belonged to what my Keepers often called the *Collective* ☹

I ran out of the bar, no longer caring if my Keepers were out there. Calling and calling his Name, though I heard the Poets shouting for me to come back. They were still laughing in wicked Delight at the bright, jumping Fire I had made of their Poet Trees.

VI

Outside of the burning Inferno, there were blue and red Lights flashing everywhere. Sirens, just like the ones I had heard after I killed the Wrong Allan, screamed all around me, fast approaching. There was also the Sound of actual Screams. People had gathered nearby to point and gawk at the Blaze. They were so caught up in looking at the Fire that they did not notice me taking my hasty Leave, keeping an Eye out for Jonah and my Keepers. No Sign of Them ☺ Or of him ☹ Not Anywhere in this flashing, screaming World ☹

Oh god, why had I come out here? Risked my Pelt in this Way?

And then I saw him in the Distance, Reader. Sitting on a dark Hillside. Smoking his Cigarette and watching the Fire.

"Jonah," I cried, and ran toward him.

He appeared to be languishing in some sort of very large, somber Park. A sloping Expanse of Grasses and Weeping Trees. Many gray slabs of Stone grew out of the Earth like strange Flowers. Names and dates were etched on them. The Dead, I knew, lay sleeping beneath. Jonah sat in their Midst, seeming to grow out of the Earth like the flowering Stones.

"Jonah," I said, quite out of Breath.

"Hey," he said, but he did not look at me. His Voice was cold and flat.

I sat beside him on the cold Grass. "Why did you leave? Is something wrong?"

He shook his Head at the Blaze, sighed.

"I just don't love that you burned the bar down, I guess," he said at last. Pulling the Grasses out of the Earth idly with his lovely Hands. I heard the screaming of each Blade.

"And all that Poet Tree," he continued. "I mean, I love a lot of those Volumes, you know?"

The table of sad Books came back to me. "You do?"

"Of course. I'm a Poet, remember?"

Oh yes. I had forgotten this ☹

"So. You didn't like my Reading, then?" *You don't like me?*

He looked at me. "I'm just not into *Destruction*, you know? I like *Creation* way more."

But I am a Creation, I could tell him. For had my Keepers not told me repeatedly that I was? I didn't quite understand what they meant by this, Reader, for they never explained. But perhaps Jonah would like me again if he knew. Perhaps he might even love me. But then I would also have to tell him about my Keepers and the Attic Times and the Lost Self I believed I once was, the Lost Place from which I had come, and this I did not wish to do ☹ This I felt I should keep to my Self.

"But I created a pretty Fire," I offered at last, lamely.

"Yeah. It was pretty. It's just . . . you destroyed so much to make it."

"Creation inevitably involves Destruction," I whispered, thinking of all the Violences I had endured in the Attic ☹ The many Violences of Revision ☹ "Axes. Ropes."

"Ropes?" he repeated. "Jesus. Look, I know it's a kind of Style, but it just seemed kind of recklessly provocative and violent to me. Unnecessary. I didn't understand the Point, is all."

I recalled some of these very Words on the Letters of Feedback that my Keepers received from Allan about their Writings. I looked back at the bar, still burning brightly, though Men in helmets with hoses were now storming the Place in large numbers.

"I've disappointed you," I whispered.

"No you haven't," he said, looking away. "The Fire was cool. It's . . . just different. Than what I normally go for, is all."

"Different," I repeated. And this Word to me seemed worse than all the Words he had used before.

Different, Pony repeated sadly in my Pocket. *I see.*

"But hey, my Peers were super into it. Still are, looks like." And he gestured at them, still standing outside the bar, still cheering in a Trenchy huddle. "And they're not easy to impress, trust me." He shook his Head at the clumps of dead Grass in his Hands. "You're in with them forever."

"I don't care about them," I mumbled, still looking at Jonah.

"I don't know if that's true." Jonah smiled, nudging me. "You seemed pretty into their Reaction. Pretty happy with it."

I shook my Head, even as I recalled my Self smiling on the Stage. Delighting in their roaring Claps. Basking in all their Cruelle Eyes on me. My Fatal Flaw, Reader ☹ My Undoing ☹

"I don't care what they think," I lied. *I care about you.* "I care about . . . "

"What?" He looked at me now, waiting.

"I care about . . . what you think," I stammered at last.

Jonah laughed sort of painfully. "Oh man, you really shouldn't. I'm Nobody really. No One likes me. My Work, I mean," he added quickly. "You should hear them in Workshop. Not that I let it get to me or Anything." He shook his Head again at the Grass.

I love you.

"I loved your Reading," I told him.

"You did?"

"Yes. I thought twas beautiful." And I prayed that he would not ask me to repeat a Line of it, Reader, to ask what about his Reading I particularly enjoyed. For I had taken in none of his Words. Only his beautiful Mouth making Word Shapes. Only his sculpted Arms and his golden Pelt Hairs shining in the Light. If he asked me such a Question now, I'd be in Trouble ☹ Twas something my Keepers often did, Reader, whenever they shared their Writings. *What did you enjoy SPECIFICALLY?* they would ask me. *What Aspect IN PARTICULAR?* And their Eyes were Wild with Need, their Faces quite shiny and slick with a kind of Wanting Sweat. *What did you enjoy MOST?*

Twas a fine Receptacle for my Defecations, I was often tempted to say. Though mostly I stayed silent, which made them wilder still, more desperate for my Specificity. But Jonah would not ask this sort of Question of me, I knew. Twas enough for him that I had found it beautiful.

"Beautiful?" he asked. I could see him blushing even in the Dark.

"So beautiful," I said. And I brushed his golden Hairs away from his Eyes. And he let me, Reader. His Gaze locked with mine. Side by side in the damp, cold Grasses in which no Dandy Lions grew. But for the first Time I cared nothing for Dandy Lions or for Grasses.

He smiled. "Really? You think so?"

"For Real," I said.

The Flames leapt higher in the Sky, making the Night's deep Blue look licked with a kind of Orange Light. Sirens roared somewhere below, but to me in this Moment they were a kind of Music. Someone, in the great Distance, might even have been screaming my Name, and I cared not. Jonah lay back in the Grass, and I lay back with him. Both of us looking up at the cold Moon.

He turned to me and smiled. I felt dizzy. Was he going to tell me he loved me?

"I wish Sam thought so," he whispered.

"Sam?" I said.

And then he turned away from me quite suddenly. Looking down at the Flames, the many Men attempting to put them out with hoses. A Coldness suddenly. I felt the Night's chill Wind.

"Who is Sam?" I asked in a small Voice.

"She's in the Program," Jonah said. "A Fiction, supercool. I guess you haven't met her yet?" He lit another Cigarette, took a drag.

I shook my Head. "I have not."

He nodded. "Yeah, that makes sense. She kind of keeps to herself." And then he sort of smiled to himself, Reader. I did not like that we were talking about this Sam. Or the Look on his Face when he talked about her. It did something quite painful to my Heart. Twas like the Ring of Arrows on my Chest had become Real. I suddenly felt their sharp Points digging into my Flesh.

"She doesn't like my Poet Tree," he sighed. "Or me, I think. She likes my Cigarettes, though." And he sort of laughed painfully again.

"She sounds very stupid," I said quietly.

He smiled at the Sky. Turned back to me.

I reached out and stroked the side of his Face. "She sounds very fucking stupid," I whispered.

"She's really smart," he whispered back. But his Eyes were on my Eyes. The Grasses there Soft and Bright. Forgiving me for my Fire, for my Destruction. Full of *Yes.*

I leaned in farther.

And he closed his Eyes, parted his Lips. And this was full of *Yes* too.

There are Times, Reader, when there are no Words at all. When only the Language of before Times will do. The Language of Wind and Grasses that I can no longer speak. Now I have only this broken Language of my Keepers that cannot capture what I felt. Jonah's hot Mouth on mine, our Bodies pressed together on the cold, fragrant Grasses beneath the low Moon. His soft Hairs between my Fingers, and his Fingers running through my own Hairs. If I close my Eyes, I am back there. Back to the Feel of his golden Arms around me and my Arms around him, and his velvet Pelt so hard and warm against mine. And him quite into me, I have to say. *Oh my god,* he whispered each Time my Mouth or my Hand touched him. *Oh my god, oh my god, oh my god. I love you,* he whispered. I think he said these Words to me. Though perhaps I imagined it, Reader. Pony claims to have no Recollection at all of this Moment. My only other Witness was the Moon, and she speaks that other Language.

I imagine he said *I love you.*

Sometimes, my Keepers said, we imagine the things we want so very vividly that we think they are Real. But they are not. Tis a Cruelle Game of the Mindscape we cannot help but play. When we are lonely, especially ⊗

Yet I do imagine it, Reader. Here now, alone in the Writing Shed, I imagine again and again that Jonah is still with me. That we are still there on the damp Grasses of that Hill, on that Night of Monsters and Fire, lying together among the many Dead and their flowering Stones.

I imagine or remember all of it again, though whether tis *Real* or not, I cannot tell now.

It felt Real, is all I can say.

It still does.

VII

Mother, as I have said, does not wish me to write a *Romance* ☹ Tis not at all the Purpose of this Project (Mother sometimes calls what we do together a *Project*). Or rather, this *Collaborative*, her preferred Term. No, no. This Book, Mother says, tapping the Vaginal Flowers shimmering so forbiddingly on its Face, is where I am to record the Violences and Wonders of the Lost Self, the Lost Place alone. Record them for Mother's eventual Perusal so that she may soon distill and elevate them into Art. So that she may make what she calls her great Comeback. So that she may give a great roaring Fuck You to those who have forgotten about Mother, who have mocked and underestimated her many Talents. This is why I must Tap the Wound, and the Lost Self alone is what I must Tap. *All you can remember of your Experience in that Other Body, in that Other Life. The Violences especially.* Anything else, Mother says, is merely a Rambling. A Digression. My own Selfishly Indulgent Whimsy ☹

But ... I cannot help it, Reader ☹

I cannot help but write about Jonah, if only to return to that magical Night in my Mindscape. Do you understand this, Reader? Do you have a Night like this in your own Life? One you return to? Play over and over again like a much-beloved Song? Even though you know you cannot go back, any more than I can. And so to go back, to *imagine* it, as my Keepers or as Mother might say, is Bittersweet. A painful, futile Exercise. But this is my Book, is it not? Tis in my Hands for now. And so for now I will write what I desire. To you and you alone, Reader ☺

Given that you are my Friend, I know you will forgive me.

———————

So let me go back again, to a low Moon over a hillside full of cold Stones and Flowers. Lying on the Grass, tangled up with Jonah, his Pelt warm under my Hands. Jonah's Fingers tracing my chest Arrows, each one pointing to my Heart, a Heart he already owned. Jonah's Lips crushing mine, I could be crushed forever. Jonah's Ear, which I nibbled softly like a Cowslip. His hard, lovely Cock in my Mouth, better than any Keeper Candy I'd ever sucked. His golden Body against me and how I felt I could never get enough of his Pelt and he could never get enough of mine, and unlike with my Keepers, I offered him every last bit of my Self. Quite willingly. And he offered himself to me, too, Reader. His Breath shuddery in my Ear, warming me through even as I shivered, whispering that I was beautiful, that this was such a Trip, the wildest Thing he'd ever done.

We lay entwined together for several Hours, stopping only now and then to smoke Cigarettes, to blow the vaporous Clouds into each other's Mouths, which was my new favorite Thing to do. And if there were still Sirens screaming in the Air, I heard them not. If my own Name was being cried out by four Mouths all Night long, I tuned it out mostly.

Aerius, where the fuck are you?

Aerius, come back!

Aerius, I love you.

Aerius, I have so many Dandy Lions, please come and eat them all from my Hands.

None of this was especially Audible to me. I heard only the soft Breathing of Jonah. I heard only the many Musics that he played for us both on his Phone. He, like my Keepers, enjoyed what he called a Playlist. *Sort of my Dreaming Songs,* he said. *But they're good for this, too.* Because of my previous Associations, I did not care much for Playlists, but twas not torturous to hear (mostly) because the Sounds were all braided together with Jonah's Sighs, his Moans of Pleasure, making a larger transcendent Music that I replay in my Mindscape still.

My own Moans and Sighs too.

Indeed, there were Moments in this Night when I felt such Happiness, such Ecstasy, such Love, that a strange Animal Cry escaped from my Lips over which I had no Control. Flashes kept coming back too. *Memories*, as Murder Fairy called them. Of velvety Grasses. A soft Wind through my Pelt Hairs. A Mud at my Feets for kicking. A delicious Strawberry Leaf between my Lips, and the taste of the Berry itself. These Flashes overcame me so powerfully as we held each other that I had to pull away from him at Times. For I felt I was falling, Reader. And if I did not pull away, I should fall forever.

"What's wrong?" he asked later, tracing my Lips with his Finger.

"Nothing, nothing," I lied.

"This is so Wild," he said. "I know it's crazy, but I almost wonder if I'm dreaming you."

"Dreaming me?" Which was funny, Reader. For I wondered if I was dreaming him, too.

"You're just so . . . "

And I waited. Breath held. *What?*

But he just shook his Head in Wonder. "Where did you come from, anyway? Besides Morocco and Japan and the Isle of Man and Argentina, I mean. It's almost like you're . . . " He broke off, Eyes lost in looking at my Face.

"What?"

"I don't know . . . like you're from some other World," he whispered.

I felt my Heart jump. "I am," I said softly. "From some other World." And I longed to tell him Everything then, Reader. About the Flashes. The Lost Place.

"Tell me," Jonah whispered, as if he'd heard my Thoughts. He kissed me softly, as if to give me Courage.

"I don't have the Language," I breathed, shaking my Head. "But it's beautiful," I said, looking at only him. "And you're taking me back there."

And he smiled and kissed me again.

VIII

I awoke for the first Time in my Life with a Smile on my Face, Reader ☺ As I felt the bright Sun warming my Pelt, I wondered if the Events of the Night before had been Nothing but a wild Dreaming. If I was still, after all, trapped in the Attic, firmly in the Realm of my Keepers, who would be coming in at any Moment to bring me my Morning Pixy Stix ☹ I became afeared to open my Eyes.

"Hey," Someone whispered, a Smile in their Voice. My Heart warmed.

I opened my Eyes. Jonah. Wearing my white Nightdress. Behind him, the Sun streaming in beautifully through a large, unwashed window. His Dandy Lion Hairs a glorious golden Chaos. Bits of Grass still stuck in them from making out on a Hillside with me. Oh how I smiled then ☺ How my Heart burst with Joy ☺

"Hey," I whispered, reaching up to kiss him. For the Feel of his Lips on mine, in the warm Light of the Sun, *this* would make it fully Real.

But he quickly got up before I could kiss him, Reader. Walked into the kitchen, mumbling something about making Coffee ☹ He really needed it Today, did I?

"Me?" No, I did not need it Today. I only needed to kiss him, to understand why he'd suddenly walked away from me. "Sure," I said.

For a while I watched his Back as he made this Coffee, my Dress falling off his lovely Shoulder, exposing the tender Flesh that only last Night I'd lightly scratched with my Talons. There were raised pink Etchings on his Pelt. And yet I felt he was very far from me now.

"It looks beautiful on you," I said of the Dress. "So much better than it does on me."

"I don't know about that." And he turned back and smiled. But something was off in the Smile; I felt it in my own Heart. He came back with two chipped mugs of steaming black Bile. Set one on the little table beside me. *Visit Alaska*, the mug read. Quickly I reached up to kiss him. "Thank you," I said, but my Kiss was not reciprocated. He had only allowed me to kiss him, as I sometimes allowed my Keepers to do, a look of Patience, Tolerance, on his Face. He then took his mug and went to sit on a large beany bag in the far Corner of the room.

"I hope you like it," he said.

I looked at him, sitting in his Corner, as far away from me as twas possible to sit, cradling his cup of Bile. "*Like* it?"

"The Coffee?"

"Oh." I took a sip and tried not to make a Face at its bitter Taste ☹ For it had been made by my Love and I must drink it, even if it did taste like the vilest of Acids ☹

"Delicious," I lied miserably. *What is happening?*

He looked at me. Smiled sadly. "Look, Aerius," he began. And already I could feel the Breath leaving my Body, Reader. Could feel my Pelt turning to cold Stone, even as I lay in the bright Sun.

"I really enjoyed what we did," he whispered. Not even looking at me, Reader. Looking down into his cup. "And I like you."

Like, Reader? Last Night hadn't he said he *loved*? I thought of my Keepers. So nakedly disappointed when I did not reciprocate their Affections. I took another Sip of his hot, bitter Poison so that he would not see my Face, any Evidence of my Heart breaking there.

"I like you, too," I said. "I liked what we did too." These were Lies. *I love you and I love what we did*, I wanted to scream into the Sun. Present Tense.

"But I have to tell you." He looked up at me now. And I knew what he had to tell me. Could even sense it. Like a Story, a terrible Fiction I was trapped in.

"What?" I whispered.

"Well, I sort of have Feelings for Someone Else, too." He looked away from me, Reader. Took an impossibly long Sip from his cup. Surely he would die from such a Sip. Surely it would poison him.

"Who?" But I knew, of course. Remembered the Name from the Night before. How he'd uttered it smiling and how, for the first Time, I had not liked his Smile.

Sam? Pony hissed from the Pocket of my Blazer, hanging on the wall. I must have said it aloud with him, for Jonah nodded.

"I'm sorry," he said. "I just ... I can't help what's in my Heart, you know?"

"I do," I said. *Because you are in my Heart. And I can't help that.* "And am I there too, in your Heart?" And for the first Time in my Life, Reader, I truly hated my Self. For asking such a Question. For not being able to help it. I thought of Goldy Cut, her Face punched in with Misery, looking possessed by some awful Spirit. *Am I in here?* she'd whisper, pressing her small, gloved Hand to my Chest. Sometimes I took Pity on her.

Of course, I'd lie. And she saw the Lying in my Eyes and wept.

"Of course," he whispered now, looking away.

He stood up, walked back over to me. Took my Hand, Reader, that dead Thing, and brought it to his Lips. How my Body stupidly caught Fire. I closed my Eyes, felt sick at the Warmth of his Touch melting me. The sudden, terrible Leap of my Heart.

"I should get to Class," he said. And then he let go. I opened my Eyes.

He went to the bathroom and emerged in black Denims and another Joy Division T-shirt that read, very appropriately, *Love Will Tear Us Apart.* Threw my Dress onto a chair near my Blazer, where Pony sat in shocked Silence.

"Let me go with you?" I offered. I knew I was behaving ridiculously, quite like my Keepers. And yet I couldn't seem to help it ☹

He shook his Head. He was putting his Trenchy Coat on now, gathering his Books. "I don't know if it's safe. Campus is pretty crazy. Apparently, there was another Murder last Night."

"Oh yes?" My Turn now, Reader, to look awkward.

"Yeah, at some Frat Party. The same Frat we were at, actually, if you can believe it." And he looked at me strangely. So strangely that I looked away. Mumbled that I could not believe it, and how terrible twas.

"Good Thing we didn't get killed, I guess."

"Yes, good Thing," I murmured, looking back at him. He was staring at my Blazer, where Ax was neatly tucked.

"Everyone's pretty freaked out," he said. "The Guy's still on the loose, apparently."

"Is he?"

"Yeah." He looked at me.

"Oh dear," I whispered.

"The whole Campus is still on semi-Lockdown. Probably swarming with Police and Reporters and stuff. It's going to be a Circus. Might be safer for you to go Home."

"Home," I repeated, and felt an Ache. Where was Home? Not the Attic. Certainly not the Greek house. And as for the Lost Place, there was no going back there ⊗ I did not know the Way Back ⊗ I looked at Jonah, his grassy, earthy Eyes. *There* was the closest Thing to Home I had found, Reader, but twas strangely forbidden now, beyond my Reach.

"Unless you have Class?" he was saying.

"Class?"

"Sorry, I don't know much about the Exchange Program. Maybe you're the kind of Exchange Student who doesn't have actual Classes?"

I recalled the absurd Lie my Keepers had told him when they were first escorting me to the Attic ⊗ I shook my Head helplessly. "I'm not sure," I said.

"Well, most Classes are probably canceled Today anyway. David's still keen to do Workshop, though. I guess he figures if he canceled Workshop for every Campus Killing, we'd never have Class, you know? And I just heard from Sam that Allan's still going to do his Fiction Workshop too."

"Allan is? Really?"

"Yeah, our Classes are right next to each other, actually, which is cool."

I looked at my Blazer now, hanging on its hook. The blue velvet seemed to glow in the Light of the Sun with a new kind of Purpose. My Blazer, which held Ax. In the throes of my Love, I had forgotten all about how I must still Kill Allan. But now the Recollection sang through me. The Dark gripped my Heart, the familiar Refrain pounding through my Blood, briefly drowning out my Pain.

"I just remembered, I do have Class Today. Actually." And there was a new kind of Singing in my Voice.

"Really?"

"Oh yes. A very important Class, in fact. So I should definitely go with you to Campus. Otherwise, I'll worry about you. What with this crazy Ax Murderer on the loose," I said. "You never know what might happen."

Love, I have told you, made me a Liar.

It also made me a Fool.

IX

I stood in the Rose Garden, just outside a building called Narrative Arts, waiting to Kill Allan. Was I waiting to Kill Allan? Or was I waiting for Jonah? Jonah, to whom I'd just said goodbye, my Heart skipping inside my Self. He was inside Narrative Arts somewhere, having his Workshop. This pained me to think about, Reader. But Allan was in there too, I knew, and this was a bit of a Balm to my Soul. For I was here to kill him, yes. Not to wait for Jonah, because that would be absurd after this Morning's Happenings ☹

Our Walk to Campus was strange, Reader. And our Parting even stranger. The School was indeed Chaos. A sea of Polices and Yellow Tapes and Blondy Women who looked quite like Goldy Cut talking into Microphones, looking into Cameras. But they were not reciting Poet Trees into these Microphones. They were News Reporters, and what they were saying, Reader, was far worse than Poet Trees ☹ Possible Homicide ☹ Maybe Murder ☹ There was much Murmuring, too, among the many student Bodies we passed. Jonah and I caught Snippets as we walked across the Green. "Alleged Beheading." "Some fucking Psycho with an Ax." "No Body found, can you believe it?"

No Body? I thought.

"With no Body at the Site of the supposed Crime and only one very inebriated student Witness, Police are really scratching their Heads," said a Blondy we passed, almost as if she'd heard my Question.

But I saw his Body on the floorboards, I thought. I saw his Head roll down the stairs. Perhaps his Body rolled away too, to follow the Head?

"You okay?" This from Jonah. Touching my Shoulder. Making my own Body catch stupid Fire again.

No. Not at all okay. Never okay again. "Oh yes."

"I told you it would be Chaos here. I'm surprised they're even letting us through. Maybe everyone's just used to it at this point. This School used to really have a Problem with Murders."

"Really?"

"Oh yeah. This one seems like a Weird one, though."

"Very Weird," I agreed. Tricky for the Polices to crack, apparently. Possibly even a Prank or a Hoax, they said. Still the Psycho was on the Loose, a Blondy Reporter said, and everyone had better keep an Eye out for a giant Rabbit Man with an Ax "who allegedly resembles actor Jacob Chamalord, Hollywood's latest Leading Man." As a Blondy Reporter said this, she bit her Lip, as if to keep from smiling.

Reader, I went cold at her Description ☹ For though I did not know who this *Jacob* was, I recalled his Name from the Attic Times. Goldy Cut would often utter it in a State of Sighing whilst ogling my Person ☹ *Has anyone ever told you you look like that Actor?* I remembered the Wrong Allan whispering. *In all the Movies right now. The hot One.* Perhaps he too had meant this Jacob. I must tread carefully, I thought. Keep Ax hidden deep inside my Blazer lest anyone think I was the Psycho ☹ For everyone was looking at me, Reader, and this made me a little afeared ☹

Had I not properly hidden Ax after all? Did they suspect me? Would they point their Fingers and cry for the Polices to take me away?

But no, they were only looking at me, more like how my Keepers did. I could feel Longings of various Degrees in all their Eyes as I passed, Teachers and Students and Blondy Reporters and Polices alike. This should have made me feel happy, these Eyes, despite the murderous Atmosphere of the Morning.

But it did not ☹ Because Jonah's Eyes were not on me, Reader. His Head was bowed, typing into his Phone a lot ☹ I sighed quite heavily, which made everyone around me sigh most dreamily. For I saw the Wrong Allan everywhere. His Face, Reader, plastered on every wall and lamppost and window and door.

HAVE YOU SEEN THIS BOY? the Poster read in very large red Letters. And beneath these Words, a grainy Photo of the Monster with whom I had jumped at the Greek house. Tyler Fields was his Name. There was the black Patch over one Eye, and he was grinning red facedly, just as he had grinned at me in the red room. *MISSING*, it read just beneath the Photo. "Until a Body is found, we must presume he is missing only," a Police said to many nodding Reporters.

"Hey," Jonah said softly. "You've been looking at that Photo awhile."

I realized we'd stopped in front of a lamppost and that I was indeed staring.

"Did you know him or something?"

I looked at the grainy Picture, the Eye that had smiled at me. *Say no but mean yes.* I shook my head. "No."

"So weird," he whispered, looking at the Photo himself now.

I turned to him. "What?"

"Well, just that we met outside that Frat house where that Guy supposedly got killed with an Ax. And you had that Ax. And that whole Backstory about killing Someone. And..."

"And?" I said.

"You do kind of look a little like Jacob Chamalord." He looked at me and blushed. I smiled. Though I knew twas not good News that I did indeed resemble this Jacob, I was obscenely happy in this Moment, Reader. For clearly he, like Goldy Cut and the Wrong Allan, had a Fondness.

I came in closer to him. "Do I?"

He looked so beautiful when he blushed, Reader. He nodded, still staring at me as if lost. Then suddenly he looked away. "I mean, I *guess* if I didn't know better, I might think, you know, you did it." He sort of laughed. Then glanced up at me, Reader, a little warily.

"How do you know I didn't?" I asked, moving in closer still. His Face now inches from mine. Yet there was something mean and challenging in my Voice. A Coldness, I did not know where it came from. I expected him to run from me.

Instead he held my Gaze.

"Because I know you," he said. "And I know you would never do something like that. I mean, it's just . . . not you." He said it hopefully, shaking his Head. His Eyes holding mine for the first Time this Morning. Melting me. "Right?" he whispered.

I looked at him, his beautiful Face a little afeared, but wanting so much to believe I had not killed the Wrong Allan. I wanted to believe it too. I nodded. "Right."

He sighed with Relief. Smiled. "I knew it. I mean, you're a Performance Artist, not a Murderer, obviously." He leaned in closer, almost as if to kiss me. "Right?"

"Exactly," I whispered, closing my Eyes. Grazing his Lips now.

"Plus it was Halloween," he breathed. "A ton of People went to Frat Parties with Real Axes, I'm sure."

"I'm sure." *Liar, Liar.* Moving to his Ear. Brushing my Lips against the tender Flesh of his Neck. He gasped and pulled me to him. Kissed me once, passionately, then pulled away.

"Look," he whispered. "I wouldn't go around telling anyone just in case, okay? You don't want to get arrested. A case of Mistaken Identity or something. It's such a good Thing you changed Clothes."

"Yes," I said quietly. I was wearing Jonah's Clothes. One of his Trenchy Coats and what he called Cargo Pants as well as a T-shirt that read *The Damned* (*He has very appropriately named Shirts,* Pony observed). I still had my Pearls on, and the Blazer beneath the Coat, which I could not do without and which made me feel a bit more like my Self. Whatever that was, Reader. Today I was no longer so sure ☹

"Sorry my Clothes are so boring compared with yours," he said now, and smiled.

"I hope I look okay," I whispered. Still reeling from the Kiss, from him pulling away.

"You look beautiful," he said. And once more I saw a Flash in his Eyes of *Yes,* he did find me quite beautiful. So all Hope was not lost. He was still looking at me intently. I almost thought he would kiss me again, especially now that he believed I was not a Murderer. His Face still so close to mine in the Bright Sun, the Wrong Allan smiling at us from the lamppost. But he turned away, looked at his Phone. A text from Sam, he said. "She's heading over."

I asked if this *Sam* knew about Clothes.

He laughed. "Oh, I don't think so. She always wears the same black T-shirt and Jeans."

She sounds very boring, Pony said from my Pocket. And I agreed, she did sound that Way, and I almost said so. "How interesting," I said instead, which was the Opposite of what I'd meant to say, Reader. I was caught between the Truth and not wanting to show it to Jonah lest he find it ugly of me. There was a Cattiness to my Voice, quite like the Cattiness of my Keepers when they spoke of one another. I did not like it and yet I could not help it ☹ But Jonah didn't notice. He was still smiling about Sam.

The Rose Garden had changed since my last Hop here, Reader, my first happy Meanderings. Back, way back when I knew nothing of Love or even of Killing Allan. When I knew only the Sun and the Grasses and the taste of bright Flowers (until I met the Mind Witch ☹). Now the Flowers were fewer and they appeared shorter, huddled closer to the Earth, which looked quite cold ☹ The Blades of Grass appeared to have shriveled. But all seemed to shine vividly under the Sun, all seemed to whisper that I must Kill Allan. Except Pony, who whispered, *But what about Jonah? What about our Heart?*

He'd waved to me as he made his Way, at last, through the doors of Narrative Arts. Said I was welcome to come in, say hi before I headed off to my own Class. *I'm sure David would love to meet you. My Peers really talked you up. Apparently, he's thrilled that you burned down the bar.*

But I said, *I had better not. I hate Poets, remember?*

I remember, he said, and smiled. *Except me, right?*

Except you, I said, the Truth of it breaking me. I watched him skip off to Class. Watched, like a Fool, even long after he'd disappeared through the doors.

I did not have much Heart left in me to murder that Day ☹ It being quite broken ☹ Yes, this was becoming increasingly clear to me. For my Hand on Ax was unsteady. My Pelt shivered in the Sunlight. My Feets were most wobbly in the cold Grass ☹ My Thoughts kept roving from Killing to Jonah. He was somewhere in Narrative Arts, I knew. Through one of these windows I might see his Face, his grassy Eyes that looked like Home. I wanted to run to him. *I love you. Please forget this Sam person and I will forget Killing Allan and let us run away together. Perhaps with you I might find the Lost Place.* Yet I remained where I was, keeping an Eye out for Allan, gripping Ax. I knew not what Shape he would take this Time, so I really did have to keep an Eye quite peeled.

I was standing out there, so very torn, when I heard Voices, Reader. Familiar ☹ Terrible ☹ They made all my Pelt Hairs stand on end ☹

"And what about the Park, Bunny? Did you look in the *Park?*"

"No, I didn't fucking look in the Park, *Bunny.* I was out in the Field, okay? I thought *you* were supposed to look in the Park."

"Oh my god, we're never going to fucking find him this Way."

"Don't lose hope, Bunny, okay?"

Oh god, Reader ☹

Them ☹

Coming closer. Their awful Voices growing louder. The sound of crunching Grasses beneath their heeled Feets, the Clicks of which I knew in my Bones ☹

"Wait did we check in the Garden? We should check in the Garden." Goldy Cut, her Voice a wavering Razor.

"But we're running late!" Murder Fairy, her Voice high with violent Panics.

"Oh, who fucking cares, it's only Workshop, for god's sake." The gravelly Nihilism of Insatiable ⊗

I dove behind the Rosebushes then, Reader. Shocked at the Speed at which I was able to go from standing forlornly in the Middle of the Garden to crouching quite low between the Fence and the Bushes full of ouchy Thorns. Through the fragrant Petals, I beheld Them, my former Keepers ⊗ How it made my Blood cold to see Them again ⊗ Goldy Cut in her Garden Dress with its many ominous-looking Poppies. *Here are some Petals for you,* she would say to me, resting my Head in her Lap full of warped orange Flowers⊗ Murder Fairy, whose bright Eyes brimmed with Murder and Worry in equal Measure ⊗ Insatiable, smug and unwashed in her soiled Flannel and Denims, right now sniffing the Air as if she could hunt for me with that Implement ⊗ And of course the Mind Witch, her Dagger glittering around her Neck, in her flowing white Dress, whose twin was right now in Jonah's rinse cycle. Her Eyes were closed, and I knew she was looking for me with her Mind Witchery, the sharpest Huntress of all ⊗

"Well, he's not here, surprise, surprise." This from Murder Fairy. She looked strangely smaller than I remembered without her Ax. Yet still formidable ⊗ "I told you guys."

"Oh like you knew," Goldy Cut said.

"I did know! Just like I know he's the one who beheaded that Boy last Night."

Oh no ⊗

"Will you *stop* saying that, Bunny," Goldy Cut said, putting her gloved Hands over her Ears. "He would never ever do such a Thing. Don't you talk about him like that!"

"I'm just stating facts, Bunny. He stole my Ax and the Boy was Axed. We need to go to the Police and tell them."

"Tell them what exactly, Kyra?" Goldy challenged. "That he escaped our Attic and beheaded some Frat Boy? That we conjured a Man out of a—"

But she suddenly fell silent as a Siren screamed past. *Conjured?* I thought in the Bush. *Conjured me out of what?* With held Breath, I waited for her to finish.

"Anyway," she added quietly, "it's absurd. Far out of the Realm of Possible Things." And she laughed a wavering Laugh.

Conjured me out of what?

"Preposterous," the Mind Witch whispered, her Eyes still quite closed.

"I mean, if anything, he should have killed Allan. Not some rando Frat Boy," Insatiable said.

"Exactly," Goldy said.

"Well, he still might," Murder Fairy whispered. "And it's our Fault. We have Blood on our Hands, Bunny."

"Oh relax, they didn't even find a Body yet," Insatiable said coolly. "So it might just be some Frat Prank."

"But the Boy's still missing, isn't he?" Murder Fairy insisted. "Tyler or whatever."

"Well, he might be in on the Joke, who knows?"

"The *Joke?*"

"Or maybe he ran away or something," Insatiable offered. "Cracked under the Pressure of School."

"Yes!" Goldy cried. "School is so hard, Bunny. I mean, it's sad if he's missing, but it's not *Murder*, okay? You're so eager to make Everything murdery! And I have to say, I find it very hard to take? Like, aesthetically."

"They found a Bunny on the Scene," Murder Fairy said at last, quietly.

They all looked at her now. The Mind Witch even opened one Eye, quite in the Way Mother likes to do. "They did?"

They did? I thought.

She nodded. "Hopping around the living room."

"So what does that even mean, Bunny? That they found a Bunny."

Murder Fairy shook her Head. "I don't know, Bunny, okay? But I think it's . . . weird."

They grew quiet then. I did too, Reader. All of us as quiet as the Roses in which I crouched. I chewed a Petal thoughtfully, taking in this News. Had I seen this Bunny of which they were speaking? I had been too busy jumping and then killing the Wrong Allan to properly take in my Surroundings ☹ And what did they mean when they said they had *conjured* me? *Conjured me out of what?*

Twas then I saw a Creature, Reader. Crouched in the Bush, right beside me. Long-eared. Small and white, a black Patch over his right Eye. His furry Body quite trembly. He, like me, was eating a Rose Petal. Chewing quite thoughtfully, as though musing on its bitter floral Taste. His blue Eye was fixed on me with a kind of strange Recognition. Tis funny to say, but he looked like he knew me. And very funnily, I felt I knew him, too.

"I don't believe that for a fucking Second." This from Insatiable. Shaking her Head.

"I'm sure that's just Urban Legend, Bunny," Goldy said, patting Murder Fairy on the Shoulder. "Rumor. Or just part of the dumb Prank, k?"

"You know these Frat Boys, Kyra," Insatiable said, rolling her Eyes. "There's a far more *rational* Explanation, I'm sure."

"Rational," the Mind Witch murmured in a low Voice, amused. Which afeared me ☹ I looked back at the Bunny beside me in the Bush, still chewing thoughtfully on his Petal, still looking at me. *I know you, I know you.*

"Oh yeah, like what? *You* tell me," Murder Fairy said, challenging.

"There are Bunnies all over Campus, okay? It's no Surprise at all that one hopped into a Frat house. Not out of the Realm of Possibility at all. The Truth is always more simple."

"And what's the Truth in this case, Bunny?"

Goldy Cut's Chin quivered. "That he ran away from us. Because he hates me." And she cried into her gloved Hands.

Murder Fairy hugged her now. Insatiable, too, both of them vying for her Body. "Oh now, Bunny," they both said most soothingly, "I'm sure that's not true."

Oh no, tis true, I thought from the Bush. *Most definitely.*

"My Heart is broken." And she wept most piteously while they stroked her Shoulders.

"We know, Bunny. Us too." Then they began to cry also. And funny to say, but Tears fell from my Eyes too. Which was odd, Reader, for I did hate Goldy Cut, I hated all of them. Still, their Sadness strangely moved me. Reminding me of Jonah, my own broken Heart.

But then the Mind Witch suddenly opened both Eyes. "Shhhhh," she said. "He is nearby."

They looked up from their Weepings. "*What?*"

I locked Eyes with my Fellow in the Bush. *Oh god.*

And then Insatiable began sniffing the Air quite like a Dog. I froze, Reader. And beside me, the Bunny froze too. *Oh god, oh god.* Twas then I heard a bit of Language coming from his Body. Heard it Singing along my Pelt. *We cannot leave here now. We must stay crouched in the soft Mud, among the Roses and the cold white Spores of withered Dandy Lions. We must pretend we are Dead, otherwise we definitely will be.*

I nodded. And the Bunny seemed to nod too.

"I feel I know you," I whispered to him. "Why do I feel this?"

The Creature twitched his Nose, continued chewing the Rose Petal. He had no more Language to speak. Or if he did, I did not grasp it.

Meanwhile, Insatiable, sniffing wildly, began to move toward us, Reader. The Bush where we were both crouched. I felt her kneel down in the Grass before this Bush. I could smell her deodorant of rancid Lavender, her cinnaminty Gums. I pressed my Self back against the Fence.

"I don't see him," she said at last miserably. "He's not here."

And how I breathed a sigh of Relief for both of us, my Self and this Creature with whom I felt a strange and powerful Kinship, a strange Knowing I could not place, as though I had met him once before in some other Form. He continued to eat from the Bush, most oblivious.

"Wait!" Insatiable cried, her grabby Hands now poking through the Bush. "I think I feel something." I pressed my Body further against the Fence, watched those Hands grasping the Air wildly, only just out of the reach of my Flesh ☻ But my Bunny Friend was still in the line of Fire. *Move away from there*, I tried to mind-speak to him. But he just stared at me quite stupidly, a kind of dull Animal Contentment in his Eye now. He continued to nibble the Petals like he was not at all afeared. I closed my Eyes, for this was a Nightmare and I could look no more ☻

"I got him," she cried.

Oh god, Reader ☻ Twas over ☻ My Freedom over and I must kill them now. But when I opened my Eyes, twas not me but my Bunny Friend that she had seized. And he allowed himself to be quite taken into her Arms.

Through the Bush I watched Insatiable carry the poor Creature toward them, a horrible Triumph on her Face. The Bunny, for his Part, was still eating his Petal. Most innocent of the Horror into which he had hopped. Goldy Cut looked at the Creature in Insatiable's Arms and frowned. "Um, what the fuck is this, please?"

"What does it look like, Bunny?"

They all looked at the Creature with their Keepers' Eyes. "Where's Aerius?" Goldy whispered. "I thought you said he was here!"

"Look," Insatiable sighed. "I think it's Time for us to move on."

"*Move on?*"

"Aerius was way too out of our Control. He ran away from us, for fuck's sake. I say we cut our Losses and try Another."

Another?

"Another?" Murder Fairy cried. "Um, I don't think so, Bunny. I already have enough Blood on my Hands, Thanks. I'm so traumatized, I didn't even do the Reading for Today. I mean, I did, but I totally skimmed the last Chapter."

"I don't *want* Another," Goldy Cut screamed, shaking her Head. "I just want him back."

Insatiable's Face grew sad. "I do too. We won't give up looking, Bunny. This is just for in the meantime, k? To see if we can. Don't you want to see if we can?"

Can what?

Goldy Cut scrunched her Nose at the Creature. "This one looks weird to me. What's with that black Patch over his Eye? He's not nearly as pretty as Aerius." But her Eyes were on him all the same, eating his Petal. They all watched him munch, a little hypnotized. All except the Mind Witch, whose Gaze was fixed on the Bush, on me, I felt. I swear she saw me crouched there with that Third Eye, Reader ⊗

"Forget Aerius for now," she said, and I felt the Eye directly on me as she spoke. "Let's try making Another first. I like this Idea. Very much."

"Maybe if we make Aerius a Friend, he'll come back to us. Like in *Frankenstein* or something," Goldy Cut offered.

"But in *Frankenstein*, Victor destroys the Friend because he can't bear making two of them, remember?" Murder Fairy said.

"Well, this isn't exactly fucking *Frankenstein*, Bunny."

I watched my Keepers leave, carrying their new Spoil in their very white Arms, this Bunny. He kept his Eyes on me as he was led away. Looking a little afeared now perhaps, but excited, too. Still munching that endless Flower. Twas in my Heart to run after him, Reader. Save him from himself, ascertain the meaning of our Telepathy, the strange Soul Connection we seemed to share. *Why is it, Bunny, that I could hear your Words in my Pelt?* And why had I felt that I knew his Face, that black Patch over his Eye? Had smiled with him? Jumped with him even, perhaps, in another Time? But my Body was quite frozen, Reader ⊗ I could not move from the Bush ⊗ Could only watch him being carried away ⊗

"Goodbye, Bunny," I whispered.

Now alone in the Garden, I felt I should run and never look back. Far too close a call ⊗ To hear their shrill Voices again, Reader ⊗ To see their grasping Hands and hungry Keepers' Eyes ⊗ How it reminded me all too clearly of the Attic Times, the terrible Time of Revision ⊗ I quite forgot about killing Allan at this moment, Reader, though I still held Ax in my Blazer, her Blade cold and sharp against my Heart. I'd been too caught up in the Preservation of my Self. Too confused by this Moment of Communion with the Bunny, as well as some of the Things my Keepers had just shared. About *conjuring* me. Having Blood on their Hands.

What can it all mean? I asked Pony, pulling him from my Pocket.

But he only stared at me with his large and ever-sparkling Eyes. Perhaps he, too, had been struck Mute by these Revelations. *You're from some other World*, Jonah had said to me. Oh god, more than anything I wanted Jonah. Hadn't he kissed me, even when he was accusing me of Murder with his Eyes? I smiled at this Recollection, filled with Hope. I would wait for him to finish his Workshop. Share with him some of my Confusions and Fears. This Love for him that I felt deep in my Heart (I felt it so strongly that sometimes it killed the desire to Kill Allan). In his bedroom, with the Moon shining on us and his Dreaming Songs playing for us, his Eyes looking into mine, so full of Desire and Wonder, I might find the Courage. The Idea of Killing Allan lessened its Dark Grip on me the more I thought of Jonah. Yes, I would go to him now. Find him somewhere in Narrative Arts. Kiss him in front of the Poets, to show him I cared not what they thought. I would make him forget all about this Sam person.

But just as I rose from the Bush, I heard more crunching Grass, more Voices ☹

Quickly I ducked back down. Peeked through the Leaves.

My Heart leapt. Jonah! Oh how I wanted to run to him, Reader, but he was not alone ☹ He was with a tall frowning girl in Black.

Sam, Pony whispered.

"Sam," Jonah sighed. "So glad I caught you running out of Workshop." He was staring at her in a Way that hurt to see. She appeared oblivious, glared at the Ground. Snatched the Cigarette he extended, and he lit it for her, quite like he had lit mine. Tip to Tip, that she might suck it and catch his most erotic Fire. She did not appear terribly moved by his Gesture. She just took Jonah's Fire and blew the Smoke straight out of her Mouth. He watched her do this, utterly entranced.

"Thanks," she said coldly, quietly. Staring very hard at the Grass. Her

long dark Hairs hung in her Face, a most bleak Curtain ☹ "I really needed
to get the fuck out of Workshop, Jonah."

He looked thrilled by her Recognition. "Oh, me too!"

"It's just driving me crazy Today."

"You mean because of all this Killer stuff?"

She looked at him like he was mad. "Because of *Them*. The . . . Bunnies."
She closed her Eyes, took a drag as if the drag might take her away. "They
brought a Rabbit to Class Today. An actual fucking Bunny, can you believe
that?"

He shook his head, in Awe.

"They'll probably sacrifice him later or something. Poor little Fucker."

"Bunnies are cute."

"Bunnies are terrible, Jonah," Sam hissed. "Never forget that."

"Cute things can be terrible for us sometimes, I guess." *Cute things like*
you, said his Eyes. "That's what makes them so cool." The Look on his Face,
Reader, when he looked at her ☹ Twas the Look on my own Face now, I
knew, as I looked at him ☹ Twas the Look of my Keepers when they looked
at me ☹ Pain twisted up with such Longing ☹ "Speaking of cool," he said,
"do you, um, like Jazz?"

But the Girl, Sam, was just staring into Space now, lost. "I don't know.
Sometimes I'm afraid that I'm going to go crazy here, Jonah." She shook her
Head. "Like, for Real."

"Don't be scared, Sam," he whispered. "I'm here for you."

Had I heard these Words, I would have died, Reader, of Happiness ☹
But this Sam didn't seem to hear him at all ☹ She looked even more sad,
more scared, if twere possible.

"I should head back, I guess," she said.

"I'll come with you," he said, breaking me afresh.

She threw his Cigarette on the Grass and stomped on it, like it might as
well have been his Heart. And he immediately followed her, stomping on his
own Cigarette, which might as well have been mine.

My Heart, Reader.

X

After leaving the Garden, I was quite Inconsolable. Wandered lonely as a Cloud, through a Sea of flashing Lights and Police Tapes, for I knew not how long. Forgetting about killing Allan, though the Blade was still cold against my broken Heart. There were fewer Blondy Reporters about, though several remained. When they saw me shuffle past, their Eyes lit up.

"Would *you* like to comment on your Experience of Campus Violence?"

"Was this a Beheading or an elaborate Prank?"

"Did you know Tyler Fields?"

I shook my Head, walked hurriedly away.

The Sky grew much darker and colder as I ambled farther from Campus, through the Town and then beyond, to its surrounding Woods and Fields. At last I neared a highway, where cars and trucks roared past. *That is a poor-people car,* I imagined my Keepers saying. *That is a bus, which you must never take.*

The Lights of the truck stop swam out of the Dark, seeming to call out to me in my Loneliness. I moved toward them. Maybe I was drawn Inside by the smell of Sawdust and Alcohols and Oblivion ⊗ Or perhaps twas the sad Music coming from the half-open door.

The Place was dark, empty but for the Barman himself. There was another Man sitting by the bar too, his Hand cupped around a glass of rust-colored Liquid. He wore a Hunter's Cap, casting his gaunt, gristly Face mostly in Shadow. They stared at me when I entered.

I do not like this Place, Pony whispered. *I have a bad Feeling.*

But I was already Inside, Reader, walking toward the bar.

"Hello there, Friend," this Barman said. Smiled like he'd just been laughing.

Friend. I warmed at this Word.

"Hello, Friend," I whispered.

"Getting cold out there Tonight?" He had long dark Hairs and a silver chain with a small glass vial round his Neck. This vial, I saw, was filled with tiny Twigs and dried Flowers.

"Yes, very cold."

"Winter. She's a-coming." The Man in the Hunter's Cap sitting at the bar chuckled at this like twas a Joke he'd told. Which was strange, for I did not find it funny, Reader.

"What can I get for you, Friend?" the Barman said, nodding at me. Though I liked that he called me Friend, Pony was suspicious. *We don't even know each other,* he whispered.

"Do you have a Goldy Liquid?" I asked him hopefully.

My new Friend looked puzzled. Then he smiled and held out the very bottle. I nodded gratefully, watched as he poured me a most generous glass. *Do you see, Pony?* I whispered. *Look how generous he is with his Goldy Liquid. This Man is most definitely our Friend.*

I don't know, Pony whispered. *I have a bad Feeling.*

"You talking to Someone in your Pocket there, Buddy?" Hunter's Cap said. I perceived he was looking at me, smiling like he was ready to laugh again, why was he always ready to laugh?

Pony said nothing now.

"Yes. My only Friend in the World. Apart from you," I added to the Barman as he slid the glass of Goldy toward me.

He and Hunter's Cap looked at each other and laughed.

"Oh hey, I hear that," Hunter's Cap said. "I got my only Friend in the World in my Pocket too, Buddy." He patted his Jacket, where I noticed there was a Bulge. "Apart from him." He nodded at the Barman and downed his glass of rusty Liquid. His Skin, what I could see of it, appeared quite rusty too, quite weathered.

Like his Soul, Pony whispered.

"Six bucks, Friend," the Barman said to me, pointing to the glass of Goldy.

Oh god, Reader ☹ I'd forgotten that one has to pay for Alcohols ☹ *One has to pay for Everything in this World*, Murder Fairy often murmured. I reached into my Pocket and held out a Clump of Grass, suspecting he'd be outraged by my Offerings. Instead he looked at my Face. Quite taken with it, as many seemed to be. He put the Grass in his Pocket and thanked me, his Eyes on mine.

There at the bar, in the Cloud of sad, pretty Music and Smoke, I drank and lost my Self in Thought. Turning over the Day's Strange Happenings. What my Keepers had said about conjuring me. *From what? From what?* That Bunny in the Bush, how I'd felt his Language through my Pelt. Jonah stomping on my Heart. And now? Now I did not know what to do, where to go. In Truth, I no longer knew what I even was, Reader ☹ But I could not lose my Self entirely in these Reflections, for the Men at the bar were laughing about something, and this Laughter kept me too aware of my Surroundings. I could feel them both watching me imbibe my Goldy Liquid as I stared at the darkening Night through the windows.

We should go, Pony whispered.

But I don't know where to go, I told him.

"Better be careful, Friend," the Man at the bar said. I turned to look at him in his Hunter's Cap. He was addressing me, I was his Friend also, and there was an odd Gleam in his pale Eye now. Like he might tell a Joke or commit a Violence and one would never know which until twas done. "Better be very careful," Hunter's Cap said to me, sort of playfully-seriously.

"And why is that?"

"Apparently there's an Ax Murderer on the Loose out there," he said, winking at the Barman, who only shook his Head.

"Is there?" I said, feeling the fact of Ax against my Heart. "How frightening," I offered, without much Feeling.

Hunter's Cap grinned. "Don't want to get all chopped up, now, do we?"

"No," I said. But he was still looking at me, enchanted, amused—trying, I felt, to get to the Bottom of me. "You look like a Hollywood Boy. Doesn't he?" His Eyes lingered on my Pearls. "What's your Story, Friend?"

"My Story?"

Do not tell this Man, Pony said.

"Tis something I am trying to piece together," I said. "Tis still . . . unfolding."

And he and the Barman laughed. "Tis? What are you, a Student at one of the fancy Colleges in this Town?"

"More like an Escapee, I'll bet," laughed the Barman.

"Neither," I said.

"Oh yeah? What are you, then, Friend?"

I thought of killing the Wrong Allan. Jonah on top of me, crushing his Lips hungrily against mine beneath the smiling Moon. The Rabbit I'd seen in the Bush, that Communion of Souls I'd experienced. I looked into my new Friend's Eyes, where there was no Communion at all, where only a strange, cold Laughter seemed always ready to erupt for Reasons I could not surmise. "I don't know anymore," I said. I finished my glass.

The Barman poured me another dram. I was about to hand him more Grasses to pay for this, but he refused them.

"Thank you," I whispered, overcome by this Kindness. Suddenly I took his Hand. He looked at me grasping it. I could feel Hunter's Cap watching us with new Interest.

"Do you ever have . . . Flashes?" I asked the Barman in a Whisper.

"Flashes?"

"Of another Life, a Lost Self you might have been? Another Shape you might have taken?"

He looked at the Grasses still cupped in my Palm, then over at Hunter's Cap. They grinned slyly at each other now. "Maybe," the Barman said.

My Heart brightened. "Really?"

"You mean like Reincarnation? Sure. I think in a former Life I was probably a Witch."

"A Witch?" I thought of the Mind Witch ☹

The Barman smiled. "Sure. Hanged for growing my Garden Herbs, concocting my Elixirs." I looked at the small vial around his Neck filled with its tiny Twigs and Petals.

"And for being a fucking criminal," Hunter's Cap said. They both roared quite heartily. They were mocking me, I realized, my new Friends. I did not like their Laughter, Reader ☹ I had not made a Joke ☹ I had been asking in all seriousness. "I should go."

Yes, please let's go, whispered Pony.

"Oh no, stay awhile," Hunter's Cap implored. He patted his Pocket again, that strange Bulge. It made me increasingly uneasy. What did he have in there?

Certainly not a Pony, Pony whispered.

"Tell us about this 'Lost Self.' What were you?" His Eyes were shining, waiting.

Let's go, let's go.

"I'll bet he was a Prey of some kind," said the Barman, eyeing me. "A Deer. Even a Rabbit maybe."

I shuddered at this Word, Reader. Felt my Pelt grow hot.

"I don't know about that," said Hunter's Cap. "His Eyes have too much of the Hunter in them, wouldn't you say?"

Twas then I remembered Ax in my Blazer, Razor in my Pocket. "Do you know where Allan might be?" I asked them. The Phrases tumbling out of my Mouth quite without Thought.

"Allan?" Hunter's Cap repeated. He winked at the Barman. "And what might you be wanting with him?"

"To kill him," I said. Out came my words again. Perhaps the Goldy Liquid had loosened my Tongue somewhat.

They laughed even more heartily. And this Time I laughed with them, even though they were certainly laughing at me, Reader. Despite my gloomy Mood, I still enjoyed creating Delight ☺ Even if twas at my Expense ☹

"And how will you kill this Allan?"

"With Ax, of course," I said.

They fell silent then as they exchanged Glances. "Are you telling us that you're this Ax Murderer?"

"I am, actually. But sadly, I have killed the Wrong Allan. I am now looking for the Right One."

"Well, look no further, Friend," said the Man at the bar, shaking his Head, wiping the happy Tears from his Eyes. "Though I do hope you won't kill me."

"Or me," said the Barman.

"Are you Allan?" I asked.

Hunter's Cap smiled at me over his rust-colored Drink. And the Barman smiled too, his Pockets full of my Grasses.

"We are both Allan," they said, winking at each other.

"Both . . . Allan?" I repeated.

And they roared and roared again with Laughter.

Until I took out Ax, Reader. Which quite stopped it, their Laughter. Which quite stopped all the Sound in the World.

XI

A Black Night full of grim Stars ☻ I lay in a deep Ditch of cold Mud and Stones, quite unable to rise or even move my Feets ☻ I could only lie there, Reader, staring up at the sliver of Moon in her Kingdom of Darkness. Trying to get her to speak with me in the other Language, to make of her a Friend, for I sensed she had been a Friend once. *Who am I? I asked her. What am I? was perhaps a better question. Where do I even belong in the World? I know no longer. I only know I am afeared of my Self, of what I have become.*

The Moon only shone down on me coolly. Perhaps she was angry with me for killing both Allans at the truck stop ☻ Her Light seemed to further expose their splattered Bloods on my Clothes ☻ The many Flecks of still-quivering Flesh from their Bodies ☻ Perhaps she had borne Witness, through the window, to my Violences. How first one Allan I had killed, the one sitting at the bar, while the Other had watched in a kind of laughing Horror at the swing of my Ax. Then how I'd killed the Other, hopping over the bar in a Flash. Raising Ax over his Head, the Head of the Barman, my new Friend, who was my Friend no more, for he was Allan ☻ He, meanwhile, still looked at me enchanted, as though I, though covered in much Blood already, were a Wonder he could not help but behold, a Rainbow or a Northern Light, and not at all a Murderer of Allans. A single swing of Ax was all it took to kill this second, laughing Allan, and then he was down like his Double. And my Hands and Arms so frighteningly skilled in this Severing, knowing precisely where to strike on the Neck, so that both Heads were cut quite cleanly from their Bodies. So that I became afeared of my own Arms and Hands, the sharp, hot Magic they made with the Blade. So quickly did I strike that both Heads were still laughing in a

kind of Horror-shock as they rolled away. I watched them roll from their
bloody Bodies, Pony closing his Eyes in my Pocket. How I wished I could
close my Eyes as Pony had, Reader ☹ But I could not ☹ For I must kill
Allan, that was all too clear. Twas a Directive in my Body. Twas an Action before Thought. The severed Heads rolled away in their Sea of Blood,
quite like the Wrong Allan's had, quite with a Life of their own toward the
Back of the bar. Watching them take their leave in this Way, I started to
feel quite lonely ☹

"Wait," I felt compelled to call as they disappeared into the Dark.
"Please!"

I ran after them to the Back, toward the empty booths and pool tables.
There was a back door there, lightly swinging as though Someone had just
made their Exit. And Outside? There were no Heads, Reader ☹ Only a small
Garden, which perhaps Allan the Barman had tended in his other Life as a
Witch. Some thin, cold-looking Trees. A couple of Rabbits staring at me in
the Dark. *Did you happen to see any Heads?* I asked these Rabbits. But they
just looked at each other, Reader, as if they did not understand me ☹ Then
they hopped hurriedly away. *Take me with you!* I felt compelled to shout. But
they did not heed my Cry at all. I attempted to give Chase, but they were far
too fast on their little hind Legs, and I quickly lost them. As I watched them
hop away into the Dark, an Ache consumed my Person ☹ Wherever they
were going, my own Human Legs could not Follow ☹

And so I was quite alone again, without Friends ☹

Back inside the bar I was met with an even greater Shock. Those bloody
Allan Bodies were no longer on the floorboards, Reader. They were gone.
Gone even though my Ears still rang with their laughing Screams. I looked
all around the bar and could not find these Bodies. I checked the dusty
underneaths of chairs and tables and pool tables and even behind the bar
itself. They had disappeared quite like the Heads ☹ There was only a young
Boy in black, sitting in a booth in the Corner of the bar. I had not noticed him
until this Moment, for he'd blended so perfectly with the Darkness. He wore
Headphones, and his Hands gripped a Book called *Being and Nothingness.*

He stared at me over the top of this Book with wide Eyes, unmoving, like he was a Statue of himself. "Did you happen to see the Bodies that were here?" I asked.

The Boy Statue did not answer me. He continued to stare, frozen, as though something had awed or afeared him into Stillness and Silence ☹

I looked back at the dusty floor, Ax still hot in my hand, her Blade bloody. Had I dreamed this Violence? Did I not kill Allan twice after all? I asked Pony, but he had been traumatized and could speak no Words ☹

I began to question Reality, Reader ☹

The very Nature of Things ☹

My Head began to spin, and whether this was from the Goldy Liquid or my Violences, I knew not. The sad Music still played in the bar, so prettily. Echo and the Bunnymen, the jukebox said. "The Killing Moon." A favorite of one of the Allans' presumably. The Dust swirled around me. *Your audience of Dust awaits*, said the Poet last Night. But I had Nothing to say ☹ I had finally killed Allan. Both of him. That Darkness that had gripped my Heart should surely have lightened. I should have been Relieved. Happy. And yet something felt . . . *wrong*. Off.

I was not happy ☹

I was, in fact, very sad ☹

I felt a Veil falling between my Self and the World.

Now, in the Ditch, I looked up at the Moon, Cruelle Mute. The Violences had allowed me, briefly, to forget my Sadness about Jonah, but now this Pain came back full Force ☹ I envied the Allans, their Heads lost to the Darkness. Possibly still rolling out there somewhere in the Night. Perhaps they were making their Way to the Lost Place. It suddenly seemed very far away.

I was lying there lost in these Musings when I saw four Shadows approaching me with heavy Footfalls. I could have run (indeed I should have run), but instead I let these Shadows fall over me, Reader. Obscuring my view of the Moon. Whispering, "Look, there he is."

My Keepers, I thought ☹ They'd found me at last. They were taller and lankier than I recalled. They looked like giant Bats, swooping down on me ☹ I contemplated fighting them off with Ax, but in this Moment I had no Will to Escape anymore, Reader ☹ I allowed my Self to be taken by them, my Body gathered up, my Arms slung around their surprisingly broad Shoulders, and dragged out of the Ditch. Back to the Attic and the Ropes of Revision ☹

Anyway, what had I to live for?

XII

When I awoke, I expected to find my Self back in my Attic Cell, a Bouquet of Pixy Stix at my Feets. A heart-shaped Post-it beside my Head that read *Good Morning* ☺ *I LOVE you* ☺

Instead I found my Self on a futon. Was it Jonah's futon?

No ☹

This futon did not smell intoxicatingly of his Dandy Lion Hairs. It smelled distinctly musky, what I later learned was a Scent called Patchouli ☹ There was a large window in this musky room. Through it I saw a very sad Garden, its mangy Grasses bitten through with Frost. White Flecks falling slowly out of a white Sky. *Snow*, I knew instantly. I had felt it falling on my Pelt before (cold and bright and making me shiver in my Heart), back when I existed in that other Form, lived closer to the Earth, now white and bereft of Flowers. The World, it seemed, had turned cold overnight. As if it knew of my own Heart turning cold ☹ In the many Fictions my Keepers attempted to read or feed to me, this often seemed to happen, the Weather Systems reflecting the Characters' emotional Interiors. *Pathetic Fallacy*, my Keepers called it. *A Mirroring of the Atmosphere and the Heart.* This window seemed so to reflect my Heart that I wondered for a Moment if I might be in a Fiction my Self. But I did not like to wonder on this long. I turned away from the Glass, and what I saw then, Reader, made my Heart colder still ☹

Four young men in Trenchy Coats were sitting around me on beany bags.

"Good Morrow," one of them whispered. Colby. The Carrot-haired one whose Earring I had stolen.

Oh no, Reader ☹ Oh no, oh no. Not—

"Ah, he recognizes us, clearly," said Another, smirking. The one with

Tears falsely weeping from his right Eye. Matthias, I would later learn was his Name.

"He Pales," observed a Third. He had Hairs the dark of Jet, quite slick. The Leader, I remember having intuited. "Bring him Hydration!" he barked at a Fourth, the Blondy. Gunnar the Henchman. "You must be quite parched," the Leader said gently, turning to me.

I nodded dully. Gunnar looked at me. "What do you wish to drink?" he asked.

"Just pick something, Gunnar, do not force him to think!" the Leader snapped.

Oh god, whispered Pony. *Rhyming.*

My Soul screamed inside my Self, yet I moved not ☹ For I did not have the Heart to run this Morning, not even from Poets ☹ Imbibing all that Goldy Liquid the Night before had made my Body quite sluggish. My Head felt like I had taken my own Ax to it. So I remained on the futon. I sipped a tea of Chrysanthemums Blondy gave me. Twas in a cup shaped like a leering Skull ☹

"Where am I?" I whispered, though I already knew.

"Oblivion," Blondy said, and smiled.

"Otherwise known as our Writing Space," the Weeping one added.

"I hope you don't mind us kidnapping you," said Colby.

"I don't care," I said. "For I see no Point in Living." This was so true, it nearly brought Tears to my Eyes. They smiled, seeming quite taken by my Nihilism ☹ My suicidal Morning Musings ☹

"What were you doing out there in the Ditch?" they asked me, most dreamily.

Should I really tell these Poets about killing Allans? No, I decided. I would keep it to my Self for now. "Trying to speak to the Moon," I said. "But she would not speak to me."

They nodded knowingly. "She is very capricious."

"She is a Cow," the Leader hissed. "Sometimes she speaks, sometimes she refuses to speak."

"One cannot trust her at *all*," they murmured.

"And what were you doing out there?" I asked them.

"What else? Breathing in the wild Night. Looking for the Flame of Inspiration, so to speak." They smiled at me. "And then we found you."

"And you're quite lucky we did. There is supposedly an Ax Murderer on the loose."

"Is there?" And I feigned Innocence, that Country of Mind from which I was forever severed ☹

"He killed twice more last Night, apparently. At the very bar where we found you," Gunnar said.

"We don't know if he actually *killed*, Gunnar. There were no Bodies. Only Hearsay from an Undergraduate. A Visual Artist, no less. High on Dexedrine."

I recalled the young Boy Statue in the booth, hiding behind a Book called *Being and Nothingness*, staring at me in afeared Silence.

"He claims the Killer looked like that actor Jacob Chamalord," Gunnar said, looking from me to the Others, who stared at my Face.

"Oh yes?" I said.

Oh fuck, Pony whispered in my Pocket. And I wondered, Reader, if they noticed this alleged Resemblance between my Self and this Jacob ☹ The Poets looked at me a very long Time, indeed seemed to lose themselves in looking.

"You might have been beheaded by Jacob Chamalord, Friend," the Leader said at last. "How lucky that we saved you."

"Yes, how lucky," I mumbled.

This does not feel like Luck, Pony whispered.

"Did you not fear for yourselves?" I asked them. "Encountering this . . . Murderer?"

They chuckled at this, Reader. "Oh, we do not fear the Ax. We are Poets, after all. We live ever close to the Blade," Blondy said.

"On the dull Edge of Oblivion," Matthias added. They all smiled darkly. "By the by, we were quite impressed by your Reading the other Night."

I thought of the bar burning. Their Claps and Cheers. How they happily added to the Fire with their many Whiskeys, while Jonah sat there appalled. "Thank you," I murmured.

"We have even told the Immortal about you," the Leader said.

"And who is the Immortal?" I asked like I was interested, though I did not care, Reader ☹

They all looked very alarmed that I did not know.

"Only the greatest Wordsmith of the twenty-first Century!" spat the Leader.

"He comes to Campus a few weeks from hence as our Visiting Writer," Blondy said. "He will give a Reading in the Grand Hall."

"And he will read our Work too, don't forget, Gunnar, he has promised," Colby added.

I began to deeply pity this Immortal, Reader ☹

"We are right now preparing our Manny Scripts for his Arrival," Matthias said.

"Just prior to Thanksgiving."

"Which we protest in any case. A stupid holiday."

"A *Thanks* for what exactly?"

They all sneered happily. "You will meet him when he comes," Blondy said.

"But I hate Poets," I whispered.

"Yes, exactly. He will love this about you. That you hate Poets."

Except me, right? I remembered Jonah saying, and smiling.

Once more I felt my Eyes fill with Tears. I turned away from them toward the window. The white Flecks were now falling most heavily. Pathetically. *A Mirroring of the Atmosphere and the Heart.* "Will Jonah be there?" I asked.

Silence. I glanced back at them. They were all exchanging Looks now.

"He might be or he might not," the Leader offered at last. "One never knows with *Jonah*."

"He is in love with one of the Fictions," Blondy erupted. "It is *disgusting!*"

"Shhh, Gunnar," the Leader whispered, most consolingly. He looked at me through his thick Lenses. "Forget Jonah for now. He is not Worthy of your . . . Affection."

"We will help you forget if you stay with us," Colby said.

"You will be our Muse," said Matthias. "You've already given us some immortal Lines."

"As well as some other, stranger Sounds . . . ," added the Leader with a sly Smile.

I had?

"Uttered as you slept. In the throes of your Heartbreak. Straight from the Soul, Muse."

"Muse," I repeated. And for the first Time this Morning, I began to feel truly afeared ☹ *What is a Muse?* Twas then I noticed, Reader, that they were all writing. Blondy scribbled in a little black Notebook, clasping in his Hand a Feather, plucked, no doubt, from an unsuspecting Magpie. Matthias scratched at a pad of yellow Papers, his pierced Tongue lolling out of his Mouth with wicked Pleasure. Colby gleefully stabbed at his Phone with his Fingers. And the Leader, he was clicking on his Lappy Top, his Face a sickly Blue from the screen's Glare. All of them smiling as they scribbled and scratched and clicked. All looking at me, Reader, as though they were cold, and Pony and I were a bright Fire. Twas then I had the oddest Sensation. That my Soul was somehow leaking out of my Body ☹ That the Blood was being drained from my Heart ☹ I felt I could not breathe, that I might be Sick ☹

"He Pales again," observed Colby, still stabbing at his Phone.

"Gunnar," the Leader said, still clicking too. "Bring him whatever he desires."

Blondy sighed and set down his Feather. "What do you desire now, Muse?"

I thought of Jonah's Hairs brushing my Shoulders. His Eyes the only Home I'd found in this World. "Tenderest spring Grasses," I told him sadly. "Dandy Lions."

He nodded uneasily. As if to say, *And where am I to find tenderest spring Grasses?*

"And Pinkberry," I added in a Whisper, almost in spite of my Self.

"Pinkberry?" Gunnar repeated. "But this is the preferred Food of the Fictions! Their many hideous Toppings and Sprinkles." He shuddered.

"I would like extra Sprinkles," I said without thinking. "Though I deserve them not." Silence among them now. Their Leader looked at me, quite coolly through the Smoke of his Clove Cigarette. Then down at his Writings, which somehow, I knew, I had been feeding.

"Do as he desires," he barked again.

"*What? But—*"

"*Go, Gunnar!*"

Gunnar sighed and rose from his beany bag. "Extra *Sprinkles*," he mumbled under his Breath, quite reproachfully. Muttered about the Shame of being seen at Pinkberry, the happy Violence of the Decor. "*Tis like being raped by a thousand smiling cartoon Bananas," he grunted as he stomped out the door.

"Is there anything else you desire, Muse?" the Leader asked me. Softly now.

I stared at the dusty floor quite forlornly, all their Feets in their untied combat Boots. *To go back in Time. To return to the Lost Self that knew not Love nor Killing Allan but only the tender Taste of the green Leaf. To leave this monstrous Human Form behind.*

I opened my Mouth.

And then I vomited, Reader. Quite endlessly, while the Leader shouted for something called a Hair of the Dog.

XIII

So went my Season with the Poets, Reader. In which I was their Muse ⊗
In which I was fed Pinkberry and Dandy Lions and Grasses, which
Gunnar allegedly had to forage from Fields quite frosted over, for twas November now. In which I drank of the Goldy Liquid (which they grudgingly
procured for me) with a kind of reckless Abandon ⊗ Twas a strange Interlude. A period of Oblivion ⊗ The Poets were either completely unaware of
my Pain or perhaps sparked by it, forever writing beside me, recording my
every Utterance eagerly, as though I were some kind of Oracle ⊗ *The Immortal is coming very soon*, they said. And they must get their Manny Scripts
ready, they said, for his Feedback. And I, as their Muse, played a most crucial Role in the Birthings of their Poet Trees ⊗ When they said the word
Muse, a terrible softness came into their Eyes, Reader. A wild Wanting that
afeared me ⊗ It reminded me of my Keepers, of the Attic Times. Yet I was
not technically a Prisoner here and could go anytime, I supposed. But I did
not, could not, leave their musty Rooms, Reader. A kind of heavy Melancholy had overtaken my Spirit, you see, paralyzing my Body ⊗ I remained
reclined on a beany bag, surrounded by their thin gray Volumes, drinking
Goldy Liquid from my Skull cup, staring out the windows with Eyes quite
glazed over, while they wrote around me in a little Ring ⊗ Perhaps twas the
fact of my broken Heart. Or that I had killed three Allans (all erroneously,
I suspected) and felt no Relief ⊗ Or that my Keepers were surely still out
there in the cold white World looking for me ⊗

No One ever comes here, the Poets often assured me. *Tis the Den of Oblivion*, they said, and grinned darkly.

Jonah might come, of course, they sometimes taunted. And my Heart
would brighten briefly.

"He might? Has he spoken about me?" I asked. I watched them contemplate this, wondering if they were trying to increase my Heartbreak with their Answers.

"He fails to mention you," they said at last. "He is so very busy *writing*, you see."

"He remains indifferent. Up there with the Moon and the Clouds, as is his wont."

"So telegraph the Moon," I whispered sadly.

Telegraph the Moon, they recorded.

I knew not how many weeks passed in this Manner, Reader ☹ In the Abyss I lost all sense of Time and Space. Knew not the Day from the Night, for twas all a kind of metered Darkness. Winter was falling thick upon the World, this I drunkenly observed from my beany bag by the window. Gone were its sweet Grasses, and the Wind had a Sharpness to her now, I could feel it cutting through the Glass like Ax. Increasingly I felt as if something Vital were being taken from me by these scribbling Poets, and I had no Power, in my weakened State, to resist. I looked out at this cold and Darkening World and lost all Hope.

But this is turning into a most Dismal Story ☹

In order to spare you and my Self further Painful Recollections, I shall skip ahead now to the Day before their Immortal arrived, for something of Import occurred on this Day that is related to my Violences ☹☺ I had been lying reclined in the living room, nursing my Skull cup, lost in my Utterances (*my Pelt shivers at each white Fleck, your Absence makes of every Hour an Attic Time*), feeling my Soul drain from my Body, when we heard a Knock at the door. The Poets looked up. They had been surrounding me as usual, scribbling feverishly, recording my every Sound with bright, hungry Eyes. Now they appeared panicked. *A Knock? At the Den of Oblivion?* They looked at Gunnar, who sighed and got up from his beany bag, muttering that he was not a Servant. At the window, he peered through the torn Curtain.

"Well?" the Leader grumbled. He was sitting at the Feets of my weakened Body, hunched over his Lappy Top ☹

"Tis some sort of Mob," murmured Gunnar.

Mob, Reader? ☹

"Ignore them," the Leader snapped, clicking away.

"Do not ignore us, please!" Someone cried through the door. And they knocked again, more forcefully. The Poets turned to me, almost instinctively, then to one another.

"Hide him," the Leader whispered.

I allowed Colby and Matthias to drag me upstairs (I truly had no Will anymore ☹). From my perch on the landing, I watched the Scene below unfold, my Forehead pressed against the railing. The Knocking was now very forceful indeed. Was it my Keepers at last? Polices? *Oh god*, Pony whispered, and despite my Numbness, I had to smile. It had been so long since we'd had an Opportunity to converse privately.

Pony! I exclaimed.

Shhh, Pony said, for this was no Time for happy Reunions ☹ We held our Breaths and waited.

When Gunnar finally opened the door, twas a group of Strangers who filed in. All were wearing the same black T-shirt imprinted with giant bleeding red Letters ☹ And all appeared to be bleeding profusely themselves, for their Faces were very White and their Throats appeared slashed ☹ *Dear god*, Pony whispered. Twas as if I had taken my Ax to each of their Necks and then had attempted to affix their Heads back on their Bodies, as I'd tried to do with the Wrong Allan's ☹ Only in this case it seemed to have worked. For though they all appeared to have recently been killed, they were very much Alive. Staring down the Poets in their Den of Oblivion.

"What is this?" I whispered to Pony.

I have a bad Feeling, Pony whispered back. Which made me afeared, Reader. Pony's Intuition, you see, was almost always Correct ☹

Three young Persons stood at the Helm of this Mob. One of them I recognized as the Couch Monster from the Greek house where I had killed the Wrong Allan ☹ I had a Flash of him reaching for a Gun on the wall, screamingly accusing me of Murder ☹ Another was the Boy Statue from the truck stop, who had no doubt witnessed me killing the other two Allans, the ones who had likely only been joking about being Allan ☹ Between them was a tall, dark-haired Girl in an Army Jacket. She alone was a Stranger to me. Her Blood-splattered Face looked very pinched and serious. Her dark Hairs tied in a most somber Ponytail, but twas nothing like Pony's Tail, for I sensed it had never once swished ☹

"May we help you?" the Poets said, bowing slightly to this bleeding Mob.

The Girl pulled an Ax from her Jacket. Reader, the Resemblance to my own Ax was so striking that if the Blade hadn't just then been hidden in my Blazer, pressed against my Heart (as it always was), I would have thought twas mine. The Girl turned this Ax round in her pale Hands. "We are from the School of Visual and Performing Arts," she said gravely.

Oh god no, Pony whispered.

"And we are raising Awareness," said one of her bloody Ilk.

"About the recent Violences!" cried yet Another.

"On this accursed Campus!" finished Another.

Twas astonishing that they could speak with their serious Neck Injuries, Reader. I was about to remark on this to Pony, but he cut me off.

Tis Makeups, he explained quietly. *Theater can be very Cruelle in its Deceptions.*

The Girl smiled nastily, covered in her false Bleedings. "No doubt you've heard about the Violences, of course?"

"Violences?" The Poets looked back longingly at their Writings. They did not like this Interruption, I knew. "Oh yes, the Violences," the Leader said irritably. "Terrible."

"Dreadful, dreadful," the other Poets murmured, lighting Cigarettes.

"What's even more *dreadful*," the Girl said, her Voice rising, "is that the *Police* aren't doing anything to find the Perpetrator, can you believe this?"

The Poets shook their Heads, pretending to be horrified. Pony and I, however, were delighted ☺ Not doing anything, Reader? Twas the first good News we'd heard in some Time ☺

"Injustice!" the bloody Mob cried behind her.

"Systemic Apathy is a DISEASE!" cried one in the Back, but the Girl raised her Ax, silencing them all. She had a Mind Witchy Energy to her, quite like the Leader.

"And what exactly is . . . AAARV?" Matthias said, attempting to read the bleeding Letters on their T-shirts. Dragging out the As with his Poet's Cadence.

"ARTISTS AGAINST AX-RELATED VIOLENCE," they shouted.

"An ancient Warren organization!" cried one.

"Which we have resurrected!" cried Another.

"In the Face of these most Violent Times!"

And now they all raised Axes in the Air ☹

Such a fucking Production, Pony said. *Leave it to Performing Arts.*

"After all, one of our fellow Students has been killed!" the Girl cried. I thought of the Wrong Allan then, my awful Oops, and felt an Ache ☹ "Our very own dear Taylor Fields."

"*Tyler,*" corrected the Couch Monster quietly beside her.

The Girl frowned. "As you see," she told the Poets, "we have enlisted the Witness to his Murder." She nudged the Couch Monster, who flushed beneath his bloody Makeups. "He told the *Police,* but of course they didn't believe him. Instead they're saying it's all a PRANK, can you believe that?"

Thank Christ, Pony mused.

"I thought it was a Prank too at first," the Couch Monster mumbled. "But I saw what I saw. At least"—he shook his Head—"I think I did."

"Of course you *did!*" the Girl shrieked. "No One in this town seems to CARE that people's HEADS are being CHOPPED OFF."

And she swung her Ax, slightly bigger than the others, most wildly. *Tis a Toy,* Pony told me now. *Performing Arts must have a formidable Props Budget.*

"If the *Police* aren't going to investigate until they have a *Body,*" she said, "if they're not going to believe us until they have *Evidence*, then we have no Choice but to take Justice into our Hands, do we not?"

Oh fuck, Pony whispered.

"Absolutely," the Poets agreed.

The Girl beamed now through her Bleedings. "So you will join our Cause, then, Poets? As fellow Artists?"

Now the Poets looked at one another, panicked. "Well, we would love to, you see. Very much indeed. Only we are very busy at the Moment. Just in the Midst of finishing our—"

The Mob immediately booed.

The Girl, meanwhile, just stared at the Poets, her Expression full of quiet Fires.

"You know Narrative Arts has a very long History of looking the Other Way when it comes to Campus Violence," she said at last. "Ax-related Violence in particular." She looked at them most accusingly.

"Is that so?" they murmured.

"So the Rumors go."

"Well, we know Nothing about that," the Leader snapped.

"Of course not!" she snapped back. "Too busy writing your *Poems* in the Dark. Well, there will be No One left to read them if we are all MURDERED!"

There is No One reading them now, Pony whispered.

The Poets nodded gravely. Thankfully, I knew they did not really care at all. They wanted to sink back to their Oblivions, climb their Poet Trees. "We promise to keep an eye out," they mumbled. They were about to usher the Mob out the door, but the Girl stopped them.

"Wait! If Nothing else, at least take a look at these Pictures of the Suspect."

Oh god. *Pictures*, Reader? ☹

"Despite his recent Trauma, Trent was able to sketch the whole Thing, just as he himself witnessed it at the bar. Show them."

Trent opened his black Book. The Poets stared silently at the open Page, at this alleged Sketch of my Self, their Cigarettes smoking in their Fingers.

I held my Breath, my Heart knocking against the blade of Ax. Waiting for them to say, *Yes indeed, that is our Muse. He is upstairs right now.*

"Is this some kind of *Joke?*" Colby asked at last.

"It is not a *Joke* and maybe *you* won't think so either when you're MUR-DERED!"

"But it looks like a Violin with three Noses," Gunnar said.

"It's an *Artist's Sketch*," the Girl said. "Trent is a Cubist."

"I included this, too, if it's more helpful," the Boy called Trent said, holding out a glossy Photo that looked ripped from a Magazine.

"This is just a Picture of Jacob Chamalord with Rabbit's Ears drawn on his Head," Matthias said.

"It is a *Found Object*, and according to both Trent *and* Cody"—and here she nudged the Couch Monster—"a *Perfect Likeness!*" the Girl roared.

Jacob Chamalord ☹ Oh, Reader ☹

"Well? Have you seen him or haven't you?"

The Poets stared at this Photo. They recognized my Likeness, I know they did. I could feel it in their Silences, the crackle and hiss of their Cig-arettes turning to Ash in their Hands. I held my Breath once more as they looked at one another, then back at their Writings.

"No," the Leader piped up at last. "We have never seen this Person be-fore."

Ah, sighed Pony.

And I, too, sighed with something like Relief, Reader.

Later that Evening, after the bleeding Mob had taken their leave, I lay re-clined in the living room. High on the Goldy Liquid and its forgetting Magic, yet still very much unsettled by the Day's Happenings ☹ Normally, at this Time of Night the Poets would surround my Body in an effort to record my Drunken Utterances. Instead, Reader, they were having a great Argument in the kitchen. About me and my Murders ☹

"I really think he might be this Killer they are looking for," Gunnar was shouting.

"Absolutely not," the other three countered.

"But he has an Ax in his Blazer!" Gunnar persisted.

"Yes," murmured Colby dreamily. "For the frozen Sea within us."

Gunnar shook his Blondy Head. "I think it is Real."

"*Real?*" sneered the Leader, his Hairs of Jet glistening under the grim kitchen Lights. "Come now, Gunnar. Are we seriously going to have a Discussion about what's *Real*? What are we, Fictions?"

"But three People have been killed!" Gunnar persisted.

"Tis Tragic," the Leader agreed. "But tis also a very dangerous Town. We knew that when we applied. The more prestigie-yes the Program, the more violent and bleak the Town."

"Tis the Risk we took for Art."

"But we found him near the very truck stop where those Men were murdered!"

"*Missing!* Missing, not murdered."

"They could be missing *and* murdered," Gunnar said. "Do you not think it's a remarkable Coincidence that—"

"Enough, Gunnar," the Leader snapped. "He is a Muse. And not just any Muse. When I am near Aerius, I feel Things I've never felt before. I have a new kind of . . . Access."

I shivered at this. The Others did not know that the Leader would often wake early to be with me alone. I'd open an Eye to find him hovering over me with his Lappy Top, clicking with a Fury that afeared me so much, I closed back my Eyes and wished to Run ☹ Yet I could not Run, had no energy to Run ☹ Could only dream of the Lost Place, of Jonah waiting for me there.

"When he Dreams," the Leader sighed, "his Utterances become something else entirely."

"Oh yes? Like what?"

Like what? I wondered.

The Leader shook his Head, his Gaze suddenly misty. "I only know they are a *Language*. More Primal, more Transcendent than our Human Tongues could ever muster. And I am very close to cracking them," he whispered.

I felt my Heart lift a little then. Could it be the Language of the Lost Self? Was it still somewhere Inside me, though I could access it not?

Gunnar merely scoffed. But I felt him looking at me curiously now from the kitchen. "And what if he's dangerous?"

"A dance with the Muse is always dangerous," the Leader said darkly. "Tis a most violent and ecstatic Tango." He ran his Fingers through his Hairs, which I'd drunkenly twisted just the other Night into a Fishtail. Very surprised to find that my Hands had this particular Goldy Cut Skill. On a Lark, I'd told them that such Hair Braidings might help their Writings. Though really I'd suggested it only so that they might *stop* their Writings, Reader ☹ Give my Soul, even if briefly, a much-needed Break. I had also braided Matthias's and Colby's Hairs. Even Gunnar, perhaps not wanting to be left out, had allowed me to weave a small, twisty lace Braid in his long Goldy Locks. He'd come to me solemnly, Brush in hand, and whispered, *If you must.*

"A Journey to the Underworld," Colby said, stroking his own Dutch Halo.

"Perhaps you're not equipped for such Journeying," Matthias said, fingering his French Knot.

"I'm *equipped*. I'm just concerned he might murder us all in our Sleeps one Night."

"Silence, Gunnar!" the Leader shouted. "The Immortal comes Tomorrow, and I will *not* have you *ruin* this for me! Not when I am so close." He looked at me lying there in the living room. I immediately closed my Eyes to feign Sleeps. Felt him smile at this. *The coyness of the Muse.* He began to walk toward me.

"Can we really trust a Muse who loves *Jonah*?" Gunnar called after him in disgust.

"Love makes Fools of us all," the Leader muttered bitterly as he approached me. "Including the Muses. Including even the Gods."

And then One by One they all followed suit, resuming their usual Positions around my Person ⊗ Waiting for me to speak Utterances that would spark their creative Journeyings, grow their Poet Trees ⊗ At first I refused them, I was Silent. But my Pain was such that the Utterances gushed from my Lips quite in spite of my Self, and I knew not what I said. I thought only of the Lost Place, where I was never lonely, for I was Friends with the Mud. There my Heart did not ache for Jonah. I had killed no Allans nor wished to kill Allans. There was only the Wind in my Ears and the Cowslip on my Tongue and the soft sweet Grasses at my Feets. Then I thought of Jonah himself. Who the Poets kept hinting might come but who never came. And so, surrounded by Poets and quite without Hope, I *imagined* him there with me.

I had grown quite good at imagining, Reader, in this Time of gray Skies and Snow.

XIV

This, Reader, was the Eve before the Violences, which I must now return to in my Tellings ☹☺ Which all began the next Day with the Arrival of their Immortal. The Poets had stayed up quite late that Eve, scribbling and clicking madly, putting what they called "the Last Touches" on their Manny Scripts, while I sat, Muse-like, drinking my Self into a pretty Oblivion in their Center ☹ (They never ceased plying me with the Goldy Liquid, for which I was grateful.)

When I woke very late on this Day, I found them surrounding me in their Evening Wear ☹ Ascots gleaming ominously ☹ Eyes freshly lined and glittered. Talons painted a sparkly Black. "Tis Time for the Immortal's Reading," they intoned. "You will be our Guest."

"At the Dinner, too," Matthias added.

Reader, I did not want to go to this Reading ☹ I was not only very afeared of encountering my Keepers or this Mob, but I truly hated Poet Trees more than ever before. Also, I was very Depressed ☹ I told them this. But they said, "That is a perfect State of Mind for Poet Tree."

"You are our Muse," they said.

"We wish to introduce you to our God," they said. "Tis Time for Muse and God to meet."

"You can ask him about this Lost Place you often mention in your Utterances," Gunnar grunted.

How can a Poet possibly know about the Lost Place? I thought. I shrugged and flushed, hating that these Poets knew my Interiors.

"Also, Jonah will be there," Colby taunted.

"Jonah?" And a small, shameful Fire in me awakened. Hope broke terribly inside my Heart.

The Poets smiled. "Come along and you'll see."

Given how these Poets had spoken of *the Grand Hall*, I expected it to be grand, Reader. But it turned out to be a very small Bookstore quite like the one I'd burned down ☹ A dusty Hole full of shelves and wobbly tables covered in *Volumes* ☹ A few folding chairs had been arranged around a wooden Podium. No sign of Jonah anywhere ☹ As the Poets rushed to claim their Seats, I went looking for him, but the Place was truly empty. Even the Woman with Allergies was not there (perhaps she'd taken my advice and given up on Poet Trees). Just a pale Clerk glowering near the ancient cash register and an old Homeless hovering in a Corner. He was partaking from a plate of free Cookies on a table, stuffing them into his coat Pockets. *Lots of Homeless around here, so sad,* I remember my Keepers telling me, so long ago. *What we thought you were at first, isn't that funny?*

I went over to him, mainly to partake of the Floral Arrangement behind the Cookies. The Homeless watched me stuff limp Daisies into my Pockets just as he was stuffing Cookies in his.

"Are you here for the Immortal's Reading?" I asked him.

"The *Immortal*," he said, and laughed uproariously. "Absolutely not. Are you?"

"I'm here because I have no Choice," I told him.

But we are also hoping to see our Love, Pony sighed.

The Homeless smiled. "Me too." He took a Daisy from my Hand, put it in his Mouth, and winked at me. I watched him disappear into the dusty Labyrinth of Shelves.

"Aerius, come *here*! Tis about to *start*."

"Jonah isn't here," I whispered to the Poets as I took my seat.

"*Hush.*" They told me to direct my Eyes to the Podium, where the Immortal would soon manifest like a Sun. Colby walked up first, going quite pink in the Face as he unfolded his crumpled Introduction and read from it, his Words running together, so that I caught very few of them. *Esteemed. Genie-yes. I Con.*

The Homeless, the very One I'd just encountered stuffing the Cookies into his Pockets, walked up to the Podium then. *I knew it*, Pony whispered. A little Man he was, quite like an Elf. He wore a Trenchy Coat like the Poets', though his was quite battered looking, like it had weathered many Storms. He had a Scally Cap tilted on his Head. A scruffy Face covered in gray and black Bristles, and glittering Eyes that reminded me of a Hawk's ⊗ Could this Homeless really be their Immortal? The Way the Poets murmured and grunted appreciatively at the Sight of him, he must have been, Reader. Twas then I saw that tucked under his Arm were many Volumes ⊗ I wanted to escape, but my Head was cottony from all the Goldy Liquid I had been imbibing, and anyway, these Poets were sitting on either side of me, Reader, pinning me in Place ⊗ What remained of my Soul screamed inside my Body as this Immortal began flipping through his Volumes, each one spiky with little Bits of Paper, marking where he would read Selections. (There were *many* of these Bits of Paper, Reader ⊗) As he flipped, thanking Colby for his "most generous Introduction," thanking all of us for being "in Attendance," sneering at the humming Emptiness of the room, the Poets lowered their Heads as if about to hear a Prayer.

He read many Poems from many a Volume, while they hissed their approval after each one. Pony went into a Coma. I, for my part, became quite sleepy, Reader. Twas something in the trancy Way the Immortal was reading. Almost as if he was trying to Hypnotize with his Voice. Despite my Self, I fell into a kind of Dreaming, a Vision. Suddenly I was in the tall, grassy Blades, a sun-warmed Dandy Lion on my Tongue, a vast blue Sky over me, hearing the jumping Song of the Wind.

"Aerius."

Then a giant Hawk swooped down, eclipsing the Sun and swallowing me in Darkness ⊗ He was about to take me in his Talons and I screamed and screamed and—

"AERIUS!"

I opened my Eyes. Poets all around me. Looking disgusted and embarrassed by my Dreamings ⊗ "I told you," Gunnar barked to the Others. "Didn't I tell you we should not have brought him?" The Immortal stared at me from his Podium, smiling most strangely. A curious Twinkle in his Eye now.

He continued to smile at me at the Dinner, a most horrid Affair at something called a Bistro ⊗ It gave Pony and my Self a Shiver to enter the Place, Reader, though twas nice enough with Candle Lights and Flower arrangements and tinkling piano Music. There was a giant Rabbit's Head on the wall, emanating red Light like Fire, which Pony took to be an Omen of Ill Portent ⊗ *I feel I have been here before,* he whispered from my Pocket. *In another Time, in another Pocket. We should go.*

But what about Jonah? I whispered back.

"Aerius, do not dawdle at the Threshold, *please,*" the Poets scolded.

So I joined them at their round table appointed with Tea Lights and dying Orchids, their Immortal already sitting at the Helm like a sad, drunk King. The Poets surrounded him, each of them clutching their Manny Scripts, which they were so very eager to share. The Immortal eyed these Pages warily, mostly keeping his strange Gaze on me as I partook of the Orchids. I was keeping my Eye out for Jonah, of whom there was still no Sign ⊗ *We should go, we should go,* Pony urged. Making me nervous, and I was already quite nervous, Reader, to be in such a public Place where I might be recognized ⊗ Beneath the table, Pony continued to murmur about his Intuition and how I never heeded it these Days ⊗ The Poets, meanwhile, raided the bread baskets and attempted to engage the Immortal in Conversations. "And how is your hotel?" Colby offered.

"I am not staying at a hotel," the Immortal said wearily. "I am staying with your Poet Tree Teacher and his Wife, the Fiction. In their guest room."

That sounds horrible, doesn't it, Pony?

I don't care, Pony intoned. *Let's please go before it's too—*

"I imagine that must be much cozier than a hotel," Matthias said, most genially.

"I'd prefer a hotel, honestly," the Immortal sighed. "But it's not terrible. I'm left alone mostly. David is busy teaching, and the Fiction is locked in her Writing Shed. I'm treating it as a little Writing Retreat, my Self." He smiled sadly.

"How wonderful, Great One," the Poets murmured, nodding. They were behaving so strangely, Reader. Not at all seething, as usual. In fact, they were being most polite, which unsettled me ☹ Their Voices full of Light and Softness, like they had swept them of all Shadows. Now and then they gazed at their Manny Scripts, which were resting on the table before them. Pages they had written furiously at my Side, woven through with my Utterances, now typed and ready to hand over to their God for Feedback. He ignored these Pages, drinking his Scotch with Ice. Continued to stare at me as I ate the Orchids. "Fascinating," he mumbled.

"Where is Jonah?" I asked Gunnar at last. I was trying to avoid the Immortal's Gaze, for it only increased my Dread ☹

"He'll be along soon. He won't miss the Chance to have his Manny Script read, trust."

"At the very least, he will not miss the free Meal," Colby added.

"No Poet would miss the chance for a free Steak," the Immortal said to me, smiling.

"Unless one sees Steak as Murder," Gunnar grunted quietly from behind his Menu. "In which case, he would not miss the Chance for a free Risotto."

I could order whatever I wanted, Gunnar said to me. The school had deep Pockets, apparently, like the one in which I housed Ax.

"Do you have any more of these?" I asked the Waitress, pointing to the

Centerpiece I'd ravaged. She looked at me and smiled quite dreamily. "I'm sure we can figure something out," she said. "Has anyone ever told you you look like that Actor—"

"He looks like No One," the Leader snapped. "Please just bring him his Orchids."

"And a bottle of Goldy Liquid, please," I murmured, looking away. *We should run*, Pony whispered.

"Goldy Liquid?" the Waitress said, sounding puzzled but delightedly so.

"Goldschläger," Gunnar explained to her. "Will you not have Wine for a change?" he snapped at me. "Or Ale? Anything other than this Frat Boy *Drink*?"

"I will join the Boy," the Immortal said from across the table. "*Goldy Liquid*," he said with a smile, borrowing my Parlance. "Please bring another shot glass for me." Reader, I did not really want to share my Goldy Liquid with this Immortal ☹ He had already gone through two double Scotches since we arrived at the Bistro. But it seemed there was no Choice, there was never any Choice among these Writers ☹

"Your Reading was so wonderful, Great One," the Poets told him. Many such Words of Praise they heaped on his Person, while he grunted his Thanks, seeming quite bored. His Eye had a faraway, glittery Look. His Scally Cap drooped. He turned to me, still forlornly partaking of my dead Petals.

"And you," he said. "What did *you* think of it, may I ask?"

"Me?" The Poets all turned to me now, waiting for my Words. "What did I think?"

"Of the *Reading*," Gunnar barked.

"Well, I hate Poet Tree. And all Poets. So I am not the one to ask," I mumbled.

He laughed with Delight. "You are exactly the one to ask," he said, Eyes still on me. "I noticed the Work made quite a . . . visceral Impression on you."

It came back to me, the Impression. My Self huddled close to the Earth, its sumptuous Dirt, its Blades of Grass a prickly velvet, the Shivers through my Body.

"Twas a strange Experience for me," I murmured.

"Strange?" A Hunger overtook his Face now. I thought of my Keepers then, ever hungry for more Adjectives about their Writings. "How so?"

"It took me somewhere," I said at last, evasively, picking at a Petal. "Some Place or Self I thought I had been before. To which I long to return. Except that I cannot find my Way Back now."

"Where?" he whispered. "Tell me." He seemed very excited suddenly.

Oh god, Pony gasped. *They're here.*

"Where?" I said.

"Yes, where?" the Immortal pleaded.

There! Pony cried.

"There?" I repeated.

"Where's there?" the Immortal cried. "Where did you go, tell me!"

But I never answered his Question, Reader. Because that's when I saw Them outside the restaurant, through the windows. *The windows! The windows!* Pony shouted. Making their Way to the door, all four ⊗ Their terribly shining Hairs, their shimmering Dresses swishing in the Night ⊗ Those wildly desirous Eyes ⊗ And that sinister Scent, Reader, I felt I could smell it even through the Glass. Of Flowers not in Nature ⊗ Of False Grass ⊗

"Aerius," the Poets said. "What is it?"

But I could not speak, could only watch Them approach ⊗ Goldy Cut, her Hairs freshly golded and cut, her stained white Gloves, her Dress the Color of wrong Skies. Then Murder Fairy, brooding in her red Cloak and little clicking Shoes, ever casting watchful Glances all around her Person. Insatiable in a Victorian-looking Frock, clomping along in her army Boots, her brazen Mouth open as if trying to make out with the very Air. And of course the Mind Witch with her silvery Locks, her long white Tunic that so resembled my own from long ago. And her Third Eye, that Huntress, wide open ⊗

What Horror I felt then, Reader. A Memory of Ropes. A Triangle of Glass ⊗

"Well, look who's just arrived," the Leader intoned, noticing them.

"Why would *they* be here?" Gunnar seethed. "The Fictions don't have a Visiting Writer."

"Probably just here for Dinner," Matthias said. "They can go Anywhere anytime, remember? They're *rich*."

"Looks like they have some Companions with them Tonight," Colby chimed in.

Twas then I noticed that they were not alone, my Keepers. Four Men were walking behind Them. Each Man was quite tall, like I was, and wore a dark blue Suit.

"Prelaw, by the looks of it. Or Finance," Gunnar sniffed. "Some lovely American Psychos. In Brooks Brothers, no less. How fittingly vile."

One of the Men looked at me through the Glass and seemed to smile. He had the whitest Teeth, Reader. His blue Eyes shone in the Dark. A Wave of Dread entered my Heart. "I must go now," I whispered.

"*Now?*" the Immortal said.

"We haven't even received our Food!" the Poets cried.

But I was already running from the table, Reader, toward the Back of the restaurant, the Poets calling after me.

In a dark Alley reeking of Garbages, I leaned against the rank Wall, catching my Breath. Stared up at the cold Night. A *close one*, Pony whispered, over my racing Heart. *Too close, too close.*

Had they seen me as I had seen Them?

Don't know, think not. Shouldn't linger here in case.

Quickly I wandered away from the Bistro toward a small Park across the street. I had not been outside in a long Time, Reader, and the World had grown terribly cold. But twas lovely in its Coldness. Trees tall and glowing white with Snow beneath the Moon. Grasses sparkling with Frost as though Nature had spread her Glitter there. I drifted toward the Glitter, my Breath coming out like Smoke. As I did so, that Melancholy possessed me again, making my Steps heavy, hanging my Head low. Perhaps because I felt once more alone in the World. That I had no Place here. That I would forever be on the run ☹ I watched from between two prickly Evergreens as my Keepers were seated in the Bistro, a pretty table right by the front window. Their Companions, these tall young Men, helped them into their chairs. Something about these Companions, Reader. Their glazed Expressions and chiseled Faces. Their Eyes, so blue and bright. They felt infinitely familiar for Reasons I could not articulate. Twas a Feeling. *An Intuition*, as the Mind Witch or Pony or even Mother might say. One of the four Men looked especially familiar. He had a black Patch over one Eye like the Wrong Allan. He looked quite like the Wrong Allan too. So much so that I almost wondered if he *was* the Wrong Allan, Reader, if I had not really killed him after all. Suddenly his Eye locked with mine, as if he'd heard my Wonderings through the Glass and now saw me hiding between the Firs. Looking at him, I had a Flash of that Rabbit I'd encountered in the Rose Garden so long ago. Twas his Eye Patch, perhaps, that reminded me of the Rabbit's black Patch. Twas a Sense of Knowing as I held his Gaze, all my Pelt Hairs suddenly standing on End. Quickly I hid back behind the cold Shrubs, my Heart pounding.

"Aerius," said a soft Voice then. I screamed.

I turned to find the Immortal standing behind me in his battered Coat. Smiling at me most sadly, gripping the bottle of Goldy in his Fist. "You ran away."

I looked at him, my Heart still pounding. "I . . . needed Air," I said.

The Immortal smiled. "You don't need to explain yourself to me, Boy. Who wouldn't want to be out here among the Stars? Rather than sit in that Den of Lies." He nodded toward the Bistro, then took a long Swig from his bottle. *"Follow your own inner Moonlight,"* he murmured. *"Don't hide the Madness."*

I had no Idea what he was talking about, Reader. But I said, "This is excellent Advice. Thank you, Great One."

"*Great One*," he muttered, shaking his Head. "I am no Great One." He took another Swig, then stared balefully at the Snow. *Let's get out of here,* Pony pleaded in my Pocket. *Please.*

"I really should—"

"I know what you are," he suddenly said, looking right at me, Reader. "And I know this Place you are trying to return to."

I gazed at the Immortal, swaying drunkenly before me.

"You know?" I whispered.

He smiled darkly. "All Poets know. Well, any Poet worth his Salt knows. Many a Time I have tried to go back there my Self," he said. "To the Primal Self. The Animal Past." He took another long Drink.

"The Primal Self," I repeated softly and felt a Shiver. "Where you know the Language of the Moon and the Wind and the Grasses?"

"Where you know the Language of Everything." He looked dreamily at the Sky.

"And do you ever see yourself small and furry?" I asked him. "Sitting under Shrubs?"

"I do," he whispered, Eyes shining with Tears. "I do."

"Me too," I confessed. Tears in my own Eyes now. "How can we go?" I asked him. For what did I have in this Place but Poets and Keepers? And Jonah Nowhere in sight. And I did not love being a Muse ☹ "Will you show me the Way, Great One?"

He does not look he knows his Way Anywhere, Pony observed.

The Immortal pulled a gray Volume from his Pocket.

Oh god no, Pony said.

"This," the Immortal said, waving the Volume. "I will read you a Poem I didn't read earlier, before my Audience of Dust. The dry, Academic Setting was no Place for it. *To have great Poets, there must be great Audiences.* Here"—and he waved at the Shrubs—"is where one must read Poems. Out in the open Air among our Friends, the Trees, and our Lover, the Mud."

And he sank down to his Knees on the snowy Grass. He pulled me down with him—he was surprisingly strong. I watched as he peeled back the Grass, ripping out the Roots, and began digging in the cold Dirt with his bare Hands. He encouraged me to dig with him. I did, though twas very cold Work at first. But the Warmth from our Hands seemed to soften the Earth. I laughed with Excitement and the Immortal did too, even as Pony murmured, *I do not know about this.*

"There," said the Immortal at last, pointing to the Fruit of our Labors. I looked down at this small, dark Hole we had dug.

"This is the Way Back?" I said.

He nodded, bleary-eyed, his Scally Cap quite askew now. He stroked the Soil with his frail Hands. Quite drunk he looked at this point. I stared at the Hole. It did not look like the Way Back to me, Reader ☹ It did not look like the Way to Anywhere at all ☹

I told you, Pony whispered.

"We also have this, remember," he said. And he shook his Volume at me again, its Pages flapping like a flightless Bird.

"And is this a Map?" I asked him.

"This is a *Poem,*" he said, getting impatient with me. "There is a Poem in here that we will read together. You know, they have said I am the reincarnation of Ginsberg."

"They have said this?"

"Oh yes."

"Wow." I did not know who this Ginsberg was, Reader. But I attempted to look impressed. If there is One Thing I have learned from the Poets and Keepers both, is that tis very important to pretend one has read certain Volumes and to look impressed by a Name. "Ginsberg," I repeated with Feeling.

He nodded. "And this Poem is my Tribute. It is a Howl," he said.

"A Howl?"

"MY Howl. In the manner of Ginsberg, I have written it. Totally revolutionizing his Confessional Mode. I like to think too that I have sharpened its Symbology."

"Oh?" I said.

"We must be like Midas," cried the Immortal. "We must Howl our Howl into the Mud. The Mud is our very best Audience. She will hear us and open herself, the Earth will open, she will take us into her mineral Embrace. And this is how we will go Back."

I nodded, Reader, though I no longer knew if he and I were talking about the same Place. And if we were, did I really want to go back there with this Poet? ☹

I hate Poets, remember? I'd told Jonah.

Except me, right? Jonah Nowhere in this Night. I looked at the Immortal, extending his frail Hand to me.

"Take it," he said. "While I speak the Words aloud. Here." He gave me his Volume. "You may hold the Poem and read along with me. Though listen first, please, so that you may catch my Cadences."

So I held the Volume in one Hand and the Poet's Hand in the Other. I watched him bend his Head toward the cold, muddy Cavity. Putting his whole Face into it, Reader. He then began to shout his Poet Trees deep into the Hole. And I read along with him from his Volume. Twas the usual Poet Stuff about melodious Springtimes and curious Clouds and cosmic Fellatio and the Monster of Capitalism and the Wonder of certain hallucinogenic Drugs and the Reincarnation of the shiniest Souls ☹ And then:

"I am Allen G," he whispered into the Hole.

"What?" Suddenly a Cold swept through me. The night Sky seemed to fill with a red Fog.

"I am Allen G," he repeated.

"You are—"

"I AM ALLEN G," the Immortal cried into the dark Hole, my Grip tightening over his Hand.

"I AM ALLEN G," he howled. No longer hearing that I was not joining him in his Reading. That I was instead staring at the Page, at the word *Allen* (a variation?) beside the words *I am*. That this word *Allen* was flashing redly in the Back of my Brain Chambers.

Along with the word *Kill*.

XV

Quickly I buried the severed Head in the Hole, letting go the cold Hand of Allan, while his Blood pooled hotly around me. Allan whom I had killed again ⊗ Killed almost as quickly as I'd thought the word *kill* ⊗ Whom I had killed three times before, though erroneously ⊗ Watched as Allan's severed Head tumbled into the Hole we had dug together. Watched his headless Body gush its dark, hot Blood.

"I thought I had killed you already," I told Allan's head softly. "Thrice." I covered the Hole with clumps of frosty Grasses so he would not look at me ⊗ His Blood-splattered Face appeared to be smiling serenely. He was smiling more in Death than he'd ever smiled in Life, sitting among the Poets and their Manny Scripts, which he must review, drinking his Scotches and stealing dusty bookstore Cookies and reading from his Volumes under the gray Light. *How many more Times must I kill you, Allan?* I thought.

In the Distance now I heard the voice of Gunnar.

"Lenny," he called. "Lenny, where are you? Your plate of Murder sits cold on the table!" (*Murder*, Reader, was how Gunnar referred to all Meats.) "Your Murder grows cold, Lenny!" he cried. "As do our Manny Scripts," he muttered under his Breath.

I looked down at the headless Body lying in the Dirt, dark Blood still gushing all around us. The dark Hole in which I'd buried the Head.

Lenny?

"But you said you were Allan," I whispered to the Body. Which could not respond, Reader, for it had no Mouth.

Oh god, I thought ⊗

I could feel Pony's stony Silence in my Pocket. *No.* I shook my Head.

No, no, NO, twas impossible that I had once more killed a Wrong Allan,

Reader. I shook and shook my Head as if to make it not so, not this Time. He was Allan, he *must* be Allan, mustn't he? Hadn't he screamed this Name nearly a thousand Times into the Hole? And the words *I am Allen* were printed in his Volume, were they not? Twas *Allen* with an *e*, but surely no less Allan for that. My vision had grown swimmy, Reader, and the Pages were now sprayed with Allan's Blood, obscuring all Words. I closed the Volume. *A Lamentation by Leonard Coel*, it read on the Cover. I felt sick then. I turned the Book round. On its Back was the Photograph of the Man I had just killed. *Leonard Coel*. Looking sad and scruffy in his weathered Coat. His Eyes twinkling sadly, filled with a Longing that I knew now was for the Lost Place.

"Lenny," shouted Gunnar once more. "Oh forget it," he muttered. Through the Shrubbery now, I watched Gunnar trudge back into the Bistro, not wanting his own vegetal Risotto to grow cold. I turned back to the headless Body of Allan. Who was a Man named Leonard Coel. *Leonard. Lenny, I'm so sorry I have killed you. Please forgive—*

But the Body was gone.

Nothing at my Feets now but Grass, sparkling with Frost.

"Leonard?" I whispered, reaching out. But there was only Air and Earth. Allan or Leonard was truly gone, Reader. As if he had never been there, hunched beside me on the Grass, screaming his Poet Tree into the Mud. As if I'd never taken the hot Magic of Ax to his bristly Neck. No Sign of him, though his Blood had freshly splattered the Blade.

"Leonard, where did you go?"

I dug my Hands back into the Earth, looking for his Head, for something to tell me what was Reality, Evidence of what I had done. I was attempting, as my Keepers often said, to *ground my Self*. And I did feel something in there, Reader. But twas not the wispy-haired Skull of Leonard. Instead my Fingers grazed something warm and fuzzy and soft.

And Alive, Reader.

I jumped up from the Shock of it, this Presence of warm Life in the cold Hole.

Then out of this dark Cavity there emerged a Creature white as the Snow. Furry, twas. Long-eared and bushy tailed. Sitting at my Feets. A Rabbit. Wearing Leonard's Scally Cap on his Head. He shook it off, his Eyes looking up at me, blue and twinkling, quite like Leonard's Eyes had twinkled. Twitching his small pink Nose as if to say, *Hello.*

"Hello," I whispered. And I felt as if I were falling, Reader. The Ground seemed to sink beneath me. "What have you done with Leonard's Head?"

The Rabbit stared at me. Tis funny, but I felt he was about to speak, that he knew of Leonard's Whereabouts. I recalled my earlier Encounter with that Rabbit in the Bush, how I'd heard his Language reverberating in my Blood. Now I looked at this white Rabbit sitting by the Hole, looking up at me. I waited to hear him speak through my Pelt. I even closed my Eyes. *Tell me. Tell me the Meaning of all of this, Small One.*

"Aerius," said a Voice.

I opened my Eyes. There he was at last. Standing in the Snow before me, his Face licked silver by the Moon. Cigarette burning between his fingers. Smiling like I did not have an Ax in my Hand, a Rabbit at my Feets, like I had not just accidentally killed his God.

"Jonah," I whispered.

"What are you doing here?" he said, Eyes on mine.

"Waiting for you," I said. And I knew twas true. I could feel the Rabbit nodding at my Feets.

Jonah's Smile brightened. "It's good to see you."

You too. But all my Words were gone from me again. Hiding under Shrubs. It seemed Jonah's Words were gone too. He took a long drag of his Cigarette.

"I wondered where you were," he said at last. "If maybe you'd even gone back Home."

"Home?" I shook my Head at the dark Hole. The Rabbit was now rubbing his Face with his Forepaws. "No, I actually can't go back, it seems. Ever." Tears threatened to fill my Eyes.

"Oh," Jonah said. "Well . . . I'm glad."

I looked back at him. Still smiling at me in the Dark. "You are?"

"Of course. I'd miss you. I *have* missed you. A lot."

I've missed you, too! So much. But I stayed silent, Reader, under the Moon and the starless Sky. Even as he moved in closer to me, having just said the Words I'd so long dreamed he would say. Perhaps I still feared that his Missing and my Missing were not the same. Perhaps I feared this was not Reality. I merely nodded coolly.

"I didn't have your number or email, so I couldn't reach you," he said, moving in closer still. "I just kept hoping . . . " And he shook his Dandy Lion Head. I reached out and stroked his Hairs, so soft they made me ache. I was so relieved that I did not touch Air.

"Hoping what?" I said.

He smiled again. "That you'd show up somewhere again, I guess. And here you are." A Warmth suddenly coursed through me in the cold Night. I wanted to kiss his smiling Mouth. And he wanted to kiss me, I felt. Our Breaths, dancing Smoke in the Air, were already entwining. And then he said, "What are you doing with that Ax?"

I realized I was still holding her Handle limply. She looked suddenly like a foreign Object. Nothing that could or should ever belong to me. An awful Prop Someone had placed in my Hands. I felt Pony shaking his head sadly.

"I don't know." Those threatening Tears started falling from my Eyes at last. I looked at Jonah through these Tears.

"Aerius," he said with such Kindness it nearly broke me.

I almost told him Everything then, Reader. About Allan, how I must kill him. How I would very much like to stop, but it seemed I could not stop, my Hand on Ax faster than I could think or blink. When I only wanted the Cowslip, I only wanted the Moon to speak to me, I only wanted to hear the Song of the Wind. I only wanted Jonah's Mouth, his Pelt, his Cock, his Heart, his Love. "I do not even know what is Real anymore," I said at last. "I only know that I've done some terrible Things. That I seem to be wired for Destruction. And that I don't belong here."

And that I love you.

I waited for Jonah to run from me. But he just stood there in the Snow, staring along with the Rabbit.

"Wow," he said at last. "These Performance Pieces of yours are really intense."

"What?" When I gathered the Courage to meet his Eyes, I saw he was gazing at me with a kind of Wonder. Like I was a Poem or a Cloud.

"I dig them," he said dreamily.

"You do?"

He nodded. "Just please don't kill that Bunny," he said. He smiled at the Creature still sitting by my Feets. Looking up at us with shining Eyes.

"Bunny," I repeated. The Word caused a Fire to light up inside me. The Word was like a Tunnel opening in my Mindscape, and once more I felt I was falling.

"Aerius, are you okay? I'm sorry, I was kidding. I don't think you'd ever kill a Bunny."

He brushed my Hairs away from my Eyes. Stroked my sorrowed Cheek, and I was melting, melting under his Perfect Touch. That wanted Nothing from me. That made me want to give him Everything.

"Sometimes I feel very wrong," I whispered. "Or like the World is wrong. One of us is very, very wrong. And I want to leave, I want to go Home. But I don't even know how or where I . . . " I looked at the dark Hole. The Rabbit watched me sorrowfully now.

Then Jonah kissed me, Reader. His lovely Mouth suddenly crushed against mine, making me forget the cold Night. Hands gently caressing my Neck, my Face, as I caressed his. His impossibly beautiful Pelt pressing into me, warming me so deeply, I felt I should never be cold again. I felt the Rabbit sigh. And Everything became clear in that Moment. *I love you*, I thought. *This is who I am*, I thought. *This is Home*, Pony whispered. Ax nearly dropped from my Hand. . . .

Church Bells chimed in the Night. Jonah pulled away gently, no longer smiling.

"Oh god, I really should head to the Dinner now. I'm pretty late."

"Okay," I breathed.

I looked down at the Rabbit still at my Side. I guessed we were alone again in the World. *What about me?* Pony sighed from my Pocket. *You forget me so much lately.*

"Should we go?" Jonah said then.

And he held out his Hand to me.

Reader, may I express to you the Happiness I felt for this short Space with Jonah's Hand in mine as we made our Way out of the Park? Winter was banished at last from my Heart ☺ I kissed him once more, and he kissed me, Reader. His Mouth so soft and yielding, its cigarette Smoke filling my own. Twas a beauteous Moment, the Moon shining down, making the frosted Grass sparkle. The Bunny still following us. As if to say, *Yes, this, exactly.* And the World no longer felt wrong like Allan. And I no longer felt wrong in it.

"I love you," I told him, the Words coming out of me like Smoke. Snow began to fall lightly all around us. For a brief Moment Everything felt exactly right.

He smiled at me, his Dandy Lion Hairs glittering with Snowflakes.

"Let's get Inside," he said, squeezing my Hand. "It's freezing out here, don't you think?"

No, I didn't say. I do not find it cold at all. May I just be out here with you, the Snow falling around us forever? But I let him draw me back toward the Bistro and its lit glass windows.

And then there, through the windows, I saw Them again. They who had made me go running in the first Place, Reader. They whom I wished to forget forever. Drinking their Champagnes at a round table with their strange Companions.

"Aerius, what is it? Why are we hiding here?"

For I'd stopped us, pulled us both behind the Evergreens that flanked the Park's Entrance. I stared at Them, their small, shining Heads glowing like awful Suns ⊗ Their Companions were seated beside Them, each one chewing from his own plate of Flowers. *Lovely American Psychos*, the Poets had called Them. Who were these new blue-eyed Mates? These tall, Petal-eating Men in their blue Suits and black Gloves. Why did their striking Faces feel so very familiar to me? As if to look at them was to see something of my Self? The one with the Patch over his Eye, who'd been staring at me earlier, was now looking dully through the Glass.

"Aerius?"

Suddenly he noticed me, Reader, through the Trees.

"Aerius, what's wrong? Shouldn't we go in?"

"I can't," I said, locking Eyes with Patch through the window.

"Why?"

Because through that door is Death. And I don't like the look of this American Psycho staring at me through the window. Through that door are only Poets and Keepers, only Prisons. "Let's just go somewhere else. Please. I hate Poets, remember?" I tried to smile. But Jonah wasn't smiling anymore.

"I have to go in, Aerius. I already missed the Reading because I had to finish my Poem." I saw then, Reader, that there was a Manny Script tucked in the inner Pocket of his Trench ⊗ How my Heart sank at the Sight of those Pages, Reader, folded against his Chest so they wouldn't get wet in the Snow. "If I miss this Dinner, I won't forgive my Self. Why can't you just come in with me?"

I shook my Head, staring at my Keepers and their strange Dates through the window. Patch's Eye was still on me.

"I have to leave," I said. "I'm sorry."

"Well, I'm sorry too. Because I really have to stay. This is my Chance to get Feedback," he said, suddenly determined. The Light (or was it the Shadow?) of Ambition in his Eye.

"You won't be getting Feedback Tonight," I whispered.

"How do you know?"

Because I killed your God. "I have a Feeling."

"Well, either Way, I have to make an Appearance. It's good . . . for Connections and stuff."

I saw now that he was also wearing a Suit and Tie under his Coat. The Tie had a brightly colored Painting of a bald Man screaming on a Bridge. That feeling of Sickness returned to me, Reader.

"I'm a Poet, Aerius," he mumbled.

"I know," I said sadly. *Yet I still love you.*

"It's a rough Path," he said, the Snow sparkling in his Dandy Lion Hairs. His lovely Face turned away from me, away from the Night that waited for us, toward the lit windows of the Bistro, all those Idiots inside.

"You should come with me now," I said.

"Please don't ask me to choose between you and Poet Tree," he said. The Night Wind swirled all around us, whispering her Promises, I heard them. But Jonah, I knew, heard them not.

"Come with me," he begged.

We can't, whispered Pony. The Rabbit was still at my Feets, watching this sadly. I shook my Head. "Please don't ask me to choose either."

And then the Warmth in Jonah's Face was gone. Twas like the grassy Earth in his Eyes had suddenly frozen over. Twas like the Dandy Lions had died.

He let go of my Hand. To recall this now, his letting go, the sudden Coldness of it. How he turned and walked away from me, through the door where I could never follow. How I stood there watching him go, Snow falling around me. Falling somewhere inside me still.

"Jonah, wait!" I said.

But the Psycho in the window, Patch, he stood up from the table now, his Mouth full of pink Petal, his Eye wide with Recognition. He pointed at me, where I stood behind the Trees.

Panic thrummed in my Body. *Run, run,* I thought. But I was frozen, Reader. Frozen by Fear or by my own broken Heart, I knew not. I could only stare at my Keepers through the Glass—they'd looked up but didn't seem to espy me behind the Trees. Now Patch opened his Mouth and made a screaming Sound I could hear even from where I stood. *Oh god, oh god,* Pony cried. A scratching at my Feets. The Rabbit, still at my Side, looking up at me with his bright Eyes.

Come with me, I felt him whisper through my Pelt.

And then he leapt off into the Dark.

XVI

How long did I run after Bunny, leaping through those dark, snowy streets? Forever, it felt like, his Tail flashing ahead of me in the Night. As I followed, I thought I heard Noises behind me ⊗ Oh god, Reader, were they coming for me? I dared not look back lest I spy my Keepers and their Psychos hot on my Trail ⊗ Instead I kept running, my Gaze fixed on Bunny. I felt his Words along my Pelt. As if to say, *Hurry*. As if to say, *This Way. Okay, Bunny*, I thought. *But you are moving so quickly through these winding streets, and I can't keep up, for I can't jump like you, Bunny, though my Body wants to so much!* Legs tingling, Feets Singing with Jump. Bones and Muscles and Blood electric with Jump. The Longing to jump ringing through my Being, and not just the Longing, but the Memory. *Did I jump like you once, Bunny? Because racing through this Night together, my Body wildly straining to reach you, my Soul exhilarated, though I am so heartbroken and afeared, my Feets nearly flying off the Sidewalk, I feel perhaps I did. But if I did, I can no more. And now I am afeared I'll lose you in this endless Dark. And if I lose you, what will become of me?*

Behind me, the Noises seemed to grow louder ⊗

"Wait for me, Bunny," I whispered as I ran. Each Time I said *Bunny*, twas like a thrum through my Blood. But Bunny would not wait. Wherever he was going, he was very excited to get there. I felt him smile up ahead. Perhaps he was leading me back to the Place that Leonard and I had wished to go. Perhaps he'd found the Way.

"Have you found the Way, Bunny?"

And then? He disappeared ⊗ I could see him no more in this dark, wrong World ⊗ Just a street of sleepy houses, Reader. My Self alone on the snowy sidewalk. Nobody pursuing me after all. Which should have been a great Relief—in my afeared State, I had perhaps imagined these Noises. Yet I did not feel Relief, Reader. *Oh, Bunny,* I thought, looking at this lonely street. *Oh god, where did you go? Did you leave me? Am I finally completely alone in this Darkness?*

There is always me, Pony whispered suddenly from my Pocket. *Please don't forget. Please know I love you. Please know I am here.* And I worried, not for the first Time, that I was imagining that Pony said this to me, just as I'd imagined being chased. Because I so desperately needed to hear these Words in this Moment, Reader. Because I so desperately needed a Friend.

Twas then I saw him.

Bunny.

Perched regally before the front steps of a dark house up ahead.

A tall house, twas. Glowing a pale Purple, or so it seemed beneath this Sky, beneath this Moon that now appeared between the Clouds. "Bunny," I whispered. And he turned to me, his Eyes still very bright.

Here, said Bunny's Body to my Body, making my Pelt tingle, making the Hairs there rise. Then he hopped to the Gate beside the house and disappeared through the slats.

No Trespassers said a little Sign with cozy lettering on this Gate ☹ *Beware of Dog* said another ☹

Yet what could I do but follow?

A Garden, Reader. A Garden is where I found my Self when I followed Bunny through the Gate. So pretty even in the Snow ☺ I could smell its Life pulsing far beneath the Frost. Everywhere I looked were climbing Vines and the spiky Stems of what were once Roses. All along its Fence, Strawberry and Raspberry and Blackberry Bushes, barren now. And a very small white house in the Corner of the Garden. Like a Cottage or a Shed, I thought. It gave me a funny Feeling to look at, this Shed. A quickening of my Pulse. A Cold in my Blood ☹ And yet twas pretty shining under the Moonlight ☺

"Bunny," I whispered, "why have you come here?"

But alas, there was no sign of Bunny anymore. He had disappeared again ☹ Only Feetprints, Reader. The tiny Feetprints of Bunny turning Circles in the shining Snow, quite like a Fairy Tale. Murder Fairy used to love to read me such Stories, they were her Favorites. Because they were about Witches and Fairies just like her, she said. And there was Magic, too. *Just like you*, she said. *Me?* I said. *Oh yes*, she said, *you are very much of that Other World*. And she pointed to an Illustration of a Forest full of sly-eyed Creatures. Perhaps this was why I felt the Cold in my Blood. Because the wintry Garden, the little Shed, the Bunny Prints, all felt like a Fairy Tale to me. And though Fairy Tales have Wondrous Happenings ☺, they also have Violent Happenings too ☹ Feetprints often lead to Danger, I knew. To Witches and Ogres and such ☹ Yet they were so pretty that I was dazzled to follow ☺ Enchanted, as is often the case in Fairy Tales ☺ I followed them until they suddenly stopped and were replaced by some bigger Feetprints. Human looking. As though Bunny, in mid Hop, had suddenly become another kind of Being. Hurriedly, I followed the larger Prints, quite forgetting my Fear. They led me to the Shed in the Corner of the Garden. Right to its red front door, where they stopped abruptly, as though Bunny had gone through the door, how curious. I noticed the window of the Shed was lit up dimly, perhaps Someone inside was making a Fire. Perhaps Bunny himself. Perhaps this was the Way Back of which Leonard had spoken. The Cold grew in my Body. Why did this inner Cold grow when the lit window and the shining Feetprints drew me in so? I could not say then. Twas another *Feeling*. Which I ignored. Bunny was my Compass, my North Star, and I must follow him to the very End of his Journeyings. I could not return to the Poets, for I had murdered their God ☹ Also, I did not care to be their Muse anymore ☹ Certainly, I could never return to my Keepers, to their Revision ☹ Just seeing their shining Hairs and hungry Eyes made me want to run and never cease running. Of course I wanted to return to Jonah. But Jonah favored another World, a World where I increasingly sensed I didn't belong. Had never belonged. A Human World full of Pain and Sorrow and endless Pining and Ambition and trying to take down the Moon in a Manny Script ☹ I did not want to be in this World any longer. Could not breathe there, twas not my Air. But in what World *did* I belong, Reader?

Perhaps this door would lead me there.

Twas darker Within than it had looked Outside. As my Eyes adjusted, I discerned a dank room lit by a ring of small Fires. A scent of burning Flowers and Leaf permeated the Air. I heard a Music composed mostly of Strings, which the Mind Witch favored, and which should have been a Warning, Reader. Which should have made me run Miles away. But I dismissed it. I was so desperate. So broken in my own Soul. And curious. Very curious, too. In the center of the room, I saw now, there sat an old Woman. Cross-legged on the floor. Eyes quite closed. Long Goldy Hairs streaked with Silver. She wore a glittery Tunic like the Mind Witch. Her Eyelids were fluttering as though she were lost in Dreamings both blissful and painful. I have known such Dreamings ☺☹ And in her Lap sat Bunny.

"Bunny," I whispered.

But Bunny only blinked at me now. He seemed in a Trance. Quite happy, though she was holding him there. Stroking his long Ears. Whispering Words I could not discern, what was she whispering to him? Twas putting him in this Trance State where he could no longer communicate with me. Where he no longer appeared to even recognize me, Reader; I was a Stranger to him.

Bunny, what is she whispering to you?

I saw that at her Feets was a bundle of fresh Rose Petals and Freesia. My mouth watered at the mound of Petals, Reader. Perhaps while she and Bunny were dreaming, I could have my Self a Meal ☺

Quietly I made my Way into her Ring of Fires. Quietly I sat before the Woman, whose Eyes remained closed. A small room, twas. With only a table and chair in the Corner. On the table, a pad of Paper and some Pencils. A

Lappy Top, the sight of which made me slightly afeared ☹ Still, I reached for some Petals ☺ Delicious ☺ So fresh and sweet and peppery, I gorged my Self a little on her Bounty, Reader, and choked ☹

Twas then she opened one Eye.

The look on her Face, Reader, when she saw me, sitting crossed-legged as she was, choking on her Flowers. Tears fell from her Eyes almost instantly.

Strangely, they fell from my Eyes too.

She looked at me through this Veil of Tears. "It is Alive," she murmured.

Alive? I looked at Bunny in her Lap; his Eyes were very bright now, practically glowing in the Dark. The Woman stared at me like I was the most incredible Dreaming.

"It returns to me at last," she whispered. "It manifests." She stared up at her Ceiling as though speaking to Someone there. I looked too, but there was No One on her Ceiling, Reader ☹ When I looked back at her, she was shaking her Head in Wonderment at me.

What returns to you? I wondered. *What manifests?* But I found I could not speak. Something had happened to my Tongue, Reader. Almost as if the Petals had made it numb, or was it the Woman herself, her violet Eyes now fixed on me?

She turned to the Bunny, still sitting in her Lap. "But what of the Violence?" she asked him. "Surely there is no Creation without Destruction, is there?" She was asking Bunny as though he might answer her. She looked back at me, Reader, that Hunger in her Eye.

"Tell me your Name."

"Aerius," I whispered. When she asked for Words, I could give them, it seemed.

"He speaks, he speaks. The Reality insists upon itself." She smiled. "Aerius," she said, and nodded. "Of course. Both of the World and not of the World. And he is full of Sorrow. His Heart breaks. He is wounded, is he not?"

I nodded. For I *was* wounded, Reader ☹ For my Heart *did* break ☹ Though I did not feel it right to share with this Woman, I could not help my Self. She had a Power greater than the Poets, greater than my Keepers, greater than even the Mind Witch herself. A Way of directly drawing secret Truths from me that I did not wish to give away.

"Of course he is." The Woman nodded with me. "He is a most beautiful Wound. Aching for the Tap." She smiled.

Who are you? I wanted to ask her, but felt I could not move my Mouth now. *Are you another Witch of the Mind?*

"I am Mother," she said, as though hearing the Question in my Head. Definitely a Mind Witch, then. "Mother is what you may call me."

"Mother," I repeated. Though I wanted to run, I was frozen, Reader. Her violet Eye had a kind of paralyzing Effect. A strange Fire spread through my Body, pinning me there on the floor as she drew closer, marveling at my Face. What she called "the Beautiful Wound" of me. How marvelous I would be to Tap. She had not Tapped in some Time, she said. She'd felt so dried up, barren. The Marrow of her Soul had been sucked dry by her Students, those little unrelenting Vampires. Though I did not know what Mother was talking about, I nodded along. "But here you are," she said hopefully, crawling toward me on her Knees.

I nodded, very afeared now ☹

"I am so humbled," she whispered. Though she did not look humbled, Reader. She looked, in fact, quite emboldened. Crawling ever closer to me in this Ring of Fires. "I will never again question," she murmured, crouching down before me. "And he bears the Mark of the Crystal Thief," she gasped, looking down at my Forearm, the horned Rabbit drawn in ink. "A sign, a sign." She wanted to touch my Face, I knew, but she was afeared to. Lest I might disappear, vanish under her Hands. I knew this Feeling. She did not yet know if I was Real or if she was imagining Things. At last she reached out her Hand, so tremulously, to touch my Shoulder—

Twas then we heard the Sound of Boot Crunches in the Snow outside. The Swishing of Trenchy Coats. The Poets. Their deep Voices calling distantly. "Lenny, Lenny!"

"Fuck," she growled. "Interruptions!"

"Lenny, are you there?" But they did not call my Name, Reader. I wanted to scream, *I am here! In the Shed with Bunny!*

"Silence," Mother told me, putting her finger to her Lips. And twas like my own Lips were suddenly sealed, like she had cut out my Tongue. Gathering Bunny into her Arms, she rose and left the Shed, closing the red door behind her with a click that said, *Stay*. The Moment she was gone, I could move again. I ran to the single window, open to let in the Night Air, concealing my Self in the dark Shadows lest Mother or anyone Outside see me. Peering through the Glass, I saw the Poets standing in her snowy Garden like wilted Bats. Jonah was not with them ☹

"Gentlemen," Mother said, holding Bunny close to her Chest. "This is an unexpected Surprise. What brings you here so late?"

"We're sorry to bother you. It's just that . . . " They broke off, looking at one another.

"*What?*"

"Leonard Coel has gone missing," Gunnar said at last.

Mother did not reply. I could not see her Face, shrouded as twas in the Shadows of the Winter's Night. She only continued to stroke Bunny by the Ears, which he appeared to quite enjoy from my Vantage Point. Her Silence seemed to say, *Continue*.

"We were . . . having dinner with him . . . at the Bistro, you see," the Leader began, stammering. I had never seen him look so flustered. "And all was going just fine, just fine. He ordered the Steak, was drinking Scotch. We were complimenting him on his most brilliant Reading. Then he went outside for a Cigarette and . . . did not come back."

"We waited until the Bistro closed," Matthias said. "We had no Choice but to eat his Steak lest it grow cold. And to order more Food and Drink, otherwise they would not have let us stay as long as we did."

"Meanwhile, *one* of us looked all around for him," Gunnar said pointedly.

"But we could find no Trace," the Leader said sadly. "Except this." And he held up the Immortal's Scally Cap. "We found this in the Park."

"Twas like he just vanished into the Dark," Colby said nervously. When the Poets got nervous, I recalled, they rhymed.

"And he was supposed to offer us Feedback." They held up their Manny Scripts. Mother glanced at these crumpled Pages, gripped in the Hand of each Poet. I felt her Soul shudder.

"I see," she whispered.

"He said he was looking quite forward to reading them."

"Did he?" Mother smiled at Bunny as though they were enjoying a private Joke. She scratched his Ear.

"We can't imagine that he just *disappeared* when he still had to give us Feedback."

"Of course not," she said. "How could you ever imagine that?"

"We wondered if perhaps something had happened to him."

"In fact, we think he may have wandered off with a Friend of ours," Gunnar said, though the Others attempted to shush him.

"A Friend?"

"He has also disappeared, you see. And he may be dangerous."

"Really? And who is this dangerous Friend?" Mother sounded amused, but her Interest was piqued.

"Our Muse," they whispered in one Voice.

And Mother laughed. "Yes, that's exactly right. He has run away with your Muse."

They looked at her as if they did not understand.

"Boys," Mother said. "You needn't worry. Leonard Coel is here among us." And she stroked Bunny's Ears, which twitched and twitched.

"He is?"

"Yes, yes, he came home a little while ago. But he doesn't wish to be disturbed at the Moment, I'm afraid. He's busy manifesting, you see. Exploring his Animal Past and such. Being with you all was just so inspirational to him that he is currently in another State of Consciousness entirely."

The Poets looked at one another. They did not appear relieved. "But what about our Manny Scripts?"

"We have polished them up."

"We have been getting them ready for *weeks*," the Leader murmured.

"One cannot ignore the dictates of Inspiration, Joaquin," Mother said to him. "The Call of the Wild must be heeded, as you all know from your own Dalliances with your . . . dangerous Friend, the *Muse*. Now if you will excuse me, it is quite late. And I am actually working on something new my Self."

Their Eyes glazed over at the Thought of yet more Fiction in the World. "Cool," they lied. "May the Muse be with thee." They bowed and turned away with a Swish of their Trenches, a rustle of Pages. Trudged off morosely into the Night.

"I hope you'll come to my Showcase this Spring," Mother shouted after them. "I didn't think I'd have anything to show, but Inspiration has struck this Night for me as well as Leonard. Landed in my Lap, so to speak." And she smiled at the Shed. "Must be something in the Air."

The Poets stopped then. Frowned. Gunnar turned to look back at the Shed. For a moment I wondered if he saw me in the window. But he did not.

"In the Air," they echoed wistfully.

And with that, they left the Garden. Mother watched them go, still stroking Bunny's Ears. And then she whispered to him, I heard the Whisper. All down my Pelt, Reader. "A close One. A very close One, Lenny. But I covered for you," she said. "Me, the *Fiction*. You're welcome."

Lenny?

The Rabbit's Ears twitched more nervously.

"And just think," she said, "at least you don't have to read their Poet Tree now. There is a bright Side, isn't there, to the Rabbit Life? 'The Animal Past,' as you so often said." She laughed and turned back to the Shed, her violet Eye catching mine through the window. Twas an Eye far more hungry than all the Eyes of my Keepers and the Poets combined, Reader ☹ All's Child's Play compared with the Hunger I saw there. With what was bent toward me now, still stroking the trembling Rabbit in her Arms.

Part Three

We

B unny, we'd like to pause just for a sec here, k?
First of all, *hi.*

How are you?

Still sitting comfortably in your chair? Enjoying the ropes (we jest)? Still following our poor monstrous boy into his darkest night of the soul? Oh, we hope so. And we actually think you have been, Bunny, by your face! You look riveted (and not just by ropes!), gagged (and not just by a literal gag!). And also like you've been, you know, crying a lot. Your one eye that we can see (will you ever stop hiding behind your hair, Bunny?) looks wild with emotion. Are you connecting with his journey? Is it touching your dark, twisted heart? Well, let's just set the book down for a minute, k? We'll keep the ax where it is, of course, the blade right at your throat, where it belongs. We're deep in the wee hours of our story now, by the way. We're deep, too, in the wee hours of this night. Sometimes it feels like the dawn will never break, doesn't it?

We bet it feels like that for you right now.

Now, we should say we're *aware* that we're not always coming off so great in these pages we're reading to you, Bunny. Still, we wanted to show you the Source material. Wanted you to hear it all from the horse's mouth (the rabbit's mouth?), so committed we are to authenticity, to giving voice. And it really does look, by your tearstained face and trembly body, like it's striking a chord. We have to admit that pleases us. We're enjoying these tears of yours as *artists*, you know? What we live for, really, we do. We've shed one or two of our own tonight, trust.

But at this point? We feel we should interject with a little interlude of our own, k, Bunny? Lest you think we're the fucking monsters he paints us out to be. Our boy exaggerates, of course he does. He's a Fiction, after all, isn't he? Our most beloved Fiction, but a Fiction nonetheless. And though we forgive him for his many lies (just like we'd forgive our own future child for spitting in our face one day), we do need to supplement his narrative here. Say some words on *our* behalf. About where *we* were at this particular juncture. Both in our minds and also in our hearts, Bunny.

Which by then were really one mind, one heart.

And so we'll tell this next part as one voice. For verisimilitude. For *effect*, as it were. One voice from four mouths ever shifting, just like the old days. Remember those old days, Bunny? Maybe it's the magic of this attic or perhaps the transformative power of story (ha!), but we feel we've sort of become One now again in the telling, isn't that lovely? We'll pass the ax around as we tell, how's that? Just to, you know, make it more fun for you, our captive audience. Put our masks back on and turn out the lights. For vibes, Bunny. So you'll never know who's telling, where the ax is going next.

Oh, but you'll feel it.

That's a promise.

15

Now, where were we?

Oh yes.

Let's go back a stitch in time, shall we? Back to that Hallows' Eve, Aerius's escape from our triangle window. *If* we can even call it an escape, Bunny. (We still call it the result of a certain person's negligence, don't we, Vik?) Of course we were pissed that he left us. Hurt too, Bunny. We felt empty and lost and so terribly unmoored in the world, we really did. And also just, like, *really* sad. That night we searched every last fucking garden and field and stretch of grass in this hellscape town, didn't we? Screamed his name (most lovingly) into the dark until we basically had no throats left.

Because he must surely be so lost and afraid out there.

Because how would he even survive in the cold, wide world without our loving care?

There was also, of course, the matter of Allan (Aerius wanting to kill him and such), which weighed on us too, sure. Though not as heavily, we confess, as other concerns. Like who would feed him his dandelion—Pixy Stix diet now? How might he procure his daily Woolf? Or just how mundane the world suddenly seemed to our eyes without him, Bunny. Kyra's attic lost its glittery look; the dust became just fucking dust. The sun was just the sun and the moon was just the moon and everything seemed to whittle back down to itself, so that we were living in the actual world, in *fucking reality*, as Coraline called it, and it was horrible. A most unmagical, terrible twenty-four hours.

But then?

Vik found that other ugly bunny in the rose garden the next day, didn't you, Bunny?

Trying to atone, we guess, for losing Aerius. (But you can't atone for the unforgivable, Bunny, as you well know.) "Time to move on," she said hopefully. "Try another."

We looked at this ugly bunny with his eye patch, munching his pink petals. We had our doubts, of course, that we could ever find Love again. Took him back to the attic with the heaviest of hearts. Because some of us weren't fucking ready to move on, k?

And we did wonder, we *worried*, could we even do it again?

Back in Kyra's attic, it was with little faith (and in Coraline's case, several French 75s) that we lit the candles and incense and such. Stood in a circle and such, surrounding the ugly bunny. Watching him munch those never-ending petals so very shamelessly. He was making serious eye contact with us the whole time. Our thighs quivered a little, we'll admit. We felt our hearts open slightly, like the legs of a whore. A violent trembling overtook our bodies, Bunny, and Bunny, we knew, was responsible. We closed our eyes.

A sound like the end of the fucking world.

When we opened them, we were blood-spattered, covered in animal gristle, and Kyra's curtains were on fire, weren't they? We were screaming most dreamily, and there was a gentle *knock, knock* at the door. And? And a beautiful man in a dark blue suit waiting on the other side. He had an eye patch quite like the one he'd had in bunny form.

"Hello," he said, "is this, uh, Intro to Philosophy?"

"Fuck yes," we think we whispered.

And after that?

Well, we were sort of on a roll.

How many rabbits did we fulminate that November with the power of our collective mind? Don't really know, Bunny. Kyra was our counter, but she sort of lost track once we started doing four at a time, k? The trauma of

loss had brought us even closer together, you see, and this resulted in many
a lovely Manifestation. Or as Vik liked to jokingly call it, a *Man Fest* (being
the crudest among us, she enjoyed such reductive wordplay).

We called it fucking Literature.

Were the explosions upsetting at first? Of course they were, Bunny, in-
nards are ick. Hence the aprons and bunny masks Coraline bought us online,
which were really protective wear. Hence our painting a bright blue sky on the
attic walls, complete with cumulus clouds. Because there is no Creation without Destruction, no heaven without blood—Else always reminded us of this as
we waited, splattered with rabbit, for that knock on the door. How the sound
of this knock thrilled us, Bunny! How we wish to exist forever in the holy space
between the gristly explosion and the wondrous knock! That moment when,
bloody and grinning so hard that our faces hurt, we'd skip to the door and there
he'd be waiting on the other side. Beautiful as Brando maybe (in his heyday,
obvi). Smiling at us—a little vacantly, perhaps, but still. Always dressed in that
dark blue suit and pale blue shirt that matched his eyes, so lovely-strange. (We
did not know whose soul was responsible for this eye/clothing combination,
for no one has fessed up to this day.) Their black leather gloves freaked some of
us out a little at first, sure. But Else convinced us to see such recurring features
as our haunting artistic stamp, quite like O'Keeffe's floral clit. Vik was more
freaked out by how polite they were, weren't you, Bunny? They were always
saying such nice words to us, it's true. *Hello. How are thee? All my heart is yours.
You burn too bright for this world. How amazing that you are so super talented
and single.* Staring at us so worshipfully with those pool-water eyes. "Hot," she
admitted, "but creepy, Bunny."

"Not creepy," Coraline snapped. "Better."

Way fucking better, she insisted, than the aloofness of Aerius. It made
us more civilized, certainly. We did not need to tie them to a chair, for instance, no, no, for they were quite willing to perch beside us on the fainting
couch and discuss, at length, which Brontë sister or Austen heroine they
believed we most resembled. *You are Emily sometimes*, they mused, *Charlotte
other times. Sexy all the time.* Not at all like Aerius. Not literally fucking run-

ning from us, Bunny, and screaming. Instead, so well-bred. So *appreciating* what we had to offer. *Tell me everything*, they would entreat. *Fascinating*, they would marvel, even if we said nothing at all. *Thou art as wise as thou art totally beautiful.* They actually *wanted* to hear our playlists, Bunny, k? Begged for us to play Taylor again, to play Lana again, to play Stevie and Charli and Chappell, not to mention the whole of Kate Bush and Heart. *This is my very favorite*, one of us might say of "These Dreams," and they said, *Oh, my very favorite too. May we have this slow dancing?* And they rocked with us in the attic to the watery music until we were quite seasick. They said, *Love is a smoke and is made with the fume of sighs.* They said, *You are so fucking beautiful, it actually hurts me physically to look at you. Ouch*, they said, looking at us still. *Ouch, ouch.* They said, *You have bewitched me, body and soul, and I love, I love, I love you, k?* And we said, *Really?* And they said, *omg, totally. May we fuck you?* Yes, that's right, Bunny, they asked to fuck. You got this part so wrong (you got SO MANY things so wrong) in your little novel, by the way. They weren't *afraid* of sex with us, not at all, k? In fact, make no mistake: they begged for it just as fervently as they begged for more Bush on the Bose. And naturally, our answers varied, Bunny.

Yes, please fucking fuck me and let me also fuck you?

You may fellate my Aura until it turns the color of Primroses.

How comfortable are you with an entity orgy?

You may spoon me, and should this result in a kind of dry fucking at some point in the wee hours, I am not averse to this. I am, in fact, wildly consensual.

But there *was*, of course, an issue with that in the end. The fucking, Bunny, dry and otherwise. For as it turned out, as we quickly discovered, one by one by one, none of our Manifestations were quite equipped for that. Anatomically speaking. Where there should have been a dick there was only a small, smooth bump, quite like a Ken doll's. As you well know.

Was that disappointing to us?

Yes.

Yes, it was fucking disappointing, Bunny.

And therein lies *the rub*, so to speak.

Aerius, you see, was quite well equipped that way. Aerius also did not have small paws for hands. Aerius, our Happy Accident, came into the world ungloved and beautifully fucking five fingered. And?

And quite *significantly dicked*, as one of us loves to mention.

(Never lets us forget, in fact.)

No, Bunny, she never had sex with him as we said, despite her vulgar boasting. None of us did, we're not *rapists*, k? We only know because we peeked once or twice. Maybe a dozen or so times. But what we glimpsed in that peeking. *Twas* enough to launch a thousand ships in our hearts. Fuck Helen of Troy and her alleged face, Bunny. Aerius's cock, that was a true masterpiece.

The most genius thing we've ever made. *Fact.*

But speaking of *facts*, we had to remind ourselves of others. He ran away from us. Did not wish to slow dance with us. Did not enjoy Touching Tuesdays or Prom Thursdays. Did not fuck us or even want to make out with us. Whimpered at the mere thought of it, Bunny. Screamed, as we recall (fondly now). And yet: he *could* fuck us. That *could* was always hanging in the air, Bunny, like so much untouchable glitter. The *anatomical possibility*, so to speak. His hands, though they never willfully touched us, when they did, by accident perhaps, well, we *still* shiver to recall it.

It was like being physically grazed by God.

Like our whole body became a kind of glitter, sparkling and weightless.

A few weeks later we found ourselves with a basement filled with what we liked to call our Darlings. Or Hybrids—Else much preferred this term, which captured the experimental nature of our enterprise, both literary and scientific. Drafts, Kyra insisted, because they were absolutely a kind of writing, Bunny, only fucking better, going beyond the LePen. But though they were all compelling in their way (we cannot stress this enough), and though we were conjuring magnificently (had it down to an arty science, essentially), we were still somewhat dissatisfied (shall we say?) with the Results.

We pined for that glittery feeling. For the world to feel imbued with magic, as it had with Aerius. For the sun to be more than itself once more.

Hence the ax.

Which, as you know, was ultimately necessary, Bunny.

That's the curse of being a Creative, isn't it?

Which brings us, of course, to the night we'll never forget. End of November. We'd decided to take four of our Darlings out on a lovely dinner date. *Test-drive them*, as Vik would say, which we did love to do. Fyorg, Rainbow, Armand, and Deviant, we *believe* were their names, though who fucking knows, Bunny. Hard to keep track after a certain point, it really is. Which we were already past, we're afraid to say. Definitely Fyorg was there, though. The one-eyed boy we'd conjured after Aerius. (He's sort of important, k? There's a little foreshadowing for you.)

We'd mostly gone to Mini in the past, but Coraline suggested we branch out that night and go to the Bistro. She'd had a lovely lunch there with her mother back in September, she said, before she'd lost her soul to this. Okay, Bunny, we said, sure, we're down. The Bistro was surprisingly very accommodating of our needs, the servers most understanding, almost as if they'd dealt with such occurrences before. They were happy to give our boys plates of flowers, for example, make them Shirley Temples in plastic to-go cups with lids so as to minimize spill.

But the date itself was a disaster. Our Darlings were listless before their foliage. Picking at the petals half-heartedly. Complimenting us quite half-heartedly too.

"Your hair is so hairy," they offered.

"Love your whatever," they said idly.

The conversation was, shall we say, *wanting*. There was a kind of electricity in the air too that had not been there before. "And what did you make of *The Waves*?" Coraline pressed. We'd left our beloved book in the attic for them to ponder, along with a sticky note that said *Dinner Convo Material* ☺

"Make of it?" Rainbow said, and looked worried. Continually staring out the window at the dark. The others, we noted, were doing the same.

"Um, what are you seeing out there?" Kyra asked. Worried, always, that the police were on their way, you see, that we were going to be arrested imminently for breaking all the laws of the natural world. But when we looked, we saw nothing, Bunny. "What, *what?*" And they would not say. It was insolent, and we did make a note of it with our LePens. How they usually feared the sight of these LePens, Bunny. Whimpered at the sound of their scratching. (The LePen was a kind of nonviolent ax, really. It had a wonderfully pacifying effect.) But on this night they paid them no mind. So consumed by some outside happening we could not see. Perhaps their rabbit vision continued on even in human form, which was a question fascinating to ponder.

We often wondered where the rabbit ended and the man began.

And then Fyorg surprised us all by suddenly standing up from his chair. Pointing out at the dark and screaming. "He!" he shouted. "He, he, he!" His one blue eye so wild with seeing.

He? What the fuck is he seeing out there? we asked ourselves in the hive.

But all we saw when we looked out the window were our own reflections, four women with so-shining hair and very haunted eyes. Four rabbit men sitting around us, eating their petals worriedly now.

Defective, we concurred on the drive home (in Else's Jag, obvi). Absolutely, no fucking question. We conferred about this with a series of glances. Rearview mirror to side mirror, all our eyes meeting there, us nodding soberly beside our rattled Darlings, who were still screaming all the way home. *Only one thing to do in this case*, we silently agreed. Alas, they left us no choice, Bunny. Screaming at windows. Not knowing what to make of Woolf. If they couldn't go out in public, then what was the point of this exercise, really?

When we got to Kyra's, we told her, Bunny, time to do your magic. Take them up to the attic one by one by one and do what needs be done, please.

Meanwhile, we'll watch TV in the living room, k? We'll keep the others distracted until it's their turn to meet their fate. Maybe start with Rainbow, whose screams were really starting to drive us fucking insane in the Jag.

But Kyra just stood there in her pretty red cloak, hesitating, didn't you, Bunny? Didn't love her job as Executioner anymore, you see, now that it had become more full-time. "Can't we just drive them out to a field or something?" she said. Totally resisting her artist's calling.

"Um, no, Bunny."

We'd tried this just the other week with a couple of them. Waved goodbye as they turned their scared circles in the corn or whatever, their blue suits suddenly looking too big for their bodies. "Not these ones," we said, turning on the television. "Too screamy." The boys settled at our feet, chewing their twigs, hypnotized by the TV's light, its bright colors.

"What about Elsinore's basement?" Kyra said.

"We're only putting the ones with *potential* in the basement, remember?" we said, and yawned, clicking the remote. *The Bachelorette* was on, thank fucking god.

The Bachelorette was always on those days, strangely.

"I don't know if I can do this tonight," Kyra murmured. She looked tired, it's true. We were tired too, of course, Bunny. But we fucking rallied.

"Of course you can, Bunny," Else told her gravely. "Because you must. This is the Work, and we all must play our parts." She gripped her diamond dagger pendant and smiled.

"We believe in you, Bunny," we all whispered.

"I can't," Kyra whined. But she was already putting on her *Kitchen Bitch* apron with its fake string of pearls. Taking her new ax from off its hook on the attic door. Saying to Rainbow, "Come upstairs with me where I have many a Pixy Stix." She had all manner of dandelions up there too, she said, untouched by the winter's frost. Not to mention the very best Shirley Temple, and wouldn't he love a sip? "Yes," he said. They always believed her, Bunny, it was kind of heartbreaking. Followed quite willingly. Didn't even seem to notice the ax behind her back that she took barely any pains to conceal. Which supported Else's hypothesis that defective Darlings *want* the ax, really they do. Kyra clicked shut the door, and shortly thereafter the screaming began. The sound of ax meeting flesh and/or bone. The sound of ax being itself, really. The other Darlings grew more nervous beside us, understandably so. Squirming in their seats. Tugging on their silk ties. Trying to smile at us, but those smiles were like ticking bombs.

Murder?

Oh, we don't really care for that term, Bunny. Doesn't even seem fitting in this case, right? More like hitting delete a lot. Literally. Because you have to kill your darlings, don't you? We are instructed to do this all the time in Workshop, are we not? Isn't that what all the writing manuals, both lame and elevated, tell us? Isn't that what all the famous Fictions are quoted as saying? Well, fine. *Exactly.* Ultimately, we were just taking that very sensible writerly advice. And it's not like we killed *all* of them, Bunny. Some we kept, as you know, sure. Put in a bottom drawer, so to speak (a.k.a. Else's basement). Telling ourselves maybe with some revision or time or both, we might revisit. Which was kind of a lie. After our experience with Aerius, we were a bit sour on revision, that whole humiliating fucking enterprise. Far more violent, far less merciful, truth be told. And anyway, there was only so much room in Else's basement, after all.

There was only so much room in our hearts, too, you know?

Did the sounds above our heads bother us somewhat? The blood, dark and vital, that sometimes trickled down the steps from the crack under the attic door? It did a little, Bunny, though it was astonishing how quickly we grew accustomed to it. Used the time to decompress, really, to journal. Reflect on the Work and its purpose. But on this night the noise actually did irk us a smidge. There were four Darlings to kill, you see, so the ceiling was practically vibrating with Bunny's Violences. We contemplated wearing earplugs, or better yet, noise-canceling headphones, but Bunny had insisted we listen. That we always hear the screams and the swoosh and the all-important crack. So important for our Growth as Artists, she said. Okay, Bunny, *fine*. We killed time instead by watching *The Bachelorette*. Though we couldn't really hear what was going on between Dirk and her many tuxedoed candidates over the screams, we had a few ideas of whom she might eliminate next. Wished she could eliminate more than one candidate per episode, really. Cut to the fucking chase, get to Spencer, his sly smile and cruel-kind eyes. Vik asked Deviant, sitting at her feet, whom *he* might eliminate, just to, you know, make conversation. Or to fuck with him, you never knew with Vik. Or perhaps she, like all of us, was genuinely curious about his perspective, Bunny. Our Darlings often got quite lost in *The Bachelorette*, as though it were a horror from which they could not turn away. Deviant, staring transfixed at the screen, said no one, he would eliminate no one. "Or maybe *she*," he said, pointing at Brindy herself, looking so lovely in her red sequined strapless.

"*What?*" Coraline looked predictably horrified. "Why would you ever eliminate the Bachelorette herself?"

"I do not care for her bangs," Deviant said. "Also, she is a cunt."

"*Cunt?*" Coraline clutched the ghost of her pearls. And how Vik blushed, slouched on her usual chaise longue. We knew, of course, that she, being a shameless bitch, had fed him this awful word, hadn't you, Bunny?

"Cunt," Deviant said again. "*Cunt, cunt, cunt,*" he sang.

"Oh look, Deviant," Else said, "Bunny is calling for you to join her in the attic now. Looks like there are some treats up there just for you."

And then there was only one Darling left. Fyorg. Beautiful, but from the moment he knocked on the door, he'd been a bit of an odd duck, Bunny. Rattling on about ravens and a philosophy class he was late for. About the nature of reality and what was for real. Asking if we had any Jäger, which *no*. Too bad we had to kill him, for aesthetically we were quite drawn. He had a dreamily psychotic look to him. Very Christian Bale circa 2000. A little Elvish, too, in the *Lord of the Rings* sense, Bunny, like he might be capable of eerie forest magic. Kyra liked to point out that he also looked a little like that missing frat boy, Tyler whatever, and didn't we think so? No, Bunny, we didn't. *You're imagining things*, we lied. But he sort of did, it's true. In certain lights. Which of us had been thinking of him during the conjuring, we wondered. Perhaps seen his posters, plastered all the over the school that morning, something of his face sinking into our subconscious? In any case, it was really only the very mildest resemblance, Bunny. He really looked way more like Christian Bale meets a hot Scandi elf.

Fyorg was kneeling before the television, watching *The Bachelorette*, quite rapt. Blowing bubble gum, his favorite sweet, sipping on his sippy cup. Vik sometimes added a shot of absinthe to their cups before the ax, sort of a send-off beverage. He had been the screamiest one at the Bistro, but now he appeared quite calm. "Fyorg, are you enjoying the show?" Vik asked him, winking at us. Loving to poke the bear tonight and always.

"Nevermore," he whispered, staring at the screen.

"Nevermore?" we repeated.

"Nevermore," he said again, shaking his head at the TV, "is watching this."

Which, what the fuck? No Darling had ever insisted on a name before.

"You're *Fyorg*," Coraline insisted, like she was a child putting a rogue doll back in its place. And we felt funny, Bunny. Was he fucking with us?

"Nevermore's too hot right now." And he took off his leather gloves and threw them over his shoulder. We all stared at his naked hands, Bunny. Fleshy. Manly. Five fucking fingered.

"Too hot," Vik whispered, fanning herself. "Definitely." How had we not noticed this before?

Just then Kyra appeared from behind the attic door in her bloody apron. She looked exhausted, understandably. The ax, covered in so much blood now, quite limp in her so-small hand. But she also looked beautiful, as she always did postkill, when she was deeply engaging the Work like this. Sinewy, we often complimented. Triceps and biceps like you wouldn't fucking believe, Bunny, the definition was Madonna level, so much so that some of us were a little jelly.

"Fyorg," she whisper-sang. "Time to go up to Attic. To have a treat."

But he kept staring at the TV. Brindy was making her choice now. A long-stemmed rose in her red-nailed hands. Her smile was *sorry, not sorry*, and a few tears shimmered prettily in her so-cold eyes.

Fyorg shook his head. "Leave my loneliness unbroken."

What, Bunny?

Then he noticed the ax in Kyra's hand. Screamed and jumped behind the couch, oh dear. We sighed collectively, walked as one body to where he sat cowering behind a ficus. As though he wouldn't be plainly visible there, Bunny. As though he could actually hide. (All these bunny men had a very skewed sense of their own physical proportions.) We held him down most lovingly while Bunny made her slow way over, dragging her feet and the blade of the ax along the floor, which she sometimes did when she was super tired.

"Hurry up, he's strong!" we hissed. "He's wriggling in our hands!"

Not that we were terribly worried, Bunny. There was no escape from the living room, we'd made sure of that. Hid all the potential weapons. And bunnies, perhaps because they are natural prey, do not think to defend themselves anyway. Fyorg shook his head while Kyra raised her ax in the air.

"Not again!" he shouted. "Not again, not again! Please don't kill me!"

Which was a strange utterance for him to make. Normally, they didn't scream like this, beg for their lives like this, and it was super traumatizing, Bunny. For us. What did he mean, *Not again*? Perhaps just babble. More evidence that he was truly defective. We told ourselves we were growing as artists, this was the season of our flourishing, as we tightened our hold on his limbs, closing our eyes because most of us really don't love violence, Bunny—we're always closing our eyes at the bloody part of any movie. We waited for her to finally strike, hit fucking delete, *do it*.

But she was hesitating now. "What do you mean, 'Not again'?" she said, her ax wavering over her head.

And Fyorg saw this wavering, Bunny, saw the hesitation on Bunny's face and shouted: "KILL AERIUS! Kill the BUNNY MAN!"

And just like that, Bunny dropped her ax.

16

W hat did you just say?" Else whispered. Threateningly, Bunny. Her otherworldly voice suddenly a fucking growl. For truth be told, we did not ever utter his name aloud back then. The name of our First Boy. First Draft. First Darling. First what-the-fuck-ever. First humiliation, Bunny, really, that's what he was (though he still had our hearts).

"You *know* Aerius?" Coraline asked him, still gripping his limbs tight.

He nodded. He didn't fucking know, we thought. How could he possibly?

"Aerius is the one with the ax," he said.

What the fuck, Bunny?

But he was staring off into space now. "Aerius is the one who jumps to many jumping songs," he said dreamily. "And I jumped with him."

He looked at us sadly. "Aerius is the one who kills."

"Kills?"

"And my soul from out that shadow . . . shall be lifted—nevermore," he whispered. "For real." And then he burst into tears.

We felt cold then. The creeps, oh god, we had them. All down our bodies, Bunny. We looked at this defective Darling. Drunk from sippy-cup absinthe. Still staring tearily at Brindy on elimination night. There were two suited men waiting to learn their fates, but she had only one rose left. "This is so hard," she was saying, and we thought, *Yes. It's very hard, Bunny.* The work of elimination takes its toll, absolutely. Else shook Fyorg's shoulders most violently—*What are you saying, what are you fucking saying?*—and then he just began to babble, Bunny. About reality and philosophy and how he'd once had a pet raven but it wasn't for real. He burst into tears again. Quite inconsolably. We patted his hulking shoulder, said soothing words.

All the more reason to kill him, we thought, saying as much to Kyra in the hive mind. *Finish him off, he's making no sense. And obviously suffering, Bunny. So put him out of his misery, k?*

But Kyra was staring at him, interested now. Curious, even though curiosity killed the cat, and we telepathically reminded her of this. Still, she asked: "Do you really know Aerius, Fyorg?"

"Nevermore," the boy corrected, staring at her with his one eye. He nodded.

Kyra pulled us into a huddle then. "What the fuck? Is he our conscience or something? Fucking with us? Or does he really actually know something?"

"I don't know, but I like being fucked with," Vik said. "They don't fuck with us nearly enough."

"*Of course* he doesn't know anything," Coraline snapped. "Now can we please just *delete?*" She was extremely cutthroat with the Darlings when they got screamy, weren't you, Bunny?

Fyorg, meanwhile, was crouched behind the ficus, still worriedly watching *The Bachelorette* from between the leaves. "Nevermore," he kept whispering.

We all looked at Else, who was staring intently at Fyorg, her crystal dagger shimmering quite like her eyes. "I wonder," she murmured. On the screen, the eliminated man was hate-hugging Brindy now, wishing her luck on her journey. His bleached smile full of sting.

"*Nevermore*," Else said, smiling, "do you know where Aerius is?"

He nodded again. Our hearts froze in our bodies, Bunny. We blushed furiously at the thought of him. Those lovely cold eyes, that accidental fucking touch.

"Where?" we asked as one voice, calm as calmest seas, not at all betraying the roiling desperation beneath.

"There," he said, pointing out the living room window at the black, just like he'd done at the Bistro. We peered out at this black. Seeing nothing, Bunny. The silhouettes of surrounding houses. Our neighbors inside probably wondering, *What the fuck?* But again, probably not. *Art project,* Bunny had explained to them once, after the first axing. *We're experimenting with different methodologies. If you ever hear screaming up there, that's all that is.* And the neighbors smiled. Understood or pretended to. Fine art students demand such indulgence. They thought we were such kind, well-mannered girls. *Lovely*, they often said, seeing us skip by, gathering twigs for our Darlings.

And we agreed, we were. Fucking lovely.

Into the cold, cold night we allowed Fyorg/Nevermore to lead us. He was moving pretty quickly, Bunny. Practically skipping down the cold, snowy streets, so that we had to skip too. To skip after him brought such wild smiles to our faces, even though this was very serious, this was so high stakes. We tried not to smile or, god forbid, laugh. For if we were to laugh now, it might break something like a spell, and then it might all disappear. Our skipping Darling. This night suddenly imbued with a magic we thought we'd lost forever. This tenuous path back to our First Boy. Bunny brought her ax just in case. Not that we would do any killing out here in the open, no, no. But just that this was sort of a dangerous city, Bunny, as you yourself observed in your little novel. Especially after a certain hour. Lots of maniacs out there, you know? Lots of psychos and such. So much violence and some of it so terribly unnecessary. The recent beheadings on campus and at the truck stop, for instance. Which we were certain had nothing at all to do with Aerius. Mostly certain. Okay, so we were a little divided on this question, truth be told. Kyra, for one, *really* thought he might be involved. He did run away with our ax, after all, she often reminded us. And she'd had to buy another online, which was annoying. But ultimately, we simply did not think so, no. Because he'd come from us and we were lovely.

As has already been stated.

"Here," our Darling said, stopping his skip at last. And we saw we were in a park, just across the street from the Bistro. We were standing, in fact, before a hole in the grass. Freshly dug. Quite like the one Vik had dug long ago in the rose garden with her so-gross hands. We all crouched down and sniffed the earth. Oh, Bunny, how the tears instantly stung our eyes as we sniffed. For we could smell him in the mud, yes, the spring flowers and grasses of him. The man and the animal. The *manimal*, as it were. Unmistakable. Like a bit of glitter in the air, and we were intoxicated all over again. None of them had ever smelled quite like this. Quite so . . . foresty. So of the earth, rich and sweet and deep. So . . . *real*. Yes. That was the word.

"Aerius," we all whispered, wild-eyed and hunched by the hole. Our lovely dresses torn, our skin exposed to the snowy night, yet not even feeling the cold.

Fyorg/Nevermore, perhaps out of his own animal curiosity, bent down and sniffed the ground with us. His nose went rabbity, twitched. His ears twitched too, as if recalling the memory of what they'd once been. Suddenly he sat up on his haunches, or legs rather, looking around at the dark.

"Where is he? Where is he?" we begged desperately.

Down the dark and turny streets we ran, with the moon high above us and Fyorg/Nevermore racing ahead, openly hopping now like the animal he once was. We thanked god there was no one out and about to witness this, Bunny. Because they would definitely have been startled by the hopping man in his Brooks Brothers suit, his silky tie flapping backward in the breeze he made. At this very late hour it was too dangerous for most to be outside, even here, in what appeared to be a fairly nice neighborhood, that's where he was leading us. It had a professorial boomer vibe, Bunny. Stately houses, boastful oaks. Tibetan prayer flags hanging from eaves, and so many Teslas glimmering ominously in the driveways. Wind chimes swaying in the night air, making a familiar tinkling music. The sound told us we'd been here before, yes. This was Ursula's street. *Um, why are we*—and then he stopped right in front of her very house.

We stared at her Gothic turrets aimed sharply at the night sky. "What are we doing here?"

But he just pointed with his trembling human finger. His one eye wild with seeing. *Seeing what?*

"Aerius," he whispered.

We exchanged looks then. *Should have axed him back home*, we thought. *Waste of time. Bullshit.* When we could be watching another episode of *The Bachelorette.* See who Brindy eliminated next, our dresses splattered beautifully with the evening's Work. Toasting her choice, whatever it was, with some well-earned bubbly. Watch the eliminated boy hate her quietly, even as he embraced her for the cameras. Going in for that vengeful boob crush (a final *fuck you*). Such a great show.

We were asking him, "Why have we stopped here? Why, why, why?" when a little dog, a long-haired terrier, came bounding out of the pet door, barking his head off. He immediately raced toward Fyorg/Nevermore, who screamed and ran away. The dog bounded after him, barking more wildly now, like it sensed the animal in the man, that was all the dog saw. We watched them disappear howlingly into the dark, moving so fast that there was no human way to follow.

And then it was just us again. Standing on our teacher's porch, between two rabbit statues made of stone—had those always been there? Looking up at that cold bitch of a moon.

What now?

A light on our faces suddenly. The front door open. Ursula standing in her winter smock the color of glittering snow crystals, her voice sounding surprised. "Girls? Is that you?

"Oh my, oh my," she said. What were we doing out here? And was this blood on our clothes? Whatever happened? We looked at her, staring at us so kindly. Maybe a little impatiently, too. Maybe even a little furious (it was very late, and we'd no doubt woken her up). But mostly just wondering, *What the fuck?* And this curious kindness in her eyes, it broke us, Bunny.

Emotionally. Suddenly we felt as cold as we probably were. And helpless. And fucking lost.

We shivered collectively. And then? We sort of broke down quite embarrassingly. And everything—the house, Ursula, the snowy night—blurred into a twinkling snow creature. Who told us gently, gently to come inside.

"And tell me. Tell me everything."

17

Ursula's living room looked especially witchy on this night, the air heady with incense and candlelight and flower arrangements, each a kind of fragrant, vaginal *come hither*. A bowl of clementines so very ripe, they were on the verge of rot. A Norse music composed mostly of drums and chanting. Her pervy husband was nowhere in sight, thank god. Probably upstairs somewhere dreaming up more obscure poems that would ultimately be lost to darkness. *May he sleep forever*, we thought. *Forever and ever and ever*, we thought as we sipped the floral tea she'd made for us. Brewed in a black clay pot patterned with dancing rabbits, alarmingly long-eared. "Marigolds and dandelions," she said. "Both fresh picked from my garden this summer, along with some rose petals and wild thyme, a most restorative concoction."

"Yes," we agreed, breathing in the steam. Which smelled of him. So potently. We almost expected him to manifest suddenly, for the steam to become flesh. Tears swelled behind our eyes again.

"All right, now," she said, stirring, "what's this about, my dears? Tell me."

My dears. Sitting before us on her lavender armchair, smilingly waiting for our words. Yet distracted also, we noted. She kept staring out the window, at something in her backyard. What the fuck, Bunny?

"Um, are we . . . *interrupting* something?"

"I'm afraid I *was* in the middle of working. The Witching Hour being my hour, you see. But when I heard the barking and saw you out there, the state of you, I couldn't very well turn you away, could I? Compassion being my fatal flaw. Now go on."

"You're going to think we're crazy, though," Coraline whispered. Clutching her teacup like it was the only solid thing left in the fucking universe. Undermining our narrative, Bunny, before we'd even begun.

But Ursula just shook her head. "Please do remember that I went to Bennington. And I was a student here once myself. Long, long ago. An MFA candidate, no less. Just like you. You're safe with me."

And it was funny, but for the first time we wondered if, in fact, we were safe, Bunny. Something about Ursula tonight, her energy. The witch of her was truly in the air everywhere. In the swirling smoke and the quivering candle flames and the floral tea steam. Alive in her voice and in her eyes, which mesmerized us. *Tell me.*

Else took it upon herself to speak for all of us, of course. Which, fine. We let her hijack our collective narrative, Bunny, knowing that she must have her little God moments. Bit our lips as she grandly recounted finding that first bunny in the rose garden. How he seemed to flirt with her (with *us*, hello?) so flagrantly—such a strangely flirty bunny, that first one. How she (*we*, Bunny) turned his eyes an eerie blue with her (our!) embrace. How that hug got us dreaming, dangerously maybe. How he led us, hopping, back to our very own attic ("Um, my attic, actually," Kyra interjected) and the happy, sweaty accident we had there. The terrible violence and then the wondrous discovery, not so long after, in the garden behind Narrative Arts, of the creative Result. Standing among the dandelions in her very own nightdress and pearls ("My pearls, by the way," Coraline said).

We described him physically, which brought fresh tears to our many eyes. And funny that Ursula had us repeat this description, Bunny. Several times. Asking follow-up questions: "What color hair *exactly?*" "*How* tall roughly, in terms of inches?" We shared our revision process, so painful to recall. He was so rough, you see. So raw. Wildly resistant to our various narrative and stylistic approaches. How probably we loved him too much. How he eventually ran away from us (we glared at Vik). Leaving us no choice but to—

"Sit down at your desks at last?" she offered. "Put pen to paper? Fingers to keys?"

"Explode more rabbits in the attic," Vik whispered sadly. Yet shuddering with pleasure, as she always did, at the recollection of this violence.

"I see."

We shared our tender hopes of conjuring another just like him. Spoke of rabbit guts and bloody aprons and wondrous knocks on the door. Our desperate longing to return to the wild joy and even wilder despair of that first Happy Accident. The many rituals we'd made in the service of that.

"*What* rituals exactly?" she asked sharply.

And then she had us name our conjuring tools, Bunny: the candles and incense and films and music and such. The Smut Salons, in all their hot pink confessional wonder. The tight circle we made around Bunny's body, our bodies and minds and hearts aligned and humming with desires like an engorged clit.

"And did it work?" she asked eagerly. Too eagerly, Bunny.

"We *were* able to conjure more, of course," Else said. "Many more, in fact."

"More of *the same*," Vik mumbled under her breath. Sort of bitchily, Bunny. Like it was one of *our* faults that we were always making "the same dickless dude in a suit," as she put it. For the record, we did *try*, in our Conjurings, to go beyond boy creatures, by the way. Of course we fucking did, Bunny—our desire is not a monolith, despite the gross insinuations in your little novel. Sure, we sometimes thought of girls (we thought of all manner of creatures, tbh). And yet. And yet, and yet, and yet: no matter how much we attempted, in our creative intentions, to push beyond certain . . . *shapes*, as it were, something inside us—or perhaps it was in Bunny or the very nature of the magic itself—was spitting out this . . . okay, yes, this dickless man-in-finance type. And, um, we didn't know why, Bunny. We still don't. Surely not our *own* desires, which were so very rich and varied and mysterious. A speculation worthy of its own story, perhaps.

Ursula smiled now. "More of the same," she mused, repeating Vik's cruel words. "And what does that mean?"

"It means none like him," Coraline snapped, glaring at Vik.

"And what do you mean by 'none like him'?"

But we couldn't very well tell our writing teacher that we couldn't make a dick, Bunny. Or human hands. Or a soul. So we beat around the bush, as it were.

"We're artists," Else prevaricated. "We just want to love what we make. And to make something that loves us. Is that so wrong?"

We looked up at Ursula now, so terribly vulnerable. Waiting for her to tell us, *Absolutely not wrong. You are, in fact, the greatest geniuses I've ever known.* But Ursula wasn't looking at us at all anymore. She was looking through the window, at her writing shed. "Wrong?" she sighed.

"We just want him back," Coraline pressed. Desperately, Bunny. Her hand was in her bloody dress pocket, and she was licking the balm from her lips with slutty abandon now.

"We don't even care anymore that he's dangerous," Kyra blurted. Then covered her little fucking loud mouth with both hands. Like, *Oops.* But it was too late.

"Dangerous?" Ursula turned back to us.

And then we had no choice, Bunny. We told her, very quietly, about the ax. How he'd taken ours on his way out the window. Possibly killed a few people, a frat boy and a couple of barflies, we weren't totally sure, though. Warren and its environs being a violent place overall.

"Things happen here," we said to her floor.

Ursula agreed quietly. *Yes,* her eyes said. *They did.*

"So, um, he might be a murderer," Kyra said.

"But also he might *not* be," Coraline retorted.

Ursula stared at us over her steaming cup. "And if he is?"

"Well, that would be so terrible," Else murmured. "But it might also just be a most unfortunate misunderstanding. A miscommunication or something tragic like that."

"Like in *Frankenstein* or something," Vik offered.

"Have you read *Frankenstein*?" Ursula asked us.

"Yes," we lied, looking back at the floor. "Lots."

"Well. This is a *fascinating* story, ladies. A very fascinating story indeed." She stroked her glittering shawl. We waited for her to tell us that we should be expelled or arrested. For her to call the police. Or to give us a writing medal, we didn't know. We really felt in this moment that she could go either way, Bunny. Her eyes were so very inscrutable. She kept staring out at the dark, then back at us, then out at the dark.

"I do wonder," she said at last, "about the *plotting* of all this."

Our fairy tea had grown cold at this point, Bunny. We stared down into the floral mulch. "Um. What?"

"Well, I admire the allusions to *Frankenstein* and fairy tales and so on. But the whole story seems quite . . . oh, I don't know, very genre, no? Whorish."

Whore?

"A little *too* whore, frankly. Probably Allan has you reading too many slashers and such."

"But—"

"And the violence is quite gratuitous. Axes are such tactile instruments, which I appreciate, but the allusion to Kafka is a bit . . . *convenient*, don't you think? A bit heavy-handed. As for the magic, the transformations . . . I hate to use the word *wacky*, but there you are. It's a stitch too wacky. A touch too camp. *Zany.* A sort of zany *romantasy*, isn't it?"

And there they were, our very least favorite adjectives in the English language, Bunny. Falling from her mouth in one tacky string. We felt sick.

"Of course, I'm only *one reader*," she humbly qualified. Not looking at all humble, Bunny. "But for me, the plausibility feels a bit . . . *stretched*, don't you think? And as for this *boy* character of yours . . ."

Not boy—Darling, we wanted to correct. *Hybrid. Draft.* And not a *character*, Bunny.

"Him *running away* from you and such." She used air quotes around the phrase *running away*. "It makes you all seem almost a bit . . . clumsy, doesn't it? As creators? A little desperate."

"No." And it was our turn to shake our heads. "You don't understand, Ursula. What we're telling you isn't Fiction. It's . . . *real*."

She smiled thinly. "Confusing metaphor with Reality is an all-too-familiar trap for young artists. And of course the metaphor always reveals us, reveals the real. More powerfully even than the merely real. So it's tricky. Very tricky not to lose one's way, one's grip."

Her eyes staring into our eyes, so red and puffy and brimming with tears. We were gripping her armrests, her handleless cups, as though we were literally fucking sinking.

"Sounds like you had a difficult semester creatively," she said with great pity.

The hardwood floor sort of began to give beneath our feet then, Bunny. Grow soft as grasses. The witchy room itself seemed to swim.

"But . . . but," we blurted softly, "this really was . . . *real.*" But the word suddenly seemed like so much silly fairy dust on our tongues. A bubble we were blowing into the dark, so easy to burst. And how she was looking at us, Bunny. She was Mother saying, *Just some silly stories, Button.* She was our surgeon sister scoffing at our psychic powers. She was our ballet mentor filling our unbridled body with so much instructive shame. She was our typewriter, its cold keys unyielding beneath our fingers. Whispering, *Not worthy.* Whispering, *Never again.*

"*Real,*" she repeated, smiling. Looked at her wrist, that ever-invisible watch there. "In a sense, absolutely. Despite the madcappery of this *whore story,* this *rabbit romance* that you are describing to me, ladies, the underlying creative crisis actually seems very common."

"*Common?*" We could feel our mothers shuddering at this word even from a thousand miles away.

She poured herself more fairy tea, smiled at something out in the dark. "You made a thing. A raw and powerful living thing. But it wasn't *perfect,* or so you thought then. Perhaps because it didn't *love you* the way you wanted, to use your own crude phrasing."

Um, did we say that, Bunny?

"Because it was difficult to shape or control. Or perhaps because it was simply . . . beyond you in some way." She looked at us sadly. "So you tried, in the meager, amateur ways available to you, to fix it. And it escaped you, of course it did." Her smile grew world-weary. "And now you're trying to re-create it and you can't, of course not. Everything seems but a Pale Shadow of this First Attempt, for all its flaws."

"Yes." We lowered our heads, our faces hot with shame. All but Else's. (For God will never be shamed, will she, Bunny? You did look pale, though.)

"Well, let's extend the metaphor, shall we?" Ursula continued. "Probably it needed more-experienced hands. Probably it went elsewhere, to seek such hands. And who knows? Maybe he found them. It's the nature of Art to seek the right hands for its making, after all."

We stared down at our own hands, so very small. So very pink and puls-ing with want. Covered in a film of sweat. No grip at all.

A bark ringing through the house now. Her demonic terrier back from his hunt. He trotted adorably into the living room, bearing a little scrap of dark blue fabric between his teeth. From Fyorg/Nevermore's pants, we immediately recognized. The dog laid this scrap before Ursula's feet like a spoil. She picked it up and smiled.

"Brooks Brothers," she said. "A favorite brand among a certain ilk of undergraduate. Orpheus has been harassing our young Republicans, no doubt."

We watched Orpheus go barking away, disappearing through the kitchen door flap into the backyard. The moon had come out, illuminating her garden. Once more we saw her shed, that little house in the back corner of the snowy grounds. An electricity passed through our bodies when we saw this shed, Bunny. How the dog immediately ran there, turning maniacal little circles just outside the door. Barking and growling his head off. A light we saw now, flickering in the window.

"Tis getting late," Ursula said.

Tis?

"But what do we do *now?*" Coraline pressed.

"Go away," she snapped. "For winter break," she added quickly. "Take a much-needed pause from the Work and from one another. We can re-visit this in January, once I've had an opportunity to process this . . . *story* of yours. In the meantime, I should really get back. To my own Work, that is."

"What are you working on?" Kyra asked, playing politely interested even though we knew she didn't really care, Bunny. None of us did. We were too devastated, too vulnerable, too embarrassed for reasons we couldn't even name. Just going through the mannerly motions of conversation now. But Ursula took her query seriously. A light in her eye brightened. So desperate are writers, all writers, to converse about their Work. It made us sad and sick even then.

"It's only just revealed itself to me," she said, her eyes on that shed in the dark. "But perhaps you'll see it when you come to my showcase in spring. I'll be presenting on the Work I managed to manifest. When I was given time to do it, of course." And she looked at us now, like, *Fucking go. I have given you enough of my Self.*

We looked back at the shed, that flickering light in the window. Our skin still humming strangely. *What's in there?* we almost asked her.

But Ursula was standing up now, beckoning us to move along. "Leave the hothouse of campus, the hall of mirrors that is Narrative Arts. Get some Reality. Perspective. A grip."

And then we were back out in the dark.

Our hands empty of everything but one another.

18

The last two weeks of the semester were something of a blur for us, Bunny. We floated through those final days on campus as if in a kind of dream. Somehow we managed a Friendsgiving, survived (barely) our last workshop with Allan. Turned in our portfolios, as if those bound pages (or panes of glass), hastily compiled at the eleventh hour, were actually the true sum of our creative Oeuvre that term.

The Narrative Arts Christmas party was an understated affair due to the Violences, obvi. "So scary, right?" we said to anyone we passed, shivering appropriately in our holiday wear. We attended the party despite our ennui, Bunny, of course we did. Unlike you, we're not antisocial freak shows, k? We swapped out Kyra's cat ears for festive reindeer antlers, and Coraline even baked gingerbread men for the occasion, didn't you, Bunny? Complete with blue icing eyes, our little inside joke.

"And are the police doing anything to find the killer?" Kyra asked those with whom we mingled, the bells on her antlers tinkling with concern.

"They aren't? How terrible," we all murmured.

"Systemic apathy is fucking crazy," Vik said, and we agreed, Bunny, as we sipped the rainbow sherbet punch we'd made. It contained every alcohol under God's sun. Drunkenly, we stared out the window at fucking New England. Still hoping against hope for any sign of his wondrous silhouette in the bleakly falling snow. For his mellifluous voice to call out to us. *I am so sorry I ran away! Twas only because I loved you so much, it afeared me.*

"What are you looking for out there, Fictions?" the Poets sneered. They'd sallied up to us like spiders, donning their usual military vampire bat wear. One of them, Evil Jesus, was wearing a *Santa is Satan* sweater. We noticed that they were also hovering near the window, like they, too, were looking for someone out there in the cold.

"Nothing," we lied. "You?"

"Nothing," they sighed, sounding uncharacteristically forlorn. They'd had a bad semester, so we'd heard.

We turned back toward the window. There were some very angry-looking people out there suddenly, Bunny, in bleeding black T-shirts. Protestors, it looked like. They were shouting into megaphones (we couldn't hear the screamy words), holding up giant photos of Tyler Fields. In some photos he had an eye patch. We stared at his handsome jock face, so fratty-pretty in his polo. Smiling yet also sad-seeming at the same time. And strangely familiar-looking, both with and without his patch. We thought of Fyorg/Nevermore, lost somewhere in the world with that hole in his pants. The resemblance had always made us a little cold, Bunny.

The protestors appeared to be shouting at us now through the window, what the fuck? One pale girl in particular was glaring and gesticulating wildly like she thought she was in the French Revolution or something, Bunny. Pointing judgily at our lovely seasonal attire, or perhaps the celebratory cups of high-octane rainbow booze in our hands. She looked like she could have been your friend, Sam. Her ponytail was the saddest fucking thing we ever saw, and her army clothes screamed champagne socialist. She looked ready to set something, anything, on fire. In the name of "justice" or whatever, but really more just to watch it burn, Bunny. She wanted to burn the world with her anarchy eyes, you could tell. We stared at her sort of screaming at us, poor uncomprehending Marie Antoinettes, with what looked like a little toy ax in her hand.

Um, what the fuck is this, please?

"AAARV," the Poets mumbled, seeming to hear our thoughts.

"*What?*"

"Artists. Against. Ax-Related. *Violence*," Matthias enunciated with his Poet's cadence.

"Ax-related?" And for a moment, in the hive mind, we screamed. But we gathered ourselves. Smiled bemusedly. "Ax-related," Kyra sniffed. "*Huh.*" Antlers tinkling.

"They seem to think Narrative Arts is somehow involved in the Killings," offered Colby.

"How funny," Else said, gripping her dagger, which had turned a disconcerting shade of vermilion. "When art making is such a peaceful enterprise. So *monkish*, really."

"They came by our house and interrogated us," the leader said bitterly. "Perhaps they'll do the same to you."

We looked back at the group, chanting and waving their toy axes around quite wildly, as the police appeared to be dragging them away. We smiled, even as the hive mind was now ringing with *Interrogated?! Don't want to go to jail! This is all your fucking fault, Bunny!*

"We look forward to it," Else said. Her smile daring fate.

As the Poets turned away, probably in search of free food, we noticed the braids in their hair. The fishtails, the medieval ropes and knots. *Plagiarists!* we heard Coraline shriek in the hive mind. Her shocked rage ticking in all our fingers. *Is this a fucking joke? Where did you—*

But then Allan was before us, eating one of our gingerbread men headfirst.

"Glad you could make it to the party," he said. Or some such genial nothing. Being a prick, he wanted to engage. To wish us well before subjecting us to the Catherine wheel of his grading rubric. "And how did you enjoy your first semester?" He hoped we'd learned something with him this term.

"Oh we *did*, Allan," Coraline slurred drunkenly. "*Truly.*" Not at all keeping her shit together like we'd talked about. She raised her glass like she was about to throw a punch.

"In fact, in many ways, Allan," Kyra added sweetly, taking Coraline's sloshing drink from her hand, "you're sort of responsible for everything we've done this fall."

He licked an icing eye from his lip. Glanced out the window, where the screaming protestors were still getting dragged away. And then he turned to us and smiled, sort of bowed in his *milady* way. Self-deprecating but not really. Not fucking really, Bunny. "Cool," he said. "Well, I'm looking forward to reading your portfolios."

We smiled. *Sure.* Of course we'd done the final assignment, Bunny, *click, click*. Name and year in the top right-hand corner of the front page, table of goddamned contents, *here you go*. But our souls were not in those double-spaced pages (or glass panes), Bunny. That was no longer where we spilled the heart's blood, where we housed the pulsing clit. *That* lived between four steepled walls covered in rabbit guts, painted with bright blue sky and fluffy white clouds. It lived in our held hands and in our shuddery breaths and in our awed silence before the knock on the door. Where he and his smug red pen would never fucking find it.

Unless he ran into a beautiful boy with an ax, of course.

"We hope you *enjoy*," Coraline said, snatching her drink back, smiling bleary daggers. Her voice was *Fuck you forever*.

Allan was staring at us sort of funnily now.

Why is he staring like that, Bunny?

The party had suddenly emptied, only us first-year Fictions left (the Poets having found and promptly taken off with all the food). And you, Samantha. You showed up late, as was your socially delinquent way. Hovering in the periphery, waiting for your moment alone with him, remember that? Not surprising that you didn't mention the protestors in your screed of lies, Bunny. You were kind of checked out by then, weren't you? Living in your head mostly, which apparently is quite the little whore novel of its own. You'd brought all Allan's novels with you, tucked under your black lacy arm. You wondered if he might be so kind as to sign them? Only if he had the time and was willing, of course!

Allan nodded absently. "Sure, Sam. I'll meet you in my office."

And you blushed, Bunny, shamelessly.

But he remained standing with us, almost like he was waiting for something. What the fuck was he waiting for, Bunny? It crossed the hive mind then that he might know something. *Do you know something, Allan?* But we just stared at him tipsily as he stared at us, not at all afraid.

"How are those allergies, by the way?" he murmured at last. "Under control yet?"

"Not exactly," Kyra confessed. And Coraline kicked her. Like, *I love you, but shut up, k?* We couldn't trust Kyra with authority figures, that she'd keep those wintry cherry lips shut. Did Allan notice the scuffle? No, he was staring out the window again now.

"Allergies," he mused. "A terrible affliction. And it seemed to be really affecting this cohort. Creatively." He watched the protestors, some of whom were now resisting arrest. A few of them ran desperately toward the window, Bunny, toward us. Thumped the thankfully thick glass and mouthed *Murderers* right in our lovely faces. Our turn to blush, Bunny. We looked at Allan like, *Omg, the world. Crazy, right?* He, meanwhile, sipped his wine in his withholding way. "Well, maybe you'll bounce back in spring. With Ursula," he offered.

"Maybe," we murmured. *Bounce?*

"Or you might need to go back to the rose garden," he added quietly, turning back to us. "Try another approach."

And that, Bunny, is when our hearts exploded like rabbits in our bodies. *What?*

But he just looked at us. Smiled his infuriating smile that had made us want to kill him in the first place. Slugged back the last of his wine in its little plastic cup.

And then? He left us.

Vik called after him, "Hey, Allan." Fucking loving to poke that bear. To not just disturb the shit, but to roll around in it, Bunny, orgasming grossly.

Allan turned back, brows raised inquiringly. Almost playfully, like he was fucking with us. Was he? It was on the tip of our tongues to say, *We conjured a bunny boy who wants to kill you, by the way. Please do keep an eye out for a handsome young man in a blue velvet blazer and pearls, brandishing an ax. But then maybe you already know?* Instead we all just raised our rainbow punch, the pretty colors of which had melted into a sad brown sludge, and whispered, "Merry Christmas."

He winked, making our souls cold. "Merry, merry, Bunny."

And with that mic drop, he was gone.

We watched you scamper down the hall after him like a puppy. If the puppy in question were a tall, nihilistic bitch-goth, obvi. Definitely you two were fucking, though clearly, he was holding all the psychosexual cards. We almost felt sorry for you, we really did, but mostly we just felt sorry for ourselves. And worried. *What does he know? What does he fucking know? Nothing, he knows nothing.* We looked back at the window. Just our own reflections there now, poor lonely Marie Antoinettes. Pressed against the cold glass and staring out at the dark.

Which was violently empty of magic.

Violently empty of all but snow.

19

And so? We took our leave of one another for winter break, Bunny. *Reality, perspective, a grip.* We needed them now more than ever before. Left our remaining Darlings in Else's basement with a bounty of sweet provisions and *Love Actually* playing on continuous loop on the wall, not to mention a playlist that was really just Wham!'s "Last Christmas" on shuffle and repeat. "Stay here while we're gone, please," Coraline warned them. "The world is a cold and terrible place full of murder, and you are safest in this cozy basement with all this delicious candy." They nodded dully at the wall with their lovely, vacant eyes. "Terrible," they murmured, shivering in an imagined winter. "So beautiful you look in your candy murder." Sitting in their blue suits and silk ties, like they were about to do serious business, Bunny, with stocks.

Vik, being a borny whore, offered to stay with them over the holidays. "My mother *really* doesn't need to see me," she pleaded.

But we said fucking no, and Coraline nearly throttled her, and Else was most adamant.

"*Reality*, remember?" she said, quoting Ursula.

To that end, we locked Else's basement door. Double-bolted it, Bunny, then cracked a window. Got into our various Ubers and then on our various planes and trains and cruise liners.

And bye.

In our respective homes, we attempted to decompress. *Reality, perspective, a grip*, this was our mantra. But it wasn't easy, Bunny. We were met with all manner of questions from our loved ones.

How was school? our parents or siblings might ask us over dinner. *Did you write anything?*

Oh, lots, we prevaricated. Picking at our plates of whatever.

Like what? some asshole at the table might press.

Mostly experimental stuff.

I heard about the violence on campus, another might say. *Some beheadings around town? That a boy went missing? That true?*

Here we'd shrug evasively. *Don't know for sure. Probably just a prank.*

Our loved ones would exchange looks then. Chastise us for our life choices. *I told you, darling,* one of our mothers might say, *didn't I tell you not to go Ivy? All these Ivy schools are in such terrible towns. Why didn't you go to that other program—you know, the one in the little nowhere town where they grow corn?*

May I please be excused?

Because it was too hard, Bunny, to answer this question. To answer any question, really. So we stayed in our rooms mostly, k? *To write,* we explained importantly. *So much writing to do, oh my god.* And we lay there and cried into our duvets, listening to our various playlists, which so perfectly soundtracked the falling of our tears. We barely even partook in the caroling, the sleigh riding, the mulled wine making, the Mariah Carey–ing, etc. That year, all the Christmas cookies tasted like so much sugary fucking dust. In fact, this season actually reminds us of that part in your own novel, Bunny (the saggy middle part, remember?), when you're alone over winter break, and you're ill and heartbroken over your many, *many* creative failures. And as you lie there, plague-ridden on your poor-people mattress, you imagine *us* (of course you do) thriving and celebrating in a so-pretty elsewhere, happy and rich and way better dressed than you. When we read that part, we belly-laughed, Bunny. I mean, *yes,* we were rich and better dressed by comparison (obvi), but you seem to think you're, like, the only person in the world who's ever been sad? And even worse, that this saggy sadness of yours is what makes you, like, a *real* artist or something? (You *would* tell yourself this palliative lie.) Well, guess what, Bunny? Fuck off. We're artists too, real honest-to-god suffering ones, k? And that Christmas was proof. Hard to take part in any rejoicing when your heart is broken into a thousand unmendable pieces, Bunny. When you're perpetually, achingly aroused for something you realize you'll never touch again. Because he didn't love us—yes, this baffling fact was finally sinking into our souls. Because he was also maybe a murderer. Because ultimately, even in the very best-case scenario, we were still essentially sharing him with three other bitches (no offense, Bunnies).

Mostly, though, because he was gone.

We actually *did* try to write during this time of pain, by the way. Perhaps the Muses would be kind to us, we reasoned, after all we'd endured. Compensate us for our great loss. But alas, even Muses can be elusive cunts, Bunny. A tender adjective or just-so clause might find us and we'd jot it down, sure. But mostly not. Mostly, we . . . *grieved.* Watched the snow fall over New Hampshire, the palms shiver in Monterey County, the Virginia sky go gray with sickly clouds, the red sun rise bloodily over the Kona volcanoes. We closed our eyes and dreamed of that cold blue glare, that accidental touch. *Reality, perspective, a grip,* we told ourselves as we sank into our so-soft beds and kept sinking, losing ourselves in ceiling fantasies, grabbing our phones. Because we could not reach for him, you see, we reached for each other.

Miss you, Bunny, we texted.

Miss you too.

Did we maybe make a murderer?

Maybe ☹

Did I lose the only thing I'll ever love again?

Will my Aura never again turn the shade of Primroses?

Am I ruined spiritually and sexually for all future entities?

Was that bloody autumn in the attic the happiest fucking time I'll ever know again?

Don't know ☹

Our loved ones worried for us. Whispered about us behind closed doors, we heard them. *Unstable. Not herself. Taken a turn down a dark mental road.*

In Virginia, our mother was deeply suspicious of our lack of appetite. "How come Button isn't eating Mother's holiday blondies?" she asked with a murderous sweetness. "Not hungry," we said, and for once, Bunny, it wasn't a lie. We attended her book club meeting under duress, wearing a dress the color of a dead sky that hung on us. Watched her get drunk on wassail, flirt flagrantly with the arborist attending to her evergreens. Watched her with a new kind of seeing, Bunny. Thinking, *You made me.*

On a foggy beach in Big Sur, we got gutter drunk on diet prosecco, then did detox yoga with our mother. Loving for the first time how deeply uncurious she was about us. Asked us no questions apart from whether we were hydrating enough. "I do wonder about this writing thing," was all she observed once, between our Downward and Upward Dogs. "You seem a little too in your head these days." We grunted noncommittally, though later on, alone in our dark bedroom, cradling our old, bloody toe shoes to our fucking heart (that empty vessel), we wondered about it too, Bunny. *This writing thing.*

Across the country, under a New England moon, we lay on our quilted bedspread the color of blood, praying for the old entities to enter us. "Please," we whispered to the air, "please fuck me like you used to." And nothing, Bunny. We just lay there in the swirling fucking dust, empty. Our shelves of typewriters looked like what they were: rows of cold, dead clicking machines. We could hear the mundane sounds of our Austrian Japanese mother making strudel in the kitchen, our Irish father, who taught us everything about storytelling and axes both, chopping firewood outside. Every strike made us fucking shudder with arousal and PTSD.

In a volcanic mountain lodge on the edge of the abyss, our surgeon sister took one look at our pale, smiling face and said, "What have you fucking done this time?" "Nothing," we murmured, because Denial, at this tender juncture, was our spiritual survival, Bunny. Thankfully, she was too blind to truly see, let alone attend to our psychic wounds. And so we wandered alone by the crashing white shore, looked to the natural world for healing. For the Universe to smile upon us once more. To tell us, in her language of Signs and Wonders, what surely must be true: *You are so very special. What you are doing is terribly important Work. We fucking love you, Bunny, we do.*

We closed our eyes and opened our third one to the Yule moon.

We thought about our creative crucible.

We begged for guidance, a way forward. *Reality. Perspective. A grip.*

Even though we weren't so sure anymore, Bunny, if we really even fucking wanted those things after all.

20

In late January, as you know, New England is a horror show of snow and ice. Especially in this town named after God and fate. And yet we were anxious to return to campus for spring semester, Bunny. Would we come back to find all of Warren beheaded? To find him waiting for us in Kyra's attic, turning a bloody ax in his hands like a rose? Saying, *So sorry. I love you. Dance with me, please.*

We would have danced with him even then, is the sick thing.

There had been no Violences over the break, no more beheadings, which, *phew.* We told ourselves it was a good thing, Bunny, that he seemed to have vanished into thin air.

That there was basically no evidence of him in the world, like, at all anymore.

We returned to a basement full of sleeping Darlings huddled together for warmth, surrounded by Pixy Stix dust. George Michael still giving his heart from our pink Bose and *Love Actually* still playing on the wall. "Beautiful Aurelia,'" our boys quoted lustily, rising from their rabbity slumbers. Looking not at us but at one another. They'd stripped out of their suit jackets and shirts and were wearing only their silk ties now, which appeared slightly chewed. We gaped at their very cut bodies while they took us in coolly, their pale eyes more hollow than ever before.

"'Sometimes things are so transparency, they don't need evidential proof,'" one whispered.

"I have been perusing the works of Austen," another called from his shadowy corner (and we observed the gnawed pages by his clawed foot).

His lovely mouth was flecked with paper and sugar. "I find you to be both the Senseless and the Sensibility."

Cringing, we shut the door.

As for the attic, how different it looked to our eyes after so much time away, Bunny. In the wintry afternoon light, it seemed smaller than we remembered. Less holy. The blood spray on the walls, the painted clouds, did not fill us with dreams but instead an anxious dread. Had we gotten reality, perspective, a grip after all?

Not fucking really, no.

Well, what was it, then? What had caused this atmospheric shift?

We looked at one another in our slouchy cashmeres, breath coming out of our mouths like so much cold, minty smoke. And we knew that something essential had flown from us. Our creative fire, the heat of our hearts' blood, had grown cold. The hive mind was dark, Bunny. And in its place? A deadness. A sick desperation.

"Spring Workshop tomorrow," Kyra said in a hopeful voice, her words a tremulous cloud in the cold air.

"Yes," we murmured.

It couldn't come fucking soon enough.

21

We arrived at the Cave early that first day, of course we did. Waiting, breath held, for her to appear out of the dark. Notebooks and mind vaginas wide open, Bunny. LePens fucking gripped in our hands. Because this was serious, k? This was a goddamned creative emergency. Way worse than we'd first feared. Last night Vik had snatched a rabbit from a neighbor's bush and brought him upstairs. *Just to see, Bunny,* she'd said, cradling the creature in her arms, which were shaking as ours were fucking shaking. *Can we still?* He didn't even break a sweat, Bunny. Though we circled him, stared at him, until we felt like our eyes were bleeding. Else let out a most unholy shriek, and Coraline shook her golden bob, crying, NO BUNNY NO BUNNY NO BUNNY, not stopping even after we'd slapped her. She was still whispering it in the Cave now—*no bunny no bunny no bunny*—like a nightmare she was trapped inside of, Bunny.

We all were.

A judgy cough from the opposite shore of the table. You, Samantha. Sitting across from us in your cardigan of despair. Blinking through your bitch curtain like a bitch. Bracing yourself, probably, for the arrival of the Word Witch. You were in a nightmare of your own, we guessed, what with your boyfriend, Allan, being gone and Ursula now taking the reins. We remember how you winced when at last her voice pierced the dark. And we? Smiled for the first time that year.

"Creatives," she intoned from somewhere in the shadows.

Fucking finally, we thought.

Oh how our souls brightened briefly at the sight of her shimmering toward us in her art smock! A North Star on this blackest night of the soul. What we'd come here for, dreamed of for so long.

She came into the light, murmuring apologies for her lateness (she was very late, that should have been the first clue). She looked much younger than we remembered. Taller, strangely; thinner, too. A pinkish glow to her graying cheek, like when one of our mothers got a vampire facial. Weird. When we'd last seen Ursula that snowy November's eve, you see, she'd seemed positively grandmotherly.

"Welcome to spring semester," she said in a so-rich voice. And smiled at us. Wildly, Bunny. Ran a hand through her witchy locks, which seemed to have far more gold in them now than silver.

"Thank you," we murmured. A little discomfited by her distinctly unmotherish appearance. By that unbridled grin, which seemed just not very . . . professorial enough. Which seemed far too . . . *happy*. Flustered. Almost like she'd just been fucking or something, Vik said later. Her lipstick, one of us observed, was an alarmingly wanton magenta.

Still, we smiled back, gripped our LePens. Awaited her nurturing guidance. For her to go around the table widdershins, perhaps. Draw out our personal stories with tarot cards and birthing gestures. And yes, we know you made cheap fun of her admittedly unorthodox pedagogical gifts in your *novel*, Bunny. Her occultisms, her gynecological metaphors, her use of sock puppets, her deep love of what you called Trauma Porn. Well, sometimes you fucking need that shit, k? *We* needed it. Wanted her to Tap our Wounds, oh so tender but generative. Reanimate us from the creative dead with a choice writing prompt or an all-seeing crystal. We closed our eyes. Ready, so fucking ready, to be Unearthed.

Instead, Bunny, she handed out syllabi, remember? *Please pass these around, thanks.* Went through her attendance policy for what felt like five hours. Pulled out some handwritten notes from what looked like 1989 and read us her very long list of Workshop protocols, do you recall those? Each week we would be submitting pages (or Wounds, as she preferred to call them). "Handwritten only, please," for she liked the Wound "raw and freshly bleeding." And no submitting drafts "until the day before Workshop, please." She wouldn't read our Wounds before then because, and here she smiled, "I like to have them fresh in my head." She preferred a paper clip to a staple, by the way. A double rather than a single space, k?

Um. K. But—

"Wonderful. Well then. Let's go Tap, shall we?" And she rose from her chair like, *Dismissed.*

WHAT? we almost screamed. You were already out of your seat of course, Bunny, gleefully fucking running out the door. Meanwhile we watched, panicking, as Ursula hummingly gathered those ancient notes and shoved them back into her witchy satchel.

"That's *it?*" one of us couldn't help but cry. Coraline. Blood dripping darkly from her dress pocket. The hand in there a fucking fist.

Ursula looked at us perhaps for the first time since she'd entered the Cave. Witheringly, Bunny. "*Excuse* me?"

"Well, but . . . aren't you . . . going to give us, like . . ." This from Vik. Trailing off, poor Bunny. Fumbling for her words for, like, the first time ever.

"Give you *what* exactly?"

Oh, the shame we felt, Bunny. But also the righteous outrage, k? *Um, some guidance maybe, hello? As our teacher? Because we took your creative advice, by the way. Reality, perspective, a grip—we tried to get them. And now look at us. Broken of heart. Empty of attic. And no bunny, NO BUNNY!*

"Maybe a writing prompt?" Kyra blurted at last.

A flash of annoyance in Ursula's eyes then. Pity too. Like, *Oh my, oh dear.* What did it say about us, as artists really, that we needed our creative hands held in this way?

"*Tap,*" she said at last. "How's that?"

And we felt psychically smacked in the face.

The hive mind went completely black then, Bunny. The candle of hope nearly snuffed.

"Ursula?" Else whispered desperately. Yes, even Else sounded desperate. A crack in the otherworldly bell of her voice. The dagger around her neck pale and limp looking. "Could we please speak with you for a moment?"

"Oh, I have to run today, I'm afraid," she said. "Engagement." Her voice very *sorry, not sorry*. A kind of singing in it that made us sick.

"But it's about that conversation," Coraline pushed, she loved to fucking push. And today we loved her for it. "You know, the very important one we had just before break, remember? Where *you* told us to—"

"Engagement," she snapped, cutting her off. "As I said. But perhaps you can come see me during my office hours."

Office hours?! Um, were we fucking FRESHMEN, Bunny? But we played grateful. "Oh *of course*, thank you! And when are they?" And we waved our LePens, cracked now like our smiles, pretending to take such mindful note. Feeling this whole time like we were fucking drowning.

"By appointment," she sang, not even looking at us.

"So can we make the appointment *now*?" Coraline cried. Dress pocket dangerously bloody from gripping that new razor of hers. A breath away, perhaps, from losing a finger entirely.

Ursula smiled coldly, snapping her satchel shut. "Email me."

What could we do, Bunny, but sit there, stunned, watching her wrap herself in her many shawls, watching her leave us. Practically skipping toward the exit. Just before she was about to disappear through the doors, she turned to us. "Oh, girls, I almost forgot."

And for a moment, Bunny, hope rekindled so stupidly in our hearts. *Is she finally going to be curious about us? Our mind vaginas? Our lives?*

"Yes, Mother?"

"Toward the end of term I'll be presenting a showcase of my new Work. I hope you'll all attend? I'm quite excited to share it with you." That unnatural smile stretched her lips again, painted that too-bright slut shade. *Fuck no*, we thought. *Don't want to attend, Bunny. Don't care about your new Work. This is about US, OUR Work. That's in fucking crisis right now, k?*

"Of course we'll attend," one of us simpered. Kyra of course. We hated her for it even as we all nodded along, smiling so hard, our cheeks would ache later from the fake. "So exciting," we said, or some such writer lie.

"Thank you. It's just come pouring out of me recently."

And we thought of shit, Bunny. Glistening, sickly rivers of it. "How wonderful for you."

"It really is," she agreed. "*So* wonderful to feel connected again." She bit on her bright lip, like a girl talking about a crush. How terrible writers looked, we thought, when they were happily working on their *Worlds*. When they were deep inside those Worlds, utterly immune to Reality, seeing only glitter in the dust motes. We watched her literally bound out of the room without another fucking thought or word for us, her dearest students. Just sitting there in the dark Cave, still clutching our cracked LePens, still hunched over our open notebooks.

Which were more blank than they'd ever been.

22

S pring semester sort of went downhill from there, Bunny.
January, February, March, April.

The days, weeks, and months ticked by like a most terrible clock.

We spent the long, cold hours together, mostly. Holding our collective breath. Waiting (dare we say hopefully?) for more beheading news. For some evidence of Aerius. For our love, our soul, to return to us. But the Violences had ceased, Bunny, along with our Art. AAARV stopped their daily protesting and outcries, which, thank fucking god. And still no bodies found. Still no confirmed sightings of Tyler Fields, either, though some students had claimed to have spotted him on campus, near the Philosophy building, looking lost. Perhaps he'd run away was the general consensus.

Young people today, so very unstable.

Yes, very, we agreed with whomever, *truly.* The posters of his face, once plastered all over campus, started to wilt and peel from the lampposts and walls and corkboards. Got covered by new play advertisements, announcements of poetry readings and visual art exhibits.

Visit the Hall of Infinite Reflection!

Attend Dr. Ursula Radcliffe's Spring Showcase!

Tickets now available! Pay what you can! Bring your friends!

Pathetic, Bunny. The exclamations. The blatant begging. Artists, we started to think, in the winter of our Creative Standstill, were truly a little gross.

Last fall began to feel like a kind of dream, Bunny, a Fiction. If we didn't have those hollow-eyed Darlings in the basement, demanding Pixy Stix, offering to slow dance with us (however clumsily) to our harp-forward favorites, we might have thought it really was.

Sure, we did our best to move on, to start fresh. But it was fucking hard, k?

We couldn't seem to even hunt rabbits these days, you see, let alone explode them anymore. We tried, desperately, to gather the little fuckers into our arms and lure them back to the attic. But they no longer came to us so willingly, Bunny, and we had to give literal chase. Racing across gardens and fields and sometimes streets and driveways and other people's yards, our backs and pits and underboobs sweating so profusely beneath our lovely outerwear, arms outstretched wildly to catch, gloved hands fucking clawing the air. Whispering, *Come here, Bunny, please come fucking here, k?* Kyra was the best runner among us, which is funny because she had the littlest legs. But she was quick on those legs, Bunny, like a magic millipede or something. Still, the creatures would elude her, disappearing into some big bush or ducking coyly into the nether regions of the earth.

"What the fuck are you girls doing?" an old man once asked from his doorway, shotgun cocked in his hand. He'd caught us in his garden, in pursuit of a wily winter hare, now hiding (we suspected) among his evergreen shrubs. We froze before the cold gun barrel aimed right at our faces, Bunny, stared into the man's dead eyes.

"Writing," one of us whispered.

"Fucking," said another of us, at the very same time.

"Tapping the Wound," another offered, chin quivering.

"Trying so very hard to find Love again."

Tears fell from all our eyes from the truth of it. He shook his head and shut the door.

Eventually we had no choice, Bunny. No choice but to make our way to the mall, to fucking PetSmart.

"Hello, good day, how are you?" Else told the clerk most smilingly. "We'd like to purchase all your rabbits, please."

We stood hovering by a cage of them, all cuddled so sweetly together like Easter. And us smiling just as sweetly, Bunny. Quite like Easter ourselves.

"*All* of them?" And the clerk just looked at us, in our lovely dresses, like we were, I don't know, *weird* or something. Admittedly, there may have been a wildish sheen to our faces. A want, unholy and bottomless, gleaming in our many eyes.

"We just love rabbits so very much, you see," Coraline said very reasonably, "that we want to provide them with a beautiful, loving home."

"With lots of flowers to eat," Kyra chimed in.

"And grasses to munch," Vik added.

"And candy to suck," Coraline finished.

The clerk frowned now. She reminded us a little of you, Samantha. Depression lipstick. Suspicious bitch blink. A silver ankh dangling from her neck on a cheap black rope. "I don't know that I'm allowed to sell *all* the—"

And then Else slapped down the platinum credit card, Bunny. Smiled her mother's smile that meant business. That pushed open every door. Demanded it be pushed open for her to glide through, so prettily, not suing you this time.

Back in the attic, we lowered the lights. Lit the vanilla cream candles and the lavender-rosemary incense like we were on a date, which, *weren't we?* Played Bush, we were bringing out the big guns this time. The whole of *The Sensual World*. Gathered in our hot pink circle, lips balmed, bodies spritzed with various scents emulating the natural world in all its fucking wonder. Stared unblinkingly at our box of fuzzy bunny until we couldn't fucking see anymore, Bunny.

Were there explosions?

Oh yes, there were explosions in the end.

After hours and hours and hours.

But the Results, oh god the Results. We still shudder to recall how they came into being screaming or else frozen into a kind of open-mouthed silence. All of them a pale, eerie blond, like the children in *Village of the Damned*, haircuts like Little Lord Fauntleroy. Pink eyed and wearing pretty lavender suits, with furry white paws for hands. "Hot," Vik said, and she really wanted to keep one of the less screamy ones, but we said fucking no. They creeped us out, k? But not in a good way at all, Bunny.

Off with their heads, please.

The PetSmart bunnies were kind of a new low for us, Bunny. Creatively speaking. (Our basement Darlings seemed like pontificating geniuses by comparison.) We grew more slaphappy with the ax during this time—what else could we do? We were lost, k? Lost and at a loss. In the dead of fucking February. In the crotch of rainy, never-ending March. In the wet blush of April. And then there was that terrible spring day when we'd run through all the pet store rabbits, and all the wild ones eluded our grabbing hands. We watched a last little runt run away from us into the spring dark, into the wide world.

And we, stunned, just stood there in the cold mud, watching him go.

No longer even giving chase.

We recalled Aerius running away from us into the autumnal night.

It was triggering, Bunny.

Of course, it wasn't our lack of innate talent—how could it be, given our amply demonstrated genius? No, *circumstances* were blocking our Potential, Bunny, as Else so often pointed out. Our ongoing heartbreak, for one. Not to mention sheer fucking teacherly neglect—first Allan's and now Ursula's. The *indifference*, Bunny, likely systemic to Warren as an institution, was stifling our burgeoning Greatness, totally.

Case in point: Spring Workshop.

You stopped going to class, remember? In your novel you cite us, our laughter, our togetherness, as the reason, and it's so funny, Bunny, that our laughter's what drove you away. Maybe we *were* laughing on the outside, k, but on the inside?

That was a whole other fucking story.

We hated Workshop, maybe more than you, which is saying a lot. We didn't whine about it like you or stop going like you, because unlike you, Bunny, we didn't live in an '80s high school movie of the mind, we didn't sit smoking and brooding in black on the other side of the fence of Life, wearing so-scary eyeliner and listening to too-cool-for-you music, skipping class and talking to swans, k? We took our graduate careers and opportunities, like, seriously. So whatever weird text Ursula assigned, we fucking read it, rainbow highlighter in hand, from that treatise on the fornication of flowers to the photography collection of overexposed torsos. Whatever writing prompt she gave us—from *Gushing the Blood* to *Turning the Wheel of Fortune Widdershins*—we did it in good fucking faith. We were there every week with bells, basically, cooing at her dog, our paper-clipped, double-spaced Wounds in hand, waiting-dying for her to tell us something promising, something specific, something beautiful about ourselves.

But she never did, Bunny.

Instead, she was . . . fucking strange. Daydreamy. *Distracted.* Always *smiling* to herself. Humming a jaunty song whose lyrics we could never catch. Coming to the Cave late and leaving early. Ignoring our very courteous emails, our carefully worded, oh-so-mindful-of-her-time requests to meet outside of class, *during your office hours, which, um, aren't you supposed to have those?* Getting *us* to lead the discussion on the readings in class. (*Why don't I turn it over to you?* That was her very favorite phrase.) Offering only the vaguest of feedback on our Wounds. *Tap more deeply*, she said of every Wound, not even fucking looking at it, Bunny. Not even looking at *us.* Just sort of staring into the middle distance at something only she could see. *Gush the Blood*, she whispered. *Find the throb, the bounce, if you will, of raw life.* She smiled dreamily, her whore lipstick painted thick, thick. Ran a hand through her long golden hair, which seemed to be getting more lush, more golden by the week. Her line notes were equally baffling. *The authorial musicality prevaricates* ☹ *Let the Source speak* ☺

She wasn't a prick like Allan, of course. Didn't overtly eviscerate us, fill us with a dark shame that left us paralyzed in the rose garden for hours afterward, imagining murder scenarios.

It was more like she just . . . wasn't really there at all, Bunny.

Be with it always, she murmured distractedly as she bolted toward the door.

What the fuck? But she was already turning away, Bunny. Gone before we could blink. And we, in the dark of the Cave, in an even deeper dark of the heart, watched her go.

We always seemed to be watching something escape us that spring.

Broken, we'd return to our basement Darlings. Sought their company and consolation in the evenings, on the makeshift dance floor. They said, "Tell me everything," and we did tell, Bunny. Lowered the lights and cranked the Bush. Got drunk and leaned on their hulky (if slightly misshapen) shoulders and told them every fucking thing under the sun.

"She fails to facilitate our genius," we whispered into their very hard arms, watching the April rain fall through the window, the frost slowly unfrost on the branch. "We are cruelly thwarted in our artistic growth."

"You're so hot, though," they offered. "Also, what does the brain matter compared with the heart?" They smiled beautifully, emptily at us. Squeezed our side boob. You could drown in the bright blue nothing of their eyes, Bunny, you really fucking could.

"Sometimes when we think of Aerius," we whispered, "we are so sad, we feel like dying."

"No dying," they said, bringing our wrists to their lips, nibbling the orchids we wore there. "Not when you're this pretty and delicious, k?" Speaking more to the flowers than to us, truth be told. "Forget this Aries," they whispered, mouths full of petal.

"*Aerius*," we corrected, practically screaming. Sometimes we'd admittedly lose it mid-Bush, Bunny. Right on the dance floor, under the prom party lights. *Why can't you be more like him?* we'd hiss. And we'd shake them like we were angry mothers and they the most disappointing of children. Shake them until they bit us sometimes. Fucking hard on the finger or wrist, *OW*.

We grew incredibly adept at first aid that spring too, didn't we, Bunny? Yet we couldn't mend our hearts.

23

May brought with it a scent of freshly budding green that made our thighs ache. Brought with it such lush grasses, such blooming flowers, we almost couldn't bear it, Bunny. So many bunnies hopping around Narrative Arts, taunting us. Mocking us, really, we felt, for the moment we drew close to them, they'd run. *Fine*, we thought, *fucking run*.

Don't even care anymore, we lied.

Last day of Workshop. After class (which was a joke, we hate to say it, Sam, but you missed nothing) we lay in the rose garden, now positively brimming with life, which only sharpened our sense of spiritual and artistic death. That hole in the earth that Vik had dug was still there. Where we'd first seen him smiling slyly at us, not so very long ago. Long ears twitching with promises, beckoning us, most flirtingly, *Come on, let's go*. We gazed at this muddy hole, mourning all we'd lost. Pondering the vicissitudes of Creation and Destruction.

"Well, it's fucking over," Coraline sighed. She'd been in a shit mood for weeks, Bunny.

"*What?* Please don't say that, Bunny, okay?" we whispered.

"How can I not say it, *Bunny?* We have to face *Reality*."

And we, lying in the Ivy grass, had to smile darkly at that word. *Reality*.

"We're just not Magic anymore," she whispered, shaking her head. No longer so bobbed or blond, she'd let the dark roots creep in again most wantonly. "Aerius was a fluke," she pressed, articulating our very worst fear.

"And an ax murderer, don't forget," Kyra said. Twisting the knife as she so liked to do then. Perhaps she missed her axing days.

"Who didn't even kill Allan," Vik said, adding salt to the wound.

"But at least he was alive," Coraline shrieked. "At least he had . . ." And here she trailed off.

A dick? we thought. *Human hands? A healthy hatred of us?*

"*Substance.* And now? He's gone. And we . . . can't even make pale shadows." She was thinking of those PetSmart bunnies, we knew, those Little Lord Fauntleroys with their bright pink eyes and white-furred paws. Or was she thinking of our basement Darlings, growing ever more hollow eyed, ever more confused in their compliments, ever more stiff in their slow-dancing skills? Probably she was thinking of the last bunny, the one we'd tried and failed to transmogrify into Tom Cruise circa 1983, who, despite our staring at him for fucking hours, just kept eating his little mound of wood chips and grass. Eventually hopped away like, *Later. Thanks for the snack.*

She cried now in the rose garden, in that bright May sunlight, exposing the many cuts on her skin, her bloody gloves and lying hair.

"Maybe we should just forget about trying to explode rabbits for a while," Kyra whispered now among the thorny pink flowers. "Try actually writing or something. Beyond those dumb prompts of Ursula's, I mean."

"Oh, very funny, Bunny," we said. "Don't be silly. No, no. *Writing?*"

That can't possibly be the way forward, we thought. Artistically or otherwise. But what was?

Just then Ursula emerged from Narrative Arts, almost as if we'd summoned her with our question. Bounding out the door in her Stevie Nicks priestess wear. Reeking of ungodly gardens—we could smell the mugwort from here.

Our first instinct, of course, was to ambush her. *Can we please talk to you? Why have you been avoiding us, your beloved students, all semester?* But we were arrested by the sight of her skipping across the green, smiling obscenely. Clearly deep inside in her own dreamworld. Clearly a music to everything only she could hear and she was sort of prancing to it. She tilted her face up to the sun, appearing to bask in its golden light.

Her joy, Bunny, was monstrous to behold.

And familiar. Oh so familiar to us.

We watched as she stooped down and picked a dandelion growing in the grassy verge by the sidewalk. Snatched it most greedily from the earth. Looked both ways as she shoved it, almost guiltily, into the black mouth of her purse. The heat flooding our faces when we saw her pick that dandelion, Bunny. Like we were suddenly on fucking fire from the inside with a knowledge we couldn't name. Or could we?

We watched her clip-clop away. And there was something in her step. Something we'd noted before—all semester, in fact—but hadn't been able to put our finger on until just now.

There was a *skip* to it, yes, but not just a skip.

A hop.

There was a fucking *hop* to it, Bunny.

And then, in the rose garden, the pink cloud of our hive mind—dark for so very long—suddenly awakened.

We followed her across campus and beyond, hearts in our fucking throats. Keeping a safe distance, but we needn't have been so careful, Bunny. She was oblivious to us, to everything, smilingly lost in some sort of '70s-tinted daydream. Singing along to whatever enabling song must have been playing on her dated headphones. We caught bits of what we thought might be Fleetwood Mac lyrics. Her high, cracking voice so different from the one she wielded in Workshop, which sounded like runes if they could talk. Her golden hair shining, bouncing in the May sun. *Bouncing*, Bunny. Yes, it bounced with each hop. Giving us the strangest fucking feeling. Our hands trembled with it, this feeling.

Keep following.

By the time we approached her house, the hive mind was pulsing wildly with speculations we dared not speak, dared not even hope. We hung back at her neighbor's as she hopped ahead into her own front yard like a giddy child. Pulled the dandelion from her purse, clutching it unnecessarily close to her boob. She twirled its stem, then took a sniff like a hit while we fucking watched, hive seething. She didn't go through her front door, no, no. Instead she looked both ways (not seeing us thanks to her neighbor's poplars) and went through through the side gate.

Which led to the back garden, Bunny.

That writing shed.

The flickering light we'd seen in the window.

We must see what was inside the shed, Bunny. Now. Though at this point we fucking knew. And with the force of this realization, moving as one body now, a body electric, we tore through the side gate, ran through the back garden, all her brazen bushes and flagrant flowers, and threw ourselves, screaming, against her little red door.

A dark room that smelled like fire's ghost. We lay in a heap on the dusty floorboards, which *ouch*. Felt the bruises forming instantly on our thighs and sides. We would have to massage one another later, extensively, but there was no fucking time for that now. *Where is he, where is he?* We looked around wildly, expecting to find him naked and chained to a post, she was such a perv probably.

No sign, Bunny. A ring of unlit candles surrounding us. Some statues of rabbits on the shelves, along with some New Agey–looking texts and novels. A purple velvet curtain that divided the room. *What's on the other—*

A clearing of a throat behind us. We turned.

Ursula. Sitting at her desk in the half dark, her giant headphones still on. Looking down at us like we were fucking insane. And looking around the place now, which was clearly just a kind of witchy office, we maybe were.

"Girls," Ursula said, slipping off her headphones, "what the hell is this about?"

It was awkward, Bunny. We really didn't know what to say for ourselves. *Sorry to break in and everything. Don't know what came over us. We just really, really wanted to schedule an office-hours meeting, k?* We kept murmuring half-baked apologies to her unfinished floor while she chastised us. "Second time you've shown up at my door unannounced. This time breaking in," blah, blah, blah. She looked at us curled in a heap at her foot. Droned on and on about boundaries. But we weren't really listening, Bunny. We were too busy noticing things in this office of hers. How those rabbit statues were stare-smiling at us, for instance, causing our skin to crawl. A live bunny eating rose petals in the corner, nibbling in a way that made our thighs twitch. That purple curtain behind her, *what's on the other fucking side?* And the smell, Bunny, pervading the small space. Spring in its first flowery flush. Autumnal gardens. It made us dizzy with want. Made our nipples and clits hard, our hearts literally ache. We looked back up at her. "Where is he?" we asked as one voice. Growling now.

"*Excuse me?*"

"WHERE. IS. HE?" And we sounded fucking crazy maybe. We didn't care.

"*Who?*"

"You know who," Else challenged. Bold as fuck.

"Our cold love," Coraline said.

"Our Happy Accident," Vik added.

"The boy we conjured from a bunny last fall," Kyra clarified softly.

Ursula let the absurdity of this hang in the air. Perhaps hoping we would crumble, back down, skulk away. But we stayed where we were, Bunny, clinging to her floorboards.

"*Aerius,*" we whispered.

And then, Bunny, the look in her eye shifted.

"What did you just say?" Her voice was low, threatening. Her gaze was suddenly dark matter, swallowing us. We couldn't bring ourselves to repeat his name.

"Please," Coraline begged in the smallest voice. "Please give him back."

"*BACK?*"

She stared at us. So fucking coldly, we ourselves felt cold, Bunny. For a second she looked like she might kill us. The rabbit eating the rose petals suddenly hopped into her lap. She looked at him sitting there. Closed her eyes. We watched her bury her face in his fur. Shake her head. "No," she whispered.

We looked at one another. *What?* "Ursula—"

"I really have no idea what you're talking about," she murmured into the rabbit's body. Making us colder still. The rabbit stared at us with his bright eyes.

"With all due respect, Professor," Else said softly in her most omnipotent voice, "we think you do." Which was un-fucking-real, Bunny. It was in moments like these when we were thankful for her God complex. She was more ballsy than our Darlings.

Now Ursula looked up from the rabbit's fur. Her eyes flashed with *how fucking dare you*. Was she not our literary idol? Were her works not what had first lit up our mind vaginas so long ago? Did we not sit in her living room only last fall, looking at her like she was God? *You're why I want to be a writer. You're why I'm alive at all.* Had we not gushed these fawning words to her face? How could *she* ever possibly steal from *us* when she'd fucking made us everything that we were?

"Girls," she began gravely. "I'm afraid you're deeply mistaken."

Suddenly we felt sick. We thought of that tattoo of the Crystal Thief on his forearm. We locked eyes, still clinging to her floorboards. *Oh god.*

"And not only about this *Aries business* . . ."

Aries?

"But about the very nature of Creation in general. Perhaps it's my own failing as a teacher." She was petting the rabbit now, staring at Else.

"The nature of Creation?" Else repeated. Not sounding so much like God anymore, Bunny.

"Well, if this . . . Eros is his name, you said?"

"*Aerius*," we corrected. And why did we have the feeling, Bunny, that she had once more purposely misremembered?

"If this Manifestation is *yours*"—and now she looked us dead in all our eyes—"then, *with all due respect*, why isn't he *with you*? Why do you have to hunt him down like this? Break into my home?"

The rabbit in her arms regarded us coolly. Our hands gripping the floor-boards grew slippery and hot. Ursula smiled now. "Creation shouldn't be a *struggle*. You shouldn't have to go *chasing* it. After all, one has one's dignity to think of, doesn't one? It should be an ecstatic Visitation . . . when you least expect it. It should . . . visit *you*."

And here she flushed, as at a delicious memory.

Our eyes stung with tears, Bunny. Of Envy, obvi. And her homely, inevitable sister: Shame.

"Now, was I fortunate enough to be visited recently? Yes, I was. After a dry season. A very long, very dry season. But I can assure you that this Visitation was quite authentically my own. As you'll see when I give my showcase tomorrow night. I do still hope you'll all come?"

We stared up at her from the floor, sinking now beneath us—why were all her floors so fucking unstable? Bodies bruised and dripping with the shame of it all. And the rage, Bunny, roaring in our hearts. No grip at all.

"Sure," we whispered.

"Now, I won't further dignify this outrageous conversation with my time. But I will say that *I*, unlike *some*"—and here she looked again at Else pointedly, for two could play at this God game, Bunny—"don't need the *Collective* to conjure. I much prefer to collaborate directly with the Source itself, just me and *it*. Otherwise, too many petty human issues come up, I've found. Covetousness. Jealousy. Competing ideas. A Cesspool. One can't think for oneself. One loses one's soul. Worst of all, one has to *share* the Result. And I was never terribly good at sharing. I'm still not."

Else flushed now, finally shamed. Thinking of our many fights over Aerius. Clearly, we were also not good at sharing, Bunny. Was that why he'd jumped out the window?

We looked at Ursula, stroking that bunny. Smiling at us now, though her eyes were still dark with anger. And something else. Some other sick emotion swimming there.

We looked away. "Sorry to bother you," Kyra murmured. "We'll go now."

And then, quicker than thought, one of us pulled back the purple velvet curtain. One of our many hands just reached out and yanked it back while we all held our breath. But there was nothing there. Just a little kitchen area, a blue-and-white Finnish tea set. A chaise longue, velvety purple like the curtain, for lounging or fainting perhaps. No sign of him anywhere.

Ursula looked at us, that quiet rage in her dog violet eyes. The rabbit in her arms doing the same. "Are you quite done?"

"Quite," we whispered.

24

And so we left, Bunny. Empty-handed. Vaguely horny (that scent of him we'd caught in the shed such a mindfuck). Broken of spirit and heart. But together, more so than ever before perhaps. We took slow steps home, walking in a kind of mystical sync. United in that persistent, unquashable feeling that he was out there. That he was in fact quite close. Bunnies leapt out of the dark and followed us home, seeming to corroborate this hunch, their white tails flashing in the dark. Taunting us like he once did so long ago.

Oh, Aerius!

Was he not ours after all?

She really made us fucking doubt ourselves, Bunny. As we walked, we raked over all the proof in the hive mind (*pearls, razor, conjuring dress, Kill Allan*), but the creeping doubt maintained its grip. In hindsight, it was reprehensible of Ursula to gaslight us about our very own Creation like that. After much therapy, we now recognize her narcissistic manipulations for what they were.

But back then, as you know, we were such innocents, Bunny. Really just trying to make something beautiful in the night, you know?

In Else's basement we found our Darlings huddled together among the crushed-flower-petal and candy-wrapper debris, watching *Rebel Without a Cause*. Some were making out with each other, quite lost in that, until we cleared our throats. "Would you care to dance with us?" we asked them shyly. Even though it was not Prom Thursday, Bunny. Or even Touching Tuesday.

They looked up and smiled. Held out their black-gloved hands. "Nothing would give us greater screaming."

Having exhausted the Bush, tonight we turned on the Heart. "Alone." Put it on repeat, because technology. Rocked with them in the dark to this song that one of us (she was Music Nazi that spring) loved so.

"I love it so too," they murmured into our necks. Nibbling the flower necklaces we wore for this very purpose. "My favorite also, oh yes."

"Is it?" we said. But we knew better than to push too much. To push was to have them explode on us, literally, and we'd just had our dresses dry-cleaned. So we smiled. "How serendipitous."

"So Serengeti," they agreed, holding us closer. Rewarding us, or so they thought, with a slight boob crush.

"There must be a way to get him back," one of us whispered as we swayed in the basement dust, eyes fiercely closed to the girl/rabbit shadows on the wall.

"But why do we need this *murderer* in our lives?" Kyra asked. Even though she knew. Wanted him as much, if not more, than we did.

"Because he's the closest we ever came, Bunny," we replied most reasonably.

"To something *insane?*"

"To something real." The word echoed uncomfortably in the basement, as it always did. Our Darlings grew stiff in our arms.

We thought of his vivid eyes full of our shadow selves. Shivered.

We'd go to Ursula's showcase, oh yes.

He'd be there, we knew that somehow.

Speaking of which, let's return now to his story. Where was he at this precise moment of our basement musings? Our endless pining? Our newly hatched scheme?

We can see you're literally dying to find out, Bunny.

Part Four

Aerius

XVII

D ear Reader,
Please forgive me ☹

It has been a season since we last communed, I know. I have missed you. There is so much I have longed to share with you (for there have been many Happenings), but I could not ☹ I'm afraid I've not had much Solitude of late, my Mindscape has not been my own ☹

I do hope you have not felt Neglected by me, Friend.

Truly, you are my only Friend in the World now.

So much has happened that I am not sure where I should resume my Tellings. The Moon thrice became a Sliver of herself, then bloomed into a beauteous silver Circle in the Night Sky. Spring arrived in all her Green Glory, melting the Snows and revealing the sweet Grasses and Flowers beneath. The Wind lost her cold Bite, grew as soft and yielding as Jonah's Pelt, making me ache for him (though I dare not dwell on that here). Pony died ☹ One Day I pulled him from my Pocket, for he would not answer my Good Morrows, and I saw that a sort of Glaze had overtaken his sparkling Eyes ☹

Perhaps he is not Dead, Reader. Perhaps he is merely in a Coma of some kind.In any case, he ceased speaking to me, though I still cried to him sometimes.

Very well, I cried to him often.

Mother reminded me twas not a Matter of Life or Death, for he was a Toy. This I could not believe ☹ And so at last she took him from me entirely. Mother has grown much stranger with me. But perhaps the bigger Change is with my Self. *Within* my Self, Reader. Tis hard to articulate it, for tis not a Change visible to the Eye. But I feel it in my Heart as surely as I see the

Moon slivering, as surely as I watch the Sun stretching herself in these longer Days, as surely as I watch my new Rabbit Friend eat his rose Petals at my
Feets, his Eyes twinkling just like the Immortal's.

And it scares me.

I am not quite ready to share about this Change yet, Reader.

So perhaps I will begin by telling you about Mother, her new Strangeness.

She leaves me Alone in the Shed less these Days, hence my Difficulties
in sharing freely with you. Always poking her Head in the door, wanting to
know how my Wound Tapping (she means my Writings, of course) is going.
It Bleeds, Mother, I always tell her. If you would leave me to it, I think silently.
But Mother does not leave. Instead it has been her Habit to come into the
Shed with her evening glass of Wine sloshing. To step inside my Ring of
Fires, sit cross-legged before me, and stare. Her Gaze is misty and fixed. Her
Smile is sloppy and painted. She is in Love with me, I think.

"You are welcome to sleep in the guest room now, you know," she says
huskily.

"I know, Mother."

"Leonard," she says, pointing to the Rabbit by my Feets, "doesn't re-
quire a bed anymore."

I stare into the Eyes of the former Immortal. They look bright and sharp,
just as they did when he was a Man, before I killed him with Ax ☹ There is
so much I know now, Reader. So much I wish I didn't ☹ So much I wish to
know still.

"You do not need to sit out here all Night in the Shed," Mother whispered one Evening. "Aren't you cold?" And she shivered performatively.

"Not at all, Mother. I enjoy the Shed." I didn't enjoy the Shed ☹ But I
preferred it to Mother's house, for twas mine in a Way that her house was
not. A room of One's own, as my Keepers used to say, is so very important.

Especially for being with you, Reader ☺

But I was indeed cold, I was indeed shivering ☹

In her kitchen we imbibed her Wine the color of Blood, as Mother loves to
do in the Evenings. "Isn't it so much warmer here, Julius?"

"Aerius," I corrected.

Mother frowned. She wished I would allow her to call me by this Name,
her Name for me. Wouldn't I rather be named for an Emperor than some . . .
Allergy Medication?

No, Mother, I much prefer my own Name.

But I did not tell her this. I merely smiled. Tis important with Mother, I
have learned, to tread very carefully with my Words.

"You are right, *tis* so much warmer in here, Mother," I lied. Mother said if
I became *too* warm, I was of course welcome to take my Shirt off. She wanted
me to be quite comfortable. To embrace what she called my Wildness. Twas
Mother who'd confiscated my old Clothes ☹ In their Place she'd offered me
a Choice between a black Scottish Kilt and some very tight-fitting Pants ☹
(I chose the Kilt.) As well as a new Shirt, which was white and billowy, quite
like a Pirate's, open to the Navel like my old Nightgown, leaving little of my
Pelt to the Imaginings ☹ Still, twas better than no Shirt at all.

"I'd prefer to keep it on for now, Mother," I told her now quietly.

"By all means," she said, sounding somewhat disappointed. She said I
was a Free Agent, after all. I was not a Prisoner, was I?

"No, Mother," I said, "I am here quite willingly."

And Mother smiled again. Her Voice when she spoke to me was as silky
as the Cowslip. "How happy that makes me to hear."

"Do you know *why* I am here willingly, Mother?"

"Tell me." And there was a Hopefulness in Mother's Voice then. She
stepped closer to me, each Step making a jangling Sound due to her many
Jewelries. I smelled the faint Witchery of her, the fragrant Fire. I was enveloped in a kind of magenta Fog of the Mindscape. I nearly lost my Voice. But
I still spoke, must speak.

"Because you have promised to show me the Way Back, haven't you?"

"The Way Back," Mother repeated, a Question in her Voice. Like we
hadn't discussed this a Thousand Times before, Reader ☹

"To the Lost Place," I reminded her. "The Lost Self, remember?" To say this aloud caused a Stirring inside of me, brought a near Tear to my Eye. Pictures formed in my Mindscape. Of Sun-dappled Grasses. Swaying Spring Flowers. A long-eared, hopping Shadow. Ever since I crossed Mother's Threshold and took Feather Pen to Page, I've believed in this Lost Place, this Lost Self, Reader, like never before. That I must go back There. That this is where I belong.

I looked at Mother. Because of the Mists in her Gaze, I couldn't read what was there in her strange-colored Eyes. "Absolutely," she said.

"Because you know I can no longer suffer the Pain of being in this Human Body. Which still pines and longs for . . ." And Mother held her Breath. *Longs for what?*

Jonah. My Love. But I dared not speak his Name before Mother. I must tread so very carefully, Reader. "The Lost Self, Mother. You will lead me there, will you not?"

Now Mother appeared distracted, murmuring in a noncommittal Fashion. Pouring herself some more Wine from a very large bottle from a Place called Burgundy. (How Mother would love to take me there, she said, if I weren't in such a Rush to leave her ☹) She poured a very large Goblet for me as well. I watched her drink, thinking of my Goldy Liquid Days with the Poets.

"When will you show me, Mother?" I pressed.

She looked into my Eyes, paralyzing me briefly in her French-outfitted kitchen. Copper pots and pans everywhere, some in the shape of Fishes and Birds. An oven that was nothing but a Hole of Fire. *For Bread,* Mother says, but I have never seen her bake Bread there.

"At Mother's Showcase, as we discussed," Mother whispered, sipping long and deep from her Goblet.

"Your Showcase, Mother?" I repeated. Though of course she had already told me this.

"A very important Presentation they expect Mother to do," Mother said. "To show what Wound she has been Tapping during her Season of Freedom." She smiled at me sort of sourly. "All of Mother's many Enemies and Friends in Narrative Arts will be in Attendance, not to mention the Warren Community at Large. All of whom wish for Mother to Fail of course," Mother said quietly, and sipped. "But Mother will not Fail," she added, looking at me dreamily. "Mother will show them all via a Dazzling Demonstration of her Creative Powers. And you," she said, "will play a most crucial Role in Mother's Demonstration."

I became afeared then ☹ "And what sort of Role am I to play exactly, Mother?"

She looked at me over her sloshing glass. "You will be the Star of the Show," she said. "Mother's Great Vindication."

"Will I, Mother?"

"Oh yes."

"And then you will send me back as you promised?"

Mother walked over to me now. Came in close to my Body. She put her Hands on my Face, as she quite likes to do, and looked deep into my Eyes.

"Do you trust me?" she whispered.

I looked into Mother's misty Gaze. *Absolutely not,* I could imagine Pony saying if he'd still been Alive and in my Pocket. *In fact, with each passing Day, I grow more afeared of you.* But thanks to Mother I no longer had Pony ☹ And indeed, thanks to Mother, I no longer had Pockets ☹

"Of course I trust you, Mother."

"Good." And Mother smiled again. "Now tell me more about your . . . Wound."

The Wound is what Mother calls my Manny Script, Reader. Though she seems to believe tis *her* Manny Script, that *she* is the Author ☹ Or that tis both of ours, that we are collaborating together, even though I, Reader, have been doing all the Writings ☹

"It Bleeds, as I have told you, Mother." Twas the Answer she expected.

"And?" she asked me eagerly, her Hands still on my Face. "Do you conjure the Other World for me?"

This, of course, is what Mother wishes my Book to be, Reader: a Dispatch from what she calls *the Other World.* Directly from the Source (my

Self). In my own Words. From my own Lips, by my own Hand, she often says, looking at my Lips and Hands most hungrily.

But if tis coming from my own Lips and Hands, how is it not mine, Mother? I sometimes ask her.

And Mother laughs. This question, she says, is where I show my Ignorance. Not only of what she calls the Process, but of Art itself. *You,* she says, taking my Hand, *are a Source. Now, as a Source, what is your job?*

To bleed for you, Mother, I whisper.

To bleed what? she presses.

My Heart's Blood.

Mother beams. She loves this Answer so very much. *And what is Mother's role?*

You are the Auteur, Mother, I recite. *You will elevate my Bleedings into Art at the Showcase.*

Exactly. And in the meantime Mother will facilitate my Bleedings however she can. Keep me feeling what she calls happy and free. For tis Mother alone, Mother insists, who has the Capability of unleashing me. She alone has the Visionary Thinking to put the Pen directly in my Hand. *Above all, my role is to trust, just like you. Trust being a most crucial part of the Process, do you understand?*

I understand, Mother, I always say, whether I understand or not ☹

"Aerius," Mother said then, "you've yet to answer my Questions. Do you conjure the Other World? Do you Tap the Wound of the Lost Self? Do you *Bleed* for me?"

"I do, Mother," I lied. Tears nearly threatened my Eyes. Oh god, what a Liar I have become, Reader ☹ Love first made of me a Liar, but now tis Fear that keeps me one. Fear of Mother. Fear of what would happen if she knew the Truth ☹

Mother looked at me for a very long Time. She looked down at the Book clasped tight in my Hands. That I'd yet to let her read was a point of great Tension between us.

"You know, of course, that Mother's Showcase is very soon," she said in a low Voice. She looked out at the Pink Moon, nearly full.

"How Time moves quickly in Spring," she murmured. "Slow in Fall, fast in Spring. Tis the Rule. And moving ever faster."

"Yes, Mother," I whispered. My Throat was suddenly quite dry, Reader.

"And yet," she said, coming in closer still, "you will only ever let me read over your Shoulder. You will never let Mother take a closer, deeper Look at your ... Work."

She looked at my Body then, Reader, her Eyes full of Unspoken Appetites. This Hunger of Mother's, as I have shared, is not at all like my Keepers' Hunger. Tis Fathoms deep, fueled by Decades of Neglect and unfulfilled Longings. A misbegotten Beast ☹ And I have awakened it ☹

"I will when tis Time, Mother," I told her, smilingly echoing her own Words back. I clutched my Book closer to my Self.

Mother gripped my Shoulders. She reminded me yet again how very pressing was this Circumstance. Her very Legacy at Stake. People had forgotten about Mother, she reminded me now. They had dismissed her ☹ Her Literary Agent never called anymore, stopped calling in the early Aughts. And her Editor, Mother snorted, was a patronizing Fool. Condescended Mother ☹ Took many Moon Cycles to read her Manny Scripts, if he read them at all ☹ Mother's Writing Career was now consequently in a Shambles ☹ Twas being run by indifferent twelve-year-olds ☹

"I'm so sorry, Mother," I said to her, as I always do. "It all sounds to me like the very Opposite of Sunshine."

Mother sighed. A Tear trickled down her withered Cheek. I had a Way of putting Things sometimes that deeply Affected her. This Showcase, she insisted, must be her great Comeback. Her undeniable Proof of Genie-yes to all who doubted Mother's Capabilities. Did Mother mention that she'd also invited the whole of New York? Oh yes, her indifferent Publisher. The Presses, who'd long since laughed her off (though Mother still had Friends at *Vogue*, the *Times*, and *Vanity Fairs* who had RSVP'd). Not to mention the

Upper Administration of Warren, who did not understand Mother or her Art, who cruelly whispered of Early Retirement Packages. The many Faculties who gleefully wished for Mother to fall flat on her Face. Her copycat Students, who stole the very Marrow of—

"Yes, Mother," I interjected, "you have shared all of this with me before. But tis Essential for my own Process that I have some Privacy as I write, you know." I looked to Leonard, sitting on the kitchen counter, watching, as he always does, our evening Exchange. He nodded slightly, encouraging me.

"*You* must *Trust*, Mother, remember? Tis your job as Auteur," I reminded her.

Now I felt Mother staring at me very coldly. I was making her eat her own Words, and she cared not for their Taste.

"Your only Way Back, remember," she warned darkly.

"Your Showcase, Mother," I told her, swallowing hard.

"Yes," she said, at last loosening her Grip on my Body. "Well, what I *have* read of your Pages impresses me. I must trust the Work to reveal itself to me fully in Time. After all, you are not my Prisoner."

"No, Mother." Even as I thought, *I am, I am*.

"I shall let it write itself. As the very best Books do. As my own Works once did."

And Mother smiled sadly now, recalling her Former Glories, getting lost in her Dreamings. No longer staring at me, just her own aged Face in the window's Glass. Though I was happy she was no longer staring at me, I was sad to see Mother so sad ☹

I knew, of course, what twas like to get lost in Dreamings.

Especially Dreamings of What Once Was ☹

So each Night it went thus for many Weeks, Reader.

And though I continually asked Mother what to expect at this Showcase, what Role I was to play precisely, she told me *tut, tut, Trust*. I must Kneel upon the X on the Stage, that was All I needed to know. In the meantime, I must Keep Tapping the Wound of the Lost Self, she said. The only Way Back was to Bleed, she said. The Whole of my Heart's Blood.

Very well, Mother, I said.

And though Mother continually peered over my Shoulder to catch a Glimpse of my Writings (and my Body ☹), I only ever showed her Bits. A page or two. Whenever she wished to take a closer Look, I shut the Book, I kept it from her. Told her she must please Trust as I Trusted.

Very well, she said.

And so we both remained in a kind of Suspense, Reader. In a Place of Unknowing as to our Respective Fates. And I perhaps in a Greater Suspense than even she. For there is something I must share with you now about the Book I am Writing, Reader. Something I dared not share with Mother, not yet. Something that afears me ☹ Tis the true Reason I won't let her Read:

I am not Writing the Book she wants ☹

XVIII

Mother, as I have shared, wishes me to write Flashes from the Other World. She believes such a Text will be Groundbreaking. *Visionary.* That twill win her many Prizes and Accolades and long-awaited, much-overdue Respects. Indeed, Mother believes these Writings together with her Showcase might very well restore her to her Rightful Place as *Literary I Con* in the Eyes of All who have dismissed or snubbed or forgotten her.

Well, Reader, as you know, I am incapable of writing such a Book ☹ To write of the Other World requires a Tongue I no longer Possess ☹ A Language I can no longer speak ☹

And so when Mother first told me *this* was what she wanted the Book to be, I nearly died. Indeed, I almost told her the Truth right then. But I worried she would throw me back out into the cold, wintry Dark, Reader. I worried that I would never find my Way Back without her, for Mother had already convinced me that she alone held the Key to the Lost Place. And the Flower Book she held out to me, the Feather Pen, the Sense of Meaning and Purpose with which she imbued them, seemed like Salvation. A Home when I had None. A Friend.

So I told her of course I would write it.

Leave it to me, Mother, I said ☹ Like a Liar.

Like the Fool I have become ☹

And when she shut the Shed door, leaving me to my Darks and to the Blank Page, I wept. It felt like I was once more inside a Fiction, a most terrible Fairy Tale, Reader. Just like the ones Murder Fairy would read to me in the Attic Times. Like I was being tasked with the Impossible. A Tower full of Straw that I must now spin into Gold.

I cried about this for some Time. I did not know what else to do ☹

How could I ever go back unless I gave Mother the Book she wanted?

I would remain Here forever, in the Writing Shed, in this Human World. Pining for Jonah. (And oh yes, how I still Pined for him, Reader.)

Then one Night, when I was crying thus alone in the Shed, Leonard came hopping to my Side. His Gaze seemed to tell me that he knew the Source of my Distress. He beckoned me to follow him into the house. I did follow, Reader, though in those early Days I was terribly afeared to enter Mother's Realm ☹ But twas very late and they were all asleep, even her demonic Dog. I followed Leonard's leaping form into the guest room, to the little cherry-wood desk in the Corner. I watched as Leonard hopped up onto this desk. *The drawer, the drawer,* I felt his Body tell my Body. And there they were In-side, Reader: Pages upon Pages in Leonard's Scrawl. "What are these Pages, Leonard?" I whispered, though I knew, I knew. For I was already Smiling. My Tears were drying on my Face. I felt a Lifting in my Heart as I recalled being transported during his Reading. The Place his Words had taken me.

I looked back up at Leonard. And his Rabbit's Eyes brightened.

That very Night I began to copy his Pages into the Book, Reader. Word by Word. Page by Page. Copied them in the Front of the Book, which I'd left Blank just in case Fortune should fall upon me. And since Leonard's Writ-ings were Poet Trees ☹, and Mother does not write Poet Trees ☹, I mended their broken Lines and changed them into Prose, of course ☺ Twas my In-novation, my Contribution, so that Mother will accept them as Fiction ☺

These are the Writings Mother espies whenever she looks over my Shoulder and reads my Work. These are the Writings that have kept me from you, for tis a lot to Transcribe ☹

And are they indeed Dispatches from the Other World, Reader?

Are they what Mother wants for her Showcase?

The Truth is I do not know ☹

Leonard's Writings are lovely, they are Transportive, they whisper of the Other World, but they are not in its Language. They are very much in *this*

Language. (Indeed, they were Poet Trees ☹ until I mended them ☺) And in the Dead of Night, I also continue (when I can) to write my own Story. I write it in the back of the Book, upside down, where Mother doesn't see or think to check. Everything that you are now Reading ☺ Clutching my Feather Pen in the Dark, I tell you All. Tis *my* Book. The Truth of my own Heart as I am able to tell it, the Violences and Wonders I've experienced here in this Body, in this World, the Tapping of my own Wound. Tis indeed its Bleedings.

And thus it went. With Leonard's help, I wrote the Book Mother seemed to want in the Front ☺ And I wrote the Secret Book I felt Compelled to write in the back ☺

For you, Reader. My Friend ☺

My Great Fear, of course, was that neither my Secret Book nor Leonard's Writings would be Enough for Mother to send me back on this Night of the Showcase ☹ But Leonard's Eyes told me not to Fear ☺

That is, until the Incident in the Garden ☹

Which I shall now Recount ☹

Twas the Day before the Showcase. An afternoon in May, the Month of the Hare Moon.

I made my Way to Mother's Garden, as was my wont, taking Advantage of the fact that she was away from Home, on Campus teaching her last Classes, or as she preferred to call it, *Casting Pearls before Entitled Piglets*. Reader, I confess that I love Mother's Garden more than any Place in this World (apart from Jonah's Body). I love smelling the Spring Flowers in their first Flush, the many bright-colored Berries gleaming on the Bush ☺ Indeed, Mother's Garden is the closest Thing to the Lost Place that I've yet to Experience.

I took my Book with me, of course. Whenever Mother was away, you see, I'd try to give my Self over to my Secret Story. I'd try to Tap my own Wound so thoroughly. Writing to you, Reader, in these Moments of Solitude, was my Great Consolation. Mother, as I shared, had taken Pony from me, which at first I thought terribly Cruelle, and I said so and we had quite a Fight ☹ But Mother made me see twas for my own Betterment as an Artist. Now I had only one Audience, one Vessel in which to pour my Soul. One Tunnel in the Earth in which to whisper my Truth like Midas. I remained in a Rage when she took Pony away, but I confess that his Absence has concentrated my Creative Efforts. Now my Wound bleeds like never before, because there is only you, Reader, to catch its Drips. With the Showcase the next Day, I was motivated to write quite hurriedly. And though I knew this was not the Book Mother wanted, I could not help but write it as though twere the Book that would indeed send me Back. I must leave no Blood unspilled, no Story Stone unturned, Mother said. My whole Soul must be in this Manny Script. *The only Way Back*, she said.

I could only hope twas true.

But I digress ☺

Twas an unusually warm Day, and its blue Sky and bright Sun had me dreaming of Springs gone by, Springs in which I took another Shape. I had taken off my Shirt, the better to feel the Heat and Light on my Body, the soft, fragrant Grasses on my Pelt, something I would never do when Mother was around. How those Grasses recalled Jonah, Reader. Their mingled Perfumes were dizzying, reminding me of my hopeless Affection. Rolling with him on the flowery Hillside on that Autumn Night, his hot Mouth against mine. A Pain began to possess me that I had not felt in some Time ☹ An Ache most visceral ☹ I had not seen him since that awful Winter's Eve when he chose Poet Tree (and the dreaded Bistro) instead of my Self ☹ I had not gone looking for him. I told my Self he had made his Choice and where he'd gone I could not follow. And he, clearly, had not gone looking for me, either, Reader ☹ And so I no longer had Illusions. I no longer had Hope. Only this Ache, reawakened by the Earth and Sun, that made me long more keenly than ever before for the Other World. There I would not miss him. I would not even remember him or my broken Heart. But in the meantime, here in Mother's Garden, I would write about our Time together. I would relive it in the World of Dreamings. I would roll around in Mother's Grass *imagining* he was here with me. In the throes of such Imaginings, with the Sun on my Pelt, I might even set down my Pen, reach under my Kilt, and pleasure my Self among the lovely Flowers ☺

Which I did do, on this Day ☺

I was in the midst of such Pleasurings, whispering his Name, when I saw Someone staring at me from the Gate. A Stranger. Watching me intently through the Slats. I ceased my Pleasurings, and though I did not know this Person, I waved.

"Hello," I said. For it had been a while since I'd seen a Human Face apart from Mother's and David's. And the Stranger promptly disappeared. Almost like I'd scared them away somehow, though I'd been most friendly ☹

Twas funny.

People were very funny, I thought.

Just then Mother appeared in the Garden. Back from Campus and bearing a Dandy Lion, which I knew was for me. Everything Mother brought Home was for me. Slung around her Shoulder was her Satchel, which she called her Albatross. Full to the brim with Student Stories, which she would not read until the very last Minute. Which would make her cry when she had to read them at last. *Because they are so very good, Mother?* I would always ask, and she would snort.

Her Face, Reader, when she beheld me in the Garden in the midst of my Pleasurings. Awestruck, I knew. Lost in the sheer fact of my Self lying there, Pelt exposed, *like a Dream come to Life,* she has often said. Like a Dream she believed she had brought to Life. Taking in my muscled Pelt, its inky Universe, Mother went quite red in the Face. Her Mouth opened as if to speak Words to me, but no Words came out. I smiled at Mother's rare Loss of Language. Enjoyed that I had this visceral Effect. Wished uselessly that I could have such an Effect on Jonah ☹ But to think on this too much would deepen the Ache no Goldy Liquid could dull ☹

And then I heard the Sound—we both did, for Mother's Hearing is incredible—of female Voices nearby. All too familiar ☹ Deep in anguished Arguings ☹ Drawing ever closer to us ☹ She whipped her Head in the Direction of the Gate, then looked back at me.

"Get Inside," she hissed.

From the second Story of Mother's house, from the window of the guest bedroom, I watched Them enter the Garden, these Shapes of my Nightmares ☉ Traipsing across Mother's Grasses in their pastel Finery, their Hairs shining in the afternoon Sun. And yet how different they looked to my Eye on this Day, Reader. Shorter, I thought, almost as if their Souls had shrunk inside their Bodies. Younger, as if they'd moved backward rather than forward in Time. Their high, whispery Voices teemed in my Head. *He is Here, he is Here. We will unearth him, we will not leave without him, he is Ours. She is hiding him somewhere, but Where, Where?*

Mother, meanwhile, had disappeared from View, had crept into her Shed. They seemed to know this, for they went immediately to the door and knocked it down. Though I could not hear or see Anything, I intuited a Confrontation between Parties ☹ I intuited twas about my Self ☹

I had never told Mother of my Keepers, Reader. Indeed, I had never told her about the Poets, either. Such Confessions were for the Secret Book alone. Such Tellings, I felt, might compromise my Position with her. I had acted instead like I'd only ever belonged to Mother. Like my Existence had begun when I first appeared inside her Ring of Fires that wintry Eve.

Knowing Mother and my Keepers were together now, I was terribly Nervous. Indeed, twas a Mix of Feelings I had then.

The Desire to run still coursed through me, as it did whenever they were in my Vicinity ☹ It would, I knew, Forevermore. But a strange Pity arose in me too as I watched Them, many Minutes later, leave the Shed, escorted by Mother. Their shining Heads were hanging low, like so many Spring Flowers gone limp. I heard their sad, covetous Thoughts. *Not Mine? Truly not Mine? How could it not be so when I Love like this?* I could feel their Hearts breaking inside their small Bodies. And twas funny, but I felt my own strangely break too. So much so that I almost waved to Them. Just then Mother looked up at me in the window. And down dropped my Hand, Reader, almost instantly, so that I felt like a Marionette on a String. And Mother's Mindscape the Hand on the String ☹ Twas in these Moments that I was reminded of her powerful Witchery. That she alone was the true Mind Witch.

In any case, my Keepers did not see me.

After they'd departed, I expected Mother to run to me and tell me of this Happening. But she did not. Instead she just stood there in the Garden, Reader. I watched her pour herself more Wine from a bottle sitting on the patio table. I watched her drink and stare into Space, the Afternoon darkening around her. I don't know why, but her behavior afeared me somewhat ☹ Of course, if I am being honest, Mother's behavior always afeared me somewhat ☹ This had been a difficult Season for her, I knew. She had long been languishing in the creative Shadows. Twiddling her Thumbs, she often said, on the Edge of the Abyss. Waiting for the still, small Murmur of the Source to whisper in her Ear. And what whispered? Nothing ☹ The Wind hummed, seemingly mocking. The Moon smirked high in the black Sky above Mother's Head. The Air grew cold and the Leaves fell with such a dead Crackle. By November she'd begun to wonder if her many Years of teaching Idiots had ruined her Receptive Capabilities ☹ Perhaps her Head was so filled with the Ghosts of their needy, entitled Voices that she could no longer hear the Source's Siren Call ☹ Mother often feared this was the Case, that she had Given Too Much ☹ There was another Possibility too, which unsettled Mother even more, which she liked to think about even less: that she was perhaps simply . . . old now. Barren ☹ Her fevered Days of ecstatically dancing with the Heavens quite behind her. She had been readying herself to open her Eyes to this grim new Reality ☹

And then at long last, she said, looking at me, *I was Visited.* Tears filled her Eyes, as they often did. Mother could be very Emotional indeed when speaking of her Visitation.

Meaning me, I suppose ☺

But now I felt a great and increasing Unease. That Night, I languished in the house, thinking about my broken Heart, which Mother always said was an excellent Thing to do and would certainly help with my Wound Tapping. I wandered the many rooms, looking for a Place I might settle to write. David would be in the living room, sitting on Mother's fainting couch, reading his Pornographies. He'd raise his evening glass of Chartreuse, smile blandly at me, as was his Way. Twas a Smile tinged slightly with Suspicion. Mother had explained to David about me. Well, she had *lied* to David about me. She told him I was a young Neophyte she'd had the Pleasure of corresponding with of late, a Kerouac of my Generation. Though my Work showed great Promise, I was sadly entirely without Means, a young, hapless Destitute ☹ She was thus sheltering me whilst I labored on my great American Fictions ☺ *I have sheltered many a Duckling in the Past*, she said to me. *He will not even bat an Eye. If I told him the Truth, it would make him too jealous*, Mother said. *David, you see, has not been Visited since the Eighties.*

When I passed the living room, he was staring at me over the top of his Book. "Hello there, Aerius. Still tapping away at your *Wound?*"

"Yes," I said.

"Well, I hope it bleeds for you. I hope it veritably gushes forth. What the World absolutely needs is another Wound. Another bleeding Writer sharing their hard-earned Truths."

His Smile grew sharp, as sour as Wood Sorrel. But I only smiled back and said, "Thank you." Twas the best Way, Mother said, of handling his many psychic Thorns.

I made my Way to the Solarium. I liked this room, for there were many strange and pretty Plants to nibble on while thinking. A golden Harp, which Mother liked to strum, and many framed Pictures of Mother on the wall. She was much younger in these Pictures; they appeared to have been taken in another, olden Time. She had once been an icy Blondy. She had once lined her Eyes in the Manner of the Poets, so they looked like a Cat's. She had once been quite pretty, twas true. In one Picture she was in a Garden, the Rose Garden I knew so well. In the Photo Mother was standing in the Midst of this Garden, holding a small white Rabbit in her Arms, smiling at the Creature like twas such a Gift. Was the Rabbit happy to be in Mother's Arms, or was it afeared? Or was it I who was afeared looking at them, how they stared at me from the Photo ☹ In another she stood in a Field, surrounded by Rabbits the same gray Color as the Sky. In a third she played the Harp in what looked like a small, dark room, two white Rabbits at her Feets. There was an Ax, I saw, glinting in the Corner of this room, Blade sharp and spotted with Blood. And though this afeared me, Reader, twas her Expression in this and every Photo that made me most cold. It said, *I will plunder.* It said, *All under the Sun tis Mine.*

"What are you doing here?"

I turned and there was Mother in the doorway.

"Mother," I said, "you startled me."

Though I could not see Mother's Face in the Darkness, I knew her Question was still there.

"I wanted to eat the Plants," I lied, and whether Mother believed me or not, she did not say. She only smiled sadly, taking one of her Photos off the wall. Who knows what Thoughts passed through her Mindscape as she stared at herself. Mother's Mindscape was often inscrutable to me, shrouded in Mists like her Eyes. Now she shook her Head drunkenly at her own Image. "Tis no Wonder that as Writers age, their Author Photos become monstrous," she muttered. "Marguerite Duras, Jean Rhys. So lovely in their Youth, and then by the End? All Jowls and thin Lips and dead Eyes. I used to be quite comely in my Day, don't you think?" she said, looking at me. "Very Stevie Nicks, many used to say. Kate Bush if she were blond."

I did not know who Stevie Nicks or Kate Bush were, Reader, though their names called to mind the Wailings of the Playlist ☹ But I nodded. "Oh yes. Very pretty, Mother."

She smiled back at her own Likeness. She'd reapplied her Lippy Stick, the Color of her most audacious Flowers. Doused herself in Diptyque's L'Ombre dans l'Eau. Its dark Forest and prickly Thorns and strange Berries now enveloped me. She was wearing a long white Nightgown that was alarmingly translucent in this Light. It reminded me of my old Nightgown.

"You're safe now," she whispered to me, setting the Picture back on the wall.

"Thank you, Mother," I said. Though I did not feel at all safe. Something in Mother's Voice was chilling me. I sat down on her fainting couch. She took her seat on a little velvet pouf by the Harp and began idly plucking its Strings, an eerie Tune. I did not like this Plucking, Reader ☹ It did a funny Thing to my Body. And how she was staring at me, as if she was searching my Face for something. "What is it, Mother? Why do you look at me so strangely?"

She continued to strum, staring at me. "Is there something you're not telling me?"

"Not telling you, Mother?" I felt my Pelt grow hot. "Of course not. Why do you ask?"

"My Students came to visit me this Afternoon."

"Your *Students*, Mother?" My Keepers were her Students, then. Somehow this did not surprise me ☹ "How terrible," I said, trying to make Mother smile. But Mother did not smile. Mother looked very grave.

"They seem to think they know you," she said.

"Do they?" I grew red in the Face.

"They accused me of Stealing you from Them, can you believe that?"

I shook my Head. "That is absolute Madness, Mother."

Mother sighed with Relief. "Of course it is. You did visit me after all, did you not?" Such Desperation in her Eyes. "You are Mine."

"Of course I visited you, Mother," I said. "Twas Fate," I added, "as you have so often said."

"Yes," she said. "Yes, of course. And if there are some *Affinities* between their Visitation and Mine, it's merely because they are influenced by me," she murmured. "I influence my Students greatly, I always have. Often they arrive already influenced. Often that's why they apply to Warren in the first Place." She nodded to herself. Seeming to be satisfied. But her Face was full of Shadows as she plucked the Strings. There have been so many Times during my Season here when I thought I should run, must run. That though every door was unlocked and every window open—the casements right now open and bringing in the fresh Spring Night—Something was holding me against my Will. Something in the Music and the Mists and the lush Garden and Mother's own Eyes, I did not know what. I told my Self, Reader, that I was *imagining* this, given all my former Troubles. I reminded my Self again that I was here because this Book that Mother had given me was all I had. The only Way Forward. The only Way Back. Which I so desperately longed for ⊗ I stayed where I was.

At last she stood up and began walking toward me, still frozen on the couch. My Book was lying beside me, turned round and upside down, for I'd been about to write my Story. The Feather Pen I loved best rested between the Pages like a Bookmark. The Ink was wonderfully bright, like Mother's Lippy Stick.

"Why is the Book upside down like this?" she said.

"No Reason, Mother," I whispered.

Mother stared at me. "I'd like to take a closer Look Tonight," she said. And she slid her Hand toward the Book, toward my Body sitting beside her.

Quickly I took the Book in my Hands. "Tis not ready yet, Mother."

"Not *ready?*" she repeated.

I shook my Head.

"Julius," Mother said darkly.

"Aerius," I corrected.

And how Mother winced at this Name, as though she had eaten a bad Twig ⊗ "The Showcase is Tomorrow Night. At this Point tis most important that I see."

What was it about Mother's Eyes that made me not trust her in this Moment? What made me feel I must not Relent? Twas not simply that I had lied to her about its Contents. I felt that if I gave her my Book now, if she touched or even looked at a Page, twould no longer be mine forever after. Twas like she was asking to peer beneath my Pelt, to poke at my Interiors with a Stick. I grasped it tighter to my Heart. "No, Mother," I whispered. "If I show it now, I will never finish. And then you cannot have your Showcase and I cannot have my Way Back, which you promised to show me, remember?"

Mother stared at me, saying Nothing at all. Briefly I wondered if she might kill me. Or attempt Seduction. I did not know which afeared me more on this Night ☹

"I should return to it now," I whispered, picking up my Feather Pen.

"Perhaps let's take a Break first," Mother said, resting her Hand on my Wrist. Perhaps we could watch a Film together, Mother suggested. Which Film did I wish to watch? I could pick any I liked, for Mother had Netflix and the Criterion Channel. "*Bride of Frankenstein*, Mother," I said, for twas my very Favorite. I was surprised she wanted to watch with me. Normally, she would retreat to her Shed at what she called *this Witching Hour*. Normally, she would want me to keep Tapping. I my Self wished to keep Tapping. But she insisted a Break might do us both good.

We sat on the fainting couch, watching the Film on the wall (Mother had a projector just like my Keepers). And though I was still afeared that Mother might attempt Seduction of my Person (I was always afeared of this ☹), she kept her Distance, kept her Eye on the Film. Though I longed to return to my Writings, I *did* lose my Self in the Story, this being my favorite Film, Reader ☺ I loved the Ending best, when the Creature cries, *We belong dead*, pulls a Lever, and sets the whole Castle ablaze and crumbling to Dust. As I watched this Scene now, I recalled, with a sad Smile, setting the Poet Tree bar on Fire. Jonah's disappointment in me ☹ Our Night of profound sexual and spiritual Connection, which I can never seem to forget. When I close my Eyes, tis right there for me to see and smell and touch. To *imagine*. Or remember. With great Sorrow I remembered it now, with a Pleasure bittersweet. Remembering, Murder Fairy once said, was always thus. Twas perhaps due to this Confounding of Emotions, this Letting Down of my Guard, that I missed Mother attempting to snatch my Book from my relaxed Hands. Quickly I grabbed it back from her, my Heart pounding and pounding. And she, Reader, looking at me so darkly now. How I hugged the Book so close to my Self, as though twere Jonah's Body. As though twere my only Friend. All I had now in the World and I would never let go again. She rose from the couch and walked out without another Word. Without even saying Good Night to me. And I, shaking and shaking. The Pages clutched in my trembling Hands.

XIX

That Night I had great difficulty sleeping, Reader. Between my Keepers storming the Garden and Mother's attempts to steal my Heart's Blood, I felt deeply unsettled. I was not safe in Mother's house, I never had been, I'd always known this. In the guest room, I watched the Hare Moon come in through the window. Beautiful, bright and nearly full. Tomorrow Night, the Night of the Showcase, she would be full. *Mother has arranged it thus*, Mother had said. *The only Way Back is on this Night*, she'd said how many times. *After that*, she sometimes added ominously, *there is no Way.*

On Leonard's bed, I finished transcribing the last of his Writings into the Front of the Book. Then I turned the Book round and upside down, as was my Habit. I tried, desperately, to keep on with my own Writings, but even to open the Book this Way after Mother had attempted to steal it made me feel so strange. So I tucked it under the pillow, Reader. Attempted to lie back, to close my Eyes. Leonard was at my Side; he liked to make his Way from the Garden up to the guest room in the Evenings. There were still some of his Scally Caps on the dresser, a couple of holey Sweaters thrown over a chair, a black Composition Notebook on the nightstand by the Bed. This was his Journal, his own Secret Book, which contained but a few Scratches. Lists of Food, mostly. Items he would buy if he won something called the Pulitzer Prize (a bottle of Grey Goose, a new Trenchy, dinner at Le Bernardin). Some Quotes from Allen Ginsberg, the very Poet I had mistaken him for ☹

America I've given you all and now I'm nothing.

We're golden sunflowers inside.

A soulful Writer this Allen had been, I thought. Leonard joined me now, lying on the neighboring pillow. I welcomed him, though his Presence always made the Lost Place feel so achingly close. Tonight I felt he was trying to tell me Something. *What are you trying to tell me, Bunny?* But he couldn't say, or if he could, I could not hear him.

"Leonard," I whispered, "what if it doesn't work? What if she can't send me back after all?" He only stared at me dreamily with his Rabbit's Face.

"I am sorry I killed you, Leonard," I told him now. "I had meant to kill Allan, and I thought you were Allan. And I do not even know why I must kill Allan."

Twas then I felt I heard his Words along my Pelt. Nearly understood in my half-dreaming State. *Prefer this, actually. Thank you. What every Poem reaches for, I am already now.* And his Eyes half closed.

I looked at his small, furry Body, and a Longing consumed me. A most terrible Longing, so different from my longing for Jonah, so different from any Longing I'd ever known. *Why, Leonard, when I look at you, do I feel as if I'm seeing Everything that I have lost? Everything I wish to find again? Why do you look to me like the very Shape of Home?* Leonard merely blinked at me, sleepily, perhaps with a kind of Pity.

I spoke earlier, Reader, of a Change Within Me.

Well, perhaps now I shall tell it to you, though I am very afeared ⊗ Not so much for my Self, but for you, Reader. For I fear the News may come as a very great Shock to you (twas a Shock to me, too) ⊗ I fear too that it might change Things between us, that you might no longer Love me ⊗ But I cannot contain this Secret any longer. And you are my Friend, are you not? And I have promised to share the whole of my Heart with you (is this not what Friends do?), so share I must. I only ask that you please prepare yourself.

Tis this:

Reader, it has come to my attention that I . . .

I believe I was once . . .

That is, I feel I *may* have once been . . .

a bunny.

There.

I have said it ☹☺

I know it sounds crazy, Reader. And I'm afeared I have no Proofs for what I can only call this . . . *Feeling*. Nor do I know the Reasons why I believe I was what I was. Or *how* I came to be what I am now (though indeed I have my Suspicions ☹).

I only know that I feel it to be True.

I do hope this will not change Anything between us. I hope this will not, as Mother says, *undermine* my *Narrative* ☹ Above all, I hope that you will still be my dear Friend, as I am your dear Friend (and will always be) ☺ You have grown very dear to me indeed. You know so much of my Heart. And tis strange to say, for we have never met, but I feel that I know yours, too.

Perhaps, knowing my Heart as you do, twas not so great a Shock to you after all.

Perhaps you had already guessed, like I did, quite some Time ago.

Perhaps indeed you, like me, have always known.

For a while, I confess, the Revelation thrilled me. I knew at last what I was ☺ I had a Name at last for the Lost Self ☺ Twas Bunny! ☺

Bunny, Bunny, Bunny! I shouted until Mother told me to cease my Happy Howlings ☹ I even tried hopping with Leonard, until Mother warned that I would break her floorboards ☹ *Tis one Thing to Speak the Lost Self in a Book,* she said. *Tis quite another Thing to behave like some . . . Animal.* For I was a Gentleman now, she said. And a Gentleman *walked.* A Source such as my Self, he strolled Arm in Arm, she said, with his Auteur. And she held out her

Arm for me to take. So I stood paralyzed in my Human Body, Arm locked
with Mother's, watching Leonard hop away from me.

Bunny, I whispered.

And then this happy Knowledge, having at last surfaced from a buried
Place deep within my Heart, sat happily within me no longer. For if I had
been Bunny once, I was Bunny no longer. I was still lost from this Self. Still
lost from the Lost Place.

Still lost.

Which brings me to one last Thing I must share with you now, Reader.

Tis a lot to share in one Moment, I know.

Probably I am breaking some cardinal Rules of Story ☹

But tell you I must, for having unburdened my Heart this much, I can
leave no Shadows lingering, no Story Stones unturned. Tis Time to share All.

There was a Shadow Side, you see, to my Revelation. A Dark Wondering
came with it. And Leonard's Company, though I enjoyed it perhaps now more
than ever before, though indeed he was saving me, also began to unsettle
me deeply. Whenever I looked into his Rabbit's Face, this Dark Wondering
overtook my Mindscape. I felt it in my Body, along my Pelt Hairs. An Awful
Knowledge beginning to reveal itself to me. A Terrible Arithmetic adding
up in the very Back of my Brain Chambers. Mostly I kept it hidden, buried
deep beneath my Thoughts, where I'd kept Bunny, tried not to give it Space
or Words or even Breath. And yet now, looking into Bunny's ever-twinkling
Eyes, it inevitably rose to the Surface. As it quite liked to do in the Nights.

Twas this:

I had killed Leonard and he had turned into a Rabbit. With one swing of
my Ax, he'd assumed a different Shape. One he seemed to much prefer, that
looked to me like Home. That *was* Home, Reader.

If Violence had changed him, then perhaps it followed that Violence
might . . .

And then I thought of Ax.

Mother had confiscated her along with Razor and Pony. *There will be no Violences in Mother's house*, she said, *except on the Page*. Ax was somewhere hiding in this house. I thought of her sharp Blade. I thought of my own Neck, white as a Swan's. I looked at Leonard now, sitting beside me on his pillow, Eyes fluttering closed.

"Bunny . . . ," I whispered. "What if I were to . . . "

But Bunny was now deep in Sleeps.

And so at last I closed my Eyes too, fell my Self into Slumbers. Jonah was there in my Dreamings, as he always was. In these Dreamings he had no desire to go to the Bistro, had no Manny Script, no Love for Sam. Instead he smiled at me in the falling Snow. Held out his Hand, which was furry and white. *I will come with you*, he said. *I wish to go to the Lost Place too. Wherever you go is where I want to be.*

And he kissed me deeply.

A Sound arose me from my Slumbers. Or was it a Feeling?

I opened my Eyes. What I saw was so horrific, Reader, I thought surely I was still dreaming or that I'd moved from Dreamings to Nightmares. Mother in her iridescent Robe, sitting in the chair by the desk. My Book, my Heart's Blood, in her Hands. She had taken it from beneath my pillow, Reader. She was turning its Pages. Twas the Sound of the turning Pages that must have awakened me. The Book, I realized, was turned round and upside down. My Secret Book, Reader. Open and in her Hands.

My Mouth went terribly dry. My Heart pounded.

"Mother," I said. But she didn't look up, she didn't seem to hear me. Just stared into my Book as though lost. *You stole from me*, I should have said then. *Give it back*. Instead I lay there, frozen.

"What do you think?" I whispered at last. "Do you love it?" For though I was overcome with Fear and Anger, I was also admittedly curious. I'd never had anyone read my Words before.

"Do you love my Wound?" I asked. Reader, I was shaking.

Mother was silent. There were Tears in her Eyes.

She *must* love it very much, I told myself, to be this Emotional. She was gripping the Book, and the Tears were sliding down her Face. If she loved it, that was Wonderful. If she loved it, I should have no more Fear. Then why was my Heart pounding like this, Reader? Why was Bunny now staring at me from his pillow with such Panics in his Eyes?

"Mother, please say Something," I pleaded. "I know tis not perhaps quite what you expected, but—"

Mother's Gaze silenced me. She stared at me darkly, I felt the Dark through my Body.

"It is Nothing," she said. And when Mother said this word, *Nothing*, I felt my Self dissolving, Reader. Everything in the Room suddenly began to ripple like Field Grass in a Great Wind.

"Nothing, Mother?" *How can it be Nothing when tis the Whole of my Heart?*

But Mother wasn't listening. I watched her convulse in Despair. "Mother, I'm sorry. I wasn't sure what you wanted, so I—"

"So you wrote your own little Fiction."

"Tis not a . . . Fiction, Mother," I stammered. "Tis the Truth of my Experience . . . here in this World. I didn't tell you because—"

"Tis NOTHING but a *Fiction* written by a *Fiction*," she roared, and she suddenly threw a Crystal at me, barely missing my Head. It crashed spectacularly to the floor. I stared at Mother, shaking now as I was shaking. Her Face had never looked so cutting and cold. Yet hurt, too. Tears in her Eyes as there were Tears in my Eyes. She was holding herself in her own Arms, looking miserably out at the Dark.

"If tis Nothing to you, Mother," I whispered, "then please give it back. For tis Everything to me. All I have left." And I felt as if I were coming apart, drowning. What would Mother do with me now? Would she still show me the Way? Would she give me back the Book? Even though she'd called it Nothing, she was still clutching it so fiercely to her Body.

"Was it those Girls?" she said at last. "My . . . *Students*? Do you belong to Them?"

"No, Mother." I whispered this even though I suddenly had such trouble speaking, like Mother had made my Lips dead with her Mindscape.

"Who, then? *Tell* me whom you belong to." The Anger and the Pleading were One in her Voice. I looked down at the wavering Ground beneath me. It felt so unnaturally far. And Bunny crouched there now, gazing up at me. His Face so achingly familiar in this Moment.

I belong to No One at all, I thought. Tears fell from my Eyes.

I could feel Mother standing beside me. Suddenly very close. She was lifting my Face to meet her Gaze. Her other Hand gripped my Shoulder.

"The first half of the Book seems authentic enough," she said gently. I looked at Leonard staring at me from the floor, his Eyes flashing. "There, at least, you seem to have followed Mother's Direction. Only tell me that this other . . . perverse . . . *Story* you felt compelled to write in the Back is a Fiction. Tell me you are Mine. Otherwise, there is no Showcase, do you understand me? And I can't send you Back. And you will never go Anywhere at all."

Panic gripped me. I felt the Dark closing in around my Eyes. "Never, Mother?"

"Tell me now," she said, gripping me. Her Hand still holding up my Face, so there was Nowhere else to look but Mother. Mother the Sun and Moon and Sky. Mother the World.

"I belong to you," I lied, looking right into her Eyes. "I am Yours." Did she espy the Truth of my Heart?

I saw her Face softening. How desperately she wanted, needed, to believe I was. "You are? You really are, Julius?"

I nodded, continuing to look Mother dead in the Eyes, not daring to correct my Name, not daring to look away. Even as her Gaze bore into me—Mother's Gaze, that most terrible Huntress. Her Hand gripping my Shoulder, she was so very Strong. And I so very afeared in this Moment. That she could take away Everything from me. Could she see the lying there in my Eyes? Or did she see only what she hoped was true?

"Well," she said at last, loosening her Grip, "perhaps we should have a little Dress Rehearsal and see."

"A Dress Rehearsal, Mother?"

Relief flooded me. There would still be a Showcase. Mother believed me, still wanted me to play my Part. "So there is still a Way Back for me, Mother?"

"If you are Mine, there is always a Way," Mother said.

"With my Book?"

"There is a much quicker Way than Books."

And then? Mother took a small Key from her Pocket. Walked to the Corner of the room, to a large, dark Wardrobe there.

"Will I be going through the Wardrobe, Mother? Like that wonderful Book about the Lion and the Witch?" *Mother, are you this Witch?* I wanted to ask. But Mother didn't answer. She opened the Wardrobe door. I saw my old blue Blazer hanging there. How my Heart swelled at the Sight. Was Mother going to give it back to me, to ready me for my Journey Home? No. She reached into the Wardrobe's Dark and instead pulled out my Ax.

My Insides went cold. "Mother, what are you doing?"

Mother turned the Handle round and round like twas a Flower. She looked at me now over the Blade. "You tell me." There were Tears shining in her Eyes as she walked toward me, Reader. Shining like the Blade now pointed in my Direction, I was its North Star.

"Are. You. *Mine?*" she murmured.

And I could not move, could not speak. Mother's Mind Witchery had frozen me in Place, held my Tongue in a Vise. Or perhaps twas the Shock of seeing my very own Ax in her Hands that silenced me. "Tell me," she roared, raising Ax over her Head.

I sat there, gripping the bed's edge beneath me. Perhaps I should have been happy, Reader. Even relieved. The Awful Knowledge I'd been harboring, the Terrible Arithmetic—was this what it had been adding up to all along? Was Mother planning to send me Back with Ax? But somehow I felt, looking at Mother, her murderous, teary Eyes, that this was not the Way. That she might instead send me to a Blackness Eternal. A Nothing Place where no Wind sang or Grasses grew.

I begged my Mouth to open. To speak the Lie one more Time.

Yes. I am Yours. Of course I am.

But I couldn't. I could do nothing but close my Eyes. Brace my Self for the Blade, the Ax now ready to fall upon my Throat. Pray that I was indeed sent Back.

So this I did.

A Sound like a Roar. Followed by many Bangings on a door.

Oh god, was this Death?

I opened my Eyes. Not Death. Or if twas Death, then Death was very much like Life. For I was still here in Mother's guest bedroom, my Head tilted back, waiting for the Strike. But Mother was over by the window now, Ax lowered. She was looking through the Glass, cursing softly. "Is there no peace for Faculty?" she murmured. "These *Interruptions* are precisely why Mother is Dead Inside. Not even the Ghost of her Greatness left."

"What is it, Mother?"

She looked more closely through the Glass. Sighed and closed her Eyes. "Oh god, not again," she murmured. "I thought they had long since disassembled."

"*They*, Mother?"

"No Trust in Adults," she whispered. "Each Day a new Witch Hunt. Look at them out there with their Props, just dying to be outraged. Positively frothing at the Mouth with their perceived Slights. Such a Performance."

"Who are 'they'?" I asked again.

Mother turned away from the window and looked at me now, frowning. "Did you make yourself Visible? Were you *Seen*?"

I recalled pleasuring my Self in the Garden earlier that Afternoon. That Face peering over the Fence, how I waved. How the Face promptly disappeared, its Eyes going wide. I shook my Head. The Knocking grew louder.

"David," she called uselessly. But David didn't respond. Likely passed out from his Chartreuses and now dozing to his evening ambient Music, I could hear its Chirps and Drones in the Distance. She looked at me mostly menacingly. "You stay here and don't you move, don't you speak. You are as quiet as Mice, do you hear me?"

I watched her tuck the Ax back behind the chair. Smooth her Golden Hairs and straighten her Smock. Disappear through the door, taking my Book with her ⊗

The moment Mother was out of the room, Leonard and I ran to the window. Through its Glass we saw the Mob gathered outside her house ⊗ The same Group who had knocked on the Poets' door so long ago. In those very same black T-shirts, Reader, those ominous bleeding red Letters glowing in the Dark: AAARV. I could see their many white Necks falsely bleeding. All those Hands waving their toy Axes like Torches. There were more members of this Mob than there had been before, a veritable Storm of them ⊗ Many were holding up Pictures and Signs ⊗

"Well now, what is all this about?" I heard Mother ask sweetly.

"We received a Tip," one of them shouted, "that you were harboring the Murderer! The Man was spotted in your Garden earlier Today."

"What *Man*?"

I watched as they held up their Pictures. Though I couldn't see them clearly, I could tell by Mother's reply that they were the same ones from before. "What am I looking at?" she snapped. "A Violin?"

Then Someone shouted, "There he is!" And horribly, Reader, they all looked up, the entire Mob of Accusers ⊗ Saw me in the window and gasped. Pointed their Axes at me. "Murderer! Murderer!" they cried.

I looked at Leonard, sitting on the windowsill, his Nose twitching wildly. His Eyes saying, *Run, run.*

XX

A Forest was where we found ourselves. Very dark, though the Hare Moon shone through the Trees. I did not know the Hour, but twas late. Or was it early? *Late or early does not matter here*, Bunny said. He seemed to know the Ways of the Forest. We had been running for I knew not how long. Wandering here, Reader, in this Darkness. At first I was very afeared to be alone apart from Bunny. At first I felt so lost.

And then?

I was still lost, Reader.

Not lost, whispered the Moon. Or was I only imagining she whispered to me? She gave the Trees such a silvery Look. Even in my Despair, my Heart brightened. It reminded me (and I am sometimes wont to forget) that the World has many Beauties, even as it holds so many Griefs and Terrors. Mother with my Ax in her Hands, for instance ☻ The Violent Mob that was now pursuing me, for instance ☻ That I'd lost my Book and now I had no Way Back. For instance. That Jonah and I were never to be.

Leonard hopped at my Side. I was glad for his Company, though he wandered away from Time to Time, in search of whatever Forest Wonders, and I worried, deeply, that he would not return, that he would leave me here. But he always did return, usually with a Bounty of Flowers to share with me. Dandy Lions, other Forest Confections whose names I knew not.

"Have you seen anyone afoot?" I whispered to him. "Does she come for me? Does anyone come for me?"

Bunny looked at me. *No One comes for you*, I felt his Eyes say.

"Oh good." Twas good, I kept telling my Self, that No One was looking for me. That I was completely, utterly alone here in this endless Darkness, among these silvery Trees. *Birch*, Mother once said they were called. And suddenly I felt Sick. Thinking of Mother again ☹

"What am I to do?" I whispered to Bunny and to the Dark. "How will I ever—" But Bunny merely blinked at me. For he was well beyond the World of Books now, in another Realm altogether, the Realm of Bunny. And moving deeper into this Realm, it seemed, the deeper we moved into the Trees. Going where I could never follow on my Human Feets, with my Human Thinking. Almost like he was becoming more Bunny with each step. And I becoming more a Stranger to him.

Pony was back with me, which was little Consolation. When I first found him in the Pocket of my Blazer (I'd snatched it in my Escape) how my Heart sang! The Sight of him in this lonely Forest such a Balm to my Spirits. "Pony! Pony!" I whispered to him. "Oh god I am so very happy to see you, you have no idea what I"—but though his Eyes were ever sparkling, ever open, he didn't answer me, Reader. "Pony," I whispered, "please wake up. I am alone here. I am so terribly lost and alone here. Oh god, Pony are you dead?" *He is neither alive nor dead, he is a Toy*, Mother always said. *Just a Silly Toy, remember?* The Wind whistled through the dark Trees as I gripped him in my Hands. So very light he suddenly felt in my Hands, Reader. "I will let you sleep for now," I told his Face, forever frozen in that smiling, my Heart sinking afresh. "You have been through so very much."

I'd taken Ax, too, of course. She was back in my Coat, hanging on her hook, where she most liked to be. Unlike Pony, she seemed wide awake. Hummed with a new Energy Tonight, her Blade sharp against my Heart. Her strange Song like an Answer to all my Dark Wonderings. If only I would hearken to her Call. The Awful Knowledge, the Terrible Arithmetic thrumming through me now. *If you want to go back, there is another Way*, she seemed to say. *Right here.*

And then I saw a Shape in the Dark.

A man-shaped Shape.

Walking ahead of me. Whistling among the Trees, who was this?

Ax began to hum very loudly. Literally vibrating in my Blazer, Reader. As though she knew who twas. Recognized him before I did. I looked at his tall, hulking Frame. His shaggy Hairs going red in the Moonlight.

Oh my god, she breathed. *Him.*

And then I, too, knew who twas, Reader.

Of course I did.

"Allan," we whispered together.

Allan, Reader. *The* Allan. Just a little ahead of me now in the Forest. The very Allan I had first seen long ago in the Garden, walking toward his Subaru. His swinging Satchel and his Leaf-crunching Step, this was he. Whistling a Tune to himself, the very Tune of Ax. Allan, whom I have always wished to kill, though I do not know why, still don't know why, and yet at the Sight of him now, I suddenly felt filled with Fatal Purpose. I followed the Shape of Allan through the Trees, Ax humming hot against my Heart. *Allan*, she breathed. *Kill Allan, Kill Allan, Kill Allan.*

He froze up ahead of me. Almost as if he'd heard her Chantings. Slowly he turned round. And there he was in the Flesh. Gripping a mug full of some steaming Concoction.

How funny, Reader, that he did not seem at all surprised to see me there. Ax in Hand, her Blade bright in the now-breaking Dawn. We were of the same Height, he and I. We met nearly Eye to Eye. Allan's Eyes were the Color of wily Foxes. There was a Smiling in them, as if he'd known twas only a matter of Time before we would meet, Reader. And I would kill him.

"Allan," I said.

And he smiled at me in the first Glimmers of Morning. "So you're the one who's been causing the recent . . . Trouble," he said in his Allan Voice, which for some Reason, Reader, I hated so very much. "I thought those Experiments were behind us. But it appears Someone has awoken the Hare God. And now he wanders among us again." He looked down at Bunny at my Side. "Leonard," he said, nodding. And Bunny, strange to say, seemed to nod back.

I did not like that he knew Bunny, Reader. And that Bunny appeared to know him, too.

Kill Allan, Kill Allan, whispered Ax.

"You should not go walking through the Woods at so late an Hour, Allan," I told him, tightening my Grip.

"So *early* an Hour, you mean?" Allan corrected, still smiling. Strangely oblivious to the Threat to his Life. "Well, Allan has always risen with the Cock. He enjoys the Solitude, the Opportunity for Reflection before he deals with his Inbox. He enjoys wandering the Woods around Campus. You never know what you might find there." He bowed at me slightly. "And what brings you here, may I ask?"

"I have to kill you," I told him. Thinking surely Allan would cry, run. But he didn't move. Didn't even blink, Reader. Just stood there, looking at me.

"Of course you do," he said.

This Response unsettled me, Reader. Deeply. For a Moment I nearly lost my Grip on Ax. *Do not lose your Grip!* she cried in a Voice most familiar. *Kill Allan, Kill Allan!*

"How did you know?" I whispered.

"I'm a Writing Teacher, aren't I? This isn't the first Time I've been . . . *approached,* let's say. By Someone like you." He smiled a little more tightly now.

"What do you mean, 'Someone like—' "

"And what did I do this Time, I wonder?" Allan interjected. "Give too much Critique on a Fiction? A Novel I assigned traumatized one of them? Something I said offhandedly in Class was *triggering*?"

Ax was slipping from my Fingers. *What are you doing? Kill Allan, Kill Allan, Kill—*

"I . . . I don't know," I stammered at last. "I only know that I must—"

"Kill me, yes, yes, I heard," he muttered. He pulled a Cigarette from his Coat and lit it. "Almost impossible to be a Teacher these Days," he muttered.

"Wonder why I even fucking bother." He stared at me and Ax through his Smoke and sighed. "So what's your *Name*, anyway?"

"Aerius," I said.

And the Look in his Eye shifted.

"The Allergy Medication." He smirked, shaking his Head. "Of course. *Aerius*, do you have any Idea at all *why* you must kill me?"

"No." Ax seemed to grow hotter in my Hand. I could feel her Impatience gathering mightily. Why had I not already struck?

"And don't you think it's strange that you have this . . . *Directive* inside you? When you don't even *know* me? Don't you find it odd that you have no *Reason?*"

What does Reason have to do with it? Ax hissed. *KILL ALLAN KILL ALLAN!*

"I—"

"Of course you do. Because it's a Flaw in your Design, you see. Authorial Intent clumsily attempting to wrangle the Free Spirit of Creation. I see it in Workshop all the Time."

I didn't understand what Allan was talking about, Reader. I could barely hear him now anyway over the great Roar of Ax. Her Voice had grown more and more familiar to my Ear, was positively ringing through my Brain Chambers. I raised her over my Head, which made her shudder with Joy.

"Aerius, wait—"

"An ASSAULT!" I shouted before I could think.

"*What?*"

"I was violated!" I cried. *Violated?*

What was I saying, Reader? Tears fell from my Eyes then, and I did not at all understand their Falling. Words fell from my Lips, and I did not understand their Meaning. But I was speaking them along with Ax, for now her Voice and mine were one. "That first Day," we whispered. "When I shared the Heart's Blood. So very vulnerable and afeared. You and your red Slashes. All over my Story." *What?*

But Allan seemed to understand. He contemplated her Blade, shining sharp under the rising Sun.

"I didn't *assault*. I *offered* what I felt at the Time was very valuable Feed-back. Which is my *Job*, by the Way. As a Professor, I—"

"Stop condescending us!" I shouted through my Tears.

Us?

"Us?" Allan repeated. "Are you more than One?" He looked at me again and his Smile faded at last. "Oh god. You're all of Them, aren't you?"

And as he said this, I felt their Ghosts stir inside of me, Reader. Their shining Hairs and hungry Eyes. Their balmy Lips mouthing the words *Kill Alan, Kill Allan*. Those Words now on my own Tongue, coursing through my Blood and making Ax scream. I had a painful Flash then, Reader. A *Memory*. Of being in the Rose Garden. My Body once so much smaller and closer to the Earth, One with the Petals and the Grass Blades and the Light. Their girl-shaped Shadows suddenly falling over me. *Oh look, what an adorable—*

"No," I whispered, shaking my Head, even as I felt their Pearls cold on my Throat. Even as the Flashes kept coming, Reader. Their Keeper Hands reaching out to grasp my Body. The Darkness that followed, swallowing me Whole. And then? I was back in the Garden again. The bright blue Sky above and the grassy Earth beneath, yet my Orientation to them had suddenly shifted. Everything had shifted. I had shifted, Reader. The Grasses were so far below me now, so achingly far from my Nose and Eyes. The Wind cut through my Pelt, suddenly so thin and smooth and useless, and I could no longer hear its Song. And how cold and alone and afeared I was. Alien to my Self. Yet I was smiling. For the World was newly Wonderful. There were new Wonders to behold all around. My Hands were turning a Dandy Lion Stem in their slender Fingers. Just as now they turned an Ax.

I looked at Allan.

He stared at me, Pity in his Eyes. The Smiling there now tinged with Sorrow.

"They may have conjured you, Aerius," he said quietly. "But you are also a Free Spirit. With your own Heart and your own Mind and your own Soul. Your own Desires, too, I'm sure."

Jonah flashed briefly in my Mindscape. My Heart ached. I thought of the Grasses to which I longed to return, from which I felt forever banished. I stared at Leonard, sitting in these Grasses, looking up at me like a Stranger.

"Surely, you're more than just their Henchman," Allan pressed, his Voice so terribly gentle.

"I do not know what of me is mine anymore," I said. "I don't know where I am going anymore. I don't even know what I am." More Tears fell, and if they were my Tears, I did not know either. I stared at the Sea of silvery Trees. The low Moon and the rising Sun. Ax was growing heavy in my Hands. *Do not drop me*, she growled.

"I am . . . lost," I said.

"I think you are less lost than you imagine yourself to be," Allan whispered.

Imagine. That Word again. "I am done with imagining," I told him. Pony sighed a little now in my Pocket.

"Perhaps I can help you find your Way," Allan said, his Eyes on Ax. "I've been teaching Fiction for over twenty years now, you know. Perhaps we could do some Exercises together. We could—"

NO, NO, NO! Ax shrieked through my Skull.

"Enough, Enough!" I shouted, as if to shout her out of my Head. But she would never go, I knew. She would stay Forevermore, Reader. Keeping my Hands clenched round Ax, ever ready to perform her Violences. Her Banshee Cry coursing through my Blood. Her Dark Grip on my Heart.

"I have to kill you," I told Allan quietly. "Now. I'm sorry."

YES, hissed Ax, and I felt their Wills coursing through me in one singular Purpose. I clung to it, Reader, as I clung to Ax, though she wavered mightily now in my trembling Hands.

Allan just smiled as if I'd told him a sad, dark Joke.

And then?

He tilted his Neck back as if to help me. Closed his Eyes, rather dramatically, Allan did, as if this were his last Moment in the Sun. I stared at this Sun, rising redly behind Allan, his Throat exposed to my Blade. And suddenly the Awful Knowledge, the Terrible Arithmetic, revealed itself to me. Of course this would not be Allan's last Moment. After his Head rolled away from his Body, twould become a fuzzy Bunny. And he would enjoy this Sun in a new Way, I knew. He would open his new Eyes to a new World, the one I so longed for. He would hear the Wind Singing to him through his long furry Ears and hop happily in its Breezes. He would Speak the Language of Grasses I could no longer Speak. His human Pain, the considerable Pain of being Allan, would cease entirely. And then the Question arose: Why, Reader, would I ever give him this Gift?

I lowered Ax.

Allan opened one Eye. "Problem?"

I nodded. Hating that Allan was right. That he had so precisely articulated my Feeling. The Sun had now risen above the Trees. Under her soft pink Light, I held forth Ax.

"Kill me instead, please," I said.

NO! NO! NO!

And I sank down to the damp Grasses, Reader. Tilted my own Head back.

Allan stared at Ax like twas a Trick. "Why would I do that?"

"Tis the only Way Back for me," I said. "I was afeared to do it before. But I'm afeared no more," I lied. For I was afeared, Reader. Terribly ☹

Allan breathed a small Sigh of Relief. There was Triumph in his Expression. Which almost made me stand up and raise Ax again, but he quickly snatched her from me. Turned her round slowly in his Hands, shaking his Head. And then? He threw her away. Quite far away from himself and my Self. Bunny and I watched her silver Blade wink in the Dawn's Light. Watched her fall into a nearby Pond—making its Surface ripple, the Swans there glide away. My Heart sank. "What have you—"

"I can't send you Back, Aerius," he said, shaking his Head. "I'm sorry."

"Why?"

"Because you're not Mine. Only your Creator can send you Back. And if you are a Creation, you can send Someone Back, as you've learned."

He smiled at Leonard, crouched beside me in the Grass, Ears twitching. "Otherwise..."

"Otherwise?"

"It's just Murder, Bunny," he said.

I thought of Mother then. Her desperate Face. *Tell me you are Mine. Otherwise ... I can't send you Back.* I recalled her holding Ax, the Blade sharp and wavering above my Head. "Then I am doomed," I said.

He smiled down at me kneeling in the Grass. The rising Fire of the Sun behind him, blinding me. Casting him in such professorial Silhouette.

"Violence isn't the only means of Transformation, Aerius. There are other Ways Back. A Book is an Ax too. 'For the frozen Sea within us.' 'The Pen is mightier than the Sword,' and so on."

And in my Mindscape, I saw my Book. Now in Mother's Hands. How she'd hugged it so close to her Body even after she'd called it Nothing, a Fiction. "My Book a Way Back," I whispered. "All by itself?" My Voice echoed in the Forest, small and alone.

Allan looked down at me, suddenly quite enchanted. "All by itself," he repeated softly. "They are one of the oldest forms of Transformative Magic. They have the Power to change Everything. Hearts. Bodies. Minds. Souls. Whole fucking Worlds. People burn them for a Reason, you know."

I thought of my Self writing in the Dark. The Changes I'd begun to feel Within as I shared my Story, deep in the very Essence of my Soul. Truths that afeared and excited me rising to the Surface of my Mindscape, bleeding onto the Page. And Mother desperately looking over my Shoulder, Hands always reaching to take.

"But Mother has stolen my Book."

Allan nodded. He took a long drag of his Cigarette, which he had been smoking slowly all this Time. "She has her big Showcase Tonight, doesn't she?"

The Hare Moon, I saw now, was lower still in the Morning Sky. Nearly Full.

"Yes," I whispered, looking at this Moon. "I am supposed to be in it. I am the Star of the Show."

"Of course you are," he said. "You're what she's wanted for so long. What we all want, frankly." And he looked at me, Reader, quite longingly himself. I felt a Moment of Fear. Then he lowered his Eyes. Took another drag. "I was wondering what she was going to do for that Showcase of hers," he mur- mured. "They used to be notorious back in the Day. She was always trying to incite a Riot. Always going for *The Rite of Spring*. I guess it's just her Re- lationship to . . . the Process." He gazed down at my Body. "It's always been deeply intimate. Violent. Dare I say a little delusional."

Tell me you are Mine.

"Truly, I wonder how she or anyone else survives it." He shook his Head. "Well, you should go."

"I can't go back there," I whispered, thinking of Mother wielding Ax. "She will kill me."

Allan smiled at me darkly, as if to say, *What Choice do you have?*

"There are other Dangers," I said. "I am wanted by an angry Mob."

"Oh, right, of course. For your . . . Murders." And he winked at Leonard, still sitting by my Feets. "The students take Violences so seriously these Days."

"I am wanted by Others, too," I added quietly, picturing my Keep- ers. The Poets in their Trenchy Coats. My Heart glimmered briefly at the Thought of seeing Jonah there.

"There will always be Risks, and yes, even great Dangers, Aerius. This is Art School, after all. But perhaps you'll find a Way. You're charmed, you know."

"I am?"

"Of course. You're a Fiction. Serendipity is naturally on your Side. The Universe, if you like." He smiled again. "Goodbye, Aerius. Good luck." And then he sauntered away, Allan did. Into the Morning Fog broken here and there by beams of Sunlight.

Bunny and I watched him go whistling away. Allan, unkilled by me. Ax no longer pressed against my Heart or heavy in my Fist, but somewhere far away on the silty Pond floor. And my Hands, Reader, for the first Time, felt light and empty and free.

XXI

Twas Twilight Time when I returned to Narrative Arts. Entered the Rose Garden with careful, quiet Steps.

Axless. Pony still Comatose in my Pocket. My Hands empty, my Heart full. Of Fear, Reader. I stared at the Entrance to Narrative Arts from the Garden's mercifully lengthy Shadows. *SHOWCASE: RIOT OF SPRING* it read in big Letters on a glossy Poster on the door. Twas a Poster of Mother, much younger than she was now, smiling at something just beyond the Frame. How I shivered, Reader, at the Sight of her. Grew angry and more afeared all at once ⊗

But this Poster was the least of my Worries.

The Mob, Reader, surrounded the Entrance ⊗ Wearing their bleeding T-shirts, covered in their False Bloods, waving their Axes. Screaming, "She harbors a Murderer! Do not see her Showcase!" Some were holding blown-up Pictures of me, the infamous Drawing and Photograph. Everywhere I looked, I saw these "Representations" of my Self, Reader, beneath the words *HAVE YOU SEEN THIS MAN?*

Twas lucky I did not really resemble the Man in the Drawing at all. (It truly did not look like a Man so much as a Violin.) But I did somewhat resemble the Photograph of Jacob Chamalord with the Rabbit's Ears on his Head ⊗ To make matters worse, the Mob themselves were surrounded by Polices and Reporters. Indeed, the Mob's Leader, the Girl with the sad Ponytail and the Eyes of Fire, she appeared to be shouting at the Cameras. "The Murderer is being housed by Narrative Arts! Narrative Arts is Murder!" she cried.

"Murder!" intoned the Mob.

Reader, how my Heart pounded wildly within me.

And then, as if to multiply my Nightmares, I saw *Them*.

My Keepers in the Perfumed Flesh.

My alleged Creators ☹

All Four walking up the Pathway toward the doors, where Mother's Poster Face glowed most threateningly. Their shining, knotted Hairs and Cruelle Eyes. Their heady Scent of bogus Grasses. Each wearing the same sort of horribly adorable Dress, even Insatiable, whom they appeared to have groomed, for she looked washed and trussed up in a new Way. And they were not Alone, Reader. They were with four male Companions, quite like the American Psychos I'd seen them with once before. All tall like I was. Suited in deep blue. Pale eyes that glowed in the Twilight like mine did, these Men could very well have been my Brothers. My Keepers were holding their Hands, tugging them toward the Entrance like unwilling Toys. Meanwhile, these Men looked as afeared as I felt in my Heart. And then in my Heart I knew: my Brothers were being held quite against their Will, Reader. *Kept* ☹ Perhaps they, too, were Creations.

How cold I grew within me then ☹

"I thought we were going for Pinkberry first," I heard Murder Fairy say. Twas strange, Reader, that I could hear Them from where I stood in the Shadows, through the Mob Shoutings. As if they were indeed quite close. Twas as strange as how these Garden Shadows seemed to so perfectly conceal my Body.

"We'll go after," the Mind Witch snapped. Her silver Hairs spiky with hothouse Flowers. Her Eyes cold and sharp. "Remember, if you see him, grab him."

"Grab him," they all echoed, nodding.

"Do you really think he'll be there, Bunny?" Goldy Cut asked, looking around quite wildly. *Bunny.* To hear her use this Word now caused a Rage within me, though she'd said it, they'd all said it, countless Times before. I looked at her Dress, bright with Flowers not in Nature, the furthest Creature from the Petals and the Light I had ever seen.

"Of course he will," the Mind Witch said.

"And we'll be waiting." This from Insatiable, who grinned. "To fuck her Shit up. Take back what's Ours."

Not yours, I thought. *Never yours again.* And yet, in this Moment, I contemplated running to Them. Begging Them to please take an Ax to my Neck. *Please do me this Kindness.* But I could not bring my Self to approach Them, Reader. For one, the mad Throng would likely have descended on me before I could reach Them ⊗ And in Truth, even to look upon Them from this Distance made me ill ⊗ Of course they would never be willing to kill me ⊗ What they wished to do, I knew, was to keep me ⊗ Carry on with their terrible Revision ⊗ And anyway, I didn't know which One to beg, for I did not know who among Them was truly responsible for my Entry into this World. They had always quibbled about this among themselves back in the Attic Times. *He is Mine! No, he is Mine!* Whose was I, Reader? Which Hand among their many could successfully wield the Ax in my Favor? Which Hand would be my Death?

I did not know ⊗

And so I kept my Distance as they made their Way through the doors. Sighed with Relief as they disappeared at last through the Entrance.

They were followed closely by the Poets, muttering in their Trenchy Coats, taking last drags from their Cigarettes, their Talons painted and sharp. They were looking for me too, I could tell by their searching, cat-lined Eyes, ever glancing over their Shoulders. I did not see Jonah among them ⊗ Nor did I see that Girl. Sam. *She kind of keeps to herself*, I remembered Jonah had said. Perhaps they were together right now. But to think on this would only increase my Sufferings, Reader. And they were already quite Immense ⊗

Then Mother herself appeared in a shimmering Caftan. She was with a small Group of grave-looking Elders in dark Suits. The Administrators, I guessed, who were there to evaluate Mother *though they have no Respect or Understanding for my Art.* Mother was smiling at them, making Conversation, ingratiating herself. She seemed very nervous. Of course she would be; she did not know where I was. "Looking forward to this," she was saying.

"Should be very exciting." Making her Way along the Path through the mad Throng, who screamed most dramatically at the Sight of her. She smiled patiently as Polices held them back, allowing her, the true Criminal, to walk along with her grim Entourage. My Book was somewhere on her Person, I knew, though I could not see it ☹ I felt its Presence as surely as I felt the pounding of my own Heart. She, too, looked over her Shoulder as she approached the doors. Paused there, as if she saw Someone. Did she see me, Reader? No. Only Allan, walking up the Path toward her. Tall and hunched by his own Allanness. Hairs Wild, as they had been in the Forest. His Eyes smiling with Secrets.

"I'm looking forward to your Showcase this Evening, *Mother*," he said to her.

Mother? Mother's Eyes seemed to say. She stared at him, suspicious.

"Are you?" she said in a low Voice. "Well, I'm very looking forward to showing you." She smiled. I saw a Glimmer of Fear in her Eye then, the Fear of the Thief. I watched them disappear through the doors together while the Mob roared ☹

Reader, how could I ever hope to cross this Threshold? When literally Everyone hunting for me was now assembled in the same Place? ☹☹☹

WANTED it said beneath the pictures and photographs. MURDERER.

No, I wanted to cry. Not me! My Keepers are the Murderers! They wrenched me from the Garden. Planted their Violences deep into my Heart like so many false Flowers. Made me kill Allans until Allan himself took Pity on me, threw away my Ax. And now I am lost in your Human World of Thieving Fictions and Soul-sucking Poets. Lost perhaps forever.

Security Guards now stood unsmiling on either side of the doors. Guns in their Belts.

Oh, Reader ☹

The Moment I was spotted, I would surely be arrested. Killed. Or worse yet, *kept* ☹

There was no Way I could go through these doors. No Way I could enter the Theater like the rest of them. Storm the Stage and snatch the Book from her, as I'd been thinking. I would have to go through the Back Way, as Mother had instructed, the hidden door from the Garden that led directly to the Stage. Indeed, the only Way to my Book, I realized then, was to be in Mother's Showcase. To play my Part (whatever twas ☹) until I might get close enough to the Book to take it from her and run. Twas the only Way Back. Even then, I might get discovered. Caught by one of these Factions. Or die by Mother's Hand ☹

I crouched down to Leonard, sitting beside me in the shadowy Grasses. Though he continued to follow me, he'd grown more distant since our Time in the Forest.

"Leonard," I said softly. "If I run into Trouble, will you save me?"

Leonard looked at me. His Eyes flashed.

And then?

He hopped away from me, Reader, deeper into the Dark of the Garden.

XXII

M other had never been willing to bring me to the Theater. *Too risky,* she'd said. *We might be discovered.* Instead she'd shown me some Photos she'd taken of the Stage, drawn some crude Maps. And though Mother was not, by her own Admission, the best Artist or Photographer, this combination of Visuals did help me to find my Way through the snaking Dark. *There will be a Costume waiting for you on a chair in the greenroom,* Mother had said. *You will put on the Costume,* Mother had said. *You will make your Way backstage. You will find the X on the floor and kneel there.*

And then what, Mother?

I will be waiting for you there. Like Providence.

I found the Costume right where Mother had said it would be. A black Suit, a gray Shirt, which I quickly put on. Surprised that for once Mother wanted so very much of my Pelt concealed. When I entered the Back of the Stage, I found my Self in a kind of Garden, Reader. Though twas dark, I could see Bushes all around me. Many Beds of tall, bright-colored Flowers. Small, strangely twisting Trees. Grasses at my Feets. It all looked so Real that I thought I had taken a wrong Turn somewhere, that I was back in the Rose Garden outside. Or indeed back in Mother's Garden. But then I saw the Red Curtains, I heard the Crowd on the Other Side. I saw the X where I was to stand, marked with Black Tapes on the Grasses, just as Mother had said twould be. On this X lay a Mask. A Rabbit's Mask quite like the one I once wore at the Greek house. Yet this one was entirely white and featureless. No Lashes or Whiskers. Two black, unadorned holes for Eyes. Long Ears sharp like Swords. Twas formidable. Yet I was relieved to have it. Perhaps together with the Suit, it might save me from Notice.

I slipped it on.

And then I saw Mother herself among the false Trees and Flowers. Pacing the Grasses nervously. She had a little Microphone taped to her Mouth, and she was whispering into it heatedly. Pressing her Hand to her Ear. She stopped when she saw me standing there in my Suit and Mask. I could not tell what was in her Face then, as I couldn't see her Eyes. But I felt her Smile in the Dark. Could feel her great Relief coursing in my own Blood.

Fate, I could feel her thinking. *Serendipity.* Here I was at last, in all my Beauty. Evidence of her Genie-yes. Her Vindication. *Almost Mine.*

"Where is the Book, Mother?" I whispered.

For I saw it Nowhere on her Person. I would have taken it from her then. I would have run out of the Theater, run out of this World of Writers forever. Just the Sound of them on the Other Side of the Curtain was enough to put Fear in my Heart. But Mother didn't answer. I felt her Face frown in the Dark.

I would have to play my Part for now, I knew. I would have to wait for my Moment.

"Kneel," she said in a low Voice.

So I kneeled, Reader, upon the X in the Grasses.

And Mother smiled again. Whispered something into her mic.

Out went the Lights. Smoke filled the Garden like a Fog.

And the great Red Curtains were drawn.

Twas so dark that at first all I could see was Mother, standing beside me on the Stage in her Fineries. Her Hairs a great Goldy Cloud, her Caftan glowing importantly in the Light. I kneeled on my X, still swallowed in the Black. The Audience could see me not, though I could begin to make them out in the Dark. An endless Sea of Heads ⊗ What Mother had called *the whole of New York* amounted to a few bored-looking young People in Black slouched in the front rows. "Assistants," I heard Mother whisper beneath her Breath. A couple of them (the Presses perhaps) holding

Cameras, ready to click. Beside them, those grave Administrators I'd seen Outside, who did not understand Mother's Art and wished for her to Retire, the Faculties who wished for her to Fail—all these Aged Ones seated dourly in the front rows, all frowning, apart from Allan, who seemed to espy me kneeling in the Dark. Who seemed to smile. My Keepers and their Psychos seated just behind, wide-eyed and waiting, I knew, for any Sign of me ☹ The Poets glowering in their Trenchies on the opposite End of the Theater. The Mob standing grimly in the Back, the Security Guards at every door ☹ And Jonah? Jonah Nowhere at all among these Factions. My Heart sank, even though how could I possibly run to him in these Circumstances? I was grateful for the Darkness, which concealed my Body. At least for now ☹

Mother stood smiling at her Podium, a single deep blue Light shining down on her like she was God. She welcomed everyone. Thanked them all so very much for coming Tonight. "I am most humbled by your Attendance," she said, beaming at her many Enemies and Friends. "You will forgive me if I am a bit nervous Tonight. I have not had a Showcase in some Time."

She sighed quite performatively. Gave a great Speech then, Reader. About Creativity, the Process. And all the while that she was speaking about Bleedings and Wounds, I kneeled beside her in the Dark, looking, looking for the Book. Twas difficult, for the Eyeholes in my Mask narrowed my Vision. There was a Smoke, too, continually filling the Garden, obscuring all Shapes. But the Book was Nowhere on her Person or on the Stage ☹ There was only Mother in her Caftan, standing most theatrically in the Fog. Attempting to Enchant. To Captivate. Thus I had no Choice, Reader, but to stay kneeling upon the X. And listen. And wait ☹

"I came to Warren long ago as a Student," Mother was saying. "Now I am a Teacher here. For me, Warren has always been a Charged Place. A Magic Place. Or perhaps there is a Magic made between my Self and it. A *Serendipity*, if you will." She smiled. "I was Fortunate, in my long Career here, to be Visited many Times over. Indeed, the Transformative Powers of Creativity seemed to course through my very Body like Blood."

She held up her Hands to the Heavens. Quite dramatically, Reader. "But alas, of late, if I am being Honest, it has not come so easily." Mother lowered her Arms sadly now. Bowed her Head in an Attitude of Great Humility. "It has been a Struggle," Mother admitted. "Perhaps," she mused, "because my Process is so deeply tied to the Natural World. And as the Earth struggles to survive, to thrive, so do I. As its Rivers run dry, so too does my own Blood. As its Soil Corrodes, so too does my own Heart." She pressed her Hand emphatically to her Breast. I heard some Coughs in the Audience.

Oh my fucking god, came a whisper from my Pocket. *Where is the Book already? Let us take it and run.*

My heart soared.

PONY!

Awake, awake at long last! ☺ And right when I was in most need of him, *Oh Pony, I have missed you so terribly! Pony, thank god, thank god, I am in such—* But he shushed me ☹

"But thankfully," Mother thundered, "by the Great Generosity of my Warren Fellows, who perhaps sensed that my Creative Journeyings were not over yet, that I had still more to Bleed, to give, I was able to take a Leave last Fall. To Tap the Wound once more." She smiled again at the Audience.

"Nothing happened for a Time," Mother confessed, her Face falling. "I worried indeed that the Wound had gone Dry. That I was doomed like the Earth itself. And then, most unexpectedly, I was Visited. By a most vital and dynamic Source."

And now she beamed at me in the Dark. My Blood, Reader, went cold.

Dear fucking Christ, Pony whispered.

"Beautiful," Mother said. "Primitive. Wily and Mysterious as Nature itself. And Wounded, deeply. Brimming with Heart's Blood. What could I do but Tap?"

I looked out at the Audience. My Keepers, I saw, were on the Edge of their Seats now. The Poets, too, were leaning forward in Anticipation. The Faculties and Administrators in the front rows were glancing at their Watches. New York looked mildly amused. The Protestors lining the walls were ready to cry to Murder, while the Security Guards were yawning by the doors. Allan, meanwhile, watched me intently.

I looked back at Mother, smiling most triumphantly. Basking in this Tension. "This Source," Mother said, "provided me with the Purest of Language. A Dispatch from our precious, much-endangered Natural World."

And here at last she pulled it from her Caftan, Reader.

The Book, the Book! Pony cried.

My Book. Right there in her Hands. Those Strangling Flowers, which had always afeared me, catching the Light. Could I grab it now?

Not now, not yet, Pony whispered. *We could be intercepted.*

I looked back at the Audience, all of whom were now watching Mother as intently as Allan. Some of New York, I noted, were rolling their Eyes.

"I shall read it for you now," Mother cried, waving the Book in the Air. "Direct from the Source's Lips to your Ears! Untainted by my Authorial Hand. Before I begin, let me say that I know many of you expect a mere *Reading.*" Mild Laughter now in the Audience.

"Just you wait," Mother said, gripping the Book, my Book, so tightly in her Hands. So close but so far away from my Reach ☹

And then? She opened it.

She began to read Leonard's words in a great booming Voice. I could almost feel Leonard somewhere cringing at her Fiction's Cadence. But she did not get very far, Reader. For a great Murmuring erupted as soon as she began. A buzzing like a Drone from the Audience.

The Poets.

"What is she doing?" I heard them hiss. "What does she think she is doing? Those are not her Words!" I looked back at Mother, who was pressing on despite the Murmurings. She could not or would not hear them. On she read until a great Shout cut through the Theater.

"PLAGIARIST!"

Mother looked up from her Readings. "Excuse me? *What* do you call me?"

"You are plagiarizing Leonard Coel! Those are his Poet Trees!"

Twas the Leader. Risen from his chair in the Theater. Gunnar and Colby and Matthias scowling beside him. "*Plagiarist, Plagiarist!*" they now began to cry.

Mother looked at me kneeling in the Dark. And I knew she knew Everything. Her Eyes went as hard as Stones. The Mists there grew thick. She looked back at the Audience. The Presses were snapping Pictures. The Poets were all on their Feets now, pointing at her, chanting madly now, "PLAGIARIST, PLAGIARIST!" even as the Administrators and Faculties told them to settle. "Settle down, please."

"YES!" Someone Else shouted. The Mind Witch, rising from her seat, surrounded by my Keepers, all on their Feets too. "She has also stolen from her Students! Plagiarist! Thief!" Chanting and chanting, the whole Throng, while the Presses clicked and New York cringed and the other Elders in the Audience continued to make lame Gestures for "Order, Order, please." Except for Allan. Who only sat there, smiling.

And Mother watching it all, horrified. Mesmerized. Defiant. Still gripping the Book, which I must take from her, Reader.

Now, Pony whispered. *Now, now, now!*

I began to reach out my Hand from the Dark.

"SILENCE," she suddenly cried. And she held up the Book then. High above her Head. I froze. All froze and fell quiet for a Spell. Mother's Anger was quite formidable in this Moment. Mother herself was formidable. A *Book is an Ax,* I remembered Allan had said. And indeed, Mother held up my Book like she could strike with it. Like she could kill.

And yet she was smiling.

"It seems," she said, "that we must have ourselves a little Witch Hunt Tonight. Very well, this is Warren, after all. I shall *accept* your Slings and Arrows. I am used to playing Monster, Medea, Mother. I'm a female Writing Teacher, after all. I am used to your Projections, your INGRATITUDE. Even though I *made* this Place what it is! I *first* brought its Magic to Life, and any of You who now reap its Gifts are but PALE IMITATORS. So go ahead. Go ahead and *BURN ME.* I have been burned many times before. But before you tie me to the *Stake,* HEAR ME NOW."

Silence in the room. Mother was Smoldering them with her Gaze. The Mists in her Eyes had never been so Thick. When she looked at me, I saw a Stranger. Lost in her own Performance. *Too late*, said her Eyes. *Too late to Turn Back now.*

"WORDS. ARE. NOTHING!" she cried. "You actually THINK that there is Ownership over WORDS?" She snorted now like a Pig. "Words are such feeble Representations of Experience. What really matters is the FLESH. What matters is the HEART. THAT is my true Medium. I wrote these Words in Ink, but make no Mistake, I WORK IN BLOOD."

And she turned to look at me in the Dark. As though I were a Great Exhibition, Reader. As though she were about to unveil me. "The Heart's Blood is what my Work Gushes Forth," she whispered, turning back to the Audience.

My own Heart, Reader, was leaping inside of my Body.

"I know many of you doubt my Creative Powers are Real. Well, after Tonight I can promise you, you will doubt no more. For I will demonstrate them to you right here, right now on this Stage! I will show you the transformative Wonder of Art. The Violence and then the Transcendence. And is there a Risk?" She looked back at me now. Her Expression lit up by Madness, a most disturbing Ecstasy ☹ "Of course there is. All Art is Risk! Without Risk, we give Nothing! Without Blood, there can be no Wonder!" And with that, she threw the Book down onto the Stage.

The Book, the Book!

And then she and her Podium were swallowed in Darkness.

A Light suddenly filled my Eyes. It shone down on me, surrounded me like a Sphere. I was blinded by it, Reader. Twas a Light brighter than any I'd ever known. So bright, I could see Nothing at all. Not the Audience, not the Stage—only this Light and then the Great Darkness beyond it. A Fog surrounding me like the Mist in Mother's Eyes.

I heard gasps from the Crowd. Sighs and Murmurings.

For there I was, Reader, suddenly terribly visible to Everyone ☹ Alone ☹ Kneeling before them all. My Mask hot on my Face. My Heart leaping and leaping in my Body. They were all staring at me, and though I could not see, I could feel their Eyes. I took no Enjoyment from them, Reader. Knew this might be the Death of me. *The Death of us both*, Pony whispered. I heard more Murmurings, Whisperings among them. "Who is this? Who is this?"

Oh god, did they recognize me?

The Book, Pony whispered, *look for the Book! Our only Way Back.*

But the Light still blinded me, Reader. Smoke still filling the Stage like a Fog. Twas then I caught a Scent of Wild Flowers. Forests. Close to me.

The Book.

I began to feel around for it on the Grassy Stage below, my Fingers searching its false Blades. I began to smell for it. My Nose twitching, coming Alive beneath my Mask. But I was too far from the Ground. I hunched down lower. There the Scent of Wildness grew stronger. The Book was near me, but where, where? "Where are you?" I whispered.

I heard little Gasps in the Audience. "What is he doing now?" "What is this?"

I hunched down lower still, pressed my Face into Mother's false Earth and sniffed. Now I caught the Scent of true Flowers amid the fake Grasses. I caught the Scent of Blood. *My* Blood, Reader. Closer, I was getting closer.

Suddenly the Light began to pulse above my Head.

The Audience gasped.

"Oh my god, oh my god."

"Jesus fucking Christ."

Which was most strange, Reader. I could feel them Squirming in their Seats, watching me now. Wincing as though they were truly afeared. *Why do you all seem so afeared?*

And then in the Pulsing Light I glimpsed the Book lying in the Grass just ahead of me.

I held out my Arms to reach for it. More Gasps from the Audience, paralyzing me.

"Oh my god, oh my god, DON'T!" Someone cried.

Don't? Did they not understand that this Book was my only Way Back?

I lunged forward now, reaching for it once more.

That's when I heard Mother hiss, "Stay on the X! Stay on the X as I told you."
I turned.

There she was standing behind me in the Fog. A large Ax raised mightily in her Hands. "Don't move," she murmured. Her Eyes on the Lights, her
Smile for the Theater.

"Mother, you cannot send me Back," I whispered to her. "I am not Yours,
I am not Yours—"

But Mother was not hearing me. She was too caught up in playing her
Part, relishing the Horror and Wonder of the Audience, their Gasps and
Murmurings. Drunk on this Demonstration of what she believed to be her
Powers. Her Gaze was for the Cameras and the Crowd alone, many of whom
were now shouting "Thief," "Murderer," "Liar," "Genie-yes," "Witch," while
the Security Guards looked alarmed, awake now. Caught between Fear and
Curiosity. Was this Real? Or was this merely more of Mother's Art? And
Mother delighting in it all. No One dared to approach the Stage, for Mother's
raised Ax was most formidable. Larger than any I'd ever seen. Certainly
larger than my own, lost somewhere in the watery Depths of the Forest
Pond. It shone in the blue flashing Light like a Thing Irrefutable, a most Dazzling Truth. And Mother lost to it. Nothing in her Eyes but Defiance. Shining,
blinding as the sharp Blade itself.

Which was now poised over my Neck.

And looking into Mother's Eyes, I knew that she could send me Nowhere.

That she could only kill me.

That she would rather kill me than admit Defeat in front of these Factions, her many Friends and Enemies in Narrative Arts. New York. These
Presses with their clicking Cameras. These Faculties and Administrators, some of whom were now looking quite nervous, some of whom were
looking bored. Allan, meanwhile, was watching me closely. Not smiling
anymore.

The Book was lying just ahead of me on the Stage floor, Reader. Smelling of Wild Flowers and my own Heart's Blood. Just out of my Reach. Too far for me to grasp with my Hands alone. Mother had done this on Purpose perhaps, so that in my Reaching, in my Longing, I might extend my Neck most beautifully, most dramatically for her Strike.

So that I might be best Positioned to receive her Blade ☹

A Sound of Crying now in the Audience. Roaring above the Human Sounds. Male, Animal. Strangled. Mother's Ax above my Head wavered at this Sound. She herself wavered, her Smile cracking, looking out at the Dark. Most annoyed. Who was intruding upon this Moment of her Authorial Thunder? Upon her Murder?

I looked out at the Audience. My Keepers' Dates, my Brothers, had risen from their chairs. They were screaming up at the ceiling, and freezing Mother in her Strike. Allan's Eyes caught mine in the Theater. I felt his Message like a Lightning Flash through my Pelt, just as I felt Pony stirring in my Pocket.

Now!

And looking from Mother's Blade to the Book, I jumped, Reader.

In the flashing blue Light, I took a Great Leap toward it, into what felt like the Void.

A Hop, if you like.

And everyone screamed and screamed.

Time suddenly began to move slowly, Reader. Just like one of those Moving Pictures my Keepers used to play for me on the Attic wall. I had never quite believed Time could move like that in what we call Reality. It seemed like an all-too-Human Manipulation. It seemed, indeed, like Art. I had never believed it, that is, until this Moment.

Then I learned Time could move very slowly indeed.

It could freeze as I froze on the now-bloody Stage, after my Great Leap.

Feeling and seeing so many Things at once.

The Whoosh of Mother's Ax, like a most terrible, sharp Wind. How it roared past me as I leapt, cutting so very Close. My Mask suddenly felled and lying by my Knees on the Grassy Floor. Its long white Ears severed by Mother's Blade. Splattered with Blood, as if they were my true Ears, Reader, for Mother had nicked my Flesh. The Blade of Mother's Ax now stuck in the Stage floor. The Press Cameras clicking and clicking as she, cursing, attempted to wrench the Blade from this false Earth where Nothing grew.

And then the Screaming.

All of them screaming so very wildly.

Screaming my Name. Screaming "Murderer." Screaming "Muse." Screaming "Mine." Rushing toward the Stage, toward me ⊗ Believing they owned me, Body and Soul, each one had a Claim ⊗ They would take me back to the Attic, to the Den of Oblivion, to Prison ⊗ Security Guards and the Administrators and Faculties attempting to hold them back, to block their Ways to the Stage, even though I could tell they themselves did not know, was the botched Swing, was this Chaos, part of Mother's Showcase? Or was it simply Chaos now?

I braced my Self for Capture. For the greedy Grab of the Keeper or the Soul-sucking Poet ⊗ For the Mob to storm the Stage and Arrest me ⊗ Allan seemed to have vanished from the Theater. Stupidly, I hoped for the saving Call of Jonah's Voice. And underneath these Human Sounds, those strange Animal Cries from my Brothers rising to a feverish Pitch. Suddenly I felt a hot Breath on my Neck. Mother. She'd wrenched her Ax free from the false Earth, she'd raised it high again, she was going to kill me this Time. She no longer cared. Not about Creation nor Vindication. Only Blood. My Blood. And this Time, Reader, I tilted my Head back. Extended my Throat to her. All right, Mother. "Kill me," I said. For I would rather die here, Reader, than be caught by any of these grasping Artist Hands. I waited for Mother's Blade to descend upon me, to put us all out of our Misery. Braced my Self for the Black.

But something stopped her. A new and great Chaos now rising behind us. And Mother was beholding it, a true Horror on her Face.

I turned, ready to meet the Horror head-on, whatever twas. Mob, Keeper, Poet, I was ready. What I saw were the Rabbits. Pouring into the

Theater from all doors. Storming the Theater floor. Hopping through the Auditorium like my very own fuzzy Army. And Everyone pointing and cooing or else struck dumb by the long-eared Creatures. Twas like the Rabbits were casting a kind of strange but potent Glamour over the Throng, Reader, which no longer seemed to notice Mother or my Self at all. I thought I saw Leonard among them, bounding happily down the Aisle.

Leonard, are you saving me?

Perhaps he was, Reader.

Or perhaps my Brothers had summoned these Rabbits with their Cries. They were still shrieking up at the Ceiling, their blue Eyes glowing as more and more Rabbits stormed the doors.

Or perhaps twas something to do with what Allan had said. About my being a Fiction. *Serendipity* naturally on my Side. *The Universe, if you like.*

I will never know, Reader.

I only knew Bunny.

Bunny everywhere ☺

And the Book. My Book.

No longer out of Reach, but back in my Hands ☺

"Aerius," I heard now in a Whisper. My Keepers standing at the Foot of the Stage. Staring dead at me and Mother. Immune to the Rabbitry. Immune to the Ax. Immune to Everyone and Everything but my Self. Kneeling before them ☹

Suddenly, the Lights went out in the Theater.

Under cover of Darkness, I ran.

XXIII

Narrative Arts, Reader, is a Labyrinth. I do not know how long I ran, breathless, through its twisting Dark. Up and down its ever-winding Corridors and Staircases. Gripping my Book close, twas all I could feel now in the Black. How dearly I wanted to escape Mother, my Keepers, this terrible World, for good. Leave and never look back. Yet there was no End ⊗ The building seemed to go on Forever, to extend infinitely, twas a Maze of Halls and doors. And none of these doors leading to the Outside ⊗ And each one more terrifyingly named than the next, their Signs glowing in the dark Halls.

GALLERY OF PARADIGMS

THE METAPHORICAL CHAMBER

POETRY LIBRARY

Oh, Reader ⊗

Serendipity, the Universe—had they deserted me?

As I ran, I could hear my Name being screamed somewhere in the Labyrinth. I saw another door up ahead. HALL OF INFINITE REFLECTION read the Sign. The Words gave me a very bad Feeling, Reader. But of course, all of Narrative Arts by then gave me a bad Feeling ⊗

We must go through, Pony whispered in my Pocket. *There is Nowhere else to Run.* Speaking my exact Thoughts. Twas strange, I thought, that he should have awoken Tonight, to reassure me with my very own Words. But I could not wonder on this Miracle now, for we must go through this door.

And so we did, Reader.

A Chamber, dark yet luminous. As I entered, strange-colored Lights bubbled down from the ceiling. I found my Self surrounded by Walls of Glass, a

Sea of tall young Men. All of them looking at me very curiously through the falling Bubbles of Light.

"Who are you?" I asked them.

But they seemed to be asking me the very same Question, Reader. Their Mouths moving in Time with mine. Each one clutching a Book to his Chest like I was. Gasping for Breath like I was. *Who are you? Who are you?* Though our Answer was now as clear as this Sea of Glass.

My Self.

My Self a Thousand Times over, Reader. Irrefutably Human. Reflected all around me, seemingly to Infinity, twas quite literally a Hall of Infinite Reflection. *DO NOT TOUCH* read a Sign by the door.

Oh god, Pony whispered now. *Will the Artistry never cease? Do not look. Mirrors are very dangerous. And Artist Mirrors worst of all.*

Yet how could I help it, Reader? These Mirrors were all around me. I was all around me. Beautiful, how many times had I been told I was? And I was, I knew, even in my Ruin ☹ I stared at my Selves now in the Dark, bleeding, breathless, broken—their muscled Bodies in their torn Clothes that Mother had chosen, their Actor's Faces a product of my Keepers' Lust, their Pelts so eerily smooth and their Ears so terribly small—and the Word that came to me was not *Beautiful*. Twas *Conjured. Hunted. Lost.* So that I stared at these Selves in a kind of Horror through that falling Light. And they stared at me just the same. Our Hearts leaping in our Chests. Our Arms still hugging the Book so tightly to our Bodies. And then I remembered.

My Book, Reader.

My Friend.

I had taken it back from Mother.

I had it in my Hands at last.

I looked down at those strange Flowers on its Face. How disturbingly small and light it felt in my Hands now. Almost like Nothing at all. *The Way Back*, Pony whispered. Was it? And there among the Bubbles of Light, surrounded by my Reflections, I felt a Coldness begin to spread through me, Reader. A Doubt I dared not name.

Go on, then, Pony whispered. *Open it. Quickly, before we die here, please.*

Again, echoing my very Thoughts. Just as he'd done in the Theater. Which should have been a Comfort to me, a Balm. But it only made this Doubt grow in my Heart. My Hands trembled mightily as I opened the Book.

Just as I did, I heard a Sigh. Which was curious. Had the Book sighed at my opening? Was my Friend so happy to see me?

"Aerius," said a Voice.

I looked up, knowing what Horror my Eyes would meet. For it seemed I must meet Them, Reader. Thousands of Them. All around me. Four for every One of my Army of Reflections. Dresses torn and Hairs wild from giving Chase. Eyes fevered and brimming with what they called Love. Whispering, "Oh my god. You."

And there was Nowhere to run, Reader.

For they were Everywhere.

I was frozen, paralyzed before this Sea of my Keepers. And they appeared paralyzed before this Sea of me. Dazzled by the illusory Plenitude of my Self. They stood there, turning dumbstruck Circles, hunting wildly for my actual Flesh among the Reflections, who were all shaking their Heads like I was, mouthing my own Words as I spoke them. "No. Please. Let me go."

Tears shone in their Keeper Eyes as if I'd slapped Them.

"But I love you," all the Goldies whispered. "So much, I can't breathe." Her many Mouths trembling. Her Voice sounding so very raw and pained. She shook her Goldy Heads, none of which looked so Goldy anymore.

"We all do," they said.

And their Thousands of Bodies began to approach me, Reader. Step by terribly tender Step, I felt each Click in my Bones. A thousand Mouths now trembling. All this monstrous Love moving toward me, encircling me, all my Selves now frozen in the Glass.

"We love you, we love you," they whispered wildly. Eyes bright, as if they were deep in Dreamings. As if we were right now in a Romance and this was the Moment of our Great Union. And whether I wanted to be in such a Story did not matter to them, Reader.

"I am a Free Spirit," I whispered, all my Selves whispered, petrified before this Awful Sea. "I have my own Story."

Shh, Pony said. *You will discover us.*

But my Keepers didn't seem to hear me, Reader. Or if they did, it did not matter. They were coming for me anyway, I knew, whether I loved Them or not. Not to kill me. Never to send me back. But to torture me and themselves in the Dark forever. I could already feel their Attic Ropes encircling me. *Yes,* I heard Them say somewhere in my Mindscape. *No Choice, Bunny. We're Writers. Can't help the fucking creative Heart. The Heart that loves, oh it Rages wildly within us. Possesses us. So we must Possess you. Please god, let us.*

"But what of my Heart?" I shouted, and again they seemed to hear me not. So lost they were in looking for me among the many Reflections. Perhaps more lost than I ever was. And yet they did not seem to know which Face was truly mine, which was Real. Where to direct their most terrible loving Energies. Where to reach out their Hands.

"Where are you?" they called, touching the Glass, only Glass. Only my horrified Reflection looming there. They began to whimper in Frustration.

"I LOVE you," they cried. "Please."

Well, this is very inappropriate, Pony whispered. *They are not supposed to touch—there is a Sign right there that says so. Can they not read?* It seemed they could not, Reader. They were banging their Fists on the Glass now, on my Faces, all of which mouthed, *Please let me go.* Banging on them so very hard, we at last began to crack. Yet they didn't stop.

"I LOVE you," they shouted, pounding. "Where ARE you? WHERE THE FUCK ARE YOU, BUNNY, I FUCKING LOVE YOU, CAN'T YOU SEE? YOU BELONG TO ME, I MADE YOU, I MADE YOU AND YOU MADE ME AND I LOVE YOU SO MUCH, CAN'T EAT, CAN'T SLEEP, EVEN THOUGH YOU'RE A MURDERER, BUNNY, AND YOU HATE ME, WHY DO YOU HATE ME WHEN I LOVE LIKE THIS OH IT PAINS, IT PAINS, BUT DON'T CARE, DON'T CARE, BECAUSE YOU'RE MY MURDERER, BUNNY, OH YOU'RE MY LOVE MY HATE MY BLOOD MY SHADOW MY DREAM MY ECSTASY MY SOUL IN ALL ITS DISEASE

MY FUCKING MAGIC, BUNNY YOU'RE MINE! MY HAPPY ACCIDENT. THE VERY BEST AND WORST OF MY HEART, ALL SHINING THERE IN THE DOG-AND-WOLF HOUR OF YOUR WONDROUS—"

And so it went. I watched as they beat wildly at my Reflections, at the cracking Glass, their Hands growing bloodier and bloodier. And whether twas me or themselves reflected in the Glass, they seemed not to know any longer. I watched Goldy make out with her now shattered Likenesses, even as she was screaming. Insatiable writhing pervily on the floor with giant Shards of her own Reflections. The Mind Witch, ecstatic with Rage and Blood, stabbing at her many Faces with her many Daggers Singing "LOVE LOVE LOVE." Meanwhile Murder Fairy, all of her just stood there. Watching the Violences like I was. I wondered indeed if she was watching me, Reader, the Real me. All of her Eyes seemed to be looking right at me, at my actual Body in this cracking Den of Illusions. Suddenly, she pulled out her thousands of Axes. A sea of Blades surrounded me, surrounded us all. Her many Hands gripping, all of her Faces very solemn indeed.

"What are you doing?" Goldy cried, her Mouths full of Blood and Glass bits.

Murder Fairy turned her Heads toward Them all. "Sometimes you have to kill your Darlings, Bunny," she said. "Before they destroy you." And then she turned back to me and smiled.

"NO," they all shouted.

I looked at Murder Fairy, her many Bodies gripping her many Axes. Was she really going to do it? Was she going to at last take that Blade to my Throat? Could she even do it? Could her Hand alone send me Back? Or could she, like Mother, only kill me? I did not know. I knew Nothing in that Moment. Only that I did not want this, Reader. Not anymore. Certainly not by her or by any of their Keeper Hands. Not with my Book pressed against my Heart like this. Not with A Way Back that was mine. Finally mine alone.

Not like this, Pony whispered. *Please.*

"Please," I whispered to her.

She raised her Blades in the Falling Lights.

My Breath froze in my Body as they all screamed for her to "fucking stop STOP STOP."

"I'm sorry," she murmured, shaking her fairy Heads, and whether she was saying it to me or to Them I shall never know. "But this is for the Greater Good."

"NO NO NO—" they cried, and we all braced ourselves as, with one fierce Swing, a thousand Blades struck the Great and Illusory Sea of me and my Keepers. This Sea came raining down on their Heads in so much shattered Glass, our infinite Eyes and Hands, Bodies and Mouths. A sharp and painful Storm. And in the raining Glass, I saw that all my Mouths were now smiling, Reader. As my Real Mouth was smiling. For as the Mirrors all came crashing down, laying my Keepers low and leaving me miraculously standing, I saw a Sign at last, Reader, glimmering and red, of Serendipity. *The Universe, if you like.* Right there on the blank walls that lay behind the Illusion, that lay behind Everything.

EXIT, it read.

XXIV

I left Them, Reader. Drowning in their Sea of Glass.

Ran though my Legs could run no longer. Ran though my Heart was giving Way. Found my Way out of Narrative Arts once and for all. Into the Outside World at last. An Alley, grim and dripping. Crushed Cigarettes at my Feets. Sirens wailed and blue Lights flashed. Yet the Night air was cold and sweet.

With Freedom, Reader.

Or near Freedom.

Tears stung my Eyes to taste it.

My Arms were still wrapped around the Book. *The Book, the Book*, Pony said weakly. He was in his Death Throes, like I was. This Night had surely been too much for his poor Heart.

Or was it my Heart, Reader? Had it always only ever been my Heart?

I thought of my Keepers kissing their broken Reflections and felt cold.

The Book, Pony whispered again now, in a Voice so like my own. Desperate. Shaking his Head as I shook mine. *Hurry, hurry*, he said, even as the sinking Doubt returned to me, even as I sensed twas only my own Voice speaking to me in the Dark. I looked round the Alley, then down at the light and flowery Book still clutched in my Hands.

It hit me then, a Blade to the Throat. For how the Book worked, I knew not. Had indeed never known, for neither Mother nor Allan had ever explained and I had never asked. Had only ever trusted. Like a Fool ☹ *I don't know, I don't know*, I told Pony, sliding down to the Ground.

We must try. For what else can we do? Where else can we go? Please, Pony whispered. Or was it I who whispered? *For me.*

Once more I opened the Book. Flipped to the very last Page, which strangely contained all my Happenings to this very Moment, Reader. How was it possible? But there it all was, scribed in my own spidery Hand.

Tis a Magic Book, Pony said. Was it Pony who said this after all? *It writes itself, you see.* I thought of Mother's Words. *I shall let it write itself. As the very best Books do.* And there in the dark Alley my Heart brightened a little. The Wild Flower Scent of the Pages called to me. *Go on.*

I closed my Eyes. Tried to *imagine.* The Song of the Wind through the Grasses. The Moon speaking to me, no longer Mute. The tender Cowslip on my Tongue. And no more Human Pain or Sadness. No more Unbelonging. No more Dreamings and Longing for Things that could not be. No more Artists, above all.

I longed for it to swell all around me, this Other World. To envelop me like an Embrace, this Lost Place and its Light.

But Nothing came, Reader.

Nothing but the great Dark that lay behind my own closed Eyes. The Sirens were growing louder now. I heard Cries of petty Anguish. Felt the fact of my own Human Flesh sitting so heavily on the Earth. The dull, lone thudding of my broken Heart. Dread filled me, Reader. A sick Feeling like Drowning in Black.

Nothing is happening, Pony said.

Not Pony, Reader.

Me.

I said this to my Self.

Again and again and again in the Dark. Alone in the Alley with a Toy in my Pocket. And in my all-too-Human Lap, a most useless Book. Whose Magic was a door I could never open. No Way Forward. No Way Back.

"Nothing, Nothing, Nothing," I said. And I was drowning, drowning in the Black.

"Aerius," said a Voice. My Voice, Reader?

I opened my Eyes.

Dandy Lions.

Earth and Grasses.

His golden Face like a Sun in the Dark. Smiling, impossibly, like he was so happy to see me. For a Moment I forgot the Black, I forgot Everything.

"Jonah," I whispered. "Are you Real?"

He beamed at me through the Smoke of his forever-burning Cigarette.

"I was just asking my Self the same Question," he said. "About you."

So beautiful in that Alley. His Face so close to mine that surely I must be dreaming him, like I'd dreamed so much else. "Probably I am just Imagining again," I said, shaking my Head.

He reached out and touched my Face. A Warmth spread through me, cutting through the Cold. "If you are," he said, "I'll take it."

He kissed me then, Reader. Right there in the grim and dripping Alley. His Hand on my Neck, drawing me close, crushing his soft Mouth against mine, the most perfect Flower that ever was. And whether twas Real or not, I cared no longer. For Nothing, Nothing, had ever felt more Wonderful.

"Oh my god, Aerius," he whispered.

"Jonah," I murmured.

"You're bleeding," he said, touching my Chest.

I saw that indeed I was. A Gash where a Shard of Glass must have cut me. Right across the inky Sun that smiled over my Heart. He ran his Fingers gently over the Cut. Kissed it lightly. And I breathed sharply from the Pleasure and Pain.

"What happened to you? Tell me. Did you go to the Showcase? I was going to, but it sounded Intense in there."

And what could I say, Reader? Where could I even begin to begin? I only shook my Head. "Please just kiss me again," I whispered. "Then let's get out of here."

And he did kiss me, Reader.

And then, Hand in Hand, we ran.

XXV

ove, Reader.

Tis a Word that holds so very much inside of it. It can make you kiss broken Glass. Have Impossible Dreamings in Rose Gardens. Gush your own Heart's Blood and not even feel the Wound. It can make you forget who you are. That you were ever Bunny. That you will never belong here. It can make you forget the Drowning Black that waits behind all our closed Eyes.

And then, just like that, Reader, it can make you remember.

Tis a Mind Witch like no other, really.

As Confounding to me as Real.

Love is what I felt when I kissed Jonah in the Alley. His lovely golden Arms around me, as I'd so many Times dreamed in the Shed, in the dark Den of Oblivion. Telling me all the Things I'd so longed to hear. How much he'd missed me. Regretted how we'd parted that last Night, he'd been so stupid to walk away. He'd been a Fool. Lost in his own Book. His own stupid Dreamings, you know?

"I do know," I said. My Chest hurt terribly, twas a mighty Gash, but I told my Self I felt not the Pain, or if I did, that this was Love. Jonah kept saying we should go to something he called Health Services. He was very worried about my Bleedings.

"Let's stay here for a little while," I told him. For we'd left the Alley together, left Narrative Arts forever, I hoped, arriving at a quiet Stretch of Green before a great gray Building. *The School of Philosophy*, Jonah had told me. *I guess it's not very popular.* Nothing here but ancient Trees and their leafy Shadows swaying in the Wind. Untouched Grasses and dew-slicked

Flowers shining under the Moon. The Sight tugged at my Heart, made it ache. Though why should it ache, Reader? When I was here with my Love at last, whom I kept stopping to kiss, for surely this would make the Pain go away. My Love, Jonah, who was squeezing my Hand, apologizing again, unbelievably, for that Night.

"It's just Poet Tree's Everything to me, you know?" he said. "It's saved me, I can't tell you how many Times. It's how I stay sober. How I stay sane, really." And he laughed like he'd told a Joke. And then I knew how True twas. True and painful.

"But you," he said to me, stroking my Face. "You're another kind of Poet Tree, Aerius. And only a terrible Poet would have chosen the Page over you that Night. Nights like that are what make the Page worth Anything at all."

Is there a Word, Reader, for when you feel so much Joy and so much Pain at the very same Time? And the Joy is Pain and the Pain is Joy? Twas like a thousand sharp Pinpricks of Light waterfalling through my Body ☺ Love, of course. *Love* is the Word for what I felt then. So why, then, did I also feel a Shadow still circling us? A Darkness hovering just on the Edge.

"Oh hey, isn't that your Friend over there?" he said.

"Friend?"

He pointed to the Rabbit now sitting in the Grasses near our Feets. Leonard. Like he'd never once left my Side. His ever-twinkling Eyes shining up at me. Watching me with his Rabbit's Face.

And that, Reader, is when I remembered Everything Love had made me forget.

I looked back at Jonah, now lighting another Cigarette.

"What about Sam?" I asked him so uselessly.

"Sam's all about the Page," he said. "I guess we all are in this Place." He looked at me clutching my Book. I was still clutching it, Reader, after all this Time. "Aren't we?"

The Pain in my Heart suddenly grew sharp. I met his Gaze through the Smoke. I knew then that there was no Way I could stay in his World. Twas a terrible Place where everyone was Lost in their own Tunnel of Dreamings, their own Manny Scripts. And they'd commit all Manner of Violences to make those Dreamings come just a little more sharply into Life, to make them Real. I knew this, hated this, even as I held my own Book to my bloody Chest. I held it tighter than I'd held Jonah's Hand, though twas unfinished and leading me Nowhere at all. Nowhere but that Drowning Black.

"Speaking of the Page," he said, "what were you doing with that Book in the Alley? I heard you whispering."

"I was trying to go somewhere with it," I told him. My Voice cracked on *somewhere*.

He did not say, *With a Book?* He just looked at me, very seriously. "Where were you trying to go?"

"This Place," I said, looking away.

"What Place?"

I gazed down at Leonard. His Eyes flashed at me.

"Where I belong," I said. "More than I've ever belonged here."

I could not bear to look at Jonah as I spoke, Reader. But I felt him listening, watching me. "I was trying to get there," I said, shaking my Head now at the Grasses, "but I couldn't find my Way. I really thought my Book might lead me there. But now . . . "

"Now?" he said.

"Now I don't know if tis a Way," I said. "Now I don't think there's any Way at all." I felt the Moon come out from behind her Cloud. At last I looked back up at Jonah. His luminous Face was full of Tenderness.

"I get it," he said softly. "I really do."

"You do?"

"Of course. It happens to me all the Time with Poems."

I frowned.

"Books, then." He smiled. "It's so hard to not have Expectations. To not think about the Outcome. To let go. Then I remember something Lenny Coel used to say."

Leonard, who was chewing a Clover nearby, perked up his Ears. *What did I say?*

"Ultimately, your Book isn't for you," Jonah said.

"*What?*" My Friend? Not for me?

"It's not for you to keep or get something out of it, I mean. It's for Someone Else. A Stranger maybe."

And I wondered, Reader, if he meant You ☺

"May I see it?" he asked me. And so I let go, I handed it to him. Blood had seeped from my Wound onto its flowery Face. I smiled darkly, thinking how much Mother would have loved to see it.

"Creepy Flowers," he said, grinning. "I dig it already."

And watching him flip the Pages, his Eyes falling on my Words, I felt my Heart swell in a new Way.

"Wow. I didn't even know you wrote like this," he murmured.

"Me neither," I said. I was smiling now. I felt light as Air, Reader, as though this were a new kind of Dreaming. One I'd never experienced.

He looked up at me. "This looks fucking amazing," he said. "Hey, do you think I could read it Sometime?" Dandy Lion Hairs glowing beneath the Moon. Those kind Eyes of Earth and Grass. Eyes that always seemed to say, *Yes. Whatever you are, my Heart is open to you.*

"You can have it," I told him.

"What? No, really?"

"Tis for you." And somehow when I said it, I knew this was true.

"For me? Oh my god. Thank you." He hugged it to his Chest. Tighter than he'd ever held me. But I could strangely feel the Embrace around me all the same. My Chest ached with the Joy/Pain Feeling. Certainly it ached with the Wound. But it ached with Love above all, Reader.

"I should go," I said.

He reached out a Hand to me, still clutching my Book to his Heart. "But I want you to stay."

I stared at Leonard, gorging on his Grasses ecstatically. "This isn't the Place for me."

Jonah sighed. "Right, I guess now that the Semester's ended, you probably do have to go back to Argentina. Or Morocco. Or Japan. Or the Isle of Man."

I smiled sadly. "Exactly."

"It feels like whenever we run into each other, one of us is always leaving," he said. "Almost like we're in some weird Romance or something. Like we're Fiction."

"Perhaps we are," I said.

He smiled and hugged my Book. "Thank you for this. And for the new Friend." He looked down at Leonard, who'd hopped over to him. Was now sitting at his Feets.

"He's actually a very brilliant Poet," I said. "He may give you Feedback yet. Just listen to him."

"I don't know that I speak or understand Rabbit," he said very earnestly.

"Oh, I think you can," I said.

And I kissed him gently, Reader, one last Time.

XXVI

And now?

Now I have no Way Back, Reader.

Now I am writing to you with my Mindscape alone.

I am only hoping Someone can relay these Words of my Experience—of walking along the Path called Philosopher's Walk, into the big wide Night, away from Jonah and the Horrors of Narrative Arts and Mother and my Keepers. Having literally shed my Heart's Blood. And still shedding it, it seemed, though I no longer felt the Pain. I felt light as Air. Hands empty of Ax, empty of Book, empty, empty, under the Light of the Hare Moon. She seemed to shine a little lower to the Earth Tonight.

I almost felt her smile upon me.

I almost felt a kind of Warmth from her Light. Felt it on my Pelt and all around me, illuminating my Path, my long lone Shadow there. A little long-eared, twas. Like perhaps my Shadow knew of my Lost Self. Perhaps he and the Moon would lead me there.

I parted ways with Pony. Set him down by a Rabbit Statue I passed along my Path. For wherever I was going, I knew he could not follow. *Tis for the best*, I told him gently. *For it might be dangerous. It might be dark.* Here, at least, he was far from Narrative Arts. He would have a beautiful view of the Grasses and Flowers and the Skyscape. Could hear the pretty Musics coming from the nearby Conservatory windows. *Tis pretty here*, I told him.

Yes, I knew now that I was Imagining our Connection. Thanks to Mother and my Keepers, I began to understand all too well the difference between Imaginings and Reality.

But it did not matter to me, Reader. I loved him all the same.

Goodbye, Pony, I told him. *I love you very much.*

And I love you, he said.

And whether I imagined he said it made no difference at all.

Twas Real enough for me.

And then, on the Path, I noticed I had two Shadows.

The second Shadow was nearly the same as my own, Reader. Tall and sprightly. And a little long-eared, like there was Bunny in this Shadow too.

I turned. A Man walking beside me, walking in Time with my own Steps.

He appeared startled by my Presence. As if he, too, had thought he'd been walking alone. He, too, had suddenly seen two Bunny Man Shadows on the Path. When his Eyes met mine, when mine met his, we startled at the very same Time.

For we were not Strangers, Reader.

He knew me just as I knew him. Tears filled his Eyes as they filled mine.

"I have jumped with you," he whispered, "to many a jumping Song."

"And I have jumped with you, Wrong Allan," I said through my Tears. For that's who he was. The Wrong Allan, with a Patch over one Eye just like he'd had the Night we met, though no Bird on his shoulder now. Reader, how happy I was to see him again. Alive! With his Head affixed to his Body ☺

But the Wrong Allan seemed very sad ☹

He nodded sadly now. "Twas fun until you tried to kill me," he murmured. Still continuing to walk by my Side.

"I know," I said. I shook my Head at my Oops. "Twas my own warped Wiring. But look," I pleaded with him. "You're alive again."

"Yes," he agreed, nodding at the Dark ahead. "But I am so very lost."

I took the Wrong Allan's Hand. "I am lost too," I told him.

We wandered through the Dark for a silent Spell, looking up at the Moon, now warming us like the Sun.

"She smiles on us Tonight," he whispered.

"She does."

"I used to know her Language," the Wrong Allan said. "When I was Bunny."

"I knew it once too," I said.

"I shall know it now *Nevermore*," he said pointedly.

I reached down and pulled a Dandy Lion from the Grass, and handed it to him. "I am so very sorry I killed you, Wrong Allan."

He snatched the Dandy Lion from me. "Tyler," he said to the Flower softly. "My name was Tyler."

"Tyler," I repeated tenderly. "Twas an Accident."

He nodded. Ate the yellow Petals sullenly. "Please don't kill me ever again."

"I promise," I said.

And he squeezed my Hand. "I actually dug where you sent me," he said. "It was a beautiful Plane of Existence, in some Ways way better than this. But then I was . . . brought back here." He looked afeared suddenly. "And now?" He shook his Head. "I can't take Intro to Philosophy seriously at all anymore."

"Twould be difficult after all you've experienced," I agreed gently.

"Whenever anyone mentions Reality, I laugh and laugh. Also, how can I ever go back to playing Beer Pong when the Wind has sung her Song in my Ears?" He sighed longingly at the Moon. "Now I feel I am neither Here nor There." He shook his Head again sadly. "Actually, even before you killed me, I felt that Way," he murmured, turning the Stem of the Weed prettily in his Hands.

"I have always felt that Way also," I told him.

"I want to go Back," he whispered. "But I do not wish to go by Ax ever again," he said, looking away. "Once was quite enough, thank you. And also what if—"

"There is only Black?"

He nodded. I did not tell him I was afeared of that too ☹

"I know what you mean, Friend," I said. For we were Friends now, weren't we? "But perhaps there is another Way," I felt compelled to say, for he looked terribly afeared. I wondered if I was lying. Or was I dreaming again? Being hopeful? Braver than I felt for my new Friend?

"A Friend once said there are many Ways Back," I said, thinking of Allan. His professorial Words in the Forest. Though could I really call Allan a Friend?

"Many ways," the Wrong Allan repeated. "Really?" And he smiled a little. I watched our Shadows, now swinging held Hands. Were our Shadows growing shorter or was I imagining this? Furrier? Our Ears lengthening? Something, anyway, seemed to be happening to our Shapes on the Path.

"Yes," I said. "So we only have to find one Way."

And holding Hands with my Friend, I felt we were getting closer.

Are you still with me, Reader?

I hope you are. I really do.

My Pelt began to hum strangely. I smiled as he smiled. Our Shadows seemed to be rethinking Themselves. And I knew we were not quite as lost as we felt. I knew we were on our Way somewhere. Where, I did not know, for the Moon was illuminating only a few Feet ahead of us at a Time. But I felt she might shine us There.

And then he whispered—or was it me who whispered?—"Shall we jump again together?"

"But there is no Music."

"There is the Wind. Perhaps if we jump together, she will play for us."

And so, Hand in Hand, we jumped. Hopped, Reader.

I and the Wrong Allan. *Tyler.*

Whom I no longer wished to kill.

Whom I knew I would never wish to kill again.

And as we hopped along the Path, giddy, laughing, I forgot my Wounded Heart, and the Wind did suddenly begin to sing. The Moon, too, above us, and the Grasses at our Feets. All chimed in, a Song that was always there for the Hearing, if only we had the Ears to hear it, Reader. And now as we hopped, our Ears stretched to hear it. And it sang through our Pelts, which grew suddenly softer, our Hands furring back to themselves, and we met our own Shadows, now so much closer to the Earth, no longer a Stranger, and my Heart was full, Reader, no longer broken, as the Wind's wondrous Music grew and grew in our growing Ears. . . .

Part Five

Bunny

H ey.

Are you still with us, Bunny?

Are you awake?

Pretty hard to sleep with a blade at your throat like this, right? But let's lift that chin up with our sharp little friend here, push the bitch curtain back and see.

Oh wow.

More than awake, looks like.

Your eyes, Bunny, we've never seen them quite like this. It's almost like you're . . . *not* being a bitch in your mind right now or something? It almost looks like you're . . . *moved*.

Are you really, Bunny? Moved?

Is your heart fucking breaking like the dawn? We're so glad. That's all we can hope for, really, as artists. As storytellers. To move people, right? To connect. Reach out a hand (or an ax) in the dark, just like this. (Not that revenge isn't great too, Bunny.) It *is* a lovely little story, isn't it, about the wonders and terrors of creativity?

About learning to let go, really.

The dawn has come at last, Bunny, look. Right there in the triangle window. Finger by pink finger, isn't that how you described it once in your little novel? So pretty to watch it break, right? We bet you thought it would never come.

We never thought the dawn would come that night either, did we? The night we tried to take back what was ours. The night of the showcase. You didn't even go, did you, Samantha? Off in your own goddamned world somewhere probably. Probably better off. It was a hard night for us, obvi, Bunny. A dark night of the soul, so to speak. Well, you know. We do have to say that he exaggerated that final moment in the mirror room, Bunny. He makes us sound so violent and delusional, which is, like, *insane*, you know? He'd no doubt been poisoned against us by the Word Witch. For really we were most loving and writerly about the whole thing. A little turned around by those fucking mirrors, sure. Who wouldn't be? That's the mindfuckery of Art. But the physical injuries we sustained were totally superficial, Bunny. In fact, when we went to Health Services, they only rolled their eyes as they unspooled the gauze. *Narrative Arts*, the nurse guessed almost immediately. *Hall of Infinite Reflection*. The injury to our Hearts, on the other hand, when he so cruelly left us again?

That cut deeper than any fucking shard.

And yet we didn't give up, did we?

After we'd gathered ourselves, we looked for him all over campus, like the true artists we were. Our Drafts (we'd left them grazing in the rose garden) were screaming for Pinkberry because we'd promised, and we had to be like, *Fucking wait*, while we searched every flower bed. Poked through every bush. By the night's end we reeked of springtime and we were fucking wet with dew. But our bandaged hands came up empty, Bunny.

Except for Pinkie Pie, of course. Whom we found exactly where he'd left him. The hare statue beside Philosopher's Walk.

Coraline immediately sniffed the horse like she was taking a hit, we all did. And for a flickering, trancy moment he came back to us. A million fucking field and forest flowers, we could smell them. The sky in its many shades of day and night, we saw them all at once. Sun-warmed fur, we felt it in our hands. Evidence of God, Bunny. Evidence of us.

Our magic.

Our most wondrous love.

And so many tears filled our eyes, we thought we might never see again.

At last we fell into a heap in the rose garden. Collapsed there after god knows how many hours of hunting. Awoke with the sun the next morning. That dawn we never thought would come. We all opened our eyes at once to its pinkening light. And we knew that he'd gone for good. An emptiness suddenly, not only in our hands but in our hearts. Our Drafts were gone too, for it was only the four of us left in the garden. They'd run from us perhaps. Or turned back into bunnies, we had no fucking idea.

Or?

Or maybe we'd dreamed the whole thing—we contemplated this. That we were actually fucking crazy. Which *of course* we weren't. You know because you joined us soon after, didn't you, Bunny? Saw what was possible in the attic with your very own eyes. But that's another story, isn't it? On that May morning we really didn't know anything anymore.

We only knew there was no one left to hold but each other.

So we did, Bunny.

Even though, *ow*.

Ursula extended a kind of olive branch through email. Invited us over for fairy tea and krumkake or whatever. After everything that happened, we were certain she'd be fucking fired or something, you know? That all of New York would be burning, the whole of the literary world aflame.

But, um, no. New York was fine. Warren was fine.

Just an echo in a teacup, Bunny.

All had blown over, apparently, passed off as part of the Show, as Art rather than Life; it's a very fine line, we're learning.

And she?

Was nicer to us, actually, after that. Oh yes, much. More subservient eye contact and everything. Ever so anxious to refill our cups, which we did enjoy.

And so, over tea, we just sort of danced around any residual awkwardness.

Like she'd never stolen from us. Like we'd never broken down her door. Never accused her of plagiarism and watched her take an ax to our boy's throat on a stage in Narrative Arts. All the violent vicissitudes of the Process, ours and hers, seemingly forgotten. All the chaos of the showcase, she said, was really meant as a teaching lesson just for us. To model the chaos of the artist's life.

"An important lesson," we said. "Thank you so much for teaching us that."

"Did *Vanity Fair* contact you, by chance?" she asked us over her cup.

They hadn't, but we sipped our cups cagily. "Not yet," we said.

"Well, it's still very possible they might reach out. For a quote. Should they decide to run a story about me."

"Oh yes?" They never ran a story, Bunny.

"But you really shouldn't indulge such requests. The outsiders, the machinery around the arts, you see, they don't understand us." And here she sighed, stirring.

Us, Bunny.

"We artists have to stick together. You'll learn that such relationships will serve you far more than any flitting bit of fame." *Serve me and I'll serve you*, said her eyes.

And we smiled. "Absolutely."

There was, of course, a very large part of us that thought all of this was bullshit, Bunny. That knew she was a thief and a liar and maybe even a bit of a hack now. But then we thought of the dark window of her writing shed, those pictures of herself in the solarium with her many rabbits, and we smiled at her all the same. Delighted at the thought of how she might serve us.

Friends close, enemies closer, Bunny, we observed in the hive mind.

"We are so very grateful to have another year with you," we told her. "So very lucky." We watched her exhale with audible relief. Sip happily from her cup.

"And who knows?" she said. "Perhaps you will be visited again next year."

"Perhaps," we agreed. "Though we think we'll probably just go back to writing now," we remember we said. "For real."

"Real," she repeated, and smiled.

We smiled too. Because what a funny word that is, Bunny: *Real.*
Sometimes when we say it, we really just have to fucking laugh now.
Don't you?

Speaking of writing for real? The *book*, Bunny.

You might well wonder how we got it back, mightn't you?

We'd noticed it at the showcase, you see; how we could miss it? Saw
those strange sea-witch flowers on the cover—it looked like a mind vagina
at the hot pink height of its flourishing. Saw him snatch it from the stage.
Saw it again in that hall of mirrors. Our boy, a thousand of him, clutching it
so tightly to his chests. Holding it like we wished he'd held us. Just fucking
once. We asked Ursula about it when we saw her, and she predictably gaslit
us. *I don't know what you're talking about,* she said, stirring her tea. But her
eyes grew rabbity and frightened. She fucking knew. And we took mental
note. For what else could we do at the time?

Our boy speaks of Serendipity being on his side, the Universe, if you
like. Well, turns out it was on our side too, Bunny. And you actually played
a little part in that, oh yes. Because fast-forward to an afternoon in late May,
or was it early June? Just before we parted ways for the summer, anyway.
That summer was so existential for us, by the way. We were wandering the
city like the zombies we'd become. You thought you were the only lost girl in
town; well, you fucking weren't, Bunny. We saw you that afternoon, by the
way, we did. Walking by on the street, you didn't see us. But boy did we see
you. Tall as fuck. In your usual funeral wear. But smiling, quite uncharacteristically. Because you weren't alone for once, Bunny. You'd found a friend, it
seemed, good for you. Another weirdo, by the looks of it. Cooler-seeming
than you, though, in her fishnet veil and ripped black dress. Taller, too, which
creepy. Bleached feathery hair, a townie maybe? Or was she something else?

Something about her, the way you were looking at her, Bunny, gave us
pause. Like you were a fucking goner. Enchanted body, mind, and soul. Like
she was your dream come to life, maybe.

We looked at this strange girl more closely, and then we looked back at you. So happy and lost. No fucking clue.

And then we knew.

We knew exactly what sort of, um, *friend* she was, Bunny. The hive mind flashed with electricity, with possibility then. Our fingers and napes tingling. And we thought, *Huh. Interesting.* Perhaps we'd say hi to you next fall after all. Get to know one another a little better, you know?

We might have approached you right then, for we were about to cross paths, but you were just so oblivious (we've been there, trust) that we were sort of embarrassed for you. Also, we wanted to sit on this for a bit, let it cook, this tasty morsel, this new knowledge of you. So we ducked into a used-book-and-record store before you or your *friend* spotted us. So very uncharacteristic of us to thrift, we know (the germs and finger grease of the preloved object make us far too sad in our souls).

Yet we did it on this day.

And how amazing that we did, how serendipitous.

Because there in that dank hole of a store was the fucking Universe, Bunny. A.k.a. Jonah. Flipping through the saddest pile of dog-eared books and jazz records you ever saw. Smiling his poetry-cloud smile to no one but himself. We wouldn't have talked to him, honestly, except that luckily he saw us and waved. And then, Bunny, as we approached—had no choice but to approach now, because we're actually really very nice and polite people— we fucking smelled it. The forest and field flowers of Aerius. Suddenly all around us in that musty store.

Jonah was blah-blah-blahing at us, but we didn't hear a goddamned word, Bunny. Because there was all this glitter in the air now, we could see it. And then we saw something else. Poking out of a knapsack at his feet.

The book. Those strange sea-witch flowers. Stained with blood. *His* blood, Bunny; we could smell the beautiful Wound of him as if it were still freshly bleeding.

"How's your summer going?" Jonah was saying to us or some such.

"Fantastic," we told him. "So amazing."

But the only word in our hearts was *Mine*.

We distracted him with, we don't even remember what anymore, isn't that funny? Who cares about *logistics* when the Universe is right there beside you, in all its glitter and blood and flowers, basically saying *Take*. Maybe Else led him away, offering to buy him one of those sad records or a used book about magic. Maybe Coraline and Kyra covered for Vik as she crouched down and nabbed it from his knapsack, that sounds about right. Yes, even goody-goody Kyra was in on it. Even *she* saw the Universe was at work, Bunny. Not stealing at all. Stealing *back*.

We all knew what it would contain, of course. Exaggerations, sure. Lies, definitely. Some very damning and flagrant and embarrassing. But also: *evidence*. Nestled there among the prickly, tricky thorns of Fiction.

It is a Fiction, is it not? (Are *we* not?) Just like you and your little novel, Bunny.

Except this one's ours. Our Fiction.

And he's lovely, isn't he?

We're so very glad you agree.

And this brings us to a bit of an awkward place, Bunny. In fact, let's lower the ax from your neck for just a sec, k? Because there's something we sort of want to ask you before we kill you—we *were* actually really thinking of killing you, Bunny (we still might). But, um, seeing your reaction to the literature we made has given us *pause*. Made us, you know, wonder something.

If maybe . . .

I don't know.

You could *show* this book of ours? To, like, your hotshot agent or editor or whatever?

I mean, it's sort of the least you could fucking do, right?

And you love it, right? The story? We *saw* you were moved, so don't fucking pretend you weren't now. We saw the emotion on your face. We see it now. It's still there in that weird eye of yours.

Also, we think this deserves to be in print, don't you? Because it's such a—wait, is that a . . . *nod*, Bunny?

Okay, that was fast. Wow.

Bunny, you're not crying again now, are you? Oh my god, you are. Well, fuck. *Thanks.* That touches us, it really does. That's making us cry too, for real. What's that, Bunny? You really look like you're dying to say something. All right, fine, we'll take the gag out for a sec. We're actually kind of dying to hear your words about us.

"Wow," you say, sort of hoarsely.

Yes, that's right, Samantha. *Wow* is right, we're so glad you—

"Wow, wow, wow," you whisper. Nodding like crazy now. "Um, maybe let me go? So I can show it to my very hot agent or whatever. I'd really love to."

And we're not dreaming, Bunny. You're really saying it. Your mouth making those shapes, and the words are like music to our ears. Like the jumping song of the wind to our ears.

"Wow. Okay, Samantha," we say.

So we untie you, Bunny, we do. Most lovingly. As lovingly as we tied you up, we untie you now. And you're fucking giddy in your chair watching us, making these weird, whimpering little noises that are sort of like restrained squeal-honks. They sound like happy squeals, though, they do. And we're feeling so happy too. Because we made a mess of your soul with our words, didn't we? With our Fiction. That you're now going to help us publish, Bunny, you fucking agreed, remember? We should probably talk about the logistics of submission, right? Like who among us should type it up and what font we should use, and should we keep his weird capitalizations for the sake of authenticity or no? Too literary? (We think we're actually pretty commercial, Bunny, like we have wide appeal!) And should we include our own stories in there? Weave them in as we told them to you tonight, what do you think? Too bad we didn't have, like, a recorder, you know?! Omg, it's all so fucking exciting, Bunny! Now *we're* going to be the famous ones finally! We're crying, nodding messes too now at the thought of that. Our turn at last! *Our* turn to go on fucking tour! Our turn to make the weird squealing sounds as we untie that last cord from around your throat. And once you're free, well, you kind of jump right up, don't you? I guess we don't blame you at all. You *have* been sitting down for a while, in your own pee, no less.

We forgot how tall you are, Bunny, like a fucking tree, aren't you? Amazonian, like in a scary way. And that long dark Cousin Itt hair that hides one eye. We don't love it. Should have braided that bitch curtain back when we had the chance. Even though your eye, the one we can see, well, it also betrays nothing now. Just a sky-blue void.

Did you always have blue eyes, Bunny? Isn't it funny how we don't remember? That's how much you've hidden behind your hair historically.

Looking up at you, we're a little nervous now. A thrum of panic inside us as we face your just-now-liberated body. We wonder if you'll punch us or something. But you open your branch arms wide and you just fucking hug us. Rocking us from side to side, really putting your boobs into it. Lifting us up off our feet (we forgot how strong you are) and sort of spinning us around like in a movie or music video. It's nice but a little scary (and smelly). We have to remind ourselves that you're overcome right now, quite violently, by Literature. Our Literature. And while your response is a bit much for us, it's beautiful, too. We fucking moved you. And we're moved by having moved you, wow. That's the magic of reading, isn't it? That's how it works. The wonder of the author-reader fucking relationship. And that's how—

Wait.

What the fuck are you doing with our ax, Bunny?

Oh my god, Bunny, how the fuck did you get our ax? (*How did she get our ax?*)

Oh my god, during the hug, wasn't it? In the ecstasy of our trusting embrace with you, wasn't it? Yes. It must have just slipped from our so-trusting hands. Along with our book—fucking Christ, you took our *book*—we see it fucking tucked there inside your coat like a fucking baby, oh my god, what the fuck, Bunny?

Empty now, our hands.

Shaking now, our hands.

Cold suddenly. Cold all fucking over.

And you, smiling so widely. Gripping the scratched handle of the ax tight. The blade shining over us like the most god-awful sun.

Why are you raising your ax over your head like that, Bunny? We don't like that look in your blue eye at all, it looks fucking crazy, it—

Oh my god, what are you doing now? NO!

No, no, NO don't walk to the window, Bunny, why are you walking to the goddamned window? Stop, stop, STOP— But we can't stop you, can we? We're fucking paralyzed, hands empty of book, of ax, our bodies so small in the dawn light. No choice. No choice but to watch you skip to the window, are you fucking skipping? Stand giddily by our very own triangle of glass. Waving that glinty blade so wildly around. Still laugh-crying like fucking crazy. Screaming, "Thank you, thank you! I am free, I am free! There are many ways back, and your tale is the Way, your tale is changing me, Bunny. Thank you for telling me about the wind."

What the fuck are you saying, Samantha? We're asking you, but you're looking at the ax now, your eyes brimming with another kind of tear.

"The tale is a Way," you say.

What?

"A Way out of being Samantha."

What do you mean a—

"Just this one stop," you whisper, "just this one hellscape stop on the New England leg, and she said, 'You do it for me. You go there for me, Bunny. You take the train to the town named after God and fate. You go to that accursed campus, to the Warren Bookstore that is right beside Narrative Arts, and you walk the gangplank to the podium. You smile and do your reading (no Q and A, no signing), and you make no eye contact, and then you Uber back to your haunted hotel by the pretty river. And if I don't hear from you, Bunny, we go to plan B. Because I? Can't fucking go back there, sorry. I have enemies, I have four enemies, and ghosts, too many ghosts. Too much murder and love's memory in every swan gliding on the water, in the light on the leaves and on the rooftops, and my heart breaking all over again, still broken. But I've left these fanged shadows behind me now, I've left them all behind me now, my love and my enemies. I've shed the heart's blood, turned it into a book. But I know, I know, that somewhere out there my enemies are seething, waiting for me to come back, to show my face if I dare. Of course I'm fucking afraid of them, Bunny. Because what I wrote in that book? It wasn't Fiction at all. It was real, all of it from the bunnies to the boys to the axes to the blood, so much blood. How they're fucking psychopaths. How much I miss her, I'll never forgive them. How, in the end, I chose the mud, I'll always choose the mud, Bunny. So you'll be brave for me, won't you? You'll go to this one place in the world I can't go, with its wrong trees and its mind-fucking light. Here is a black dress, here is a toothbrush, here is a Google Doc from my publicist. Please be careful, promise me. Please know I'll be here cheering you on in the dark, please know I'll save you if I have to, Bunny, I'll take the train, I'll run from the station, we'll go to plan B, please remember I love you. And if you see them tonight? And they smile and offer you a drink? You fucking run, Bunny. Run like the wind that once sang in your ears that sings no more. I will bring you back there, promise. I've learned the Way. It's in your tale, I'll tell you when it's time.'"

"Oh my god, what are you talking about, Bunny?"

You look up at us, snapping out of your trance for a second. Remembering we're here with you in the attic. "But your tale is changing me already," you whisper, turning the ax around and around in your hands. "It's already happening, just like she said."

We watch as you burst into tears we don't fucking understand anymore.

"So long since I heard the song of the wind," you whimper, and raise your ax high—what?

Oh my god, oh my god, Samantha, NO.

But what can we do, Bunny? We watch as you strike the window glass with the ax, it makes such a shattering sound. And we scream, and you laugh and cry what seem like more joy tears and shout, "FREE, FREE, FREE."

And you stare at the shattered window, at the creeping dawn, with such a dreaming, happy face, and god, it frightens us, you've never frightened us more than in your ecstasy.

"Stop it, Samantha, STOP IT," we scream at you. "What are you doing? What are you fucking—"

"Goodbye, Bunny," you say, smiling like crazy.

Goodbye, what do you mean, *GOODBYE?*

"The tale is the Way," you whisper in some creepy joy trance.

No, Bunny. Don't jump. Don't you fucking jump with our book, that's OUR BOOK, you BITCH! You're supposed to send it to your agent, hello? Bunny, please don't jump, don't jump, don't—

And then? It's like a dream, Bunny.

Are we dreaming, Bunny?

Sometimes we still think we are.

We run to the goddamned window. Expect to see your shattered body lying there on Kyra's poorly cut grass. Your long limbs all twisted and broken among the dandelions, cold with frost. Your blood pooling beautifully around you in the fiery sunrise. We really don't want to see that, Bunny, even though we've seen much worse, trust. But something compels us, doesn't it? We have to see the Evidence. Or maybe you aren't dead after all. Maybe you can still show the book to your agent. If you're only very critically injured, there's a chance, right?

One last step to the broken window, shards still hanging there like the open jaws of some terrible beast. We poke our heads through the jaws, into the sweet, cold, gusty morning air. Bracing ourselves, we look down. Nothing. Just fucking grass, what the fuck? Oh god. Oh god, what—

Then we see.

Sitting there in the grass right on top of our book.

Unbroken. Alive. Small and furry and looking up at us with large, shining eyes. Smiling, still smiling, in the bloody light of the rising sun.

Long ears tuned and twitching to the song of the wind.

And then in the wind another sound suddenly.

A crunching foot. A drawn breath. Someone else is out there in the blowy dawn. We feel them skulking in the trees. Feel their wild, rageful heart beating in our heads.

You.

You, Bunny.

Slinking out of the shadows now in a long black coat. Bitch curtained. Breathless. Like you've been running all fucking night.

You dash toward the little rabbit in the grass—"Thank god, thank god"—at first she's all you can see. But then you look up. See us standing in the jaws of our shattered heaven. And we see you, don't we? Finally. For real. Right there on Kyra's lawn in the literal fucking flesh. That fire and fear in your eyes, it never left. The roar of your ever-breaking heart, we hear it from here as you gather first the beaming animal and then the book into your thieving arms. Smiling just like a Fiction. Just like the rabbit in the wildly blushing dawn.

And then you run like the wind.

Acknowledgments

To Michael Milosevic-O'Brien, who left this world too early. You made me who I am and I'm forever grateful. I love you, Bunny.

To Ken Calhoun, without whom this book wouldn't exist. Thank you for your genie-yes, love, faith, and friendship—and for encouraging me to write *Bunny* ten years ago to this day. I went down a creative rabbit hole from which I've (happily) yet to emerge. I'm grateful for it and for you, always.

To my parents, always, and to dear friends who've supported me in my writing life: Rex Baker, Teresa Carmody, Laura Sims, Emily Culliton. To Laura Zigman: there are no words, Bunny. To my real-life Avas: Alexandra Dimou, for deepest friendship and all the intentions, flimmies, and Fyorgian conjurings, and Jess Riley, to whom *Bunny* is dedicated: there would be no *Bunny* (or indeed any book) without your brilliance, friendship, and faith.

Music is always an important part of my process, but there are particular songs and artists (far too many to name here) who made the atmosphere of this book especially alive and tangible to me:

To Kate Bush, whose music was absolutely my spirit guide for this story, from the rose garden to the attic to the showcase: I will never forget walking by the water and listening to your albums as I was dreaming these scenes into being. You give me creative courage, always, Bunny. And heart.

To Trish Keenan of Broadcast, whose dreamy voice always conjures the universe of Bunny for me like no other: *Bunny* and I owe you a great debt.

Very special thanks to Chappell Roan from Pony, Aerius, and my Self for brightening our hearts as we journeyed through the dark. Also to Fleetwood Mac, Imaginary Softwoods, the Magnetic Fields, Joy Division, Heart, Weyes Blood, and Lord Huron for soundscaping our dreams.

To Ginsberg and Poe, the Allen/Allans I love most, both quoted in this book: thank you for igniting my creative heart.

To my La Jolla community, especially Julie Slavinsky of Warwick's for being a friend and champion; Jason Blitman, for helping me to let it go; Angela Sterling for the gorgeous author photos—thank you for making the light a friend.

To my incredible editors Marysue Rucci, Nicole Winstanley, and Chris White and to my amazing publishing teams at Simon & Schuster for all you do to support me and my work. Huge thank yous to Clare Maurer, Emma Taussig, Elizabeth Breeden, Rita Silva, Dan French, Rebecca McCarthy, Amy Fulwood, Laura Levatino, Erica Stahler, and Laura Jarrett. To Nicole, my Canadian editor and publisher: we've come a long way, Bunny, and I'm so grateful we're still walking this path together.

Endless gratitude to everyone at the Clegg Agency for all your support: Simon Toop, MC Connors, Rebecca Pittel, and Marion Duvert.

To Bill Clegg: thank you for taking a chance on *Bunny* and me. Thank you for always believing in us. Your championship, faith, and care take our breath away. *Bunny* and I can't even contemplate what we would do without you, Bunny. We love you.

To all the brilliant readers of Bunny: your responses have moved and inspired me more than I can say. Thank you for expanding the world of this story with your incredible creativity and connection. Thank you for keeping Bunny alive and real in my head and in my heart.

And so, my dear Readers, who have journeyed with me through this universe and made it richer with your presence: this book is for you.

About the Author

MONA AWAD is the bestselling author of the novels *Rouge*, *All's Well*, *Bunny*, and *13 Ways of Looking at a Fat Girl*. She is a three-time finalist for a Goodreads Choice Award, the recipient of an Amazon Best First Novel Award, and she was shortlisted for the Giller Prize. *Bunny* was a finalist for a New England Book Award and was named a Best Book of 2019 by *Time*, *Vogue*, and the New York Public Library. It is currently being developed for film with Bad Robot Productions. *Rouge* is being adapted for film by Fremantle and Sinestra. Margaret Atwood named Awad her "literary heir" in *The New York Times*'s *T* magazine. Her work has been translated into sixteen languages. She teaches fiction in the creative writing program at Syracuse University and is based in Boston.

ALL'S WELL
By Mona Awad

'A dazzling wild ride of a novel – daring, fresh, entertaining, and magical.' — **George Saunders, author of *Lincoln in the Bardo***

Miranda Fitch's life is a waking nightmare. The accident that ended her burgeoning acting career left her with excruciating, chronic back pain, a failed marriage, and a deepening dependence on painkillers. And now she's on the verge of losing her job as a college theatre director. Determined to put on Shakespeare's *All's Well That Ends Well*, the play that promised, and cost, her everything, she faces a mutinous cast hellbent on staging Macbeth instead. Miranda sees her chance at redemption slip through her fingers.

That's when she meets three strange benefactors who have an eerie knowledge of Miranda's past and a tantalizing promise for her future: one where the show goes on, her rebellious students get what's coming to them, and the invisible, doubted pain that's kept her from the spotlight is made known.

With prose Margaret Atwood has described as 'no punches pulled, no hilarities dodged...genius,' Mona Awad has concocted her most potent, subversive novel yet. *All's Well* is the story of a woman at her breaking point and a formidable, piercingly funny indictment of our collective refusal to witness and believe female pain.

ROUGE
by Mona Awad

'A narrative that oozes with unease', *Guardian*

For as long as she can remember, Belle has been obsessed with her skin and skincare videos. When her estranged mother Noelle mysteriously dies, Belle finds herself back in Southern California, dealing with her mother's considerable debts and grappling with lingering questions about her death. The stakes escalate when a strange woman in red appears at the funeral, offering a tantalizing clue about her mother's demise, followed by a cryptic video about a transformative spa experience. With the help of a pair of red shoes, Belle is lured into the barbed embrace of La Maison de Méduse, the same lavish, culty spa to which her mother was devoted. There, Belle discovers the frightening secret behind her (and her mother's) obsession with the mirror – and the great shimmering depths (and demons) that lurk on the other side of the glass.

Snow White meets *Eyes Wide Shut* in this surreal descent into the dark side of beauty, envy, grief, and the complicated love between mothers and daughters. Brimming with California sunshine and blood-red rose petals, *Rouge* holds up a warped mirror to our relationship with mortality, our collective fixation with the surface, and the wondrous, deep longing that might lie beneath.

Read on to discover the prologue of Mona Awad's *Rouge* . . .

Prologue

Prologue

She used to tell you fairy tales at night, remember? Once upon a time. When you were a sad, dreamy little girl. Each night you lay in your princess bed, surrounded by your glassy-eyed dolls, waiting for her like a wish. *Tick, tick* went the seconds on your Snow White clock. The moon rose whitely from the black clouds. And then . . .

"Knock, knock," Mother whispered from your bedroom door.

"Come in," you called in your child's voice.

And she did. She came and sat right on the edge of your bed like a queen, didn't she? Cigarette between her white fingers. Exuding her scent of violets and smoke.

"All right," Mother said. "Which story do you want to hear tonight, Belle?"

Belle. French for "beautiful." It's what she called you, even though you were a beastly little thing. Not at all like Mother. She was fair, slim, and smooth, remember? Like something out of a fairy tale. Like the dolls that lined the walls of your room. It was Mother who'd bought you those dolls. Positioned them in every corner, every nook, so no matter where you looked, you saw their glossy hair, their fair skin, those lips of red that were always sort of smiling at you. Like they all had a secret between them.

"Well, Belle?" And she smiled at you just like the dolls, remember?

She was wearing the red silk robe, the one you loved best. Sometimes you tried it on when she wasn't home, breathing in her violets and smoke. She had a pair of red shoes that matched. Satin, heeled, with puffs of red feathers on the toes—your favorites. You tried those on too, but it never went well. Two teetering steps and you were on the floor, weren't you?

"Which story?" Mother prompted now. Beginning to get impatient with you, your dreaminess. How you were staring at her like a little psychopath.

"The one about the beautiful maiden," you said.

Again? And she looked a little like she was sorry for you, like you were damned. Definitely. Because there were other stories, weren't there? There was the one about the rabbit and the turtle, for instance. There was the one about three pigs and a wolf. There was one about a girl who turned into a seal, that was a sweet one. But you didn't give a fuck about the other stories. You never did. You'd already chosen, hadn't you?

You nodded. "The beautiful maiden," you said. "Again."

And Mother sighed. Or did she smile? She didn't take the familiar book off the shelf with its very cracked spine. Didn't need to. Thanks to you, Mother knew this story by heart.

"Once upon a time," she began, "in a land far away, there lived a beautiful maiden in a castle by the sea . . ."

That's how it always started. You sighed too. A land far away. A beautiful maiden. A castle, the sea. You closed your eyes the better to see it all shimmering in your mind.

"How beautiful?" you asked Mother, your eyes shut tight.

"So incredibly beautiful," Mother said, "that all admired her from near and far." She sounded bored. A familiar digression. You sought this embellishment every night, didn't you?

"Yes." You nodded. "From near and far." Of course they would.

"From near and far," Mother confirmed.

"And many envied her too," she added in a low voice. The night it all began. Your once upon a time. Remember the wolf moon in the window? Two gray-bodied spiders dangling from webs on the pink walls. A red-haired doll with a crack in her face staring at you from a satin pillow.

"Envied her?" you repeated, opening your eyes. You saw Mother had moved away from your bed. She was now sitting at the little white vanity table she bought you last Christmas, the one with the three-way mirror. She was so pleased to give you this gift that you acted pleased too. But you didn't like this mirror. It was enough to have to see yourself once, let alone three times, remember? It was enough to have to open your eyes and see yourself at all. But Mother loved this mirror. She was looking at her three selves right now, brushing her hair with your long-handled brush. The brush was painted gold to match the gold trim of the vanity, another gift from Mother. The back was encrusted with bright-colored bits of plastic that you thought were precious stones. The bristles didn't work on your kind of hair, so thick and coarse. But it worked wonderfully on Mother's. Now you watched her brush her dark red hair with long, slow strokes.

"What's envy, Mother?" you asked her.

"Envy is when you hate someone because they have something you want," she said simply.

You stared at her reflection in the three-way glass.

"Like being pretty," you said.

"Exactly," she yawned. A glimpse of her red throat. "Like being pretty. Or young," she added, looking back at you in the glass. Her glossy dark red hair tumbling over one white shoulder. Her red robe brought out the bright blue of her eyes. The robe was a gift from the faraway country where your father was born. He bought her one in nearly every color, each jewel-bright and threaded with gold. You'd never met your father, but you'd seen pictures. He reminded you a little of the ogres in your fairy-tale books. Swarthy and stout, like you. You could see your eyes in his eyes. Your skin in his skin. There was a time when you even feared you might be part ogre, remember?

When you told Mother this once, she'd laughed hysterically. She'd thrown her head back and laughed until she'd cried. And then you cried too, you couldn't help it. So it was true. You were definitely part ogre, just as you'd feared. *Stop it*, she said, and then she slapped you. Right across the face. Tears instantly stung your eyes. *Listen to me*, she hissed. *Listen*. And the world grew very still while she assured you with the softest voice that of course your father was not an ogre, *of course not.* He was a lovely man, *god rest his soul.* Handsome, even, many women thought so. He was just from a place where there happened to be more sun, that was all. And people in that place were darker and they were hairier. So you were darker and you were hairier. You were *lovely.* You were *lucky,* she'd said, putting her white hands on your shoulders. Shaking them a little. *Lucky, do you hear me?* She *wished* she had your skin and your hair, absolutely. *Definitely.* And then she petted you like a dog. Smiled at you in the three-way glass. And you knew then that she was lying. She didn't wish that. Not at all.

Now you looked at her in the mirror until she looked away. Took a drag of her cigarette. Went back to brushing her hair with your gold toy brush.

"Anyway," Mother said. "The beautiful maiden. She had this mirror. And the mirror talked to her."

Yes, yes. This was your favorite part of the story. That the maiden talked to a mirror. That she had a friend in the glass who told her things. You were such a lonely little girl, weren't you? Whispering to grass. Befriending sticks. Dreaming yourself into movies and books. Every screen, every page, like a door to another world, remember?

"What did it tell her?" you asked like you didn't know. Like Mother hadn't already told you this part a thousand times.

"That she was beautiful," Mother said as if it was obvious. "The most beautiful in all the land."

You nodded. An ache opened up inside you. Deep, deep. For what? Some other life, some other self, some other body. In a land far away. In a castle by the sea.

"But then one day," Mother said, and her tone shifted. "One day, the mirror didn't say that." She was staring at her three selves in the glass when she said this.

"It didn't?"

"No."

And in the mirror, you saw a shimmer. A sparkling something that wasn't there before.

"Mother?" you whispered, your eyes on the shimmer.

Not just a shimmer now, a shape. A darkly glimmering shape hovering in the mirror behind Mother's reflection. Mother shook her head at the mirror. She took another drag of her cigarette. She was staring at the shape too. Like she wasn't at all surprised to see it there.

"It said something else," Mother whispered, her eyes on the shape. What sort of shape? Something or someone?

Someone.

A figure. Staring at Mother. You could feel it staring though it had no eyes you could see. Just a silhouette, remember?

"What did it say?"

"Something terrible," Mother said, staring at the figure who stared back. "Something inevitable. Something true."

Like what? Like what?

Mother shook her head again and again. She looked in the mirror like she was about to cry. The figure was looking at Mother sorrowfully. Fake sorrowfully, you felt, you didn't know why. And that's when it looked up. Lifted its eyes from Mother to you. Yes, it had eyes, though you couldn't see them. You could feel them on you. A coldness. It stared at you and smiled. You knew it was smiling, though it had no mouth you could see either. Just a man-shaped shadow. Just that shimmering silhouette.

You should've been afraid. You really should've been. Definitely. But you weren't, were you? When you felt his eyes on you, all of you was suddenly lit up. Like the glow-in-the dark stars on your bedroom ceiling. Like your grandmother's chandelier. You were smiling now.

"And then what happened, Mother?" Your eyes were staring right into his eyes, you could sort of see them now. He had eyes that saw your soul, you knew this. It was a he, you knew that, too, didn't you?

Mother wasn't looking at the figure anymore. She was looking at you.

"Mother?" you pressed, feeling the figure's eyes on you. "What happened?"

But Mother just smiled darkly in the glass.

"And then all hell broke loose."